SACRIFICE

Also By Catherine M. Walker

Unwanted (Emergence, 1)

Sacrifice (Emergence, 2)

Defiance (Emergence, 3)

Shattering Dreams (The Being Of Dreams, 1)

Path Of The Broken (The Being Of Dreams, 2)

Elder Born (The Being Of Dreams, 3)

NEWSLETTER

If you'd like updates of my progress, promotions and advance notice of when the next book comes out drop by my website and join my newsletter.

www.catherinemwalker.com

SACRIFICE

EMERGENCE
BOOK TWO

CATHERINE M. WALKER

Cover designer: https://www.jcalebdesign.com/

Ebook ISBN: 978-1-925776-16-4

Paperback ISBN: 978-1-925776-17-1

Hardcover ISBN: 978-1-925776-18-8

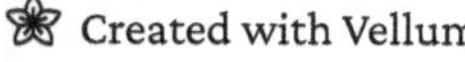 Created with Vellum

CHAPTER

ONE

The clattering in the courtyard below didn't have the courtesy to drum in time to the persistent thumping in his head. Instead, one percussive sound rose as the other fell, so it merged and formed one entity. Steven groaned and rolled over, pulling a pillow over his head. The noise of horse hooves in a cobbled courtyard of the Rathadon estate was deafening. At least the heavy drapes on his bedroom windows kept out what he guessed was the disgusting morning light. He wouldn't feel this bad if it was a civilised hour to be awake.

"Michael, I'm going to kill you for coming here at this hour," Steven cursed, as the pillow didn't seem to do much to dampen the pulsing ache.

At least, he'd kill his brother when he managed to drag himself out of bed. There was no doubt in his mind that Michael had returned home to Vallantia at this hour to taunt him. He always showed up at the worst possible time. To be that punctual, it would have to be deliberate. His little brother had always been irritating, and neither age, nor being the Warlord's pet, seemed to have changed that particular character trait.

1

Piercing screams and the clash of steel against steel made their way through the muffling effect of the pillow. Steven threw the pillow across the room and clawed at his sheets. He rolled out of bed and stumbled as the sheets caught around his legs.

With one hand grasping the window frame, he hauled back the drapes with the other, wincing as the light hit his eyes. He'd been correct. It was the early hours of the morning, but while those on horseback at this obscene hour reeked of his brother, the screaming—and what his foggy brain finally pieced together as the clashing of swords—did not.

Steven froze as his eyes finally focused enough to make sense out of what was happening below. House guards lay motionless on the ground; those that remained upright and fighting retreated as their numbers diminished. He'd have recognised the Unwanted's distinctive black and silver fighting leathers anywhere. For one thing, the fine trace work of metal woven in their fighting leathers glowed with the veil when they drew on their powers. The intruders in the courtyard below wore no house colours he could identify, which meant one thing. Bandits. Well clothed and armed, but still illegitimate.

STEVEN SAT in the formal ballroom in a chair the mercenaries had brought from the dining room. It was a large, stately room with tapestries on the walls and a platform off to one side where musicians and artisans could perform. There were doors down the length of one wall that could be pushed open to reveal a wide veranda and steps that led to a garden courtyard beyond. Old light stones, probably as old as the building itself and a symbol of wealth and power, ringed the room. The servants saw that someone with the talent with such things maintained them. He had no idea why his grandfather, however many times removed, had had a ballroom added to the castle. Given the reputation of some of his ancestors, he couldn't imagine anyone choosing to be in their company. Steven shifted in his chair and then froze as it creaked in response. The noise was overloud in the nearly empty ballroom, causing those standing guard over him to glare. His parents sat nearby, and the bandits shoved the house staff unceremoniously into the room as they rounded them up. None of the house guards had appeared in the ballroom. Yet some had survived the assault. He'd seen them being bound down in the courtyard by their attackers.

"Where do you think our guards are? We need to rally," Steven whispered to his parents, "or something."

"Rally with what?" His father's gaze was withering.

"If any are alive, they're probably in the cells under the castle by now," his mother said.

Steven couldn't stop himself from turning and staring at his mother. He'd known the castle had secrets. Places only the servants and the like visited, but he was dumbfounded by this casual revelation.

"We still have cells?"

There was that expression on his father's face again. Except this time, he could have sworn he saw a similar emotion flicker on his mother's face.

"What did you think was down in the tunnels below the castle?" his father asked.

Steven went to ask *what tunnels*, but something in his father's eyes made him change his mind. He looked away, a little bewildered as to why his father would think he'd stoop to going down into the servant areas of the castle. After all, that was why they had servants.

"I wish I had known we still had cells. There are quite a few people I could have had locked up over the years." Steven laughed, then petered off when neither of his parents laughed with him.

"I wouldn't allow you to lock someone up just because they brought out your wrong outfit for the day or mixed up your drink order." His father stared at him.

Steven realised that while this invasion was stressful for him it must be more traumatic for his parents. It was the only explanation for their behaviour. He reached out and gripped his father's shoulder, squeezing it gently to show support. He frowned, noticing the blanket across his father's legs. The chill in the room must be getting into the old man's bones. The evidence of advancing age saddened him. It must be why his father was so irritated.

"We'll get through this. You'll see," Steven said, attempting to sound confident for his parents' sake even if he didn't feel that way in the slightest.

Whatever his mother was about to say in response died on her lips as the big inner doors swept open; a woman and man strode in, surrounded by guards. All the intruders were dressed in nondescript brown leathers. He had no idea who they were, but as his parents stiffened, he realised they did.

"Warlord, good to see you well. We feared the worst after your brother's visit and the death of our son Gareth, and your people," the man said.

Steven's stomach plunged. He'd thought he was free of that mess.

"Peter, Constance, what nonsense is this?" his father asked.

Steven found it remarkable that his father sounded calm. It was only because he was sitting so close that he could feel the anger radiating from his father and mother.

"Ah, Speaker Rathadon, we considered you, but due to the injuries you suffered at the hands of the usurper, well..." Peter paused, a condescending expression on his face as his gaze swept over them all. "It was obvious that your heir was the most appropriate to lead the rebellion and take back his birthright."

"You're the patriarchs of a gambling and trading consortium. Granted, a successful one, but you have no idea what you have just done." His mother's voice was scathing.

"Mother, please, these fine people just want to help us take back our ancestral lands and help me claim my title."

"You knew about this rebellion?" Her lips compressed into a thin line as she stared at him.

"It was time we took action. I did what was right. You'll see," Steven said.

Steven was appalled at himself even as the words came spilling out of his mouth. He didn't quite know why he kept trying to justify his participation in this exploit. He didn't believe a word of it now, even if he did at the time, but somehow he couldn't help himself. His father's lips thinned as he looked back at the couple who'd invaded their home.

"You've picked the wrong Rathadon, as you'll learn to your folly." His father stared at Peter and Constance.

"Father, what—?" Steven's eyes widened as he stared at his father.

"Do you have any idea what the Warlord will do when he finds out about this?" his father asked, totally ignoring the others in the ballroom.

"What Michael will do?" His mother closed her eyes, her voice soft.

"If you'd been anyone else's brother, you'd be dead from all the stupid stunts you've pulled."

"Now, now Speaker Rathadon, Lady Rathadon, we're hardly that foolish. We've arranged a diversion for the Warlord," Constance scolded.

"It's only a matter of time. Your youngest son is about to

become very busy." Peter looked at Constance, and they both laughed.

"Now that the castle is secure, I'll have our people escort you to your rooms where you'll stay," Constance said as she gestured to some guards.

"You too, Warlord, for your safety, of course. We need to make sure nothing happens to you," Peter said.

Steven could tell there was no sincerity in the pair's words. It was yet another thing to point out his involvement in their cause had been pure folly. The sudden insight caused Steven to pause. Reading people was not his strong suit. Then he felt it, that familiar mental touch of his mother as she maintained a mental shield around his mind. She was much stronger with such skills than he was. The insight was hers.

"I'll accompany my parents to their rooms to ensure they reach them safely before I retire to mine," Steven said.

Steven stood and nodded to the servants who hurried forward, one of them grabbing the handles of his father's chair. Steven's eyebrows rose as the servant glared at the guards who'd gone to assist his father from the room.

TWO

Michael could feel the shock and fear that still hung over Ranlith. Even though the baker had earned his death, they were still reeling from watching Damien kill one of their own. He automatically checked and found that Nathanial had Damien in hand. However, all that had come from Damien since he'd killed the baker was cold-blooded determination. Michael crossed over to the hut that the Warlord had unceremoniously taken over. He acknowledged the guards outside the door as he walked between them and tapped a single rap on the solid wooden door with his knuckles before he entered. He didn't bother to wait for an answer. They didn't bother to stop him, either.

A shaft of jealousy from Aiden made him sigh. Aiden had tried to gain entrance to see the Warlord earlier but was refused. Again. It had been an ongoing thing between the Warlord and his son as far back as Michael could remember. A battle that Aiden inevitably lost.

"For such a small place, they are surprisingly well stocked.

Although I brought some of my own supplies." The Warlord gestured to the seat at the table where a flask sat with a mug. "Their lessik brew is rather good."

"It wasn't just because of Damien that we finally got around to taking this place." Michael shrugged.

Michael pulled out one of the wooden chairs and sat watching a little bemused as the Warlord fossicked around in the kitchen and opened a cupboard to grab another mug. It was commonplace for most but not something he'd expected to see from the Warlord.

"My mother had a little hut like this. Well, not quite like this one. All of this is like a palace in comparison." The Warlord joined him at the table, taking his seat again and pouring some lessik from the flask into the mug before handing it to him.

Michael accepted it, his eyes flashing up to the Warlord. He caught the image of a run-down hovel with hundreds of huts piled up together in a mass, spreading out below Yalleska as it was when the Warlord had been a child. It was a familiar story. The Warlord's mother had been a bed slave to the then warlord. She'd run when she'd found out she was pregnant. The old warlord of Yalleska slept with his bed slaves. That didn't mean he wanted their progeny to have any claim on Yalleska.

It was rare for the Warlord to mention his mother. He was obviously in a good mood, and this place reminded him of his childhood and simpler times before things went wrong in his world. The Warlord waited patiently. Michael raised the mug of lessik and took a sip of the amber liquid. The smooth, well-rounded taste—sweet with hints of spice and smoke— filled his mouth and warmed his throat as he swallowed. This drop was severely out of place here in this remote backwater. The Warlord chuckled and helped himself to some cheese and bread from a platter on the table. Michael shook his head and did the same.

"I'm guessing there was a reason for the drama with the baker. I had Damien in hand," Michael said.

"So, I take it you didn't get a good look into the late baker's mind?"

"Not really." Michael frowned and looked up at the Warlord. "He didn't like Damien much; I hadn't discovered why."

"If you had, you would have killed the man yourself."

"So, he sold out Isabella. What else?"

"The baker sold out Isabella because he wanted to possess her. He offered money to her father for the girl. Her father, it seems, is a respectable man who refused the offer. Damien had already caught the baker pleasuring himself while gazing at his sister. The only reason Mark Millar didn't die on that occasion was because the other villagers interceded."

"So, either the baker had to die, or you had to take Isabella away from here to protect her. Damien would not have understood the second option," Michael conceded.

"The man's mind was foul." The Warlord regarded him steadily.

"Fair enough. It would be better if Damien understood your motives."

"No, let him hate me for now. There's plenty of time for him to understand."

"Father—" Michael growled.

"Not now but use your judgement after you leave here. Damien still needs a degree of separation between who he was and who he will become."

While he disagreed with making the villagers fear Damien, it wasn't a matter he was willing to get into an argument with the Warlord over. There were some things he could push. Other things he wouldn't make much headway over. Besides, he was aware some here had feared Damien even before he'd killed the baker in front of them all. He pushed the concern aside. There were more pressing conversations he needed to have with the Warlord.

"This new commander has me concerned," Michael said.

"What makes you think the Sylannians have a new commander?" the Warlord asked.

"The memory of the attack was quite vivid in the minds of some of the survivors. The Sylannians were wearing maroon and cream."

"The Sylannian forces we've encountered before have always had different colours and markings on their armour. What makes the recent ones different? Other than the fact they were obviously successful."

"The memories I have from Khaliun of the commander who conquered the lands of the People and drove the Kallith from their homeland. They match the ones from the survivors here." Michael's eyes rose to meet the Warlord's. "We haven't seen them here before."

"You think they will get ready to invade soon?" the Warlord asked. "I don't know what else we can do until they invade. They could land anywhere up or down the river."

"I was hoping you had some bright ideas." Michael reached for the flask, topping up the Warlord's mug, then his own. "I can contact Khaliun of the clans and make sure they are fortifying the mountain pass and alert us if they come through that way."

"Do not burn yourself out. We can't afford for you to go down. Particularly with invasion imminent." The Warlord glared at him until he held his hand up, accepting the injunction. "I can send a messenger if needed."

Michael raised his eyebrows. "A messenger is less likely to send Khaliun to her bed cursing my name for a week or so than if I made direct contact from here. As you wish." Michael ticked options off on his fingers. "I can withdraw us to Yalleska and wait for a report to come in. Keep patrolling on a modified route, keeping to the main entry points they are likely to use. Ignoring our inland territories. Or take up a central position, halfway between Vallantia and Callenhain."

Michael fell silent as the Warlord considered options. He picked up a piece of cheese and ate it while waiting for the Warlord's response.

"Stay along the river. Get the villages to prepare as much as they can in the meantime. If they agree, advise them they can send young ones and the infirm with carers to sanctuary in Yalleska," the Warlord said.

"Good point. Either Yalleska or to inland villages far from the river; I'll advise them to take supplies deducted from their normal tithe."

"We're stocked enough at Yalleska, even to withstand a siege, although I doubt it will come to that."

"If you could send a messenger to Vallantia to alert them to prepare, I'll head to Callenhain from here."

"Easily done. I'll send a messenger. Do you want me to take Aiden back with me to Yalleska?" the Warlord asked.

"As much as I'd appreciate it, I think your time is better spent getting everything ready, our people ready, for when Sylanna hit us. You don't need to be distracted by Aiden."

"And you do?"

"His warband is competent even if he isn't." Michael shrugged. "I'll manage."

"He's been fairly bursting to try and get in to see me."

"Probably to tell you all about my brother's treachery."

"Again?" The Warlord snorted in amusement. "What did he attempt this time? Another failed uprising?"

"Pretty much. I dealt with the main conspirators who were

directly involved but got called away before I could investigate the Kastler Consortium further."

"Any more competent than the last lot?"

"These ones were killing off some of our sentries to trade with the Sylannians. That, of course, left a corridor wide open for attacks and a few holes in the communication relay. The ringleader even tried to bribe me." Michael glanced at the Warlord over the rim of his mug.

The Warlord laughed. "That obviously proved detrimental to their health. Did you find out how they've managed to trade with Sylanna and for what?"

"I was told they were receiving shipments of fine silks. There's only one commodity I can think of that the Sylannians would trade for. I only hope I'm wrong."

"So, those persistent rumours of traders engaging in the slave trade I asked you to investigate might have some truth?" The Warlord's voice was quiet, his gaze rising to meet Michael's. "You think the Kastlers are still trading in flesh?"

"I can't think of why else the Sylannians would let them live and keep their freedom. They certainly haven't shown any inclination to trade with us over the years."

Michael saw the vein in the Warlord's temple jump as he clenched his jaw. It was better if Michael traced this thread and pulled it than if the Warlord did. The Warlord wouldn't so much as pull a thread as unravel the whole thing and burn it—along with everyone else, innocent or otherwise.

"You'll follow up and check on their activities," the Warlord said.

"Of course. I tasked both Ben and Lukas to look into the rumours before I had to leave, as you requested."

The Warlord accepted his assurance. Michael agreed with the Warlord on many things, and this was one of them. People were not for sale. At least, they weren't in the Warlord's domain. It was one of the main, sweeping changes the Warlord had made as he'd conquered this land. Much to the disgruntlement of some who believed it was their right. Not that they dared to voice that opinion anywhere the Warlord might hear it.

Not if they wanted to live.

CHAPTER

THREE

Damien's shoulders tensed, the effect rippling down his back muscles. He'd thought the fear was mostly due to the Warlord's presence, but the Warlord had left after his conference with Michael yesterday and still the fear remained. It heightened any time Damien moved around the village. He realised he had always sensed it. Even when he'd lived here with tiscan dampening his senses. The tonic he'd taken had inhibited his abilities and not-so-coincidentally also dampened his perception of the constant animosity and distrust, though not entirely muted it. This background hum of aversion had been present even before he killed the baker—something he should have done a long time ago and which he had no regrets over. Damien strode across the village square. While the locals had been shocked by the revelations that the baker had given up Isabella's presence in the village for money, they were still horrified by his murder. He could feel that niggling doubt, the anxiety, and a hint of guilt from the other villagers as they tracked his movements. This, in his eyes, made them complicit in the baker's actions. If only because they had all been aware of what type of person the baker was and had made no effort to stop it.

"Damien!"

Damien spun, then braced as Isabella flew into his arms, hugging him fiercely. Everyone else might be treating him like a dangerous animal, but not Isabella. Unfortunately for the villagers, there was only one person in this village who dispatched dangerous animals, and that was his former mentor, Owen. Owen was currently disinclined to act against Damien, and the only others who were qualified were the Unwanted—his teammates. They weren't going to take any action against him for the baker's death. Which left the locals rather stuck with him until the Warleader decided it was time for them to pack up and leave Ranlith to resume their patrols.

Damien forced his mind away from villagers and concentrated on his sister. "Isa, I was coming to see you before I go."

"I wish you'd stay."

"You know that's impossible."

"Don't try to tell me I should have stayed inside. Your horrible Warlord already knows I exist. Besides, he left."

"I didn't say a word. Or even think it."

"I was getting in first. Mum and Dad are being impossible."

"Try to follow their rules, Isa. They're only trying to look after you."

"I know, but there's no point in me hiding away now."

Damien shook his head and laughed at her stubbornness. There was no point in arguing with her since he agreed with her.

He caught a hint of a smile on Isabella's lips as her attention was drawn elsewhere. Damien followed the direction she was facing to see what captivated her. That something was Michael pulling on his shirt with his back to them.

"Don't even think about him, Isa."

"What?"

"Don't try that wide-eyed innocent thing with me," Damien said, exasperated. "Michael is almost as dangerous as the Warlord."

"Well then, others wouldn't dare mistreat me, would they?" She looked up at him, her eyes wide and sparkling mischievously.

"Just…, please, he's not only the Warleader of everyone who rides for the Warlord but my band leader." Damien almost groaned aloud. Of all times for Isabella to start paying attention to men, it had to be now. Of all people to get fixated on, the members of his squad were hardly the safest. He watched as she crossed the intervening space and headed directly towards his squad mates. This time he did groan as she marched right up to Michael.

He saw Olivia speak to Michael, who faced Isabella as he pulled on his leathers. Michael's eyes caught his own; his amusement was unmistakable. He was just as aware of Isabella's thoughts as Damien was. How could he not be? She was such strong a mindspeaker, and she leaked.

Don't worry. I wouldn't dream of exploiting your sister, Michael said.

More than one person here is scared you'll kill them if you even think they might, Nathanial said.

I probably would.

Now, now, Damien, she's growing up, and you can't kill everyone she shows an interest in. Olivia's eyes danced as they rose to meet his own.

I know, but I can give it a good try, Damien grumbled.

You do realise she's decided she wants Michael to be her first? Olivia asked.

Thankfully we leave tomorrow.

She'll be of age next year, I believe, Michael said.

Damien heard the ripple of humour in Michael's tone and

didn't rise to the bait. It wasn't his business whom Isabella slept with if it was her choice, but of all the people she could sleep with in the world, he'd prefer she didn't sleep with his band leader. Or any of his teammates.

"Warleader?" Isabella said.

"What can I help you with, Isabella?"

"My brother, he's in trouble because of me, isn't he? He must ride off with you and kill people."

Damien hid his face in his hands.

"He's not in trouble. The events that transpired here ultimately made little difference to his fate. Even if you'd stayed hidden, he would still be riding out with us when we leave. The only difference was potentially in *your* fate, but I believe the issue is settled for now."

"For now?" Isabella swallowed, then lifted her head, her posture stiffening. "Does that mean you'll come back one day and take me as you did Damien? They say my powers are becoming like his."

Damien froze, eyes rising to Michael, who regarded Isabella with a grave expression. He reached out and placed a hand on her arm. He could feel the reassurance wash from Michael to Isabella.

"You may need some help controlling your powers, but I judge you'll be fine here for a little while longer."

Damien ducked his head and took a deep breath. He leaned against Olivia as her hand rested on his back and a strong sense of support flowed from her to him.

She may very well need the training and support that we can offer, Olivia said.

That's what scares me. When we leave, she'll be all alone, with no one to help her understand what's happening to her.

Concern and understanding came from Olivia. *We'll be*

passing through as often as we can. We know she's here and if her powers do continue to grow—

As we suspect they will, Nathanial admitted bluntly. *No one here is capable of training her.*

I don't want this life for her.

She is much stronger and more capable than you think. She just hasn't had much cause to grow up. You may find it is a life she wants in a year or so. Olivia pulled him into her embrace and hugged him, support flowing between them.

He wanted to protest, but there wasn't much point. His life in this village had been sheltered, but not to the same extent as Isabella's. Olivia was right. A great deal could change in his sister's life over the next few years. He just hoped they were changes for the good and didn't make her life miserable.

"You will look after him?" Isabella asked.

"I do my best to look after all my people. It's a thing with me," Michael said. Damien caught the edge of the wave of reassurance Michael directed at Isabella.

"We were about to eat. Would you like to join us, Isabella?" Olivia asked.

"I..." Isabella stopped and looked up at Damien.

Damien couldn't help his amusement at her sudden excitement at the prospect of eating with them and shook his head. "It's up to you if you'd like to join us. It will be our last chance for some time. We leave tomorrow."

"You didn't cook it, did you?" Isabella whispered, a hint of concern on her face.

"No, he certainly did not. We all value our stomachs too much for that. I'm Nathanial. You already know Michael here, and the lady who kindly offered the invitation is Olivia." Nathanial leant closer to Isabella, his voice dropping to a whisper. "She is also Michael's second-in-command."

Isabella's eyes widened as she looked over at Olivia, who looked dryly at Nathanial.

"To clarify, I am one of two seconds-in-command to the warband, and the other is Nathanial. We will also do our best to look after your brother," Olivia said.

"Come, if we continue standing here, those two will keep bantering." Michael held out his arm to her with a flourish.

Damien saw Isabella blush as she placed her hand lightly on his arm. Michael tilted his head formally at Isabella and then led her over to their improvised meal area. It was an old gesture that belonged in a court, with everyone dressed up to impress. It should have been out of place here, yet somehow, Michael pulled it off.

Do all women turn to mush when he decides to be charming?

You have no idea. You should see my mother when he's around, let alone if Nathanial is present as well, Olivia said.

Olivia's mother is scary. Although it's like she gets confused and can't remember who her quarry is, Nathanial said, then his eyes sparkled with amusement, and his mental tone lowered as if he were sharing a confidence with Olivia. *Next visit, we should also invite Damien to the inevitable ball. She'll be beside herself.*

Damien snorted and followed behind as Michael led Isabella to their campfire. Isabella settled on a low stool right next to Michael. A small collection of seats had materialised from the village and he had a sneaking suspicion the Speaker had made the order to make their stay more comfortable—if only in the hope it would minimise the chance of anyone else being killed.

Before sitting, he noticed his parents standing halfway between their home and the camp. Their concern radiated from them as they watched on, wringing their hands. With a barely restrained sigh, he went to them.

"Please, come and join us. We have plenty," Damien said as he hugged them both, repressing his exasperation as he sensed their hesitation. He understood the others in the village being fearful, but they were his parents.

"Isa shouldn't be there with them. They're dangerous," his father said.

"The Warlord was dangerous. In case you missed it, he's not here. He left yesterday."

"What if he hurts her?" his mother asked.

"Michael isn't going to hurt Isabella. Trust me. He would split in two any man who stepped out of line." He ducked his head and pushed down his impatience. "Come over, sit and eat with us. It might ease your mind."

"You... you think of yourself as one of them now." His mother's lips trembled.

"There is no going back from the Unwanted, Mother. For good or ill, it is what I am now. I will fight to keep Isa free of this life as long as I can."

"You believe they will still take her?" his father asked.

"If Isa continues to develop like me..." He paused, grappling with his feelings on what he was about to say. "She won't have a choice. No one here will be able to help her gain control of her abilities."

"We'll leave you to your friends," his mother said, a catch in her voice.

"Please, would it hurt to sit down and have a meal? The Unwanted have helped me more than you know. I'd probably be dead without them, and would have taken many here with me."

His parents looked at each other, and he was about to give up when their resistance crumbled. Grabbing his mother's hand, he led her over to the meal area. Others made way and cleared stools for them to sit on, moving over to a fallen log on one side of the fire. Callan dished up two bowls of the stew that had been made for their meal, handing one to each.

Nathanial handed Damien a drink and a bowl of food which

he accepted, grateful for that brief distraction. He was on edge, but his squad mates were on their best behaviour, and as the night wore on, a small number of villagers made their way over to the gathering. Some brought extra food, others some of their own brew to add to the assortment on offer at the impromptu gathering. Damien even saw Owen sitting not far from Isabella, keeping a careful eye on her. He gathered his mentor had been responsible for badgering some of the more even-minded villagers into coming to join them. He finally had some hope that while not all in his home village would welcome his arrival when they next rode back into town, perhaps these few might.

FOUR

J aclyn swept onto the balcony, ignoring the other houses' startlement in her brother's court. All of them were waiting for his appearance. King Samuel, her brother, was artfully late. A circumstance she had no patience for. Out here on the balcony, staring out over the canopy, was much more pleasant. She relaxed imperceptibly, bathed in the blue, veil-filled glow cast by the immature silkspiders and the webs they spun glinting through the trees.

"We met out here before we were bound," Ricardo mused.

"The first time I set eyes on my husband-to-be."

Ricardo lent down and kissed her forehead. "Your under-wives were ferocious. I still remember their scowls."

"I was terrified that night when Samuel took the throne."

Jaclyn rested her head on Ricardo's shoulder, closing her eyes against the images that flashed in her mind, prompted by their rehashing of the past. Their past. Which was, unfortunately, the cause of their problems in the now.

"I could not refuse you and leave you to die. We were meant to be, you and I."

Pairings amongst the ruling families of Sylanna were made early, yet she and Ricardo had defied their respective families. Ricardo had promised himself to another until Jaclyn had fled the Monarch House straight into his arms. He'd accepted her plea, and she'd forged the primary mate bond between their minds. Her brother's wives had been furious when they'd discovered that she was alive and mate-bonded to Ricardo. Yet they'd had no choice but to concede she was now the firstwife of her own house and beyond their ability to kill. At least directly. Her brother could keep sending her off to foreign lands, hoping she and her house met their deaths. He could send his daggerwives, wearing no one's colours, to take her life in the depths of the night, then deny responsibility. But neither he nor his wives could act directly against her in the name of the Monarch House.

"In truth, binding to you is what saved me."

Careful, my love. Some would clamour for our lives if they realised you don't exert control over me the way you should.

That way is the path of madness. I would not do that to our house.

Your brother approaches, Myra warned.

"I used to play out here as a child when I managed to escape the underwives," Jaclyn said.

"I remember," Samuel said. "Your ability to escape the restraints they placed on you made you stand out."

Jaclyn moved to face Samuel and smiled, knowing it at least appeared genuine. She was a daughter of the Sylannian high court, after all. Still, her brother and his wives understood that her pleasant expression did not go below the surface. Any more than she believed their smiles or apparent welcome. She pushed aside the sadness the sight of this Samuel provoked. He'd been her dashing older brother; he'd taught her to fight and showed her tricks to evade the underwives and escape the confines of the nursery. That boy was long gone, lost not long after he chose his firstwife. Her brother's mind belonged to his wives now.

"It seems I always had an adventurous spirit," Jaclyn said.

Samuel ignored the congregating court. Clearly they'd decided that since their king, his wives, and their most celebrated commander were out here, they should be as well. Jaclyn didn't miss the flare of what she could swear was defiance that passed over her brother's face only to be smoothed over as the firstwife's hand rested on his shoulder. Jaclyn didn't allow herself to stiffen at recognising that momentary lack of control. After all this time, Samuel shouldn't be capable of fighting the dominance of his wives. Ricardo's hand rested on her back, his presence soothing her own nerves over what she suspected was coming. Just because she'd manoeuvred for this action didn't mean she wasn't on edge about the consequences. Her brother's odd behaviour could be examined later.

As the king stepped forward, triumph and satisfaction radiating from him, her daggerwives stepped aside as she subtly urged them to. It wouldn't pay to cause a confrontation right here in front of the entire court. Her brother grabbed her shoulders and pulled her into his embrace, kissing her on the cheek. He seemed oblivious to the sudden tension in the daggerwives, both of his own house and hers. Samuel placed his hand around her shoulders as they faced the massed court.

"We owe a great debt to our sister for her courage in advancing the cause of our people. She has succeeded when so many others have failed." Samuel faced her, his expression inscrutable. "Jaclyn, sister, I order you to go to the barbarian lands and seize them for Sylanna. I appoint you as Commander of the kingdom with all rights and authority it holds."

Jaclyn tried not to let the triumph go beyond her mental barriers, allowing a nod of acknowledgement for the order.

"As you wish, my king. I am Sylanna's servant in all things," Jaclyn said.

She saw the eyes of her brother's firstwife narrow, as did

those of his other wives near enough to overhear the comment. None of them missed the slight change in the honorary wording, but neither could they fault it. It was usually phrased that she was the king's servant in all things. She passed her gaze over her brother and his wives. She didn't bother to use her powers to aid her assessment. Firstwife Chelsie would block her from doing so. It shouldn't be needed. Samuel should be deep under the thrall of his firstwife's influence, yet there was something that glittered in the back of his eyes. The stiffness of his wives, all of it screamed that something was wrong. She could see the tell-tales with her othersight, the fitful red spikes that escaped the carefully constructed barrier around him.

"You bring honour to our family line, Commander." Samuel paused, the very figure of a benevolent brother and king. "Our mother and father would be proud."

The reference to their now-dead relatives, purged by his daggerwives when he wrested control, was taboo.

I fear your concern about the onset of instability in Samuel and his wives could be accurate. Ricardo's tone was uneasy.

It brings me no pleasure to be correct, Jaclyn said.

You are not Samuel, and we have not exercised such all-encompassing control on you as his wives now do, Myra said.

I fear we will need to deal with them eventually, but that day is not today. As much as she tried to hide it, Jaclyn heard the hint of pain in her own voice.

While Samuel and his firstwife had bonded years before she and Ricardo, none of them liked the ever-present reminder of their future. That the day was fast approaching where she would have to cleanse the Monarch House. Worse, that she could be wrong about the cause of the madness that stuck down their people, and she would succumb to it as well. Unfortunately, you were the last to know when you were in the middle of that toxic spiral.

CHAPTER
FIVE

Tarkhan stood, arms crossed, repressing a sympathetic wince as the last of the wolf-eyes of the warriors of Kallith were tapped into the foreheads of the brother and sister. The tools used, made from the teeth of the wolf, sharpened and bound to sticks, imprinted using small mallets and dyes, hadn't changed for generations. This was the cumulation of painful months the pair had spent receiving their tattoos. It was a rite of passage marking the beginning of their journey between childhood and adulthood. There was always a reason for those not born to a warrior tribe, to change allegiance, and follow the warrior path. In the case of the brother and sister, it was the destruction of their tribe, being among the few of the Hallaran Clan to survive. Unfortunately, soul-destroying events weren't unique to the brother and sister. Even if it was heartbreaking. There was a part of him that wished they'd chosen a different path, but he understood why they couldn't. Khaliun, who stood next to him, was a ball of anxiety laced through with regret and failure.

This is a big day for them, try to be accepting, Tarkhan said.

It's not the ceremony.

Then what?

Khaliun didn't move a muscle, keeping her attention on the ceremony. *This isn't the time.*

When is there time?

It isn't important.

We both know each other enough to know when there is something wrong.

It's nothing.

It's something or you wouldn't be this tied up in knots. Talk to me. What's wrong?

Tarkhan saw her eyes slide over to him before her gaze fell away. He could feel the tight knot of pain and uncertainty in her. That emotion killed a part of him. They had been through so much together, and ultimately, it was the job of co-leaders to support each other. It was a little hard to do when his co-leader wouldn't tell him what was wrong. Tarkhan tried not to let his frustration show as Khaliun shut herself off and refused to answer him. Taking a breath, he focused his attention back to the initiation ceremony of their latest tribe members.

The old lore keeper dipped the sharpened tooth into the bowl of ink once more, then, in a number of rapid-fire movements, etched the final outline. The dark outer curve of the wolf eyes on the forehead of the new initiate took form at the same time her counterpart did the same on her sibling. Finally, the lore keepers eased back, standing to face them.

"The rite is complete. Welcome the new cubs to the Warriors of Kallith."

Tarkhan was relieved as the burst of welcome and acceptance came from the rest of their tribe. He'd been afraid that after all they'd been through, no one would have the energy to welcome new members of their tribe. Pushing aside his unfounded concern Tarkhan took his place to one side of the lore keepers in front of the pair. He paused, eyes flicking to Khaliun, who finally stepped forward to stand at his side.

"Welcome to the Warriors of Kallith," Tarkhan said, handing over a bow and quiver filled with arrows to each of them.

"We are your family; may you fight with honour to protect your fellow tribe members and to the benefit of the whole clan," Khaliun said gravely, handing each a sword.

Everyone was silent as the newly accepted cubs took their weapons, and then they cheered, all pressing forward to hug the pair, welcoming them to their new family.

"Come, everyone, a feast has been prepared to celebrate this occasion," Tarkhan said.

Tarkhan extracted himself and headed towards the communal tent where the food and drink had been prepared, relieved when Khaliun stepped up to his side. He placed a hand on her shoulder and steered her away from the celebration. The rest of their tribe would get by without them for a space of time. After a slight resistance, Khaliun allowed it and they wandered in silence towards the outer ring and the empty plains beyond. Their own tribe, consisting of the bulk of the clan's warriors, held a position on the perimeter of the camp. It was useful not only if they needed to fight but also for occasions like this where a conversation needed to happen away from prying ears. He could feel Khaliun's tension, but he kept his silence. She would talk when she was ready. He steeled himself. Whatever it was, she would likely be correct, no matter how much she wished other-wise, and he wouldn't like it any more than she did. If it were good news, Khaliun wouldn't be so agitated.

"I hear her."

"Hear who?"

"Delbee." She held up her hand. "I know she's meant to be dead, but I keep hearing her cry out, in anger and pain."

Tarkhan's eyes widened as he went cold. He didn't doubt

Khaliun for even a moment. He rubbed his face with his hand before coming to a halt.

"You mean we left her there? But Chono said—"

"I've been going over that conversation again and again." Khaliun took a deep, shaky breath before continuing. "He said she was tied up."

Tarkhan thought back to that day when against his instincts, which at the time had been screaming at him, they'd ridden down into Hallaran to be greeted by Chono. When Delbee hadn't joined her co-leader in the meeting hut, both he and Khaliun had been shocked. He replayed that fateful moment in his head, and his stomach plunged.

"You're right. He didn't say she was dead."

"I have to go back. If she's alive, I must try."

"No." Tarkhan held his hand up as Khaliun's face reddened, and her mouth opened to voice what would be a heated response. "If she is alive, we left her there. More rightly, *I* left her there. You were hardly in any condition to do otherwise."

"You had your reasons. If she was as badly injured as me, it's likely the Sylannians would have caught us. We all would have died," Khaliun whispered, pain rippling through her voice.

"We will go back."

Khaliun looked at him, her eyes wide. "I can't let you do that. If I'm wrong, we could both die for nothing. It makes no logical sense. That voice crying out could be them trying to lure us back."

"If you're right, you can't go alone. We both go with a small group of volunteers if any will agree to go with us." Tarkhan's narrow as she went to object. "Or neither of us goes. Besides, even if you're wrong, we get to kill Sylannians, which isn't a likely prospect here."

Khaliun took a step back, anger, determination, and devastation warring within her. It was one of the traditions of the

People: co-leaders had to agree on a course of action. While it could cause issues on occasion—they'd certainly had their disagreements—they'd always been able to work through them for the good of their tribe. Besides that, he knew his co-leader. If he said no, which he admitted he should as it was a fool's mission, she would work herself up and go anyway. By herself. It was a problem with those with exceptional gifts—they were more prone to the emotions of others around them. In their camp right now, amongst those who'd survived, grief and vengeance were the prominent emotions. Even he was prey to it. If they lived through this, he vowed he'd speak to the Warleader about getting some training for their people. Including Khaliun, so she could learn to supervise the lessons of their own, obviously, not because she needed some of the expertise the Warlord's people possessed.

The storm of emotions ceased, grief and acceptance remained. "I could lead us both to our deaths."

"You could but still, we'll go. If Delbee is alive, we'll do our best to save her."

"Should I apologise in advance if my head is just getting us both in trouble?"

"Not necessary, either way we get to kill Sylannians and resolve whether Delbee really is alive. I think our new cubs might have some input; she was their mother, but I think we should leave them this night."

"They can't come with us, even though I suspect they will want to."

"Agreed. If we are to have a chance at pulling this off and coming out the other end alive, we'll need an experienced team."

"I think we'll need to leave soon." Khaliun looked at him grimly. "The longer we leave it, the more likely the other co-leaders will find out."

"What they don't know, they can't disagree with."

"It's our right as co-leaders of our tribe to take what action we deem necessary."

"It just needed us both to agree. Which we do. We'll speak to Delbee's children, swear them to secrecy, then go before any can intervene."

"Thank you for your trust." Khaliun swallowed her tone tinged with a sadness. "We should go back."

Tarkhan and Khaliun continued in their looping path back towards the camp in silence. While it was likely their action would have been noted, none would think anything out of place. For tonight they had a celebration to go to. They needed to eat and drink with their tribe as if there was nothing wrong. As if tomorrow was just another day.

TARKHAN FIDGETED. Now that he'd made up his mind, he wanted to be gone already and the fact that Khaliun was just as edgy didn't make it any better. The door opened and their newly adopted cubs were escorted into the hut. Those that had brought them took a station on the door. The siblings looked at him; he could see their concern and he sent a shaft of reassurance at them as he waved them down. He waited as they both sank, with all the gracefulness of youth, into the piles of cushions opposite him and Khaliun.

"What is about to occur will be difficult for all the warriors of our tribe but particularly for the pair of you," Tarkhan said, trading his gaze between them.

"It is not common for us to place such pressure on a cub," Khaliun said.

"You need to give your pledge as a warrior of Kallith to keep our council."

Delbee's children looked at each other before looking back at them both. Each of them quiet and contained. They'd screamed and cried. Had nightmares and wailed at the cruelty of the Powers to land such a fate on them. To survive when their world had been taken from them. Interestingly it was the younger of the two who spoke first.

"We gave our pledge last night, leaders. Whatever you need from us, you have it." Delbee's daughter swallowed but looked back at him steadily. "None will learn about this conversation from either of us."

Tarkhan looked at the pair, old beyond their years as only children of war could be. Although neither could possibly be aware in this moment before they'd given their word how difficult this would be for them.

"We'll need your formal pledge," Tarkhan advised them solemnly.

The siblings didn't hesitate, speaking together without even a hint of uncertainty in their voices or minds.

"As warriors of Kallith, your trust is held to our heart. May the wolf seek vengeance should we betray the trust of the tribe."

"Your mother was Delbee?" Khaliun asked.

The lad's eyes widened but otherwise his face remained blank. "Yes, Co-leader Khaliun."

"She died at Hallaran due to the actions of Chono, the traitor to our clan, of all the People." The young girl's voice was soft but firm. The newly inked ice-blue eyes of the wolf tattoo on her forehead seemed to gleam.

"Forgive the question, but did you, either of you, see her body?" Khaliun asked.

The siblings looked at each other, silent communication passing between them before both shook their heads.

"No, but she was just inside the doors when the Sylannians burst in," Delbee's daughter said.

"The guards were dead on the floor when they separated me

from the others." The young man frowned. "But I don't remember seeing Mother."

Seeing the questions in their eyes Tarkhan ducked his head. He'd been half hoping they would say they had seen their mother's dead body on the floor. Because then Khaliun would be wrong, and they wouldn't be engaging in this risky endeavour.

"You know Khaliun is a strong mindspeaker?" Tarkhan asked.

The siblings nodded, staring at him intently.

"For the past few months, I've heard a voice screaming through the veil. I believe that voice to be your mother's." Khaliun's voice was low as she stared at the pair opposite them.

Delbee's children surged to their feet, half turning towards the entrance of the tent as if to run back to Hallaran immediately. The two senior warriors stepped adroitly in front of the doorway, blocking their exit.

"Hold, cubs! Sit down," Tarkhan said.

The pair looked at each other before sinking back into the cushions.

"We will be making a run back to Hallaran, if we can get there with a small, experienced group of warriors." Khaliun held up her hand as she spoke. "This could very well be a trap."

"You are cubs, and we would be failing in our duty if we allowed you to accompany us. You will both remain here," Tarkhan said firmly.

"Co-leader—"

"Enough. As your co-leaders, we have discussed our course of action and on this we both concur." Tarkhan kept his face expressionless with considerable effort. "If we find Delbee alive, and it is possible, we will seek to free her and return here."

"It is by no means assured that we will succeed," Khaliun said, her expression and tone grave.

"You will both stay here and say nothing about where our group has gone or why. No matter how pressed."

Tarkhan could see the rebellious, angry glint in their eyes, but continued to stare at them implacably until they finally ducked their heads. They both muttered their agreement. The escort who stood at the door nodded. The youngsters would find a pair of their fellow tribesmen blocking their path tonight when they tried to sneak off.

SIX

Villagers jumped in front of him, both men waving their arms, causing Michael to haul back on the reins. His horse squealed and half-reared. Michael kept expletives from pouring out of his mouth as he exercised careful control over his mount. The men in front of him had no idea how close they had come to receiving fatal imprints of his horse's hooves on their foreheads. Only the fact that he could see neither of them was armed held him back and meant he didn't signal his horse to reduce their heads to mush. Nathanial leapt from his horse, his blade clearing its scabbard before he hit the ground, with Callan and Damien following his lead. Michael's eyes narrowed and his temper rose a notch. Since there was no likelihood of any immediate attack by Sylanna in this place, he'd intended to ride straight through.

"Do you have any idea how foolish your actions were?" Nathanial asked, stepping forward, his blade pressing against the throat of one of the men.

"Sorry, I... I thought you weren't going to stop." The man was almost babbling, colour draining from his face.

"We weren't," Nathanial agreed bluntly.

"People generally breathe a sigh of relief when we ride through rather than stop for the night," Olivia said.

Silence stretched as the villagers just stared at them. Michael tried not to grind his teeth in frustration.

"What do you want?" Michael asked flatly.

"Please, Warlord—"

"Warleader. If the Warlord were here, you'd be dead where you stand," Nathanial said.

"Sorry. Warleader, please, we need you to take our village in the Warlord's name," the man said.

"We took Lutter several years back," Michael said.

"What? No, this isn't our village. Our village is Ridon, it's much smaller. You've never even bothered to ride through."

"Ridon is a few hours down the small side track off the main road." The other man swallowed as Michael switched his gaze to him.

"Let me get this straight. You're asking me to conquer Ridon in the Warlord's name?" Michael's anger drained, leaving him simply bemused by the request.

"Well, there's always a first time," Olivia said under her breath.

Michael looked down at the men, feeling the desperation rolling off the pair in waves. Other details caught his eye: their worn, ragged clothing and gaunt appearance. It was unusual, at least for those from the small villages. Even with the tithe each town had to contribute, the villages claimed by the Warlord thrived. There was something to be said for the relative peace gained from being under one Warlord instead of multiple warlords constantly bickering and fighting each other for territory. Some in the more significant population centres like Vallantia or Callenhain struggled to survive, but their circumstances had little to do with the Warlord.

Michael dismounted, signalling the rest of his people to do likewise, and handed the reins of his horse off. Lutter was deserted since the locals had made themselves scarce. However, he could sense them hiding within their small dwellings due to the slight ebb and stuttering flow of people with little talent for the veil. The muddy glow would show up in his othersight if he bothered to look—handy in small places as it meant he could pinpoint the inhabitants. It wasn't as valuable for busy places like Vallantia or Callenhain where the sheer number of inhabitants who glowed merged, forming a solid mass.

A wave of consternation from the absent, but watching, villagers emanated from the huts as they realised the warband had dismounted. Michael traded a glance with Olivia, whose lips quirked as she tried not to laugh in response. The locals, at least, had clearly hoped they'd ride straight through like they usually did. Lutter had been taken almost as an afterthought when they'd decided to stop on their way to Callenhain a few years back. One of those small villages that they collected eventually but weren't pressing. Since all these villages in this area had fallen into territory initially claimed by the Strafford warlord, they belonged to the Warlord by default, the moment he defeated the Strafford warlord.

"Now, why don't you explain why you had the pressing need to potentially get yourself killed by jumping in front of me and why you want me to take Ridon?" Michael heard the thread of exasperation in his tone.

"Set up camp. We'll stay the night," Olivia ordered the others.

His people scattered, heading off to set up their camp for the night. Except for Nathanial, Callan and Damien, who'd stayed put, blades still drawn, positioned between Michael and the ragged villagers.

"The Warlord, um, you've never taken Ridon, Warleader," one of the men said, swallowing convulsively.

"So you indicated earlier. Why do you want me to take your village in the Warlord's name? Trust me, it's an unusual request," Michael said blandly.

"If we belonged to the Warlord, the bandits wouldn't dare raid us."

"Please, we can't survive with what they take from us."

"We don't have much left, but we'll find a way to pay tithe to the Warlord somehow."

"Some of us will volunteer to ride in the Warlord's warbands, although I fear we aren't any good at fighting."

"I think we've managed to guess that part," Nathanial said.

Michael gestured, and the three sheathed their swords, moving back to form a loose detail to one side.

"I take it they've been preying on you for some time?" Michael asked.

The men nodded vigorously. All of them reeked of fear, yet he assessed they were terrified of the raiders rather than him. It was somewhat refreshing not to be seen as the monster for once.

"Yes. You've taken most other places around here except Ridon."

"Do you know where these bandits of yours are coming from?" Nathanial asked.

"No, we just figured they live in the forest somewhere." The man who'd seemed to become the spokesperson looked at his companion who hastily agreed.

"I doubt that," Michael said. "Come, you can fill us in on more details, at least as much as you know. Then we'll see what we can do."

Not waiting for an answer, Michael went back towards where the rest of the squad was making camp. He registered that the residents of Lutter, finally realising they weren't going anywhere, had become brave enough to make an appearance. He nearly sighed as he realised that one of the more courageous souls was heading in his direction.

"Warleader?"

Be nice. These folk seem a little timid, Nathanial said.

Michael suppressed his irritation and gave his full attention to a woman who stood waiting, her gaze firmly on the ground.

"I hope you'll forgive us, but our speaker is absent on business. We didn't know you'd be coming," she said, her eyes darting up to his before glancing away again.

"We weren't intending on staying until these people stopped us to request assistance."

"Our hunters did well, Warleader. We'd be honoured to share our evening meal with you," she said.

"Thank you, we appreciate it. Have you heard of these bandits that prey on these people?"

She looked up at him shaking her head. "We didn't realise, not until they came here. There are some that ride through. I'm sorry, Warleader, but we thought they were one of the Warlord's groups. I see now we were wrong."

Michael frowned. If these so-called bandits didn't come from Lutter, then it was likely they came from one of the villages around here. That was more than problematic since, to his knowledge, there weren't any other villages in this area that they hadn't formally absorbed into the Warlord's domain. This region might be sparsely populated, but it was close enough to Callenhain that they had a thorough idea of the inhabitants in these parts. It was more than likely that these so-called bandits were from a village they'd already claimed.

The Warlord is not going to like this, Olivia said.

It's a sentiment I can't fault the Warlord for, particularly since I don't like it either.

While he'd ridden in, killed, and taken villages in the Warlord's name, he didn't appreciate anyone else getting in on the act. The only people allowed to terrorise others in the Warlord's domain were the Warlord and those riding under his banner. Even so Michael knew of all the band leaders he was the only one who could attack with impunity. If the other band leaders tried without his or the Warlord's expressed permission, they'd best have a very good reason. Others outside of their ranks deciding to dabble in the practice could prove problematic. Although he wagered it was a problem, he could deal with it before the Warlord became involved.

"It doesn't sound like something any of the others that ride under the Warlord would do," Michael said.

Mainly because he'd kill them, Olivia said.

Or we would, Nathanial said.

There are plenty of undesirable people who ride under the Warlord's banner, Olivia said.

Michael resisted the urge to throw exasperated glances at the two. The poor souls almost quivering in front of him couldn't hear the conversation they were engaging in.

"Well, they don't look like you. They're mean enough, but they look ragged and unkempt next to all of you. You lot look and react like you can kill as—" The man flushed, shutting his mouth abruptly as his companion elbowed him.

A wave of amusement from Nathanial and Olivia did not help as Michael only barely prevented himself from laughing.

"Rest assured, we will do what we can to track down and deal with whoever is doing this," Michael said.

The woman, clearly realising the conversation was over, went to leave, stopped, and turned back. Michael stopped the sigh from escaping his lips as Nathanial raised his eyebrows. Nathanial always had a soft spot for those who lived in these small villages. The woman held out a basket. Damien stepped forward and intercepted it.

"It's only my brew, but I think it's drinkable. We'll get the food cooking in the central food pit. It should be ready in a few hours." The woman bobbed, ducked her head, and scurried away.

Slowly the locals materialised from where they'd been hiding. He couldn't remember the last time they'd bothered to stop here, and given the townspeople's reaction, he doubted any of the other warbands did either. By the looks of the place, they outnumbered the locals. All things considered, an overnight stay seemed to be long overdue.

SEVEN

Damien stood with his teammates out of sight from the narrow dirt track that served as an entrance to Ridon, which sat a few hours up the road from Lutter, where he and his band had been stopped. It was a sad, run-down affair with a small group of huts in various states of disrepair. It amazed him that those left here hadn't moved on elsewhere when the so-called bandits had started raiding them. Then again, there were always people like that, tied to their place of birth. Refusing to move no matter how bleak their situation became.

The careful questioning by Michael and Olivia had fascinated Damien. They'd teased out details of the attacks that Damien was certain even the poor villagers from Ridon had forgotten. As a result they had brought out the fact that the bandits had been hitting Ridon and taking what little they had on a regular basis. So regularly that it seemed to form a predictable pattern that made Michael suspect the bandits were guards who rode with one of the regular trading caravans that made its way around from Callenhain to the smaller villages. They also knew the number of raiders and how they were armed.

That insight into the likely identity of the bandits was how they'd all come to be in this village with only their leaders visible to the mercenaries when they arrived. Michael was sitting at the central firepit. Olivia was pulling weeds from a neglected garden patch while Nathanial was drawing water from the well. Damien clenched the hilt of his sword and wrenched his attention from the vine growing among the weeds in the garden bed of the dilapidated hut back toward the firepit.

The pitiful residents of Ridon had been sent to Lutter and he and the Unwanted had secretly moved in instead. They'd spent a few impatient days waiting, but finally their scouts had determined a trading caravan was on the main trail and heading to Lutter. If Michael was correct, soon after arriving in Ridon, the bandits would arrive in Lutter. At that point, they were going to get a very nasty shock.

Heads up. We have incoming. Small group, five riders.

Damien heard the riders coming before he saw the five who rode in and dismounted not far away from where he stood in the imperfect shadow cast by the hut. The group of raiders, laughing and joking with each other, strode towards where Michael sat. Damien could feel the arrogance dripping from them and the surge of superiority as they swaggered towards Michael, hands on the pommels of their swords.

"You! Go fetch the game you've hunted for us. We don't have time to mess around," the man in the lead said.

Michael stood, pushing the cloak back off his shoulders, and pulled his sword from its scabbard in a slow, deliberate motion.

Now, Michael ordered.

Damien sucked in the veil, relieved as the aching cold washed through him. The thieves in front of him spun away from Michael only to stumble to a halt, faces going pale, when the rest of the Unwanted stepped out from behind the huts and trees, effectively surrounding the bandits. The bandits went to retreat to their horses but there was nowhere to run to. All signs of confidence drained from them, as they finally faced Michael. The face of one of the men screwed up.

A hint of motion, a hand clenching on a sword hilt and beginning to draw, was all it took. Damien drew his blade from its scabbard and lunged forward, sword slicing across the man's neck in one fluid move. He snapped his shield up with barely a thought, the spray of blood from the soon-to-be-dead attacker splattering on the invisible barrier and dripping onto the ground. Fear, with a dose of horror, spiked in the bandits. Damien remembered the first time he'd killed with brutal efficiency; he'd been a mess afterwards. This time he stared down at the twitching, dying man waiting for him to bleed out.

It's surprising how much blood a body holds, Damien said.

Michael didn't look at him, he didn't have to. Damien could sense his Warleader's approval and concern all intertwined together.

Easy, Damien, Michael ordered.

He was going to draw on you, Damien said.

I know. None of them realised that, though.

Let them fear someone other than you for a change. Should give you a refreshing break this time.

Damien stared coolly ahead at the shocked thugs, dismissing the body of the erstwhile attacker. Not even a hint of apology in his stance.

"My men are a little jumpy," Michael said.

Damien nearly laughed as the remaining bandits blanched as their eyes slid from the Warleader to him.

What are you doing now?

Nothing. Just smiling pleasantly. It's amazing how threatening they find it, Damien said innocently. He felt the weight of Michael's regard as his Warleader assessed him.

Your deal with the Warlord doesn't mean you have to try and be him, or me. Just be yourself, Michael said.

Wearing the uniform of the Unwanted, and riding with our company, makes you terrifying enough to most people, Olivia said.

Nathanial moved subtly to place himself on the other side of Olivia.

"So, who's up next to explain your idiocy?" Nathanial asked in the silence.

"You all believe you are good at this killing and intimidating people business," Michael said.

"In case you're in any doubt," Damien said pleasantly, a crooked grin still on his lips, "we're better."

Damien could tell Michael was getting a little impatient as the group of bandits just stood there. Gazes going from their now dead leader on the ground back to Michael before sliding over to Damien any time he moved.

This isn't you and it's more than you trying to be what you think the Warlord wants you to be. What's wrong? Nathanial asked.

There's a tiscan vine over there, growing wild at the hut I was stationed behind. Damien bit out. *Sorry, the last few days staying here has been fraying at my nerves. I'm trying to stay focused on something, anything other than that.*

A brush of Nathanial's power rippled over his skin and mind. Damien bore the check-up calmly and didn't even bother to conceal how the plant's smell was affecting him. So, Nathanial perceived his desire for tiscan clamouring at him, that his skin crawled, and his stomach was in knots. Damien was keeping calm and staying in place by sheer willpower alone. The mental check-up didn't escape Michael's awareness. His band leader was always hyper-alert during an attack. Damien saw the moment when Michael spotted the tiscan vine as he swept his gaze over the makeshift band of bandits and scanned the edge of the village.

Will you be able to hold yourself together? Michael asked.

Damien was grateful there was no censure in his Warleader's tone. He just wished he'd get over craving the stuff. At least he hadn't even thought about his drug of choice for days, until he smelt the vine. As ashamed as his weakness made him feel, Damien was grateful for the support. With his squad around him he could stand here and not collect the leaves from the vine to make his own brew. If he was being honest, he didn't think he'd have had the power to resist if he'd stumbled on the tiscan without the others.

I'll survive, but please don't make me sleep here another night. Damien was surprised that his mindvoice remained calm.

Nathanial woke rolling out of his hammock as his brain registered that Damien was not in his bed. He relaxed as his questing mind found that Damien hadn't gone far. He was sitting at the campfire. Alone. Nathanial could feel the battle Damien was waging with himself. Yet he sat unmoving. On checking the sleeping camp, Nathanial could see one of the night guards keeping watch over Damien. At a signal from him the guard nodded and moved away from Damien back to his post to scan the sleeping town and surrounding forest for any threat. He was reassured that they had also been keeping an eye on Damien.

Do what you can; we'll not be travelling far or fast with the prisoners, a late start won't hurt much one way or the other, Michael said.

Rest, I've got this, he replied, glancing across to see Michael's eyes close.

Nathanial shook his head. Trust Michael to be aware that their problem child was up and struggling with himself.

We are kindred, all of us who are discarded. We are only as strong as our weakest member. We look after each other because no one else will, Michael said.

Always, Nathanial said.

Nathanial crossed the camp with a soft tread, careful not to disturb anyone else. He stopped by their supplies and picked up a wine skin and two goblets. Damien kept his gaze on the fire as Nathanial sat next to him. Nathanial pulled the stopper from the skin and poured some of the wine in each of the goblets. Then simply held out one to Damien.

"Is this wise?"

"I'm certain I would have noticed if you'd gone around camp sculling every flask of alcohol we have," Nathanial said.

"It doesn't quite have the same kick," Damien said, as he reached for the goblet.

"Thoughts of sinking into that soft blissful world that is tiscan keeping you awake?"

"I want more so badly right now," Damien whispered, his gaze dropping to his goblet. "It hurts."

"Yet you sit here, despite knowing where you can get the stuff."

"As soon as I smelt it in Ridon, I wanted more, but I know I can't."

"Give yourself time. You're doing well."

Damien took a sip of the wine, silence stretching between them. Nathanial watched him carefully, relieved that he was at least capable of exerting control over himself and his hunger.

"If it's not one thing it's another of late."

"What else is troubling you?"

"During the briefing Olivia said we'll be heading to Callenhain as soon as the other team arrives to take the prisoners off our hands."

"We will be there for several days, we have quite a bit of business to deal with," Nathanial said.

Nathanial sipped his drink waiting for Damien to process what he was thinking. Damien probably didn't even know himself what had really driven him out of his hammock. After all, he could be miserable in his hammock as well.

"It's a big city."

"Second biggest in the Warlord's domain. You've been there before although granted you didn't get to see much of it."

"Some of the others told me tiscan brew is available everywhere." Damien took a shuddering breath. "I don't think I can resist the stuff if I encounter someone selling it when I'm by myself."

"Believe it or not, it's good that you realise your limitations." Nathanial reached out and squeezed Damien's shoulder. "I'll detail some of your team mates to keep you company while we're in Callenhain."

It would be some time before this phase passed; Damien would be driven to consume tiscan again every time he encountered the stuff. Nathanial had discussed the issue with Michael and Olivia, and all three of them fully expected Damien would fall prey to his addiction again. Tiscan was too readily available and too easy to brew from raw. They just had to be sure to catch him when it happened.

EIGHT

Jaclyn strode toward the messenger from the trader lands who'd been briefing her brother on the progress of the war there. Ricardo was between her and Myra, and the dagger-wives had formed an automatic protective circle around them—the courtiers pressing back out of her way as she moved. Whispers and eyes followed her progress. It was unusual for her to go anywhere near her brother if she had a choice. Even Samuel stopped, the response he'd been about to make dying on his lips. His firstwife stepped forward and placed a hand lightly on his shoulder, her face impassive.

"What do you mean they have disappeared?" Jaclyn demanded.

The messenger turned to her, then back to the king, faintly panicked.

"Gone, Commander. We can't find a trace of the last clan anywhere."

"For an entire clan to up and move it would take time and careful planning, they can't just disappear. Where did they go?"

"I... we don't know, Commander. Some of the locals said they might have gone over the mountains."

"Well?"

"Well, what?" the messenger said, eyes still darting from the king to her.

"Did they go over the Heights?"

"We don't know, Commander."

"Did you check?"

"Um, I, I'm not sure. No one else seems to know the path?"

"Someone get me a map!" Jaclyn snapped.

The messenger paled and stepped back, looking gratefully at the king's firstwife as she waved her off.

"What is wrong, Commander?" the firstwife asked.

Jaclyn smiled grimly up at Chelsie. Her brother's firstwife might despise her, and she might not know what was important about one missing clan, but she wasn't stupid. She wouldn't ignore anything that might potentially be a threat to her or her husband. When it came to war, even Chelsie admitted Jaclyn and her house were the experts in Sylanna.

"Of all the clans, it is the tribes of Kallith Clan that are known to be the best fighters. When the traders send their caravans out into the world, they tend to venture out with guards drawn from the warriors of Kallith."

"What's the problem? It's one little clan." Her brother frowned, waving dismissively.

"Not just one little clan. The lands previously belonging to the clans were broken up into separate territories. There are multiple tribes in each region, and each of those regions has an oasis or lake at the heart of their ranging lands. The oasis at the heart of that final territory is Kallith. There are multiple tribes that roam there—that's thousands of fighters," Jaclyn explained, wondering how it was that after all these years her brother still didn't understand anything about the lands or people they'd just conquered.

"Those of Kallith are noted as fighters. They came late to the battle, being further afield than their brethren. But once they joined the battle…" Myra shrugged.

"If it wasn't for the warriors of Kallith, particularly the wolf warriors, we could have taken all of the lands the clans call home years ago," Ricardo said.

"Wolf warriors?" Chelsie asked.

"The best fighters and strategists—and some of their number are said to be particularly strong in the use of the veil." Jaclyn stared at Chelsie, seeing the spark of interest in her brother's wife. "They are called the wolf warriors due to the wolf-eye tattoos they bear on their foreheads…" Jaclyn trailed off as a runner came in carrying a map. A couple of other household staff followed, carrying a table between them. They placed it carefully between her and the king.

The map was unrolled, and Jaclyn stepped forward to examine it—Ricardo and Myra at her side. Jaclyn stared at the map, her finger tracing the mountain range called the Heights, and swore softly.

"What is it?" the king asked.

"The other side of the mountains leads to the barbarian lands."

"Thousands of fighters may have just joined our enemy," Myra said.

Jaclyn froze and then chuckled. She held up her hand as everyone stared at her in shock at the sudden change of mood.

"Send orders to the Overseer; I want the sister houses to scour the base of those mountains. Find the trail the Kallith Clan used." Jaclyn allowed the triumph she felt to show. "We may have just found a back door into the barbarian lands."

"See to it," Chelsie ordered, waving at one of the daggerwives of the Monarch House in dismissal.

"We can attack them on multiple fronts," Ricardo said.

Jaclyn caught her brother staring at the map with a scowl on his face. As he looked up and saw her watching him, his expression smoothed and became unreadable.

NINE

Damien trailed behind three of his squad mates as they wound their way back towards the lodging where they were staying. He was grateful they seemed to know where they were going since he was totally lost. To be fair to himself, this was only the second time he'd been in Callenhain. The first time he'd spent most of his time in the barracks where they'd been housed; he certainly hadn't been granted the freedom to go exploring. He gathered that, because the Warlord wasn't with them, they weren't staying at the Strafford family estate like they had last time. Instead, they stayed in an establishment that was maintained for the use of the Warlord's roving warbands. Although it didn't stop Olivia from having to pay a visit to the loving arms of her family.

Which was where Olivia, Michael and Nathanial had gone today. He'd been pleasantly surprised when Michael had allowed that he could go out as well—with an escort, of course. A door opened in front of him and Damien halted as a woman staggered out, eyes glazed as her hand reached out to steady herself on the door frame.

"Sorry," Damien muttered.

He continued to watch as she pushed herself off the wall to walk a weaving path down the alleyway. He shook his head and reached for the door to close it when smoke from inside wafted out and swirled around him. Damien inhaled, his breath catching, his hand clenching on the door. As more smoke surrounded him, he breathed in again. He closed his eyes as relief washed over him. Tiscan, it was tiscan smoke. His free hand shook and he darted a glance at the disappearing backs of his squad mates who hadn't noticed he'd stopped.

"Just a bit of smoke," Damien muttered to himself, "it won't hurt."

He entered, the door hitting his back as he stood in the entryway, ignoring his body trembling as he sucked in the smoke that hung in the room. He closed his eyes, disregarding the voice in the back of his head that told him he shouldn't be doing this. The voice urging him to call his squad mates or Michael or Nathanial. He'd be too embarrassed to call Olivia right now. The feeling gave him cause to pause, wondering why he thought such a thing, but as he inhaled again, all thought fled. At the sound of low laughter nearby, Damien opened his eyes to see a handful of people sitting at a table. It was a woman who was laughing and after taking one final puff of her smoke, she held it out to him.

"Here, it looks like you need some of this more than me." The woman's red hair was a mess of curls that framed her face.

Damien took a tentative step and reached out with a shaking hand, grabbing the smoke as one of the men, after trading glances with the others, pulled a chair across for him. Damien drew in the tiscan, drawing it deep inside, holding it a moment before expelling it with a shuddering breath. He sat down and sucked in more smoke before passing the smoke stick back to the woman. It occurred to him he should get back to the inn, then a fresh smoke stick was passed back to him and he accepted it, ignoring the tremor that shook his hand. Michael wouldn't be back to their accommodation for a while. He'd be back in plenty of time.

"I'm Kelly," the woman said, her hand caressing his arm. "These two are my business partners."

Feeling the tiscan relax his muscles, relief flooded him. At least it did for a moment, before his stomach began to churn, and his skin crawled with his desire for more. Damien inhaled more of the smoke.

"I'm Damien," Damien said.

"I'm guessing this isn't the first time you've had tiscan?"

"Although, I'd say it's been a while," one of the men said.

"Let me guess, some well-meaning, virtuous types objected. For your own health, of course," Kelly said as the three of them looked at each other and laughed.

Damien laughed with them. "I've always had tiscan, first time I've smoked it, though."

"Really? What was your favourite way to have that little moment of relaxation?" Kelly asked.

"My mother and some of the elders of my village used to make it into tea. I used to have a stronger brew that I made in a flask. Just an occasional sip throughout the day was enough." Damien shrugged. "I'd take a larger dose at night."

Damien found himself looking down at his hands and squeezed his eyes shut. Now that he'd mentioned his tiscan brew, he wanted some. He found smoking enjoyable, and it at least took an edge off, but now that he'd had that small amount, he wanted more. He drew in more of the smoke, closing his eyes as an easy lassitude washed over him. It was softer consuming tiscan this way. He had to admit it was pleasant. While his tonic was anything but soft, starting with lancing pain, it would merge into a wave that washed away his concerns and pushed him into ecstasy. It was a state he craved.

He went to hand the smoke back, then swallowed, startled. He hadn't been aware that any of them had moved. Yet none of them were at the table anymore. At the creak of a door, Damien looked across the room to see his hosts coming back towards him. Worry hit him as he realised he had lost track of time. He stood, concerned Michael would get back to the inn and discover him missing. He needed to be in his bed and sleeping before that happened. Otherwise, his band leaders would know that he'd started using again as soon as they saw him.

"I should go before anyone misses me. Thank you for the tiscan." Damien reached out to pass the remainder of the smoke back.

"Finish it. We have plenty," the redhead said, looking at the others shaking her head.

Damien swallowed but gratefully sucked back the remainder of the smoke stick in a few moments. Panic welled up in him as he finished it and his stomach clenched in response. He started as a hand touched his shoulder. He swallowed as he realised he'd lost track of the present. Again. The smoke might not be as strong as his brew, but it packed a punch. The kind that snuck up on you. One of the men was leaning into him, a vial in his hand, pressing it into his palm.

"Here, friend, we're businesspeople, but you can have this as a gift."

"That should be strong enough to take the edge off for you," Kelly said as she did up his vest.

Damien swallowed, looking down at her hands, wondering how and when his shirt had managed to be undone in the first place. He shuddered and pushed the worry aside then looked at the vials in his hand. One triple the size of the other.

"Thank you, I don't have much on me but..."

"Don't worry about it." Kelly's hand closed over his and she pointed to the vials. "Wait until you get back to your bed and take this one, all of it in one hit."

"You'll definitely want to be lying down when the ride hits you with that one, it's one of our strongest brews," the man said.

Damien regarded the large vial that Kelly's manicured fingernail rested on, and a tremor ran through him. He desperately wanted to swallow its contents now, but he understood their warning. They were right. He'd enjoy it better if he was in his bed.

Country boy and full addict.

Outside of a week, he'll do anything to earn his next hit.

Less, I'd wager. We'll own him in a day or so, or even by the morning.

Damien heard whispered words from all three but as he gazed down at the vial in his hand it didn't make much sense to him. The words seemed to scramble in his head, so he dismissed them as unimportant. Damien swayed and he realised either the smoke was much stronger than he'd thought, or he was out of practice after denying himself for so long.

"Save this second smaller vial for the morning when you wake. Now that you've had tiscan again, you'll need it to take the edge off. I'm sure you remember." Concern shone in Kelly's eyes.

"I used to have a sip every morning and throughout the day. My friends thought it was a water flask." Damien flushed.

"There's no need to hide with us, Damien, if you decide to come back, we'll look after your needs."

He was grateful he'd found some people that finally understood. Although he hadn't realised how much he'd needed it until he'd been ordered to stop consuming it.

"That small vial should hold off the worst of your cravings in the morning until you can get back here tomorrow," Kelly said.

"There will be more tiscan brew where that came from. As

much as you need; we even have space where you can lay back and enjoy it," the man said.

"Don't worry about payment. We run a pleasure house as well. If you agree to a few personal services, we have clients that would pay well to spend some time with you." Kelly's fingers trailed down his chest. "You might even enjoy it."

"Either way, we'll spot you some more tomorrow if you want. Free of charge," the man said.

"We can discuss business and payment after that if you decide the product meets your need," Kelly said.

Even as gone as he was with the tiscan he'd consumed he realised that Kelly meant he could work in a pleasure house in return for a supply of tiscan. His face heated in embarrassment.

"You should get home to your bed; I know you'll enjoy our special brew. We don't give that one to many, but I figure you can handle it," the man said.

"Remember, big vial all in one hit tonight and the small vial to tide you over when you wake. It will be worse in the morning after denying yourself for so long," Kelly repeated.

Damien found himself staggering down an alleyway, uncertain how long he'd been walking around. Relief washed over him as he spotted the establishment where he was staying. A nagging worry in the back of his head hoped he was safely in bed before Michael got back. He tried to scan the inn to see if Michael was inside and swore softly as his unreliable powers seemed to have faded on him again.

If they discovered what he'd done, Michael would stop him. Tremors shook him as he thought about not even getting to use the big vial of tiscan they'd given him. Pushing back the fear he continued towards the door, trying to pretend to be calm and unconcerned. He breezed past those on duty at the doors as they traded glances. Even though they'd been briefed that he wasn't supposed to be out by himself, thankfully they said nothing. He paused halfway across the common room as he saw the relief on the faces of those he'd been with that day.

"Sorry, I stopped to look at something and then I noticed you were gone." He winced and tried to appear sheepish. "Then I wandered around, totally lost. Took me the longest time to make my way back."

"Sorry, we should have been looking out for you," one of them said.

"Don't worry about it. I made it back and before Michael by the looks of it. Otherwise, we'd all be in trouble," Damien said.

As the men sighed in relief, Damien went up the stairs to the second floor and his bedroom. He could feel himself trembling as he kept his pace slow and measured. It was one of the hardest things he'd done in a long time to stay calm and not run to his room. He entered and closed the door, then leant against it, expelling a pent-up breath. Damien reached into his belt pouch and retrieved both vials of the tiscan brew, placing them on the small wooden table beside his bed. Still restraining himself from moving too quickly, he disarmed, placing his weapons carefully on the rack against the wall. As he stripped off his fighting leathers, his muscles spasmed with the need racking his body. He slid onto the bed, squeezing his eyes shut as pain and craving clamoured at him. As the tremors passed, he dragged off his clothes and dumped them on the floor.

Damien reached for the large bottle of tiscan, realising it was almost as much as what he used to keep in his flask before he'd stopped using it. He paused as he realised this amount would normally have lasted him a couple of days before he needed to brew more. Longer, if he was careful with how much he consumed.

But a burning hunger for a good dose of tiscan and the oblivion it could bring him struck again and he doubled over. He pressed his face into the pillow to muffle the groan he couldn't stifle. With hands that shook that badly he found he was fumbling with the stopper. Sweat broke out over his body when he couldn't get it off. Damien took a shuddering breath then tried again, relief and need hitting him as the stopper came off and the strong smell of tiscan hit him.

Hands shaking again, he dropped the stopper on the floor and gripped the vial in both hands, afraid to spill any of the precious liquid. He raised the bottle to his mouth and, closing his eyes, swallowed mouthful after mouthful, just as Kelly had instructed him, until he'd finished the whole bottle. Shuddering with relief as the sharp edges of the clamouring receded, Damien dumped the empty vial on the table. He slid sideways—collapsing onto his bed rather than lying down properly, but he was beyond caring. He gasped in pleasure as the tiscan hit him full force and relaxed as all his aches and worries washed away under its influence. Then pain seared through him, and his body convulsed. It had happened to him before when he'd had bigger doses of tiscan, so he endured it, knowing it would pass. Damien remembered the instructions from his new friends. Shafts of agony pierced him, but then ecstasy flooded through him. So much better than he remembered from the small sips he used to have. He moaned as it washed over his mind and body. The world seemed to recede, and the multitude of mind voices of the residents of Callenhain faded, leaving him in peace. He relaxed as the tiscan did its work, all his senses on fire, wave after wave of euphoria washing over him, chasing away the pain and pulling him down into sweet oblivion.

Tarkhan kept his nervousness to himself. Or at least, he hoped he did.

This is just another patrol, Khaliun said.

Tarkhan grimaced then paused, considering her words. She was correct, of course, it was just another patrol. Mundane. Ordinary. At least that is what anyone who caught a stray whisper or emotion from him needed to hear.

I hate the cold, he whispered back.

How did we end up with this duty? She grinned at him as she tightened the girth on her horse's saddle another notch.

Tarkhan chuckled under his breath and concentrated on the things his fellow co-leaders of Kallith would expect to feel coming from him if he leaked. Like the cold and how much he hated it. Although he hoped what he'd been told in the past was correct. When going into battle he was more focused and less prone to leaking. Tarkhan relaxed another notch as he scanned the tribe members around him and sensed nothing more than determination. They were all perfectly correct. This was just another job, and it was their job to perform.

If only we hadn't insisted on going to Hallaran alone that trip. Things might have been different, Tarkhan said.

Don't second guess. Instead of us falling into Chono's trap, the bulk of the warriors of Kallith would have gone down with us.

We might have fought and won.

I've thought on this, and I think we would all have died or fallen to whatever fate the Sylannians had in store for us.

But with the greater numbers...

We still would have ridden into a trap. With just the two of us, they discounted the threat we could be. That you could be. With our tribe at our backs, we would have been watched more closely. Khali-un's tone was grave as she stared across the intervening space at him.

Yet this time, we know what we are riding into.

We go in. We check, and we get out.

He was about to respond but spotted some of the other co-leaders approaching to see them off. He nodded at them, pushing down the urge to babble with ever-so-polite conversation. The other leaders had spent years in company with him due to the battle for their homeland, so they wouldn't expect much from him. If he started joking with them, they'd get suspicious.

"Don't look so grumpy, Tarkhan. Someone needs to go back up there to check on the progress of the new defences." Erden slapped him on the shoulder. "You and your tribe are perfect for the job."

"It's not like we're asking you to build anything." Orghana's eyes sparkled with amusement.

"I know, I just didn't think I'd be going up there again so soon." Tarkhan shuddered and threw a sour look at the pair.

Narantua closed the distance between them and pulled him into her arms. He hugged her back, then nearly swore as she stiffened. He'd forgotten how sensitive a healer could be. Narantua might not be as powerful as the Warleader's healer, but she still had enough of the healing touch to sense things from others.

Take me with you, Narantua urged, her large eyes staring into his own.

No, your place is here.

I fear for you all. Narantua's mindvoice was merely a whisper.

Tarkhan was shocked that Narantua not only sensed something was up but, somehow, also caught enough from him to know he and Khaliun were going on a run back into their former homeland.

You're not going to try and stop us? Tarkhan's eyes widened.

No. I don't need to know why. I will keep what I know to myself, Narantua said, a soft pulse of trust flowing between them. *It's troubled me that we've just abandoned the rest of the People to their fate.*

Thank you.

Don't die. Kallith needs you both.

Narantua stepped back, her face serene, not betraying even a single flicker of the conversation that had passed between them. He noticed that neither Khaliun nor Erden had even gone near each other. He caught Orghana's gaze, and she rolled her eyes. Sighing, he filed the odd behaviour of the pair in not acknowledging each other to chase up later and then mounted. Khaliun didn't even wait for more than a breath before she spurred her mount and led the way from the camp.

A DEEP RUMBLE sounded from the depths of the Heights as a rockslide crashed down the barren slopes. Workers dropped tools and scattered. Tarkhan spurred his horse, heading away from the disaster. At the last minute he swerved, and directed his horse onto the trail. He didn't slow, although he would have preferred to dismount and lead the horse down this part of the trail. Once he and those who'd fled with him were free of the momentary madness above, they slowed but kept their progress heading down the other side of the Heights, back towards their former homeland.

It would be better for them to be as far down the trail as they could get before the noise from the rockslide abated. The further away they were before the other clan leaders were alerted to their actions, the less likely any of them would be able to intervene and try to prevent their mission. Despite Narantua's reaction at the discovery of their plans, Tarkhan knew some of the other leaders wouldn't approve. The head builder had assured them both that no one would be injured but it would be enough of a distraction for them to break free without notice. Particularly since it was far smaller than it sounded—not that the work crews were aware of that little detail. There would be that brief grace period before those above would venture out. By that stage their attack group would hopefully be far enough down the trail that the sound of their exodus wouldn't travel up to those they'd left behind.

TARKHAN TRIED to keep his increasing nervous tension under control. He could explain some of it away due to finding himself on his stomach looking down at Hallaran Lake. The last time he'd been here things hadn't gone so well. At least this time he and his co-leader hadn't been completely stupid—they had some of their best warriors with them, and they'd taken care as they crossed what was now enemy territory, using all their skills and knowledge about the trails of their former homeland. Yet they'd seen very little evidence of the Sylannians. Or evidence of the members of the tribes that had been taken by their conquerors, Hallaran or otherwise. They'd kept away from the known camping and hunting grounds and trails the Hallaran tribes used but he'd still expected to see some signs of the Sylannians.

"I was beginning to wonder if they'd just packed up and deserted Hallaran," Tarkhan said.

"Me too, except I could hear their random thoughts. Of course, they could just as easily been in one of the other territories." Khaliun went bright red. "I didn't think of that before I sent us off on this mission."

"Me either." Tarkhan frowned looking down at the Sylannians and members of the Hallaran tribe below. "I know I've said this before, but something is nagging at me."

"I know, but other than there being far more of the Hallaran who survived than I thought there'd be, I'm seeing what I expected to see. But you're right, something is off," Khaliun said.

"The leaders, the Sylannians in maroon and cream aren't here," the scout said. "Always before, every single battle, every place we encountered our enemy, there were those in maroon and cream."

Tarkhan stared at the warrior who lay on the ground near them, then back down to the settlement below. The Sylannians in maroon and cream had been distinct and stood out in battle as had their leader who'd fought in their midst. Those of the clans were instantly identifiable, even though they now wore formless robes in the same uniform blue-grey colour and collars around their necks rather than their traditional furs and hides. The Sylannians wore clothing in an array of striking colours, but there were none that he could see with even the tiniest band of maroon and cream.

"She's right. The ones who commanded are nowhere to be seen," Tarkhan said.

"Well done. Don't risk yourself but keep an eye them and let us know if you notice anything else of note," Khaliun said, waiting until the scout acknowledged the order.

Edging back, Tarkhan stood and made his way carefully back to his horse, Khaliun at his side. With the sun low in the sky people were out and about around the settlement. So, while it was a good time to conduct scouting activities on their enemy, it wasn't a good time for them to head into Hallaran.

"If the Sylannians and the captives below keep to our own habits, the middle of the day, while the sun is high, should allow us to enter unobserved." He assessed Khaliun as he spoke, frowning as he noted her pent-up tension before returning his gaze to the horizon. "Can you sense Delbee among those below?"

"No, but if she's unconscious, I wouldn't. I'm not... Michael... and his Unwanted," Khaliun said.

Tarkhan's eyes widened as he heard her voice catch when she'd said the Warleader's name. If he didn't know better, he'd swear it was longing laced with heartbreak in her tone when she mentioned Michael.

"Khaliun?"

Silence stretched between them as she focused on her fingers, scraping grime from under her short, jagged nails as if she'd just noticed how unkempt they were.

"It's nothing. It's not real."

"What isn't real?"

Khaliun sighed and shook her head. "When people join minds the way Michael and I did, it's dangerous."

"I think I understand that part, particularly with what happened. You nearly died; you would have without Michael's healer tending to you."

"It can cause feelings to flare. Ones that aren't real. They will fade, but until they do..." Khaliun ducked her head before she finally looked at him, her eyes shadowed. "You don't understand what it's like when you bind yourself to another, and then they are suddenly gone. It feels like a piece of me has been ripped out.”

Tarkhan's eyes widened as he remembered the distance between Khaliun and Erden when they had departed. “Ah. So, Erden knows you feel this way and hasn't taken it well?”

A bitter smile twisted her lips. “He does, and he hasn't. We argued, and he stormed out. It isn't real, and it will fade. I know this. I don't really love Michael, no matter how it feels right now, but Erden is still jealous.”

“No wonder you've been a mess. Between the consequence of merging minds with the Warleader and hearing Delbee cry out across the veil.” Tarkhan reached out, taking her hand in his, and squeezed her fingers gently, support flowing from him. “You should have told me you were struggling. I couldn't have done much, but I could have been there as your friend.”

WITH THE NUMBER of times he'd been in this position, Tarkhan was beginning to feel right at home lying on the ground at this vantage point, looking down on Hallaran. He waited until Khaliun had settled into place on the other side of the scout before he spoke.

“You think you've found something?”

“Yes, Co-leader, I'm certain of it. If they follow the same pattern, you'll see for yourself shortly,” the scout said, not taking her gaze off the camp. “Keep your eyes on the cells off to the right.”

Tarkhan's eyes settled on the cells. He was intimately familiar with them since he'd spent time in one on their last fateful journey to Hallaran. As movement occurred on the far side, he tracked a team of Sylannians who crossed over the settlement towards the long, low building that had originally held the winter stores and excess goods for trade. They'd observed that the majority of the clan's people were kept inside its confines. They unbound the doors and opened them, a couple disappearing inside. It wasn't long before those of Hallaran shuffled out, each wearing a collar around their necks but not bound in any other way that he could see. The captives were split into two groups and led over to one side of Hallaran. One segment was led over to care for the animals, while the other was taken to tend the crops.

The scout touched his shoulder, drawing his attention back towards the cells, and he saw the door open. It wasn't long before another captive stumbled out, wearing not only a collar but binding around her wrists, waist, and ankles. Much like his own restraints during the brief time he had been held by the Sylannians. They weren't taking any chances with this prisoner since they had one person holding taut the silken ropes on either side of the person between them.

"Delbee," Khaliun whispered in instant recognition.

"You were right. She's alive."

As Delbee jerked back on her restraints, Tarkhan winced as those who surrounded her simply looked on. He sank his awareness down and heard the strange hum as Delbee's restraints became hard, the one around her neck tightening. Delbee stopped fighting, sinking to her knees, curling up into a ball and trying to grasp at her neck—but prevented from doing so as those restraints tightened as well. He felt Khaliun tug at his awareness slightly in warning before she drew him in, then focused her attention on Delbee.

Don't fight, Delbee. They'll only hurt you, Khaliun whispered in a tight communication. *Leave that part to us.*

Khaliun? How? You shouldn't be here. They'll take you.

Don't change your pattern of behaviour. Just stay alive. We'll do what we can.

Chono is here. Kill him, Delbee snarled as she staggered back to her feet.

Tarkhan was impressed that she didn't crane her neck around trying to spot where they were, simply allowing her captors to half drag her towards the lake. They tied her to a stake driven into the water's edge and stood back, yelling orders. Delbee stooped and picked up one of the buckets from a pile nearby and filled it with water. She passed it to one of her follow captives who crossed the distance between the lake and the crops to water them. Delbee stooped to pick up another bucket and filled it as she had done the last, again handing it off to the next of her tribe.

Do you know where he is being held?

Do you see the small tents off to one side of the bigger Sylannian one? Delbee asked, not missing a beat as she continued to fill buckets.

Tarkhan saw the large, colourful Sylannian tents across the other side of the settlement. They were oval with multiple peaks in the roof, probably made from the same silk as the Sylannian clothing and bindings. Just as Delbee had indicated, there were several smaller tents near the larger one.

Yes, we see them.

Those who have become traitors, including Chono, are sleeping in them.

Delbee didn't have to tell them they didn't sleep in the tents alone. Tarkhan was perfectly aware that when the Sylannians showed particular interest in a male it was to potentially use them as breeding stock. At least that is what the Sylannians had told him when they'd gotten their hands on him. He did find it interesting that they had taken Chono, though, since he'd assumed that the Sylannians only took men who were strong in using the veil.

ELEVEN

Steven didn't bother to knock as he pushed the doors open and entered his parents' outer rooms. There didn't seem to be much point since they were effectively prisoners in their own family castle. He stopped in the middle of the sitting room, eyes widening. It was clean. Perfectly clean, everything in its place. Unlike his own rooms that were starting to resemble a battlefield. The servants hadn't cleaned anything since the occupation. He hadn't even seen them except for his food being delivered to his suite.

He sighed and wandered over to the windows. Given his parents had sent for him, he guessed they wouldn't be too long. He was starting to believe, after seeing his parents' rooms, that the servants were trying to send him a message. Before now, he'd thought they'd mostly been locked up or had run away at the first opportunity.

"Steven, take a seat," Lady Rathadon said.

Steven half bowed to his mother and took a seat as she ordered. A part of him wondered how she managed to gain instant compliance from him with such simple words.

"Yes, Mother."

It seemed to be a universal thing with mothers that no matter how old you became, they could still make you feel like a child. Steven sank into one of the lounges. One of the servants assisted his father into the room and helped him settle into a large wing-backed leather chair.

With his mother and father both staring and the silence stretching between them, he shifted in his chair, and brushed ineffectively at the wrinkles in his jacket. Unfortunately, they weren't imaginary. Neither was the faintly sour smell that he was certain must be coming from his shirt. He'd just picked up what he'd been wearing the day before from a pile of discarded clothes on the floor. He felt entirely rumpled in his parents' immaculate company. This was another lesson learnt. When he threw his jacket on the floor it didn't magically end up washed, pressed, and hanging in his wardrobe.

Finally, the servants reappeared with food and drinks, depositing them on the low tables between them. One of the servants bustled around collecting a selection of the small bite-size offerings on a smaller plate and placed it on the table by his father's chair along with a drink.

Steven plastered what he hoped was a pleasant expression on his face. Even to himself, he had to admit it was a little awkward. He suppressed a sigh as his mother reached for a pastry from the platter, placing it on the plate the servants had thoughtfully placed on the side table next to her seat. His own empty plate was sitting on the low table in the centre of their seats. As the smell of the food hit him, Steven's mouth watered, and his stomach rumbled. Not needing any further prompting, Steven rose from his chair and placed a selection of the food on offer on his own plate. He wasn't about to refuse the offering after the week he'd spent with what could be politely described as slop served to him in his rooms.

Retreating to his seat he looked to either side and realised the convenient side table that used to sit right next to the chair had been removed. He tried to pretend it was a perfectly normal state of affairs and balanced the plate on his lap while holding his glass.

"What were they talking about when they mentioned arranging a diversion for the Warlord and your brother?" his mother asked.

Steven held up his hand as he chewed and tried to swallow the food he'd already stuffed into his mouth. As he coughed inelegantly, he placed the uneaten portion back on his plate and swallowed a mouthful of his wine.

"What? Why do you think I know?" Sweat beaded on Steven's forehead as he sat unable to look away from his father's gaze.

"You pretty much confessed your involvement in the ballroom. Or had you forgotten already?" His father's tone was dry.

"In order to salvage something from this mess you helped to create, we need to know what you've done." His mother sat staring at him, her pastry and drink untouched on the table next to her.

Steven swallowed, then took another gulp of his drink before he leaned over and placed it on the floor next to his seat. The silence stretched between them before he broke eye contact. He stared at the deep red wine in his glass instead.

"I was stupid."

"We gathered that much." His father sighed.

"Michael has a sentry relay out in the backwaters. It's how they've been able to stop so many incursions," Steven said.

His parents looked at each other but they didn't appear surprised. It confirmed his growing suspicion that his parents were aware of far more than they should be. Particularly since they mostly spent their days in these rooms or the gardens.

"We're aware of that, Steven." His mother's eyes narrowed. "What have Peter and Constance done?"

Steven picked up his glass to take another mouthful of his wine, barely noticing as the servants refilled it at his father's nod.

"I think." Steven found his hand was shaking and he squeezed his eyes shut. "I know they are killing the sentries, leaving the path clear for the Sylannians to attack."

"How do you know this little detail?" his mother asked.

Steven suddenly found the pattern of the rug on the floor fascinating. It was amazing the details he'd never noticed before.

"I didn't know what we were doing. Honestly." He resolutely drew his attention away from the rug, hoping to see some understanding in his parents' eyes.

"What did you do?" His mother's lips thinned, eyes flashing with anger, causing him to glance away once more.

"I met with them a few times. Then they took Evan and me out into the tributaries." Steven paused as his parents' faces seemed to harden, then carried on, the words rushing from his mouth. "I didn't know what we'd be doing."

"Just spit it out," his mother said.

"We stopped on a small landfall. There was a sentry station there. We killed the sentry."

"We or you?" his mother asked.

"*I* killed the sentry; I didn't mean to. He was rude. He laughed and said I wasn't the warlord, so I stabbed him." Steven found his head sinking again, cutting his parents out of his direct field of view.

Even to his own ears his excuse sounded weak. He'd spent so long thinking he was better than his brother because he didn't go around killing people, only to have killed someone just for making fun of him. Steven froze then, his eyes narrowed.

"Mother, get out of my head. I'm not a child," Steven snapped.

"Then perhaps you need to stop behaving like one," his father said.

"Have you even read the reports about what the Sylannian raiders are capable of?" His mother sounded just like she had when she'd been explaining things to him when he was a child.

"Why do you continue to interfere in things you don't understand? The Warlord can't live forever, and your brother is positioned perfectly to take his place on his death, you fool!" his father said. "If you haven't messed things up with your foolishness, that is."

"What do you mean? Michael is just one of his people. The Warlord has his own son, Aiden. He'll take over next." Steven wondered how his father could possibly be unaware of this fact.

"For once in your life, think things through. Your brother is more the Warlord's son than his child by birth," his mother said.

"A warlord is not decided by who is first born, Steven," his father said, his gaze unwavering.

"The warlord is the one who has the strength to take it," his mother explained.

His mother sighed as he frowned at them both and then his parents traded looks before his father shook his head.

"You were never going to be the Warlord of Vallantia." His father's tone was blunt. "I thought you would have realised that by now."

"It was always going to be Michael; even back then it was obvious," his mother said.

"No, I'm just as capable. You've always favoured him!"

"Steven, I say this with all humility. I only became Warlord of Vallantia because my siblings died of veil sickness. Each one of them would have made a better Warlord than me."

"It's not your fault, Steven, but you just don't have it in you."

"Michael has the spirit of his great-grandfather channelling through him, he always did. I remember when I was a small boy, my grandfather was terrifying." His father snorted in amusement, before it faded to leave sadness. "If one of my brothers or either of my sisters had taken over the title of Vallantia, the man who was Paul Olenna would never have taken us."

"It was an error," his mother said softly.

Steven blinked at his mother unable to make sense of her comment. His father reached across and gently took her hand in his. Steven frowned as it occurred to him that it was his father's ruined hand. Or rather, it had been. Now it seemed to grasp his mother's hand.

"There was nothing we could have done, either of us, to prevent their deaths from veil sickness, my love," his father said, his voice soft. "One such as Michael's healer did not exist then."

Steven drew his attention from his father's now-functioning hand back to their conversation. "You never intended to hand the rule of Vallantia to me?" Steven stared at his parents. They'd never spoken to him this way before.

"It has nothing to do with what we intended." His mother's sharp gaze seemed to pin him to his seat. "Listen and understand for the first time in your life."

His father shook his head. "You just do not have the capa- . bility to be a warlord. People would walk all over you."

"You can't have failed to notice that Michael's people are loyal to him," his mother said.

"Of late, it isn't just his own Unwanted. If rumours are correct, Michael now leads the combined warbands of the Warlord," his father said.

"How would I know anything about what Michael is doing?"

"There are reports delivered regularly. For someone who aspires to be a leader, you might want to consider reading some of them," his mother said.

"I know you think it is what you want but be honest. You

aren't suited to lead others in battle. What is it that you think the role of a warlord is?" his father asked.

A wave of compassion rolled over Steven, and he blinked at the moisture that pricked his eyes. He could almost forget how strong his mother was until she performed what was, for her, small acts like that. All that talent and then some seemed to have been endowed on his brother while mostly skipping him. He swallowed as he remembered that was another reason he'd spent so much time avoiding his mother: she always messed around with his head. He'd never been strong enough to push her out of his mind like Michael could.

"Well, the Warlord, um, commands, has respect. It's Michael that does the dirty work," Steven muttered.

"In these recent times, I'm told the Warlord takes a back seat and allows Michael to command. Because he's good at it. Make no mistake, the Warlord can and does fight from the front line," his mother said.

"The Warlord does not ask anything of Michael he would be incapable of doing himself. That he wouldn't do himself," his father said.

"Even in this day, with your brother to rely on, he doesn't spend all his time sitting back in the luxury of Yalleska," his mother said.

"I'd wager Michael would give the Rathadon warlords of old a hiding," his father said.

His mother sighed. "Go. Think on what we've said. Come back when you're ready to have a sensible conversation."

Steven understood everything they were saying to him. A little back corner of his mind even admitted they were probably correct in everything they said. Then he shoved the unaccustomed honesty away. They would never be willing to give him a chance, they never had been. His whole life he'd been pushed aside. Even the Warlord had overlooked him in favour of his little brother who got to run off to find glory in war while Steven remained here. Not even allowed to arrange for children to inherit the Rathadon legacy from him due to the decree of the Warlord. Steven stood and bowed to his parents before retreating to his own rooms.

TWELVE

Damien stifled a groan. He didn't want to wake any of his fellow squad mates. They might all have their own small rooms, a rare luxury, but the walls were paper thin. If any of them were even still asleep. He had a feeling it was much later than he normally woke. Swallowing did nothing to lessen the craving that hit him as soon as he realised he was awake. He doubled over into a ball, stifling the moan of pain that he couldn't keep inside as agony shot through him. He lay in misery as his body shook and desire for more tiscan rode him. Finally, when the tremors passed, he reached out blindly for the second vial of tiscan, grateful that he'd placed it, ready for use, on his bedside table. Experience had taught him he wouldn't have long before another wave of pain would hit. Hands shaking, he fumbled at the stopper until he managed to open the vial, grateful he didn't spill any. There was little enough liquid in the bottle as it was. He tipped the bottle and swallowed all the liquid it contained. He slumped back, the trembling subsiding as the drug did its work. It was enough, barely, to dampen the sharp edge of his need for more.

The dealers had been correct both in how much he'd enjoy the hit he'd had last night and how he'd feel worse than he ever had before when he woke. It was only because he'd denied himself for too long, he reassured himself. There couldn't have even been a trace of the stuff in him before he'd used again yesterday. Using every day, the way he'd done in the past, with small sips throughout the day to keep him going, then the larger dose at night at bedtime, he'd never been as bad first up in the morning when he woke. So here was another thing the dealers had been correct about: he now needed more, much more than had been in the vial, and soon. Although he was grateful they'd kindly provided it to him. Desire clamoured at him as he thought about sculling another big bottle of the tiscan. He remembered being told they had plenty of space for him to lay back and enjoy the ride. The drug they'd given him had been so strong, so good. Damien frowned, he distinctly remembered a mass of red curls, and long manicured fingernails, but her name eluded him.

He wasted no time dressing in his old hunting leathers this time. He'd be less noticeable this way than walking around in his fighting leathers, branded as they were with the symbol of the Unwanted. Damien grabbed his belt pouch and checked the coins inside, grimacing. He didn't know if it would be enough to buy more tiscan from the dealers, but it was all he had. They each received a small amount of coin when they came into towns, but it wasn't much and before now, he had to admit he hadn't needed any either. He looked at his weapons on the rack and discarded the idea of taking them. They were just as noticeable as his fighting leathers.

He opened the door with a sigh of relief when the hinges didn't squeak. The fact that he should have remembered if they did or not *before* he opened it gave him pause, but he pushed his momentary concern aside. It was only a few steps to the edge of the stairs, and he leant over the rail to peer down into the common room. Damien bit his lip at the sight of a couple of his squad mates downstairs lounging on the benches. Even if it was what he'd expected, particularly since he'd confessed to Nathanial back in Lutter that he didn't trust himself. As a consequence, Michael had issued orders that he wasn't to venture out alone. Although Damien had been surprised that instead of being confined to quarters Michael detailed some of his squad mates to accompany him when he did. A twinge of guilt struck Damien as he realised his band leader had been far too lenient. He couldn't be trusted with tiscan. Now that he'd started using again, that thought wasn't enough to hold him back.

He hesitated for a moment then took a step back and retraced his steps to his room, easing the door closed behind him. Pushing aside his hesitation, he crossed to the window and pulled open the wooden shutters. With a final glance behind him, he climbed out onto the ledge. Placing one foot carefully in front of the other, he made his way down the length of the building. Barrels stacked and waiting at the back to be picked up made the job of getting to the ground that much easier. Grasping the edge of the ledge, he lowered himself onto the topmost barrel then jumped to the ground.

With a final glance around Damien continued down the side laneway. As he stepped out into the main road, he glanced back towards the main entrance of the inn they were staying in and nearly swore. One of the guards pulling duty at the entrance was looking right at him. The man's eyes widened, and his mouth half opened to voice what Damien was sure was an objection. Damien raised his fingers up to his lips and then grinned as the man shook his head. Not waiting for him to change his mind or for anyone else to notice, he stepped out into the crowd, merging into their midst and allowing the flow of people to take him away from the inn.

As Damien walked down a back street, relief hit him as he recognised the rough door with the bars on it that he'd stumbled into the other day. He paused with his hand half outstretched to open the door and cast a look back down the row of buildings the way he'd come, then shrugged off his sudden unease and entered. A shudder ran though him as he inhaled the smoke in the air. He only realised he'd closed his eyes when arms wrapped around him, and a hand pulled his head down. A mouth locked onto his own, tiscan smoke passing from the other to him, causing his breath to catch before he sucked it down. Opening his eyes, he recognised the redhead from the other day. He searched his mind as she kissed him, a part of him noting he wasn't pushing her away. Kelly, his foggy memory responded to his prodding, her name was Kelly.

"Thank you," Damien said.

"I knew you'd be back," Kelly said.

She laughed and, grabbing his hand, dragged him over to a low couch. As he sank into it, he pulled out the coins and passed them to her.

"I don't know how much you normally charge, but, please, I need..." Damien stopped as her fingers brushed his palm, lingering for a moment, before withdrawing as Kelly took the money.

Kelly inspected the coins, then she threw them onto the table.

Damien recognised the two men who sat at the table from his last visit but no matter how he prodded his memory he couldn't think of their names. One of the men was dressed in what passed for good business attire, with a bright green coat with lace on the cuffs. The other man, more roughly dressed in muted brown and black, passed him a smoke stick, which Damien took, trying not to shake as he sucked in the smoke. As Damien inhaled he inspected the stack of wooden crates in one corner of the room and realised this place must be a warehouse. Although an underused one given the size of it, in comparison to the boxes which were stacked in one small corner.

"We are businesspeople," the man in the green cloak said, tugging at the cuff of his coat.

"But there are other ways you can pay, don't worry about it for now. We can spot you some," Kelly purred into his ear.

Damien's stomach muscles tightened as her hand ran under his shirt. He flushed as he gathered what she meant and saw the two men watching him. Indecision hit Damien for a moment, then he swallowed and relaxed back, doing his best to ignore his embarrassment at Kelly's roaming hands and the laughter of the men that rolled over him. It was little enough that she was asking for in payment for what they offered. After all, here in Callenhain, he had no other way to pay for what he wanted, and when he left this place he could source tiscan himself, like he used to. He closed his eyes and sucked on the smoke stick again. Enjoying the soothing pleasure as it enveloped him for a moment, he finally rolled his head to one side and offered the remainder of the smoke to one of the others.

"Finish it, it'll take the edge off. I'll get you some of the brew," the roughly dressed man said, then a bell sounded, and he traded a look with the man in the green cloak.

As the bell sounded again, the man in the green cloak stood. "I'll deal with our client in the shopfront, while you get our guest here a bottle of the good stuff."

Wood protested as the rough man pushed back his chair as he stood. Damien watched as the men walked across the warehouse, disappearing as they left through two different doors.

Damien relaxed back into the couch and Kelly's ministrations again, as the tiscan fogged his mind. It wasn't the oblivion that the liquid could provide—that he craved—but his friend was correct, it did take the edge off the urgency of his need for the stronger brew. His body shook as he thought about the brew, but it didn't bring any embarrassment to him as it would have in the past. A vial touched his lips and he swallowed obediently as a small mouthful was tipped in.

"There you go, just a mouthful, mind, this is our most potent stuff. Since you handled what we gave you last night we thought you might like to try it," the roughly dressed man said.

The reaction was almost instant. A scream tore from his mouth as the pain racked his body, and he was aware of hands holding him as his back arched.

"Don't fight it, you know how this works, let the drug take you," Kelly said, her hands stroking him.

Then euphoria hit him. He gasped and heard a moan of pleasure that he recognised as his own. He didn't care. As the tiscan washed over him the warehouse around him faded to the background, and he gave away any semblance of dignity or caring. He just wanted this feeling. All the time. Damien allowed the drug to wash over him as they'd told him to. Faces appeared, then faded, and snippets of conversation that didn't make any sense to him sounded distant as the stupor took him. He felt hands on his body and opened his mouth to protest, only to have more tiscan poured in.

"There you go, be a good pet and swallow it all," Kelly said.

Damien stared up into her eyes and swallowed more of the drug as she asked him to. As the desire for more rose in him, he couldn't help the whimper that escaped his lips as the vial withdrew. Her laughter echoed in his head, but he didn't care as she obligingly put the bottle back to his mouth and tipped it so the liquid spilt into his mouth. He swallowed several times, aware without having to open his eyes again that she'd given him the full vial of the tiscan. As much as he'd had last night, but this stuff was stronger. It wasn't a soft ride taking his mind away. It was pure bliss that struck him in every cell of his mind and body. He even looked forward to the pain it brought because it would be followed by the oblivion he craved.

"Pity we can't sell him to some clients while we've got him."

"It's too dangerous with this one. Besides, I think he'll be worth more to our buyers than the rest of our cargo combined."

He found himself floating, his body trembling in reaction, as their talk went over him. Damien tried to gather the threads of his scattered wits as he wondered how he was going to make it back to the inn. Then gave it up as thinking became too hard with the drug in his system. It was something he could think about after the ride subsided. He was aware those talking around him were having a conversation about him, but he didn't care. The tiscan didn't allow him to. He was well and truly lost in its clutches.

"What do you think, Sebastian? Worth the risk?" Kelly asked.

"You were right. The Sylannians will pay us well for this one. I'm surprised you let him go yesterday. What if he hadn't come back?"

Confusion rolled over Damien, and he wondered vaguely who Sebastian was. A moment of concern plucked at him with the mention of Sylanna, only to be smothered as he rode the wave of tiscan.

"He's an addict and with what we gave him, he was always going to come back here for more. Besides, now that he's consciously chosen to use again, it will make him much easier to manage," Kelly said.

"We'll have to keep him dosed until we sell him. Back off from our operations until I say otherwise, we don't want any trouble while the Unwanted are in town," Sebastian said.

"Given how much the Sylannians will pay for one like him, I think he's more than worth the risk," Kelly said.

Damien tried to stir, opening his eyes, trying to pull his mind away from the tiscan, a part of him aware that what was being said was important. He frowned at the low light in the room, it had been full daylight when he'd arrived. He tried to sit up as cold metal closed around his neck and wrists. Panic hit him and hands jerked his head back. More tiscan was tipped into his throat. He writhed and tried to spit it out, but multiple hands held him down and even more of the drug was poured down his throat. He swallowed convulsively. Then willingly. He drank all that they gave him.

"Don't worry, soon enough you'll be off to your new owners. You should be grateful, a specimen like you, you're bound to be a kept man for the rest of your life," Sebastian said.

Damien had a confused image of a man, that he guessed was Sebastian, leaning over him. Sebastian was dressed in what passed for fine clothing here in Callenhain, clothes that were an eye-bleeding combination of bright purple, yellow and orange, all adorned with lace. The colours merged to assault Damien's eyes and seemed out of place in the warehouse. As another wave of tiscan crested and crashed over him, Damien closed his eyes and sank back onto the cold stone floor. Laughter sounded around him as the world faded.

"Check him every six hours or so and give him another vial to keep him under until we can ship him out with the rest of the stock," Sebastian said.

Unease teased the edges of Damien's mind, but he allowed the drug to carry him away.

"If we keep him dosed this way he might die going through withdrawal," Kelly said.

"By the time he's going through withdrawal, that will be his new owner's problem, not ours," Sebastian said.

Hands grabbed him and dragged him across the cold stone floor, although he was too lost in oblivion to care. All that mattered was the wave after wave of ecstasy that crashed over his mind and body, taking all pain and care away. All that mattered was the promise they'd give him more every time he woke.

THIRTEEN

Kesha checked the common room where they were housed. Most of Michael's people were absent doing whatever it was they found to do in a place like Callenhain. Michael, Olivia and Nathanial were conducting business, again. They'd been busy every day, up and out the door as soon as they got up, not even bothering to greet her and not back until late. From overheard conversations, they'd been coordinating and sending out teams of the Straffords' personal guard units and the city guard to alert the smaller villages in the area to the possibility of invasion.

Her brows furrowed. They were doing important work, it wasn't personal, but she was still angry that they'd pushed her aside. It was silly. They hadn't done anything of the kind, they were just busy, and they had better things to do other than babysit her. It all sounded perfectly reasonable in her head as she laid out the arguments. Unfortunately, she wasn't in the mood to be reasonable.

Kesha realised that those who sat here in the common room were likely here to watch Damien. Which meant they probably wouldn't agree to accompany her to the market to gather some of the herbal supplies she was short of. Damien had been keeping to himself, so she hadn't even seen him around the last couple of days. Kesha gathered Damien was still sleeping, so she couldn't exactly ask him to consider taking her, along with his watchers, to the markets. She couldn't blame Damien for sleeping in, either. It wasn't unexpected for one going through what she'd traditionally thought of as "veil sickness".

She started to walk up to a couple of Michael's people who sat in the common room to request an escort and stopped. Kesha's mouth closed on her unasked request. Her eyes narrowed, she was an adult, not a child who had to ask permission to leave the house. One of them spared her a disinterested glance, before the guard returned her attention to her companion. Kesha clutched her satchel closer to her chest, and with one more glance around the common room, ducked out the doors to one side. The family that maintained this boarding house sat around the kitchen bench finishing their own meal and went to stand at her entrance.

"Please, don't bother, finish your breakfast," Kesha said, and bustled through the kitchen towards the door in the back.

She kept her head high, pretending a confidence she didn't feel as she let herself out. Walking quickly down the narrow alley that ran the length of the building, she pulled the hood of her cloak up to obscure her face. If those on guard duty at the doors looked her way and recognised her, they'd stop her—even if their main directive was to see to the safety of the inn and make sure Damien didn't go anywhere unescorted, their fate would not be anything they would want if she came to harm.

She paused at the edge of the building, almost breathing a sigh of relief to see people bustling by in the main street. It was almost easy to forget that normal life outside of the warband continued. As a knot of people passed, she stepped out and allowed herself to be swept down the road among them. The back of her neck crawled and she was certain that at any moment the guards would notice and come after her. Without pause, she walked down the next intersecting street and only when she was lost in the crowds of the main thoroughfare did she dare to glance behind her.

With a self-deprecating laugh she threw her hood back, breathing in and allowing the blue sky and sun to lighten her mood. Somehow it all combined to lower a tension she hadn't known she'd been feeling. A sense of freedom washed over her, but guilt quickly snapped at its heels as she realised those on duty at their accommodation, would get in trouble if Michael learned she'd snuck out.

"No. I'll not feel guilty. I can do what I want. I'll be perfectly fine," Kesha muttered, steadfastly ignoring the curious glances of those close enough to hear her.

Grateful that she'd dressed in her normal clothing this morning, she strode down the street towards the markets. If she'd worn the new leathers, when those around her caught sight of the sword and flame that emblazoned them, they'd know she was attached to the Unwanted. Although even if she had been wearing the fighting leathers, Kesha doubted they'd pick her as a fighter. For one thing, while she carried the dagger the Smith had crafted for her, she didn't bear a sword or any other weapon. Members of the Unwanted never went anywhere unarmed. Everyone knew that. She made it to the cross street she was looking for and went around the corner. A writhing mass of people down the end of the street heralded the edge of the market. She strode towards the first row of stalls, ducking under the edge of a tarp strung up between poles and pushing her way through, ignoring the outer tables and the assortment of pots they held.

As she broke into a narrow walkway that ran between stalls,

Kesha absently rubbed her neck. Everything appeared normal but she was suddenly uneasy, and she stood scanning the crowds that flowed around her. Then she huffed in impatience. Nathanial's assertion that she wasn't safe by herself was obviously rubbing off. Kesha pushed the niggling doubt aside when it occurred to her that those of her home village had accompanied her any time she'd left her small village as well. She straightened her shoulders, glancing around once more trying to channel the confidence even Damien seemed to have seeping from his very pores when he put his mind to it. She'd only been here a few times before, usually relying on Nathanial or one of the others to guide her to the herb sellers, but she'd been certain she could find her way back to them by herself. She paused, checking the nearby stalls as people flowed around her. There was nothing that stuck in her memory. It was all unfamiliar.

A waft of cooked meat and herbs caused her mouth to water, with her stomach growling in response. While her chore to buy some of the herbs she needed might not have quite gone to plan, she was determined she could at least have something to eat. If the rumbling of her stomach was anything to go by, it was past her normal mealtime.

She set off in the direction of the aroma and soon found herself at the edge of a large square. If anything, the madness and press of people here were worse. Smoke billowed up from stall after stall, her senses assaulted by enticing odours. Keeping a firm grasp on her leather satchel, she waded into the throng. If the food was anywhere near as good as the aromas that assaulted her, she was in for a treat.

There didn't seem to be any rhyme or reason to the food stalls. There was a fruit seller cutting up his produce on one stall. Next to it another seller with a large pot over an open fire pit was dishing out a stew and flat bread. Yet another further down was serving up fish that he loudly proclaimed was fresh that day from the river. But it was a stall piled high with cakes that really caught her attention. Each of them was topped with different coloured frostings and intricate designs. She'd never seen the like before. Some of them seemed like works of art that would almost be a shame to eat.

She resisted their allure for now, instead choosing one of the stalls that had its own seating area roped off, and took a spare seat at one of the long benches. It didn't take long before the serving man was bustling over, placing a bowl of fish stew, a hunk of steaming bread and a flagon of drink before her. She grabbed some coins out of the leather purse at her belt and paid him. As he went to give her change, she waved him off. He thanked her before resuming his rounds of the tables. That was the other benefit of being by herself. She got to pay for something. Most of the time, with the forbidding presence of the Unwanted at her back, sellers waved off her coin. She found it embarrassing and couldn't help but feel sorry for the poor seller on those occasions, though usually nothing she said could get them to change their minds.

Pushing her doubts aside, she leant down to the bowl of fish stew and sniffed appreciatively. Kesha picked up her spoon, and with a careful blow to cool it down, she swallowed the first mouthful.

KESHA MOPPED up the last of the fish stew from her bowl with the remaining piece of bread, popping it into her mouth, savouring that last mouthful. She sighed in satisfaction. The meal had been as good as the smell had promised. Frowning, she realised it was much later than she'd thought, with light fading from the sky. Standing up, she thanked the husband and wife who worked the food stall and rushed out, pressing through the crowds that hadn't seemed to have thinned at all. Torches flared around the markets as the sun sank even lower, and she hurried through the twisting alleyways, trying to make her way to the edge of the markets so she could get her bearings and figure out where the inn was.

Feeling herself jostled, she apologised as hands grabbed her and stopped her from falling. She went to thank whoever it was before instinctively shrinking back from the men that leered at her.

"Oh, I'm sorry. I didn't mean to stumble into you that way," Kesha babbled, as she tried to step away in the other direction.

A hand slapped across her mouth and she was drawn back against one of the men. She drew in a breath to scream, smelling and tasting the sickly-sweet odour from a cloth that was held to her mouth and nose. Her eyes widened even as the drug took effect, and darkness claimed her before she could so much as scream.

FOURTEEN

Tarkhan kept his breathing slow and controlled, all his senses alert. The grass rustled in the light breeze, then rocks ground against each other and leaves and twigs snapped as they were pressed between the soles of booted feet and the ground. As the boot-shod feet of the Sylannian sentries landed not far from where he lay, he sprang up, the woven grass blanket that had been concealing his presence flying back. Tarkhan struck across the Sylannian's throat with his short sword. He spun to seek the Sylannian's companions only to see his fellow tribe members had already taken them down with equal efficiency. He wasted no time as he led the way down into Hallaran. In the heat of the day, most of the encampment were sleeping. Except for the sentries, his group, and those Khaliun's group had just killed over the other side. There was only one more set of guards that needed to be dealt with and that was his job.

He led his team at a trot and they separated as they entered the settlement. Tarkhan drew his sword as he ran down the side of one of the rows of low buildings. They'd been the dwellings of the clan in residence prior to Hallaran being taken by Sylanna. Now, as far as they'd been able to determine, the buildings were empty. Khaliun and the majority of the fighters they'd brought with them were headed towards where most of the Hallaran captives were held. His own objective, with the small team he led, was the row of prisoner huts off to one side, with Delbee housed in the one at the centre.

At the edge of the row of low stone buildings he stopped, pressing himself back against the cool rock wall. There was an open courtyard around the corner of the building, where Khaliun had been strung up, with three small cells to one side. He'd been in the cell next to the one that Delbee was in. Right now, he was waiting for his team to make their way around to the other side of the open space, and for Khaliun's team. They'd originally come for Delbee but, having talked with their warriors, they were risking everything by trying to free not only her but the other Hallaran captives.

We're in position, Khaliun said.

Let's get this done and get out of here.

Tarkhan resisted the urge to run out with his sword raised and a battle cry ringing from his lips. Instead, he signalled his team. Two of his people on the other side of the small group of cells sprang into action. Tarkhan sprinted around the corner and launched himself on the Sylannians standing guard outside the cells. As he and his opponent went down, he grabbed his sword in both hands and plunged it down. There was that resistance as this blade encountered her body armour but with his full weight behind the blade it finally gave and plunged into his enemy's chest. His breath was harsh as he sucked in air; it always astonished him how much effort it took to force his blade through Sylannian armour. A quick scan of the camp showed no alarm had yet been raised. He rolled off the now-dead Sylannian, scooping up the fallen enemy's blades as he came to his feet. He crossed the short distance to the cells. Tarkhan passed two of his team who stood guard on the door and entered. As Tarkhan crossed the dark cell he signalled his other team members to stand back. His warriors complied and desisted from their futile attempt to loosen the Sylannian silk bindings that restrained Delbee. He went to his knees at the side of the low cot that Delbee was bound in.

"Give me a moment. I'll get these off," Tarkhan said.

Delbee licked her dry, cracked lips but otherwise kept her silence. Tarkhan's heart clenched at the sight of her bruised and battered body. The Sylannians hadn't been gentle. Closing his eyes, he sank into a semi-trance. As his fingers brushed the silken bonds, he heard that almost inaudible hum. He responded to it, interrupting the song of the silk until it unravelled and dropped harmlessly onto the cot. A couple of his team steeped forward and helped Delbee up.

"Thank you for your aid, warriors of Kallith," Delbee said, staring at him then the silk. "How did you manage to control that stuff?"

"It resonates a melody I can sense. I can hear and disrupt its pattern when I concentrate; don't feel bad, none of our people except me seem to have the knack of it," Tarkhan said, before addressing two of his team members. "Get Delbee back to the meeting point."

The others have been bound with Sylannian silk, we've resorted to breaking the beams they are tied to. We're doing our best to muffle the noise, but we could use your help, Khaliun said.

I'm on my way, Tarkhan said.

Tarkhan gathered the other half of his group to him, then frowned as the footfalls of the group guiding Delbee stopped behind him.

What about Chono? His sleeping quarters are the other way, Delbee almost hissed, her eyes glittering with anger.

Would you have everyone die for revenge?

No, but…

Don't throw your life away now. I don't want to get back to our new home and explain to your children how I let you die.

They live?

They do. Both have been taken in by my tribe and have just completed their rites. They are cubs of Kallith.

Chono should face punishment for his betrayal. Delbee's lips thinned as she shook her head.

Freeing you and the others is risky enough. Tarkhan stared at Delbee, not allowing any compassion or understanding of her desire for Chono's death to show. *If we attack the Sylannian tents directly it will rouse them all. We need to be as far away from here as we can be before that happens.*

But—

Let it go. Leave him to his fate.

Feeling Delbee's resistance crumble, he signalled to those assisting her and they continued through the settlement back the way they'd come in while he and his group started across the camp. He winced as he heard the splintering of wood and swore softly to himself, just as a warbling cry rang out. He spun around to see Sylannians pouring out of their tents across the small courtyard. He cursed and checked over his shoulder, reassured that Delbee and her escorts were disappearing over the hill. As more cries joined the first, Tarkhan resolutely faced their enemy who ran straight in their direction.

Khaliun, get out of here. The game's up! Tarkhan yelled.

No, we'll come and get you free, Khaliun said.

No! It's too late. Go. Get those of Hallaran and flee. Keep to the plan. Ride as far and as fast as you can. Tarkhan's eyes narrowed as he readied himself to fight with his three clan members. *Your duty is clear. Delbee and the group with her should be at the meeting point. Go.*

Tarkhan drew his sword and launched himself at the Sylannians running towards them with their blades glinting in the sun. As more of the Sylannians poured out of their tents, Tarkhan gritted his teeth. The niggling fear of what might happen to him when these women subdued him and his fellow clansmen was pushed to the back of his mind. Right now, all he had to do was fight.

"They'll want us alive. Use that to your advantage!" Tarkhan yelled.

KHALIUN'S THROAT restricted as she stared down at Tarkhan and the three warriors with him, surrounded and desperately lashing out at the enemy. With anguish and responsibility weighing heavily on her, she spun away.

"We have no time to lose, let's go!" Khaliun said, as she leapt into her saddle.

The tribe around her, Hallaran and Kallith alike, paid no mind to which horse they were mounting. She was grateful they'd spent time planning escape. The team detailed to secure extra horses from the horse yards had done their job well and as a result very few of them would have to ride double. She signalled and two of the scouts spurred their horses into the lead, heading for the nearby gully. If they could get to it and drop into its depths and out of sight, they might stand a chance of evading pursuit in its twisting and interconnecting paths.

FIFTEEN

Lilianna could sense the displeasure of the underwives. She should have been sequestered in their realm, hidden away until the birth of her child. Even if, here in the wilds, they didn't have such a place. All the years she'd spent within the trader lands had taught her bad habits. They weren't within the heart of the high courts of Sylanna where her life—and the life of her child—was at risk. The wilds were relatively safe. As far as she was concerned the reason to hide herself from everyone had been removed as soon as they had departed the Court of a Thousand Islands.

Next time she saw Jaclyn she needed to thank the First for assigning the team of daggerwives that she'd previously led as the head of her protection detail. While it might have occurred to them that she no longer led them, it was too new for the behaviour to have stuck. When they'd seen what they thought was an anomaly, they'd still come running to her. So now she was picking her path through the forest back towards the water's edge, trying to pretend she wasn't being careful not to trip over every stray twig. When they'd returned to the Court of a Thousand Islands and gone into seclusion, everything had become more real. That had been the riskiest time for her to lose her child, made worse by the king's daggerwives launching their attack. Still, some risk remained—but she wasn't going to show that to the underwives. Every week that passed without incident increased the likelihood she'd carry this boy child full term and get back to where she belonged after the birth. So, she took care, without trying to make it look like she was doing so.

She finally made it to her destination amongst the safety of the trees right on the water's edge, looking out towards the nearest island. This far out on the very rim of their original territorial home it could only house one of the lower ranked families of Sylanna.

"I presume there is a reason you've dragged me out here, incurring the wrath of the underwives?" Liliana asked.

"Wait, Primewife, you will see," the head daggerwife said.

"I'm not really primewife until my child is born healthy, you know that."

"The First declares you as a primewife. I'll not argue," the head daggerwife said.

Liliana held back her amusement as the underwives bossed around the daggerwives and in short order a fallen log was brought and placed nearby. The underwives glared at her until she sighed, reaching out one hand and allowing them to support her as she sat. It was extraordinary how difficult a simple task like sitting, let alone getting up, had become. She hoped she didn't get much bigger than she was; her abdomen was already big enough to hinder her. In the weeks to come she'd no doubt have to seek the assistance of her underwives not to mollify them, but because it was useful.

At least from where they'd positioned her impromptu seat she still had a view of the island and, as she gazed idly over the water, those who lived on the island placing boxes on the jetty. It was clear they were expecting someone. One of the daggerwives drew her attention to an incoming boat. Liliana sharpened her gaze, overlaying what she could see with her normal sight with her othersight and gasped. Hand against the tree, she stood. The approaching boat was low and flat. The people in it were wearing leather and linen. Not the trader clans, not her own people. She stepped forward, watching intently as the foreign boat pulled up to the jetty of the island. Those who resided on the island streamed out, but not on a battle footing.

Liliana's eyes widened as a handful of boys and men, all of them bound and seemingly insensible, were offloaded onto the jetty. The boxes from the jetty were loaded onto the boat. With no time wasted, the foreigners pulled away and went back the way they'd come.

"They dare." Anger blazed within Liliana.

"This is the third time we've seen this, Primewife." The daggerwife held up her hand against Liliana's glare. "I needed to make sure of what we were seeing."

"They are trading with our enemies," Liliana bit out.

"I fear so, Primewife."

"Those people fit the description of the barbarians." The sight had left her seething.

"Yes, Primewife."

"They are taking, hiding men." Liliana spun and stalked back along the winding trail.

She was so caught up in her anger, she didn't even reprimand her underwives as they subtly reached out helping hands to steady her.

Liliana lay back in the bath. It had taken them some days for the collared workers who'd come with them to craft the bath for her.

But from her perspective it was a totally welcome addition to their court in exile. With her long black hair piled up on her head, she sighed as steam rose from the bath the underwives were keeping warm for her. While she was perfectly capable of performing such a simple thing herself, she allowed them such small actions. For some reason it made them happy to look after her, even if such activity wasn't something that would bring her joy. One of the underwives gently grabbed her hand, running the soaking sponge along her arm to wash away the sweat and grime from the day's activities. Everyone was still treading lightly around her. Not that she blamed them. Although her outward display of anger over what she'd been shown had abated, it still simmered under the surface. Her eyes narrowed. Well, if she was honest, not far under the surface.

"How much longer?" she asked.

"Hopefully months yet, Primewife." The underwife guessed correctly what she was referring to.

Liliana ground her teeth. She'd known the answer but somehow had been hoping she'd get a different one.

"I'm going to get fatter and more useless."

"I'm afraid that is a situation that will not remedy in the short term, Primewife."

Liliana gasped and sat up, glaring at the underwife that tended her. Then her outrage fled. Laughter escaped her lips and she splashed water at the older woman.

"You were not meant to agree with that viewpoint," Liliana grumped.

"You are not fat or useless, Primewife, merely pregnant. Allow us to look after you and this child of our house. It is our duty."

"I know. I'm sorry, I try."

"We will protect you and your child. Then, once he is born, we will help you to become fit and strong again. Then, and only then, will we release you from our care and you can help our First and husband."

Liliana shouldn't be irritated. The underwife spoke sense. Still the words of reason the underwife spoke annoyed her tremendously. Liliana found her mind mulling over the foreign boat and the problem it represented.

"Fetch one of my daggerwives," she ordered, without directing it to any specific underwife.

She didn't have long to wait.

"Send a team of the daggerwives to follow the barbarians back to their homeland," she said to the daggerwife who entered.

"Primewife?"

"Once we know the route they are using through the river system, we'll send word to Jaclyn."

"I should have thought about this sooner, Primewife."

Liliana finally regarded the other woman. "Your role was to think of the protection of the children of the house and me. Mine, as primewife, is to look after the house." She sent a thread of exasperation laced with amusement at the underwife. "At least once the underwives release me from their care."

CHAPTER
SIXTEEN

Michael tensed as they rode up to the inn, scanning it and their surroundings for trouble.

"The guard has doubled," Olivia said.

As those guarding the door noticed the arrival of their commanders, the tension rose a notch, quickly echoed by those inside as word was passed of their return to the inn. He looked towards Olivia and Nathanial, who confirmed it wasn't his imagination as they sensed the same thing. Michael steeled himself and dismounted, handing the reins of his horse over to the guard, who came forward with his gaze averted. Michael scanned the street aware that Nathanial and Olivia did likewise. Everyone was nervous, although all of them were trying to hide it. Unfortunately for them, the tension thrummed and jumped from one to the other like a living thing.

"They've failed and are afraid of how we're going to react," Nathanial said. "None of our people want to be the ones to tell us what's happened."

"They're experienced enough to know when they've failed at a duty they've been given. So, they probably have," Michael said.

"All they had to do was stay out of trouble," Olivia said.

"They had two more duties," Nathanial said.

Michael's eyes narrowed as he entered the inn, pausing just inside the doors and scanning the Unwanted, who stood in the common room. The stillness was absolute.

"Just tell me," Michael said.

There was enough of a bite in his tone that it caused those closest to him in the crowded common room to flinch.

"The healer. It appears she isn't here," the senior-most guard, Gavrel, said.

"Appears? Or isn't?" Nathanial asked.

"She isn't. She's been gone for hours. As best as we can guess." Gavrel swallowed.

"Have you sent a patrol to the market to search for her?" Olivia asked.

Michael sympathised with her exasperated tone. The market was only place he could think of the healer sneaking out to, probably for more of her herbs. Michael mentally kicked himself; he knew Kesha was still finding her place among them and he should have made sure a security detail was assigned to take her to shop for what she needed. Instead, she'd probably believed she was being deliberately ignored and locked up in the inn.

"They visited every herb seller in the markets, and they've found no sign of her," one of the other guards, Shallan, said.

Michael swore, causing all those in the room to flinch. They all reeked of failure, and he could feel the undercurrent of further tension.

"What else?"

"No one has seen Damien for days." Gavrel swallowed, staring straight ahead. "We thought he was keeping to himself, but it seems not."

"When was Kesha seen last?" Nathanial asked.

"Today. She was here this morning, but we don't know when she disappeared," Shallan said.

"See that the gates of Callenhain are sealed and the docks are locked down, by my order. No one leaves the city until I say otherwise," Olivia said, glancing around the room.

"You lot, with us now!" Callan snapped, pointing to those near the entrance.

He then spun with the detail that had been with them on duty all day and the extras, going out once more to ensure the city guard locked down Callenhain.

Nathanial went into Damien's room, pausing at the entrance.

"Ah, my friend, what have you done?" Nathanial whispered.

The contents of Damien's saddlebags were strewn everywhere. Clothes disregarded in random piles, smashed glass on the floor and an upturned vial on the side table. This, from what he'd observed of Damien, was not normal. He generally kept his possessions—few as they were—in order. Seeing the open shutters, Nathanial picked his way across and looked out at the ledge running down the side of the lodging. That explained how Damien had managed to leave the inn without any of their people noticing.

Nathanial paid closer attention to what was thrown on the floor and groaned as he saw the fighting leathers flung to one side. If Damien didn't want to risk being identified as one of the Unwanted, it was not a good sign. He spotted the weapons stored neatly on the weapons rack and sighed. He could have wished Damien hadn't gone out unarmed. Nathanial crossed the room to the small bedside table. There was an overturned bottle with the stopper next to it. He picked it up, saw it was empty and smelt it. Nathanial recoiled pulling the vial away from his nose.

"Damn it, why didn't you call me?" Nathanial muttered.

Taking the bottle with him, he left Damien's room and went up the hallway to the larger bedroom, which had its own sitting area and table. It was Michael's room, but they also used it for private meetings. He walked in without ceremony and shook his head at Michael's unasked question, holding out the bottle. Michael smelt it and swore.

"He's using again," Michael said.

"That explains the secrecy and sneaking out," Olivia said.

"It doesn't explain why he isn't here now, unless he's passed out somewhere." Michael's tone was grim.

"I'd say he was drug addled and desperate for more. He's dressed in his old clothes and even left his weapons behind."

"Wherever he got his hands on this stuff, it's strong," Michael said.

"I haven't used in years and don't have the inclination to start up again, and even though I know I won't feel the effects anymore, I still don't really want that bottle near me." Nathanial eyed the empty bottle as if it was a dangerous animal about to attack him.

Michael handed the vial to Olivia, who sniffed it and then tucked it out of sight into her own belt pouch.

"It will, however, give us somewhere to start looking in the morning," Michael said.

"It's potent stuff, and there can't be too many here in Callenhain who could supply the drug of that quality," Nathanial said.

"We'll detail some of our other people to do that; I'll not ask you to go into drug dens," Michael said.

"I appreciate it, but I'll be fine. The stuff doesn't affect me the same way anymore. Not since the last transition attack I went through, and that was years ago," Nathanial said.

Michael shook his head. "I know but it doesn't mean it

wouldn't bring back memories and issues you'd rather not think of."

"Some of the pleasure houses in town will likely have a good notion of who the suppliers are," Olivia said.

"I'll not ask you to go into those either." Michael held up his hand to silence her protest. "Our people can do the footwork."

Nathanial traded looks with Olivia. There was no point arguing with Michael when he was in this kind of mood. Not that Nathanial wasn't grateful for the order that others would take care of that job.

Michael spun as the door opened and throttled his irritation as Aiden came in with his band leader, Derick, a step behind him.

"Hear me out," Aiden said, raising his hands.

Michael frowned. "What do you want, Aiden? In case you haven't noticed, we are a little bit busy right now."

"I know. I might be able to help, but..." Aiden paused.

"But what?" Olivia asked.

"I don't want you to kill me out of hand." Aiden's tone was entirely devoid of humour.

"If I haven't killed you already, I think you're safe," Michael said.

"But we'll put it on notice we're probably going to want to throttle you," Olivia said.

"I can't help with the healer, but I may be able to track down Damien," Aiden said, his eyes flicking between all three of them.

Michael's eyes narrowed as he worked through the implication of Aiden's words.

"How?" Nathanial asked bluntly.

"You know when you join minds with another, like you did with that woman from the clans? It's like there's a residue or something that remains." Aiden held up his hands and took a step back.

"It fades with time but yes, it is one of the complications of joining minds with someone."

"You've warned me of it before." Aiden grimaced. "On this occasion, it might prove useful."

"You can still sense Damien?"

"The connection has faded, as you said, but I still might be able to lead us to him. He is still in the city, or I don't think I would be able to feel him."

"Why didn't you tell us this last night?" Michael growled.

"You know I hate admitting you are correct about the risks of something. Besides, it took me all night prodding at that part of my head to wake it up—it's not like I've been fostering it to keep it alive and active longer. I don't want Damien permanently in my head any more than he would want me to be in his," Aiden said, looking entirely unhappy.

"Can you reach him?"

"I can sense him. It won't be fast, but I think I can lead a group to wherever he is." Aiden rubbed his temple with the fingers of one hand, seemingly ignoring them all.

Michael stared at Aiden steadily. They didn't get on, they never had, not from that first moment the Warlord had irrevocably claimed his life. But Aiden was far more capable than he showed, he was just lazy. Still, Michael couldn't help thinking there was more to this than Aiden was admitting. When it came down to it, though, whatever Aiden's motivation for offering to help, if it could assist them in finding Damien sooner, then it was welcome.

"Very well. You should have mentioned you were struggling sooner. It can't have been easy, particularly with Damien being so close at hand all this time." Michael frowned; it was a concession that was hard to make. "Get a group out front and ready to go."

Michael addressed that last to the actual leader of Aiden's warband. Derick was competent, at least, and probably the reason why Aiden had survived all these years. The other man nodded. Derick held the door open and gestured for Aiden to precede him before he walked out and closed the door quietly behind him.

SEVENTEEN

Khaliun gritted her teeth as they wound their way slowly up the trail that led up the Heights to safety. This last part of the trail would allow those below to see them. It wouldn't tell their enemy where the trailhead was, only where to start looking, but that was bad enough. The fact they'd made it this far without being caught astounded her. On this last leg they'd been forced to dismount and lead the horses instead of riding them. This, of course, had slowed them down even more as some of the Hallaran weren't in a good state before they'd rescued them, and the hard ride hadn't helped them recuperate.

They must know we're coming, the scout said.

The undertone of weariness in the scout's tone matched her own. Khaliun was grateful there'd been no recriminations from any of the warriors for her decision to leave Tarkhan behind; they'd all closed ranks and gotten on with their jobs. The senior scout had stepped up without being asked and assisted her in getting them all out of this mess.

Obviously, Khaliun said.

Why aren't they coming down to help?

Scared? Angry that we ran off on this mission without consulting them?

The longer we spend getting those we've rescued to the top, the greater the risk we'll all be discovered.

I know. However, it was always us, the warriors, who would have taken the risks in the past.

As we have done. Those of Hallaran deserved no less of us.

You know I agree. It's why we all went to help them in the first place.

Where are the rest of the warriors? The scout put one foot doggedly in front of the other as they made their way closer to the summit. *I would have at least expected them to help us.*

Prevented from helping by the others? Banished to the plateau with the others?

The others do not control the warriors.

They can if they meet in conclave.

The scout's eyes widened. She might not have known the finer details of how the various leaders of their clan all worked together. After all, the possibility of the other tribe leaders banding together to force the warriors to submit had only just occurred to Khaliun. Without her or Tarkhan to stand against the other leaders, those of their people who remained would have little choice but to follow the directions given. For the greater good of the whole. Or be expelled from the clan to survive on their own. Khaliun blinked back tears at the thought of her co-leader. The only thing that was keeping her going was the responsibility to the people she led and those she had rescued.

What have you done? Erden's mind voice snarled.

My duty! Anger boiled within Khaliun as Erden's tone unleashed all the pain she felt.

You put us all at risk for those who are nothing but traitors, Erden said.

No! Chono is a traitor, not these, Khaliun said. *Our duty was to these of Hallaran as much as it is to the other tribes of the Kallith. You know this.*

You two had no right without the authority of the conclave, Erden said.

We did, and you know it. Doesn't mean you have to like it. Khaliun's jaw clenched, uncertain if she should be grateful not to be within striking distance of her fellow leader. *We are the Warriors of Kallith. Our duty has always been to the People as a whole, not just to Kallith.*

We are the People now! Erden's anger bubbled and spat.

Enough. What is done is done and can't be changed. You lot, get down there and help them up here before the Sylannians spot them. Orghana's mindvoice cut across the argument. A talent of the other leader that Khaliun appreciated. The crunch of boots on stone and a handful of loose rocks skittering down the trail gave away it hadn't taken long at all for those up top to follow Orghana's order and come to their assistance. A handful of the tribe members who'd obviously been keeping watch came around a bend in the trail and made their way at a half trot down to them.

"There are some among the Hallaran who could use your assistance," Khaliun said mildly, and gestured back down towards those that trailed them.

She thanked the tribe member who, without comment, took the reins of her horse along with the scout's and urged the beasts up the steep part of the trail. That left her to concentrate on ascending the last part herself. She checked on her tribe members and all their charges one final time. Now, the next challenge: facing off against their fellow leaders rather than just verbally sparring.

"This moment was always coming," Khaliun half muttered to

herself, although she realised she sounded like she was trying to convince herself.

"You won't face them alone; I'll stand with you. We all will." The scout's resolve was firm.

"At the end of the day, it was me that got us into this. I'll take their censure..."

"Nice try, but no. We are the warriors of Kallith, we all had the vote on this mission, and it was unanimous. We all agreed with both you and Tarkhan." The scout paused, an echo of the grief Khaliun felt in her voice. "We supported you then. We support you now. We've spoken about this; we'll not give you up as our leader, Khaliun."

Khaliun reached out a hand and squeezed her shoulder. A sense of gratitude washed from her to the scout, moisture welling in her eyes.

"I don't know what I've done to earn your continued trust, but I will try not to fail any of you more than I already have." She straightened her shoulders, letting out a deep breath as she looked up at the last bend in the trail ahead. "Let's get this over and done with."

Khaliun saw the scout nod agreement, and they strode forward, side by side, heads high.

KHALIUN UNCLENCHED her jaw with effort as Erden droned on, spitefully glaring at her as he added his voice to those clamouring for censure of her actions.

"I say she should be removed and others more stable and suited to leadership put in their place," Erden intoned. "She's responsible for the death of Tarkhan."

She opened her mouth to respond when sudden movement commanded attention. Narantua had stood and made her way forward. The other leader stared at Erden with an unwavering gaze until he backed up and conceded the floor to her.

"The Wolves have long been the warriors of all the People, as is shown by the members of their tribe sourced from all the tribes and clans," Narantua said.

"Your heart is too soft. She risked us all," Erden said.

"The warriors gave testimony that they all voted on the mission, and it was unanimous. As such, it was not Khaliun's fault; she and the warriors did their duty to the People. They rescued those of the tribes that were imprisoned in Hallaran." Narantua pinned Erden with her sharp gaze. "Nor was it their fault that Tarkhan fell in battle, any more than it was ours that so many of the People lost their lives to the invaders during the war."

"Should we all die for them?" Erden persisted.

"I remind you all that to remove tribe leaders, this conclave needs a unanimous vote from the other leaders of Kallith Clan." Narantua paused as those gathered around her stirred uneasily. "I do not agree and will not vote for it, which makes the discussion for the removal of Khaliun moot."

The meeting tent erupted as the various leaders leapt to their feet, each yelling and trying to be heard over the others. A shaft of rage caused Khaliun to surge to her own feet. She crossed the intervening space, placing her own body between Narantua and the enraged leader as Erden lunged at her, his fist striking out. Khaliun deflected the blow and stepped in, slamming her knee into Erden's stomach. As the man grunted, Khaliun grabbed his arm and twisted, forcing the enraged leader to the carpeted floor and pinning him there. Shocked silence spread around the tent, all eyes on her as she held Erden effortlessly on the ground.

"You speak of tradition and duty, yet at the same time you would breach the peace of the meeting tent as we sit in conclave?" Khaliun swept her gaze around the other leaders who had the grace to flush. "To raise a hand in violence to another leader within these confines, during conclave—a healer, no less —is, by our own tradition, punishable by death."

If possible, the stillness, silence and shock in the tent settled even deeper. Khaliun stared down at Erden and noted that while his breathing was ragged and his face was pale, he no longer fought his restraint.

"Please, there has been enough death and hate. I do not ask for that punishment, but I stand by my stated word. So let me make it formal." Narantua's eyes were sad as she regarded the gathered leaders. "As a leader of a tribe of the Kallith, I will not vote for censure or dismissal of Khaliun. This meeting is therefore at an end."

Narantua's fingers brushed Khaliun's cheek as she passed by on her way to the doors. Gratitude, along with a ball of hurt that this action had proven to be necessary, passed between them. Khaliun bowed her head in respect, maintaining her hold on the other leader until Narantua departed the meeting tent. It was only as the doors closed that all eyes turned back. While previously those hard eyes had been directed at her, now they focused entirely on Erden.

EIGHTEEN

Aiden waited as the Unwanted scrambled to get ready. Michael wasn't taking any risks at all when it came to the chance to retrieve his lost one.

"Why are we helping them?" Derick whispered.

"I've worked too hard on setting the groundwork to make Damien my tool to allow him to slip through my fingers."

"What if they realise what you've done?" Derick persisted, his eyes on the Unwanted milling around them.

"They haven't yet."

"So that residue thing you claimed is real?"

"It's a real condition and the easiest way to cover what I've actually done." Aiden shrugged.

Aiden raised his hand in warning as Michael, Olivia and Nathanial walked out the doors to the inn. Derick gazed over his shoulder and nodded politely as the three approached them. He retreated and went to stand at Aiden's back. Even though Aiden understood his man's deference to the three, particularly Michael, it still irritated him.

"All right, let's go and see if this works," Michael said.

"Once we've retrieved your wayward squad member, I take it we'll switch to trying to find your healer?" Derick asked.

"Father really won't like it if you've lost her permanently."

"I'm aware of that, however, I'll lay odds she's still here."

"Which means we'll find her even if we have to tear Callenhain apart to do so," Olivia said.

Aiden couldn't help but stare at Olivia. Other people might have been joking or overestimating their capabilities when they said such a thing, but she was perfectly serious. Still, his father would hear of this regardless of the results. It wasn't often Michael messed up. Somehow the day seemed positively cheery. He smoothed his expression and hoped he'd been able to approximate concern on his face and tone rather than the smugness he was actually feeling.

Aiden followed along in Michael's wake, Derick at his back, the waiting members of the warband all looking to him. Aiden smiled tightly and squeezed his eyes closed. He made a show of grimacing and rubbing his temples lightly as if it caused him some pain. Aiden opened his eyes and swallowed. Taking a shaky breath, he nodded at Michael who was watching him.

"This way," he said, pointing up the road.

He took the lead, careful to keep stopping as if he was seeking that awareness in the back of his head. In truth he had a very strong sense of Damien's location. While he hadn't known what he might be able to use it for, he'd deliberately left a little back door in Damien's mind. Although with Michael and his interfering healer around, he'd been very careful not to use it until now. Unfortunately, as soon as he opened the connection, he'd discovered Damien was insensible much of the time, with only sporadic moments of being conscious. He was drugged, which made his mind a chaotic mess. The only images he caught from Damien were confused and dark. Even with all of that, now that he'd opened that connection between them, he perceived exactly where to lead everyone. It was like there was a wisp of a thread in the veil linking him to Damien. It formed a trail that only he could see.

As they strode down the street, locals scattered out of the way of the Unwanted, who were bristling with weapons and clearly meaning business. The news that something was wrong had run all through the city like a raging fire ripping through the old quarter. It was only the second occasion in recent times that the city had been locked down and the last time it had happened was when the Warlord had ridden down on them. There was a certain amount of relief at the knowledge they at least weren't the ones the Warleader was after as the warband strode right past people. That relief was followed by a waft of pity for whoever was foolish enough to warrant such attention from the massed might of the Unwanted.

NINETEEN

Damien groaned and an almost metallic sound echoed in his skull. Slowly he became aware of aches other than his head. His wrists and ankles throbbed, and there was a dead sensation right where his hip should be. He tried to roll over, guessing he'd been lying on his side too long, but pain lanced through his wrists and up his arms and the clatter of chains revealed that he was bound in place. He reached for the veil, only to find it was insubstantial and slipped through his mental fingers. The empty ache within himself where the power should reside was a counterpoint to the now-familiar need for more tiscan.

"They must fear you," a man said.

His eyes flared open at the harsh whisper. It was disconcerting knowing nothing other than the owner of the voice was nearby. The reality of growing up as he had was that he'd always known more about people—their emotions and occasionally random words or even a mental echo of what they were saying verbally. This time he hadn't even been aware that anyone was nearby until that hoarse whisper, close enough he could feel the other's breath on his skin.

"Or you have more value than us," the man said.

Damien blinked in the darkness, automatically trying to switch to his othersight and failing. His breath rate increased as he waited for the shadowy shapes to appear in the darkness. He shivered and flinched back as fingers brushed against his skin but swallowed again as nausea clawed at him. He closed his eyes, willing the familiar tiscan sickness to go away. Damien wondered, again, what had driven him to go back to the drug den. He knew, absolutely knew, that Nathanial would have helped him, without judgement, if he'd gone to him.

A harsh clatter of metal on metal sounded overloud in the darkness off to one side of him. Metal protested as the door was opened and Damien winced as the sudden light pierced his eyes. A shadowy figure was outlined in the light, carrying another in their arms. Damien had a brief glimpse of a windowless room made from cold grey stone, with people pressed against the far wall as the shadowy figure dumped their burden unceremoniously on the ground not far away. He was still trying to process what he was seeing when fingers twisted in his hair and his head was jerked back. Damien tried to struggle, but a fist slammed into his stomach and the air exploded from his lungs. Another pain added to the multitude.

"That's enough out of you," the assailant growled at him.

Hands wrenched his jaw open and he gagged as liquid spilled into his throat.

"There's a good little slave. Swallow your drugs, you know you want it."

The man let out a harsh bark of laughter and Damien tried to flinch away from the putrid breath and spit out what they'd poured into him, but his body was betrayed by his neediness and he swallowed as he was bidden. He whimpered as the vial was withdrawn and instantly hated himself for his weakness.

"Please, just a little more," Damien whispered, a note of desperation in his voice as he begged.

Shame flooded him as the man laughed but since he complied and poured more of the drug into his mouth, his shame didn't stop him from swallowing again. It didn't take long before his concerns floated away, along with the pain of his bindings. Nothing mattered other than the blissful cloud he found himself on.

CHAPTER

TWENTY

K esha groaned, wondering for a moment why she had a hangover. She didn't remember drinking excessively before bed. Her eyes flashed open, only to be greeted by darkness as the memory of being drugged in the markets came back to her. She scrambled to her feet, lurching unsteadily, still under the influence of what they'd given her. It had been an extract that healers commonly used to put their patients to sleep. Or at least, healers who only possessed a minor healing talent. She hadn't needed to use it since she'd come fully into her powers. It was times like this that being a healer frustrated her— she could heal others, but not herself.

"Hush, or you'll draw their attention."

She twisted around, seeking the owner of the voice, yet only darkness surrounded her. Kesha stumbled on the uneven stone floor then flinched as the stranger steadied her.

Kesha blinked, waiting as shadowy shapes materialise out of the darkness. She shivered and cringed as fingers brushed against her temple, pushing her own powers out as the other's talent rippled like a small breeze over her skin.

"Easy, my name is Lem. I'm not as powerful as you, but I have a little healing talent and I can ease the pounding in your head. If you'll permit," Lem said.

Kesha concentrated and pushed a small tendril of the veil out, delicately testing those around her as Nathanial had been teaching her. From the lifeforces she detected there were fifteen other people trapped in this windowless room with her. Given the store of the veil that had pooled within her, she'd obviously been unconscious for quite some time. Lem appeared as a shadowy figure to her eyes but glowed faintly in her othersight. He was correct. She could see he had little actual talent, at least not in the veil. It didn't mean Lem wasn't a fine healer. They could achieve a great deal using the old ways: needles, thin twine, potions, sharp knives, bindings, and such things. Despite herself, she shuddered. It was unlikely that Lem, being her fellow captive, had access to any such things. Except the tiny pool of the veil that dwelled within him. She judged Lem would have to use all he possessed to brush aside the effects of the drug they'd given her. Unlike Michael and his people, or even her, it would take a considerable time to collect within him again. She also didn't think Lem's talent was strong enough for him to draw the veil to him from the sources around him on purpose. She nodded, then her face heated as she realised Lem might not perceive the motion. It was only a small mercy that the stranger couldn't see her flaming cheeks.

"Please, if you will." Her voice was low and grated. A product of the drug they'd used on her.

As Lem's fingers brushed on her temple, a small burst of pride washed over her from him—his astonishment and awe followed when he perceived her own power. A breath of ice played over her skin, causing her spine to arch with her breath expelling from her lungs. The other healer didn't have the skill or power to counter the adverse reaction. It was only a moment in time, yet it seemed like an eternity. Then the icy fingers chased away her pain, and she breathed easily as the touch withdrew.

"I'm sorry, healer. It's the best I can do," Lem said.

"It was enough, I can concentrate now that the headache and lingering effects of the drug have gone. Thank you. Here, I have more than enough power to share." Kesha could hear the fatigue in Lem's voice and reached out, willing strength back into him. She gasped as he jerked away from her, holding up his hand.

"Don't waste your abilities on me. He needs it more."

Now that her eyes had adjusted, Kesha could see other shadowy figures crammed into the room. Her gaze tracked across to the figure crumpled on the ground in the corner. She squinted and realised, unlike herself and the others she shared this cell with, the one in the corner was chained.

"What makes you say that?" She regarded Lem who stood at her side.

"They drug him regularly and beat him every chance they get even though he's chained up and can't cause them any trouble," Lem said.

"Of the two of us chained, he's the only one they drugged," another voice said, with a rattle of chains.

Kesha searched the gloom for the chained speaker. If her eyes weren't playing tricks on her, he was sitting up, leaning against a wall. Her vision might be adjusting, but she still couldn't say she'd be able to recognise any of them if she met them in the streets in daylight.

"Tiscan. They've kept him mostly insensible. They've been dosing him with the stuff since they brought him in here," Lem said.

Kesha could just make out the outline of a figure, towards the corner of the room, where the unconscious person lay. She swallowed. Just because their captors had chained and drugged that individual didn't mean they were an ally to her or any of the others trapped in this room. Though he was certainly no ally to the people who had drugged and taken her.

Still not trusting that her eyes had adjusted to reveal anything that stood in her way, let alone an uneven surface, she edged cautiously forward, tapping lightly with her foot to be sure of each step before she transferred her weight.

"Nathanial is going to be so angry with me."

"Who's Nathanial?" Lem asked.

"Never mind." Kesha was certain that this time her cheeks would be bright red; she hadn't meant to voice that particular concern.

Of course, her priority should be to get herself out of this situation, but somehow, she was more concerned about how Nathanial would respond. She licked her lips. If she thought about it, Michael or Olivia would certainly be angry with her, too. Or they would be after they'd eliminated any of those who threatened her. Yet it was Nathanial's reaction she was most concerned about.

Kesha knelt beside the head of the unconscious form and laid hands on his temples. As she touched him, something twinged at the edge of her awareness. Almost a familiarity. She frowned, peering through the low light at the face of the person she was about to heal, and gasped as recognition hit her.

CHAPTER

TWENTY-ONE

Khaliun clamped her lips against the myriad of complaints that she could make. It wasn't like her current circumstance wasn't her own fault. She'd volunteered for this miserable duty for no other reason than to escape the mutterings and glares from the other leaders. Had it not been for Narantua refusing to support her demotion, she could have found herself in a much more difficult position. Such events could bring on a sundering of the clan. Since they were the last remaining clan of the People, there was no other tribe or clan for her to petition for shelter, so she'd fled up here to the Heights to help with the defences rather than staying below where her continued presence was inflaming anger and bitterness.

Remind me again why it is we are up here? Narantua grumbled.

Despite herself, the sentiment amused Khaliun.

Because my former lover is hugging his jealousy and anger to him like a new mistress. Showing support for me the way you did caused him to fixate on you as well. Hopefully, our absence will help him and the others to calm down.

137

She sensed more than heard the healer sigh her agreement. It made her feel better she wasn't alone in being out of sorts in this party. Khaliun also suspected Narantua was using her healing abilities, gently bleeding away her agony and guilt over Tarkhan's loss.

It didn't help when they found out I knew where you were all going before you departed, Narantua said.

I didn't expect them to react so badly that they'd risk sundering the clan.

She fell silent for a moment as her anxiety washed over them both.

The fortifications up here need to be completed, so it might as well be us up here supervising. Besides, Michael and his warlord are unforgiving of failure.

Khaliun blinked at the other woman's sudden change of topic, but Narantua was aware that Erden's perception of Khaliun's feelings for the Warleader had spurred his current behaviour.

I wish I could disagree with your appraisal, but I shared the man's mind.

He is dangerous, but you like him no matter how much you protest —a situation Erden is aware of.

There is much to admire about Michael, Khaliun said.

What do you think they'd do if we failed? Narantua asked. *If he finds out we might have led the Sylannians here?*

Khaliun closed her eyes. *He'd order our deaths and have no issues carrying it out himself.*

You believe he'd do that?

I do. He can be just as harsh as the man who raised him.

They rode together in silence. Others out in this miserable weather kept a careful eye on them both, but otherwise gave them space.

Everyone believes it's the Warlord who is the dangerous one, Narantua said.

The Warlord is a dangerous man. He defeated many enemies, but those acts we've heard about were not all committed by him. Who do you think did them?

Michael, Narantua said.

Khaliun shook her head. *The one they call the Warleader.*

But isn't that Michael? Narantua asked, confusion written on her face.

They are the same man, but very different people.

Except for the clattering of stones displaced by the hooves of their horses, they sank into silence. Khaliun pushed aside the nagging worry her words provided. All the more reason not to fail—or at least not to betray the Warlord. She didn't believe Michael would kill them outright for failing. The *consequence* of failure would probably take care of that. Betrayal would be another matter entirely, a future and consequence she had no intentions of courting.

We'll just have to make sure we don't fail, Narantua said.

That was a sentiment Khaliun found she agreed with. They hadn't fought so hard for survival to be wiped out at this point because of stupidity. Which she was certain it would be if they ended up on the wrong side of a battle with the Warlord again.

"At least this part is nearly done, and the teams up here will be far more protected and comfortable in this miserable duty station," Khaliun said.

She surveyed the newly completed post constructed by the working group and the detail of fighters and scouts that came with them. It never ceased to amaze her how much work it was setting up a more permanent base. Yet there was now a ring of low circular huts spaced evenly around a larger meeting hut. They had constructed the walls with stone, which thankfully was in abundance on this mostly barren mountain. Timber and hide formed the conical roofs in their normal fashion, with a pipe jutting out from the top to allow the smoke from the stoves to escape. There was now also a yard, complete with an enclosed stable for their horses off to one side, which they'd just finished today.

"It's come together well."

"Without as much complaining as I'd expected from the work crews." Khaliun had to admit, despite the inhospitable environment, the post was starting to look far more inviting than she'd ever believed it would. "Come on, I think we've done enough for today."

Khaliun led the way into the larger meeting hut in the centre, where a large pot of warming stew with bread and drinks was available, day or night, to any who wanted it. Their meals tended to be communal affairs while the stoves in the sleeping huts were mostly used to provide warmth and for brewing kaf and other small things as required. Others, seeing their leaders heading for the communal hut, took it as a sign that their working day was over. Given the conditions up here in the Heights, none needed urging to down tools and head indoors.

Khaliun sniffed appreciatively as the door to the meal hut shut out the cold behind her. The aroma of whatever was in the pot was enticing. The man on cook duty greeted them both as she and Narantua came in, then grabbed two bowls from near the hearth to spoon the enticing-smelling food into them. He carried them across to the low table off to one side, placing the offering on the table as they eagerly sat down.

"Was it the growling in my stomach that gave it away?" Khaliun asked, as she took a spoon from the container in the centre of the table.

"Working out in the cold all day, I'd be worried if your stomachs weren't wrapped around your spines and complaining." The cook's laughter was infectious.

Khaliun spooned some of the stew into her mouth, groaning at the rich flavours of meat, root vegetables, and mushrooms that carried the unexpected hint of herbs.

"Thank you. This is incredible."

"It tastes wonderful," Narantua mumbled around a mouthful of food.

The cook wandered back to the hearth and pulled back a cloth from a nearby basket, removing two flat breads and then handing one to each of them. Khaliun sniffed appreciatively, ripping off a chunk of the bread and dunking it in the stew as her stomach growled.

"Beer or wine? Leader Yangir sent some of their tribe members up with stores of both. Apparently, the wine comes from the Warlord's people." The cook's eyebrow rose as he waited for their answer.

"I'll stick with the beer, thanks." Khaliun screwed her nose up.

Khaliun had to admit, if only to herself, that she was only choosing beer because she hadn't quite recovered from the mind connection she'd shared with Michael and *he* liked wine.

"I'll try the wine since the Warlord and his people graciously let us stay and sent the shipment to us," Narantua said.

Khaliun stuck her tongue out at the healer.

"Actually, they've sent in most of our food supplies, in the Warlord's name, to help us get by until we can re-establish our own crops and supplies," the cook said as he went to the sideboard and poured their drinks.

Narantua's shock was written all over her face. Communal food and guest rights were a tradition among them, but Khaliun wasn't convinced they'd send food stocks to help support other people that weren't their own. It was confronting to realise that a people they'd thought of as harsh and warlike were more generous to strangers than her own people would have been, had the situation been reversed.

"It's a thing in the Warlord's domain. They look after their own, but he expects the villages will become viable, support themselves and others in need. As well as paying tithe," Khaliun said. It was one of many pieces of information that seemed like her own learning and knowledge, but had come from Michael when they'd merged their minds.

"So, we have a grace period?" Narantua asked.

"We have an entire season to prove ourselves," Khaliun said.

"It's more time than we need." The cook shrugged as they both looked at him, astonished. "As those of us who can't fight trusted you to keep us alive. Trust us to do our jobs now. The lands below are more than viable. We brought seed stock for crops and orchards, and there is plenty of roaming wildlife, some of which will become herd stock."

"I'll take your word for it," Khaliun said. "I was never good at such things."

"Nor do we need you to be, either of you. The tribes of Kallith survived because of our tribe leaders and your ability to do what we needed and guide us all. As well as fight for us. Now that we have the space and time, let the rest of us build this new home you have gifted us."

Khaliun ducked her head, not knowing how to respond. Particularly since her own belief was that she'd failed the tribe, her clan and the People since they'd lost their homeland and the bulk of their people in that conflict.

"We did our best for all our people. Even if we mourn the loss of our homeland," Narantua said.

"What the invaders did is beyond your control. I can't speak for all, but I'm grateful for the chance to start again. Many of our people had leaders who failed them. They don't have the chances that those of us who are of the Kallith now have." The man nodded, as if it settled the issue, then moved back to the hearth to serve others who entered the communal hall with equal affability.

Khaliun had no sooner finished her meal, mopping up the last of the stew with the flat bread, when the door opened. She took in the scout's worried expression and the fact that she made a straight line to where she and Narantua sat, and braced herself for bad news. She didn't even bother hoping it wasn't the news that none of them wanted to hear, since the scout's post had been to watch the only approach the Sylannians could use to get at them. They were nowhere near ready for what they all feared was coming.

TWENTY-TWO

Damien gasped, his eyes flashing open to darkness around him as hands restrained him. Fear flooded him as power, not his own, flared and raced through him like fire. He was in trouble. He wasn't sure why, but he was certain. The reason seemed to be on the edge of his memory, taunting him.

"Relax, I'm healing you."

Damien froze for a moment; he recognised that voice. He searched his mind, reaching out for a power that usually came easily, yet right now seemed to elude him. It was like wading through a swamp with curling mist obscuring the branches that reached out to snag him. A disjointed series of images stuttered through his mind, enough to make his breath catch in his throat. Tiscan. He'd been fed tiscan again. Damien paused as he realised that wasn't quite true. He'd been willing. At first. Dread hit him on the heels of the memory of being held and the liquid he both feared and craved being poured down his throat. It hadn't taken long until he'd succumbed to its blissful ride. He clenched his teeth against the pain caused by a fire that rushed though him now, and, in its wake, his mind cleared.

"Kesha, enough, don't wear yourself out."

"Are you sure? I can still sense your need for that poison," Kesha said.

"I'm sure." He could hear the concern in her voice and smiled reassuringly, although he doubted she could see it.

He didn't add he was afraid he might need her healing power more later when withdrawal really hit him. For now, he could at least sense the veil again. That alone helped his agitation decrease. Her healing had pushed enough of the effects of the drug aside so he could think straight. At least enough that he knew why he'd woken in a state of panic. As drug-addled as he'd been, it reassured him that some back part of his mind recognised he was in trouble.

"Where are we?" Damien didn't try to move yet, allowing the veil to run through him again. If nothing else, it was soothing.

"I... I don't know..."

"I know how they got me. I was stupid, but how did they get their hands on you?" Damien asked.

"I was stupid, too," Kesha said.

His eyes had adjusted to the dimness of the room and he saw her twisting to look around the place they were held. As his awareness expanded and he picked up the presence of others in the room, he sighed with relief. When he was young, before he'd joined the ranks of the Unwanted, it had been a relief to be cut off from the veil. Or so he'd thought. Now being cut off felt wrong and made his skin crawl, as if a vital piece of himself was missing. It occurred to him that lingering sense of wrongness had always been with him, until his recent period of abstinence from the drug. He shifted to look at the man who still restrained him, only for the hands to tighten their grip.

"It's all right, you can release me," Damien said. He caught the hesitation as the man waited for Kesha's approval before the hands withdrew.

Damien rolled onto his side, tensing as he stared towards the man, memories of being restrained and almost choking on the tiscan they poured down his throat flickering through his mind.

"Easy, this is Lem, he's a healer and was assisting me. You need to let the healing I've done settle," Kesha whispered, her hand resting lightly on his shoulder.

After another moment staring at Lem, he pushed his concern aside. Damien reasoned Lem wouldn't have helped to heal a person he wanted dead. It would have been a much easier proposition while he'd been insensible.

"We need to get out of here."

"You're chained to the wall." Kesha bit her lip, a small crease on her forehead.

Drug addled and weak as he might be, he was well aware of the chains that bound his wrists. While he hadn't known his bindings were tethered to a wall, he'd known they were connected to something.

"I know, but I need to know how much room I have." He pushed himself up to a sitting position. While he appreciated Kesha's concern for him to take it easy, and if he'd been back at their accommodations, he'd have done exactly that, an urgency gripped him. Damien knew he didn't have long, even if he didn't know how he knew it and not just because he'd come back to himself drugged, chained and in a dark cell.

"Can you reach Michael?"

"What? Michael's here?" Damien asked, rising unsteadily to his feet.

"No I meant with mindspeech. I know you're much stronger that way than me," Kesha said.

Relief hit Damien. If Michael and the rest of his squad had been locked up here as well far more had gone wrong than his own lapse back into the arms of tiscan. Damien directed his attention inward, testing the extent of Kesha's healing and his returning strength.

"No, not yet. Tiscan messes me up. I'm only just realising now how much." Damien felt a wave of despair from Kesha and reached up to cover her hand with his own. "I may not sense much outside this room right now, but my strength is increasing."

"But they'll come back—"

"They will. I haven't earned it, but trust me."

"If you'll let me finish—"

"No. Save your remaining strength." Damien shook his head, his eyes narrowing. "If they get me down and get that stuff in me again, I'll be lost without your help."

"But—"

"I can't reach Michael yet, but I can already use the veil to increase my strength." He allowed her to steady him as he rose to his feet, noting the chain that ran between his ankles. He wouldn't be able to walk much above a shuffle until the manacles were removed. "If you exhaust yourself now, there's no guarantee I'll be able to call for help anyhow."

A tremor shook her and without thinking he raised his arms, careful to grab the chain that ran between his wrists to loop over her head and pull her into his arms. Their fellow prisoners stirred and the few closer to him shuffled back. Damien could sense their unease as they realised there was a connection between him and Kesha. He pushed the nervousness of the others in the room aside, taking it as another sign that his powers were returning, and concentrated on Kesha. As a healer she was fierce and had far more strength than she gave herself credit for. Yet right now, outside the arena of fixing someone else's trauma, he could sense she was lost.

"Nathanial said if I can heal, I can kill." Kesha's voice trembled as she spoke the last word.

"No."

"I can—"

"It isn't in you, Kesha. It would destroy something in you to use your healing ability to take another's life. I'm pretty certain the reason Nathanial mentioned that your ability to heal means you can also kill someone with it, was for you to keep in mind in case of an emergency."

"You don't think this is an emergency?"

"It is, but I'm here. Let me do what I'm good at," Damien said, not even shocked that he was serious.

"You're not a killer either, yet you do what you must."

Damien caught the memory of him striding across the village square and thrusting his sword into the baker. He closed his eyes and took a steadying breath, a chuckle escaping him.

"I would have killed the baker years before if the other villagers hadn't pulled me off him." He could feel her stir to object and he shook his head. "I would probably have killed him even if the Warlord hadn't ridden into my village and engineered that little incident."

"I can do this."

Damien heard the firmness in her tone, yet underneath the resolve was uncertainty.

"You are a healer. Michael says you are the strongest of your kind he has ever encountered. Everyone needs to trust that you will do your best to heal rather than kill. No matter who they are or what they've done. You need to know that." Damien said the last softly.

"I doubt Michael would allow you anywhere near a fight in your current condition."

"I may not be the best of Michael's people, but I'm still a member of the Unwanted. You've done your job and healed me as much as you can, short of exhausting yourself. Now trust me to do mine."

"You're still not well, lad," Lem said.

Damien regarded Lem, allowing the anger he felt to seep into his tone. "As they'll learn, I'm well enough."

Damien switched to his othersight without consciously thinking about it. As Kesha indicated, Lem had an affinity for healing but was nowhere near her level. However, Damien judged this man had seen and dealt with more of the world than Kesha and had more experience with tiscan addicts.

"I'm an addict. For now, I'm better off with a little of that poison in me."

"Your friend is correct, healer. As much of the stuff as they've been feeding him, without it he'll be incapacitated," another man said. "It will take many days and intensive healing sessions, even for a healer of your power, to ease his withdrawal."

Damien searched the darkness to find the source of this speech and saw a man pushing himself up the wall. Chains rattled, giving away that this man, like him, wore manacles. Damien inspected what he could make out of the dim room they were holding him in. Either his sight was adjusting to the lack of light or his powers were back to compensate enough to allow him to see. It seemed only two of them were bound. It was also beginning to seem Damien was the only one who hadn't known of the perils inherent in consuming tiscan before he'd left his village.

"You are?"

"I'm Lukas, they caught me snooping around. Thus," Lukas held up his hands causing the chain that ran between them to rattle.

Damien closed his eyes and pushed down the sense of wrongness. Unlike the previous time he'd gone through withdrawal, he didn't have the luxury of lying back in a hammock while his squad mates took care of him. And if the recent days when he'd woken up with cravings were anything to go by, this time would be much worse. Feeling his stomach clench, he swallowed, and pushed his mind away from the drug. A hand touched his cheek and concern washed over him.

"Will you be able to stay in control?" Kesha's tone was gentle.

"Long enough," Damien said grimly.

While she'd barely be able to see his expression, she'd hear the certainty and since they were touching, she'd feel it. Or at least, she'd sense what he wanted her to. The little kernel of doubt was buried deep in his own head. Right now, doubt in his own abilities would not be useful.

TWENTY-THREE

Laughter sounded on the other side of the door. Damien checked to make sure everyone was in place. A key rattled in the lock, with a soft cursing as the bolt finally slid back with a solid *thunk*. The screeching of the hinges heralded the door opening. Damien flicked his eyes over to Kesha, reassured she held her position. Then he almost swore as loud racking sobs tore from Kesha's mouth as she threw herself at the first who entered the door. The man who entered couldn't help but throw his arms out to support her.

"You need to let me go."

"You're worth a great deal of money to us." The guard smirked.

"You don't understand..."

"No, I think it's you who doesn't understand."

Kesha sobbed, then crumpled, becoming a dead weight in his arms, and he went down to the ground trying to support her—coincidently pushing him back further towards where Damien stood.

"They'll kill you all for taking me."

"You think anyone is going to care enough to kill us all?"

"They won't let me go."

"You think highly of yourself, don't you?"

"The Unwanted will come for me."

The guard paused, stepping back a half step before he stopped. "Well, they aren't here right now, are they?"

Kesha flinched as spittle sprayed her cheek. Damien tensed as her eyes tracked over to where he stood.

"That's where you're wrong. He's here. One of them is more than enough. He'll kill you."

Disbelief shone in the eyes of the man in front of her and he threw his head back and laughed. The roar of laughter cut short as Damien stepped forward, gathered the guard's head in a vice-like grip, and snapped it around. The crack sounded overloud in the sudden silence of the room and Damien let the lifeless body slump to the floor.

"Kesha, remind me we need to talk about a few things when this is all over." Damien's eyes flashed.

"See, I told you this would work. The Unwanted aren't what you've been told. They're terribly protective." She glanced from her fellow captives to the dead man on the floor, a small frown on her forehead. "At least of me."

Lem reached down to the body of the fallen guard and, with a grunt, rolled him over. Damien's mouth closed on the protest he'd been about to utter when Lem extracted keys from the dead man's belt.

Damien focused his attention to the other prisoners gathered by the far wall. "Do something useful. Keep an eye on the door."

They all seemed frozen in place for a moment before two of the other prisoners finally edged to the door, looking cautiously out into the hallway beyond. Damien regarded Lukas, who at least seemed calm and not cowed like the others. With the dim light coming in from the open door falling across Lukas's face, he could see he was older than him, but not much else. Damien simply held out his wrists as Lem approached. Lem got to work, trying each key in the locks on the manacles that bound him.

"Can't you just—" Kesha wiggled her fingers as she approached.

Damien couldn't help it. A weak chuckle escaped him. Even that was enough to cause him to slump back against the wall as he laughed.

"No, Kesha. I don't have an affinity for metal like the Smith. That's not how our powers work. Besides, right now—" His eyes slid over to Lem and he stopped himself from finishing the thought. That it was the tiscan that was hampering his powers. These strangers didn't need to know that detail.

"Your need for that drug they fed you is starting to consume you." Kesha's hand reached up to rest on his temple.

Damien stepped back. "I'll be fine. Save your strength."

"I wish you'd let me help you," Kesha snapped.

"I appreciate your abilities, Kesha, but I know this demon a little better than I once did. Once it's clear, if I can't get more..." Damien closed his eyes, unable to prevent the shudder that shook him. "I fear it will be better for everyone, including me, if Michael, Olivia or Nathanial are around."

"You don't trust yourself."

Damien had to look away from the compassion he saw shining in the depths of her eyes. Right now, his primary emotion amongst the chaos in his head was embarrassment. Or perhaps mortification was closer to the mark. He pushed the thoughts aside. He'd have plenty of time to wallow in guilt when they were out of here and he was trying to survive the withdrawal from tiscan.

Again.

He saw that Lem had been busy and had released Lukas from his shackles.

"Come on, we need to get out of here. Stay behind me."

Damien waited long enough to see her nod agreement before stooping to pick up the chain with its manacles that had bound his wrists. It wasn't his sword, but he'd use what he was dealt. He strode out of the room they'd been kept in, Lukas by his side. At a soft gasp, he looked over at Lukas, who was still rubbing his wrists.

"So, she wasn't lying when she claimed you are a member of the Unwanted?" Lukas asked, his expression closed.

"No, she wasn't lying. Although I'm one who's going to be in a great deal of trouble when Michael catches up with me." Damien shrugged.

Lukas chuckled, and Damien regarded the only other man their captors had feared enough to shackle, his eyebrows rising.

"These men have signed their own death warrants."

On consideration Damien found it wasn't a statement that he could deny. Nor could he feel any sympathy for the likely fate of his kidnappers. They might have gotten away with taking him, possibly, but Kesha?

"All of you, stay back, let me handle anyone we run into."

Damien waited until the ragged bunch of his fellow captives behind him hastily agreed, most of them still a little wide-eyed. He tried to convey confidence. None of them needed to know he was only hoping he could stay upright long enough to kill any guards that remained. Although given the way Kesha looked at him, he gathered he didn't fool her one little bit. He led the way down the corridor towards the door at the end. He might not be at his best, but now that he was closer, he could sense there were multiple people beyond the door. Damien adjusted his grip on the chain and swung it gently, assessing its length. The weight of the shackle down the end would do significant damage.

"Have you ever fought with a chain?" Kesha asked.

"No, but Michael has." Cold determination flooded Damien. "Now, stay back."

"You can't fight them all by yourself," Kesha objected.

"I can. They won't be expecting me, let alone that I can fight them." Damien turned his attention to Lukas, guessing their kidnappers had feared what he'd do if given free rein. "Stay back, keep her safe. If anything goes wrong, make sure she lives and get her back to the Unwanted. The Warleader will pay you well."

"Come, healer, your friend knows what he's doing," Lukas said, gently pushing Kesha back behind him.

Lem also moved to place himself in front of Kesha but Damien couldn't help but feel exasperated by the others, who all shuffled back as far as they could. They could at least be useful and act as a human shield between any attacker that got past him and Kesha.

"The healers would be useful in putting us all back together if things go wrong, not so much if it's them that needs healing," he said, before shaking his head as the bulk of the captives just stared at him blankly.

He straightened and took a moment to push down the tiscan sickness, but as the bone-aching cold of the veil washed over him, he froze with his hand halfway to the door handle.

"No, not now…" Damien whispered.

It was the only warning he had before power lanced into him. He couldn't help the scream that tore from his mouth as fire seemed to rip through him. Almost as if the veil itself was punishing him for cutting himself off. His knees buckled as another peal of power hit him, flowing like a wave through him. He felt like his insides were melting under the onslaught. His breath caught as pain drove into his head and through every fibre of his being. Then his world went dark.

～

AS THE DOOR OPENED, he looked up, fire dancing in his eyes and over his skin. Every instinct in him screamed that the people in this room were a threat to him. The enemies' shock was apparent as they laid eyes on him. One enemy belatedly drew a weapon and lunged. He swung his chain and a head exploded, smashed open like a melon hitting the ground as the weighted end connected. He cleared the entrance, keeping the chain in motion so it gained momentum. He ducked, tracking the four remaining threats in the room; he could feel the waves of their terror washing over him as agony radiated from his mind and body and he lashed out with the chain. The very edge of the shackle slammed into an enemy's head. Blood and flesh sprayed as the body toppled off the chair. Damien adjusted his stance as another man stepped forward, hands grappling for a sword. He snapped the chain forward. The man screamed, a bloody wreck where a face had been moments before, and Damien moved to face the last two enemies who froze for a heartbeat before sprinting towards the door.

He paused as the name occurred to him, in a small pool of stillness in his head. Damien. He had a name, and it was Damien. As the veil tore through him again, he screamed and lashed out at the two who fled from him trying to get to the door. The chain circled up over Damien's head in a wide arc and slammed down on the back of the head of the threat closest to him, propelling the body across the floor before it toppled to the ground, lifeless, the entire back of the skull caved in. Damien switched his gaze to the last man scrabbling desperately at the door. The man screamed as it finally opened and Damien allowed the chain to stop, aware of what awaited behind the now-open door, as the man froze. What had been a man fell back through the doorway onto the cold, unforgiving stone floor. Damien's final enemy hadn't even seen the sword that had run him through.

Damien stood glowering at those who entered. They had

power like him. He watched them carefully as the calmness they sent flooded his mind and body. Tremors shook him now that he'd stopped and he fell to his knees and screamed as awareness returned.

Finally, Damien recognised it was Michael, Olivia and Nathanial, who stood around him, and wondered how they'd gotten here. How he'd gotten here. His mind was blank. All the blood and dead bodies with caved-in skulls in the room came into focus. Damien looked down at his hands, seeing them splattered with blood, and dropped the chain he was carrying. A smell hit him, bittersweet and intoxicating. Damien's head tilted, eyes sliding to the broken crate in the corner. Dark liquid from some of the smashed bottles on the floor. Damien doubled over in pain and need, sinking to the floor. He was half aware it was Olivia who caught him as he collapsed. Damien sank into her shoulder, shuddering as reaction from the tiscan and the fighting hit him all at once.

"Please, I can't…"

He looked up at Olivia as she wrapped her arms around him. Michael was on his knee on his other side, and Damien collapsed in relief as Olivia's shield expanded and wrapped around him, sheltering his mind from the chaos.

Shh, Damien, I'm here, I've got you. Reassurance accompanied Olivia's words, pushing his fear aside.

Her hand touched the side of his face as he stared into her eyes and her compulsion pushed his mind down into sleep. He didn't resist; fear rose as darkness came to claim him, but Olivia chased his fears away. Damien realised they knew he'd used again, but full confessions could wait until tomorrow or whenever she allowed him to wake.

CHAPTER

TWENTY-FOUR

Isabella woke with tears streaming down her face, a stifled scream on her lips. She wished it really had only been a nightmare that disturbed her sleep, rather than visions of the reality that Damien was living. She didn't get all of it, just a disjointed series of images, smells and emotions.

Damien, what's happening to you? Isabella whispered into the void, knowing he wouldn't hear her. He was too far away.

The first few times it hadn't been too bad. Not really. She'd been happy to see the glimpses of Damien's life. He rode through many places she'd never seen except through his eyes, laughing and joking with his new friends. She'd started to believe, with the hints of the life he was living, that maybe it wasn't so bad. Perhaps she wouldn't be miserable if his warlord came back and dragged her into that life. Except she'd never been interested in learning to fight.

Then there were the other times like this, when those visions were closer to a nightmare.

Emotions. That was the worst part. Or rather, the distinct lack of emotion while the sword her brother wielded ran through

161

the person he faced. He was cold, implacable, without a hint of regret or remorse. He'd gazed down at the man he'd run through with a pool of blood spreading out around him. There was nothing from Damien, just an awful blankness. This wasn't the brother she'd grown up with, who'd protected her.

Death. It wasn't the first time she'd seen it. Damien had killed the baker, after all. Isabella couldn't bring herself to feel terribly sorry for the man or the way he'd died. Neither could anyone else in the village, or so it seemed. She hadn't been the only one who hadn't liked him. Other villagers had known what the baker was like. They didn't know that she knew that they'd turned a blind eye to his behaviour—they would fear her if they realised she could hear their thoughts. It was only Damien who'd acted to protect her and the other girls of the village from the baker, and now the villagers feared what her brother and his new friends might do to them one day. There were exceptions, people like Owen. He'd at least looked out for her. Particularly after Damien had left, although he hadn't been around much as he was mostly in charge of checking the surroundings of the village to make sure they were all safe, and hunting.

Lately, what she'd seen and experienced in the brief glimpses of Damien's life while she slept was chaos. Damien's mind seemed to be overloaded and he couldn't track anything or function. Pain, ecstasy and confusion followed by a burning need that drove him. Last night, she'd heard him scream in agony through the veil. It was like her mind identified and latched onto that shriek. Her awareness raced across the land. Until, in a dizzying rush, he'd come sharply into focus. She'd seen him look up, flames dancing in his eyes. It was as if Damien could see her yet there was no sign of any rational thought. It was like he was empty of everything other than agony. That's when the killing started. Damien wielding a chain, taking out one person after another, implacable, deadly. She hadn't even known a chain could be used in that manner. When blood splattered on Damien, he didn't flinch or react, but she did. It was like she could feel the spray of blood on her face. She could hear the screams of those who were the target of Damien's fury. Terrified, in pain, fighting for their lives and losing. She'd reached out and tried to bleed away the excess energy, the way she'd always been able to in order to relieve his pain, but failed. There was just too much excess power churning through him. Damien had slaughtered all of them. She cried the tears that Damien didn't.

Sleep was long gone and not something she was likely to reclaim after what she'd seen, so Isabella eased herself out of bed. She pulled out the set of pants from the closet along with a new long shirt and vest that went with them. She'd had them modelled on the training gear Damien had worn. After dressing, she pulled back her thick blonde hair, braiding it to keep it out of her face, then grabbed the weapons belt and her cloak from the hook behind her door. She eased the door open, and ran lightly through the house, pulsing her power to open the front door, and fled. She'd abandoned the restrictions about using her abilities lest it attract the unwanted attention of the Warlord. It seemed pointless since he knew about her already. Inexplicably, he'd left her here and hadn't come back. She hadn't really believed he would keep his promise to her brother to leave her be. The villagers had been dumbfounded. More than one of them was constantly jumping at any sign of riders coming into the village, thinking the Warlord was coming back. None of them realised the price Damien was paying for her freedom. What the Warlord gained in his bargain.

A loyal. Willing. Son.

It was how Damien was modelling himself.

She ran through the forest. The whispery grey of the veil breathed round her, tendrils reaching out, cool power caressing her skin. She was whole in these brief moments. Branches should have snagged at her as she ran but she passed them by without a scratch. Far away from the nearest hut in the village, Isabella finally allowed herself to stop, leaning against the trunk of a tree and doubling over. Guilt hammered into her over Damien's plight. She was certain he was turning himself into a killer to make sure she was safe. Soundless sobs racked her body and she gasped. It was as if she'd forgotten how to breathe.

Isabella pulled the shimmering grey curtain to her, wrapping herself in the comfort it provided. It cut her off from the worries of her world and she allowed herself to sink into the power as it flowed around her, through her. Here, in this place, it was easy to let time slip by.

TWENTY-FIVE

Liliana rested back on the rocking chair, watching indulgently as the children ran and played. They were growing up much wilder, with greater freedoms here than they would have had in the court. She frowned, looking over to see Jaclyn's son, Thomas sitting on the ground with one of his sisters, although she couldn't remember which of the wives had birthed the girl child. She was certain the underwives could tell her, it was a part of their job after all, particularly when it came time to settle the girl in a new house. Girl children were rehoused as soon as their flow was regular and they could become pregnant and carry a child. Of course, some girls were still young in years when their bodies matured, so it might be some time before she was called to her husband's bed. While it was true that some girl children from lesser houses might never join with their husband, this was not the case for daughters of this house. The prestige of having a wife born to the Monarch House, even if they didn't have the blood of the monarch, was high. Meaning as soon as one of their daughters was old enough to be released to become a wife to another, she would likely be straight in her husband's bed. Repeatedly. Every time she was fertile, in the hope they'd gain a child with a connection to the Monarch House.

As she listened to them giggling, Liliana felt a small spurt of power and her eyes widened. She thrust out with her own power, throwing a protective shield around the boy's mind.

"Stop!" Liliana said.

She clawed her way out of the chair, then covered the distance between her and Jaclyn's son, scooping him up into her arms. She carefully reached out with her own mind, probing his. As she saw no signs of interference in his mind, she breathed a sigh of relief. The girl looked up at her, eyes wide and lips trembling.

"We were just going to play husband and wife, Mama Lil," Thomas said.

Liliana closed her eyes and breathed slowly to calm the fright she'd had.

"You will never open your mind to allow another to bind you until it is time for you to give yourself to your firstwife," Liliana said.

She stared at the underwives, who had the grace to look appalled. As well they should.

"Yes, Mama Lil," Thomas said.

"You will only practice mind bonding under the guidance of the underwives and certainly not on your brothers," Liliana said to the girl, somehow managing to remain calm, despite her fear and anger at the disaster that had nearly happened.

The girl hung her head. "I'm sorry, Mama Lil, we were only playing."

"Taking control of a husband's mind is not a game. You could have caused permanent damage to your brother," Liliana said.

"Yes, Mama Lil, I didn't mean to hurt him."

"He is not yours to bind. He will choose who he will belong to in time, but not until he is much older."

Liliana allowed some underwives to take the children off to their own quarters.

"I'm sorry, Primewife, this never would have happened back at the court."

"You've just started training some of the older girls, I take it?" Liliana said.

"Yes, that one is showing signs of maturing young. It will be years yet but it's important she begins to learn how to forge the bond, else…"

Liliana held up her hand. She was aware of the risks as well as any other. A badly forged mind bond could cause many problems. Usually there were far more underwives present to supervise the children's play, and the older girls were separated once they learned how to take their future husband's mind. It was always more problematic when the girl in question matured at a younger age.

"You've started training him as well?" Liliana asked.

"Only the simple mind calming exercises. He's too young for full training."

"Myra's son?"

"Not yet, Primewife. He is still too young. He's not of age to leave the nursery play group yet," the woman said.

Boys' training was much different to girls'. They learnt lessons in meditation from early in life to calm their minds. To open themselves, drop their mind barriers and not fight, particularly against that all-important first bond. Their firstwife would burn that initial bond, wresting control of their mind. The more the male fought, even if it was subconscious, the more it would hurt them. Once the firstwife had control of her husband's mind, it was her job, and that of the other wives, to protect their husband from harm. In addition, just before they were old enough to select a firstwife, the boys learnt how to detect when their wives were fertile and how to mate with them. Their father would normally finish their final instructions and lessons. It would be Ricardo's job to help his son in that final preparation to submit to the will of his own firstwife.

Or it would have been if Ricardo was in a normal house, but theirs was not such a house. Liliana doubted Jaclyn's son would ever submit or willingly allow another to take control of his mind. When she'd first come to the house, she'd thought it strange they'd adhered to an old custom and only the firstwife and primewife held a control bond in Ricardo's mind. In more recent times it had become a practice among their people that as soon as a daggerwife rose to the rank of wife by birthing a child to the house, regardless of whether the child was male or female, that she also forged a control bond.

She'd been proud when, in the war to conquer the lands of the traders, she and her team had pulled protective duty around their first, primewife and husband. Then she'd been horrified when Jaclyn, Myra, and Ricardo shared their secret. There was risk to all of them if others found out that Jaclyn and Myra did not control Ricardo as they should. While the bond between their firstwife and husband was in place, as was the secondary between primewife Myra and Ricardo, neither firstwife nor primewife maintained control of him. Ricardo could run wild under his own will. His fierceness in battle was his own, rather than the carefully controlled ferocity of his first and primewife. They'd shared their belief it was the very controls their people put in place to protect their husbands that caused the affliction of madness among their people. In the event of both the firstwife and primewife falling in battle, she and the daggerwives she led had been charged with a duty of seizing control of Ricardo's mind. Without someone to fill the gaping hole that would be left in his mind if the first and primewife died, he would be prey to anyone who took him first, unable to stop them. And that was if he even survived their deaths, which was uncertain. The severing of the mate bonds alone could send a husband spiralling into madness and death.

Liliana hadn't been meant to fall pregnant to Ricardo, let alone bear a male child to him. Her duty had been a trust of last defence if something went wrong in war. Yet it was that very trust that had brought her to his attention. While some wives went from daggerwife to underwife having never once slept in their husband's bed, this was not the case with her. He'd taken her to his bed every month for almost a week at a time for her full fertile period. This had left some of the other wives disgruntled since it left less time for them, but it was Ricardo's choice, not theirs or even hers. He'd persisted until she'd finally conceived.

She sighed at the memory. That would hopefully be the other bonus to giving birth to this child. Once the underwives released her from their care, her husband could call her to his bed again. Being in the beds and arms of some of her fellow wives was enjoyable, indeed some wives found having to mate with their husband a chore. But mating with Ricardo had opened a whole new experience for her. Ricardo sometimes had sex with his first and his primewife just to be with them, not with the imperative to breed. Of course, their house already had multiple sons, so they could afford that luxury. Liliana wondered wistfully if she'd ever know what that was like.

On the birth of her child and elevation to primewife, she would be expected to forge a control bond into Ricardo's mind. All the wives would witness the forging of that bond. It would be too dangerous if she didn't; it would be noted and commented on if she did not do as custom dictated. But once it was done she would withdraw and allow Ricardo the peace of his own mind other than when she was shielding him from outside influence.

If their house survived this conflict with the barbarians, the next logical step was to make a play for the Monarch House. Once Jaclyn had taken the throne and they were secure, the practice of wresting control of a husband's mind would cease by order of the Monarch House. It would cause upheaval and probably rebellion. Jaclyn had predicted it would require more than the cleansing of just the Monarch House when it was time to dispose of her brother's house. Myra would guard Jaclyn's back. As Liliana had also been forged in battle to lead and protect her house, it made sense it would be her job to go after the rebel houses to protect all their people.

Who better to wage war than the house that had been tempered in battle almost since it came into existence?

TWENTY-SIX

Olivia was used to death. Damien had done a superb job in what had turned out to be the warehouse, even out of his mind as he'd been. While Nathanial had taken a team to explore in one direction she'd gone in the other and ended up in what she'd guessed was the front of house where the establishment met and entertained their customers. Somehow this was much worse. She swallowed, scanning the room, with its bench in the centre laden with shackles, stain upon stain of blood seeping into the floor, and a tray of sharp implements on a bench against the wall. Having seen enough, she went back out and saw the huddled, drug-addled men, women and children who had been forced to work in the pleasure house. Olivia's anger flared. She didn't feel sorry for those that Damien had taken out. Or for the group of clients their people outside had corralled as they attempted to flee the pleasure house via the side alley. Or for those who worked in a real pleasure house. Except for the children. A pleasure house was no place for a child. Then again, a real pleasure house would never stoop to slavery, let alone provide children to their clients.

"In the Warlord's name, take these people to safety and they are to be cared for, including all food and medical care as they withdraw from the drugs they've been subdued with," Olivia ordered.

She watched long enough to see the acknowledgement from the Unwanted. From what she'd seen of this establishment, they'd set it up to cater to every whim of some of the most depraved of their society, so long as they had money to pay for it. She returned to the back of the house area they'd first come into, her eyes automatically tracking over to Damien, reassuring herself that he was still under her compulsion to sleep. She'd bundled her cloak under his head, while Michael's was thrown over him. Neither she, Michael, nor Nathanial were willing to allow Damien out of their sight, so he remained here, as long as they did.

Finding Kesha here as well had been a shock. Once Nathanial had calmed her down, she'd given them a rather sketchy account of what had occurred. They'd sent her back to their accommodation with a squad to guard her. There was more to sort out, but it was kinder to allow the woman to rest first. Getting her away from this blood-soaked establishment was even kinder.

Olivia wished she could believe their job was done. Unfortunately, she didn't believe it for even for a heartbeat.

"Well?" Olivia asked as Michael came into the main room.

"As Kesha said, seems like cells out the back and there is a basement that has a private dock entrance for barges. At a guess, before they became this, it used to be a trader's warehouse for legitimate trade."

"I hope we can get more information out of the *clients*." Nathanial's eyes were as hard as his tone. "I doubt Damien will be capable of telling us much. Kesha cleared a great deal of the drug from his system but, from what she and the others said, they were dosing him continuously. They kept him insensible for days."

Olivia closed her eyes.

"Liv, talk to me."

Olivia turned her gaze to Michael, found his eyes boring into her own.

"The filth that ran this place…" Olivia heard the disgust in her own tone. "They didn't set this up by themselves."

"Liv."

Olivia swallowed and throttled down the anger that burned within her. It was unreasonable. There was no proof of who was behind this enterprise at all in anything they'd discovered here so far. However, she could only come to one conclusion.

"One of the rich families must be behind this *venture*. To buy services like this costs money. A lot of it. They could not have done this without my father's or brother's knowledge, without their tacit approval. Even if it was just to look the other way," Olivia said.

"This set-up. I couldn't keep looking at the rooms out front, but it caters to people who have the cash," Nathanial agreed.

Nathanial may have seemed calm and unconcerned but it was a lie. He'd taken care to lock himself down. You had to look much deeper to see the scars he hid. It was easy to forget his past and, thankfully, occasions like this that brought back those painful memories were few and far in between. Olivia pushed aside her anger and crossed the room to him. He didn't resist as she pulled him into her arms, allowing her unconditional friendship and support to flow through to him.

Thank you, my friend, Nathanial said as he straightened.

"I know we'd normally avoid such things when left to our own devices, but perhaps we should accept your father's invitation to attend his ball. We will be in town longer anyhow. I judge

Damien won't be capable of moving for some time," Michael said.

"Hopefully whoever is responsible for this mess will be there and terrified enough they will give themselves away." Olivia conceded it was a good idea, even if she hated attending her family's functions.

"Perhaps we should co-opt one of the fashion houses to dress us all." Nathanial laughed and held up his hands, pretending to fend off her glare. "Elegant attire, not the flouncy monstrosities that pass for fashion here."

"I've worn my fighting leathers every other time I've had to attend those things. Don't see why this time should be different," Olivia grumbled.

"The Warlord keeps pressing us all to attend such occasions more regularly. Having some clothing that fits probably wouldn't go to waste. Besides that, Jenna, the Smith's daughter, settled here with her partner. He was the eldest son of a trading family. She knows as much about sword work and armour as her father and brothers."

Olivia blinked. "I'm not sure she's qualified to make a gown, even if her husband's family deals, among other things, in fine fabrics and laces. Although mixing in the circles they do, they might be able to shed some light on those responsible for this."

"That too, but she could collaborate with the dressmaker to design something that looks good but is also functional. So not only can we fight in it if we have to, but the clothing will have some protection against opponents' blades."

"Elegant and deadly?" Nathanial asked, his eyebrows rising. "Or in Liv's case, beautiful, elegant and deadly."

"Oh, I don't know. The pair of you all dressed up would pass for beautiful, I'm sure." Olivia gave away her anger. She found it impossible to stay angry when the pair of them were so deter-mined to lighten her mood.

TWENTY-SEVEN

Khaliun edged forward and raised her head just enough to peer over the rocky outcrop. Even though the logical part of her brain told her the depths of the shadows cast by the outcrops around them hid her presence, the act still made her skin crawl. Her breath caught as she followed the pointing finger of her lookout. The figures were tiny from their vantage point, but it was unmistakably people searching the mountain below. From the row upon row of tents that had sprung up, and the impractical flowing style of them, it was the Sylannians. Some of the People were among them. Khaliun pulled herself up short at that thought. Those who were helping the Sylannians below were no longer her people. They'd thrown their lot in with their conquerors and were helping to find the path over the mountains.

"There are many parties of them scouring the base and trails of the mountain," the lookout said.

"Have they gone near our old trade route?" Khaliun asked.

"Not yet, but they'll find it soon enough," the lookout said, spitting on the rocks nearby as he scowled down at those he watched. "I don't understand why any of our own would help them?"

"Probably those originally from the river lands. They've belonged to Sylanna for a long time now," Khaliun said, wondering if Tarkhan, if he'd survived, would one day be like those below. People changed when the Sylannians got their claws into them and she doubted he'd be able to resist the Sylannian ability to mess with minds for long.

"What do you want us to do?" the lookout asked.

"Your orders haven't changed. Keep watch and alert me when they find the trail."

Khaliun backed up, careful to keep in the shadows as she retreated to the makeshift camp. She wondered grimly if they'd get the time to build more comfortable lodging for those who were posted at this lookout. She thanked the clansmen who held the reins of her horse for her as she took them back. Without wasting time, she mounted and spurred her horse back towards their main outpost.

KHALIUN SLOWED as she entered the horse yard and dismounted, thanking the herd keeper who came to collect the reins. It had been useful having non-combatants up here while they were building this base. They made life easier and took on tasks like preparing the meals, caring for the animals, making supply runs and other such chores. But it was perhaps time to consider sending them out of harm's way.

She entered the meeting hut and crossed to the hearth to help herself to some of the warm spiced wine. All eyes of their small group watched her as she crossed the room and sat opposite Narantua. She took a sip of the drink and ducked her head, then grimaced in disgust at herself. So much for telling herself she'd stick to beer until she was sure she wasn't selecting wine because Michael liked it. She contemplated throwing it out, then sighed, taking another sip, closing her eyes and savouring the rich flavour that reminded her of the wild berries in the lowlands back home. It tasted so good. She just wished she was certain that really was her own thought.

"I'll need one of you to go down to the plateau and alert the other leaders that we've sighted the Sylannians looking for the trail," Khaliun said.

"Do you need me to go now?"

Khaliun assessed the fading light through the window and shook her head.

"No, it's not urgent enough to make the journey in the dark. They haven't found it yet."

"I'll send one member of my team at first light," the woman said.

"How many of them are there?" Narantua asked.

"More than a simple scouting party. Less than a full invading force. The scout says their numbers have been increasing," Khaliun said.

"So they know the path is there," Narantua said.

"Most likely. They followed our trail, aided by some of our former brethren."

"It won't take them long to find the trailhead, even if they don't know exactly where it is."

"I think we're going to have to come up with a delaying tactic for when they find it."

"What did you have in mind?" Narantua asked.

"Well, there's all those rocks that we gathered to construct accommodation for those minding those outposts." Khaliun met eyes of her fellow leader across the table. "We could always prepare a little rockfall for them."

"It won't take them long to clear it, but it should give us a little more time to get enough fighters into place."

Khaliun finally turned her attention over to those on the other table where some of the outpost construction workers were staring at them both, clearly eavesdropping.

"Do you think it's something you can help rig up?" Khaliun asked.

The small group of builders engaged in a rapid-fire conversation with each other before the head of their number nodded.

"Easily," the head builder said.

Khaliun took a deep breath, allowing some of the tension to drain out of her. Now that they had a plan, or rather a small piece of a plan that they could work on, she felt unaccountably better.

IT WAS a risk waiting until nightfall, but the risk was there no matter what time of day or night they performed this delaying tactic. She only hoped it delayed them long enough. If the Sylannians were determined to come after them, tonight's events wouldn't stop them.

We're clear, Co-leader Khaliun.

She glanced at Narantua who nodded, indicating she'd heard the scout leader's report as well. Khaliun rolled her eyes. Of course, the healer had heard. While Khaliun may have been a much better mindspeaker, Narantua wasn't that bad. Rather than be offended, Narantua grinned at her in response. Khaliun was just grateful the other leader had joined her. By tradition, it would be another month at least before the warriors could put forward another of their number to step up to the co-leader role with her. They believed such a measure helped the tribe make a better choice rather than a snap decision after losing one of their leaders. Narantua might not be the best strategist, but she was the calm presence that Khaliun could bounce ideas off.

Pull the struts! Khaliun commanded.

The two groups responsible for carrying out that action spurred their horses forward. A harness connecting them all with ropes strung to wooden beams holding the braces up either side of the trail snapped taut. An overloud splintering of wood resounded, making her wince, though it was nothing compared to what was to come. A crack echoed around the mountains just moments before the rumble of stone on stone as the boulders were suddenly freed. Dust filled the air as the giant rocks rumbled down the mountain.

Not waiting to see the result of their handiwork, others ran forward, releasing the horse crews from their makeshift harnesses, and they all ran back towards their camp in the gathering dark. Either the trail was temporarily blocked, which would delay the Sylannians, or it wasn't. Either way, they didn't have time to lose.

TWENTY-EIGHT

T arkhan watched as a fighting force, hundreds of Sylannians, passed them on the dusty road heading back the way they'd come. The road led towards Hallaran, and further afield to the trailhead that led over the mountains to the rest of his people. It was the third such unit he'd seen. One thing gave him some hope: there had been no sign of Khaliun or any who had ridden with her. He sent a muttered plea out into the world that his people would be safe. There was at least one positive impact of the wolf's eyes centred on his forehead and the leader tattoo covering half his face—the others with them, mostly from other tribes long fallen to the Sylannians, knew what they meant. Even though they followed the Sylannians' orders without question, their only restraint a simple collar, they gave way to him. None of them whispered warnings to the Sylannians, even though to do so might earn them favour. They were beaten down, defeated, but perhaps not the total traitors that he'd taken them for.

Tarkhan shuffled along in the string of prisoners, two tribesmen making way for him as he slid between them to take their place. In the last few weeks, his captors had kept a close eye on them all. They'd learnt something from the raid on Hallaran. At night, or when they camped, it was almost impossible for him to arrange enough of a distraction to effect their escape. Now they were on the outskirts of what had been the second largest habitation among their people. Traders with their goods would converge here in better years before continuing on their journey to the river. It was humming with activity even though it was crawling with Sylannians and it was while they were moving through these bustling streets that the best escape opportunity presented itself. During the day, the Sylannians trusted in the silken bindings they used to keep him and the handful of prisoners under control. He'd kept his ability to control the silk to himself since he figured he'd only get one chance to pull off an escape. Tarkan's lips pulled back into a soundless snarl as Chono's back came into view directly in front of him. If nothing else, even if his escape attempt failed, he'd achieve one positive thing.

Please, let me cause the distraction, while you attempt to escape, one of his warriors said.

You have your orders. Run hard, lose yourself in the market crowds, then go to ground until the fuss settles, Tarkhan said, not taking his eyes off the back of his target. *Now get ready. We're nearly at the crossroads.*

The citizens flowed around their group, mostly ignoring them, other than a few whose gazes slid away from him after noticing his tattoos. Through trial and error, he'd worked out that while he could interact with their silken bonds, he had no control over the garments the Sylannians themselves wore, even though they seemed to be made of the same material. Tarkhan allowed his mind to sink down until the whispering of the silk filled his head. He hummed at it, sending his counter melody not just to his own bindings, but to all those who were collared around him. He didn't have the control or time to see if he could narrow his focus. As his bonds slithered off, Tarkhan leapt on Chono, taking the other man to the ground. Mayhem erupted as he slammed Chono's head repeatedly into the hard-packed dirt road. As the man went still and lifeless under him, Tarkhan scrambled to his feet, spinning around to discover that while the Sylannians were staring at him in disbelief, they'd still had the presence of mind to surround him. He had the satisfaction of seeing that his warriors and a good number of the other captives had managed to flee, and as futile as he knew it to be, Tarkhan hollered a battle cry and charged at the Sylannian line. He dipped his shoulder and crashed into them, trying to maintain his momentum as two of the Sylannians crashed to the ground. He half stumbled, then took to his feet, trying to put distance between him and his captors. Tarkhan went down a side street, pushing people aside as he pelted down the narrow laneway, in the opposite direction from the markets. He took the risk of checking over his shoulder, triumph surging through him to see the Sylannians chasing after him. His warriors were now on their own. He only hoped they'd be able to evade their captors and make their way back to the new homeland of the Kallith.

Tarkhan slid to a halt as the narrow alleyway he'd been running down opened onto a square. The many eyes of those who sipped kaf under the shade thrown by the tall palm trees that ringed the square turned to stare at him. His breathing sounded overloud and heavy in his ears. He saw his mistake immediately. There were none of the People here, other than those serving the kaf and food from the sellers that lined the plaza. They were all Sylannian. At the cries from those pursuing him getting closer, he ran across the open area, desperately trying to reach one of the other many streets that led into this place. Aware that the other Sylannians, who'd been sipping kaf moments before, were now on their feet and pursuing him as well, the insane hope glimmering within that he might pull this off died. Hands grabbed him a moment before bodies slammed into him from behind and he pitched forward. Tarkhan's breath exploded from his lungs as he hit the hard ground. While he desperately tried to suck in air, he felt many hands pinning him down and the restraining silk winding around him again. Tarkhan struggled ineffectually as they flipped him over and he hummed the counter to the silk which, despite their efforts responded to him, slithering back to the ground in a soft pool. He had the momentary satisfaction of seeing the shock register on the faces of those who held him before another strode through the press that surrounded him. At a wave of her hand, the babble of the others stopped. Her dark-brown eyes stared into his own as she paced forward and wrapped some of the silk she carried around him. It tightened around his neck as she hummed at it.

"Easy," she said, following up her words with a pulse of soothing, which caused him to calm despite himself. "Now, aren't you a surprise? Don't fear, you are far too valuable to allow any harm to come to you."

The woman snapped orders at the others around them and he shunted her calming influence aside and tried to pull away as the wad of silk in her hand dabbed at the side of his face, wincing as the silk contacted the side of his head and an injury he hadn't been aware he'd suffered.

"Let me go. I'll never submit to any of you." Tarkhan hummed at the silk but it didn't respond, and the woman's eyes crinkled.

"Hush now, warrior of Kallith." She chuckled as he stared at her, and she tucked the now-bloody piece of silk into her waistband. "Yes, I know you are of the warrior caste. You won't be able to control these bindings. Unlike those that collar your fellow countrymen, which can be controlled by any Sylannian, I keyed these to me alone."

With those words, she stood, issuing further orders to those around her before striding across the square. Tarkhan was prodded to his feet and herded in her wake.

Tarkhan found himself installed in a cage off a small inner courtyard in a larger complex. At least he had shade from the palm trees and wasn't roasting out here. He'd seen no sign of any of those he'd originally been captured with and hoped his sacrifice hadn't been in vain. He scrambled back against the hard bars of his cage as the door opened and the Sylannian who'd subdued him entered. A little yelling and some scrambling by some collared servers resulted in a chair being positioned within comfortable talking distance. The Sylannian waited until the others left before she sighed and sank into the cushions of the chair.

He stared at her as the comforting pulses washed over him, unable to resist their calming influence despite his best efforts. For the first time, he noted the band of deep maroon and cream in her robes. It was the first time since his return to his former homeland that he'd seen the markings of the conquerors who'd led the invasion.

"Where does your Sylannian heritage come from? Your mother?" she asked.

Tarkhan's eyes flared wide, an answer bursting from his lips before he could stop himself. "I'm not Sylannian."

"You are. In all the places we of the Thousand Islands have been, there are none but our own who can control the spidersilk."

He shook his head. "I'm not."

"It matters not, other than it changes your fate." She waved her hand, her expression indulgent as her eyes swept over him.

"I'll be taking you to our primary base, where you'll be shipped back to Sylanna. Normally I'd detail others to take you out for some exercise—"

"Oh, a walk would be appreciated."

"I'm sure." Her tone was bland, humour sparkling in her eyes. "Unfortunately, with you being so... skittish, you'll have to stay caged unless I can spare the time myself. I will, however, ensure you are well cared for while you are in my keeping."

The Sylannian stood and left him in the courtyard alone. He heard her issue a string of orders and the thumping of feet as people ran off to obey her. He sank back against the bars. Now that she'd left, trembling shook his body. In all his life he'd met no one who could sway another the way she'd been doing to him. It wasn't like she'd been in his head or anything. He'd just found it difficult to maintain his defiance under the constant stream of soothing emanations. His mind teemed with questions from the small amount of information the woman had given him. She'd been correct in at least one of her claims: no one else he'd tried to teach could pick up the technique to manipulate the silk. They couldn't even hear its melodic hum, no matter how hard they tried. They'd only believed him when he'd demonstrated his control over it. Although he baulked at any suggestion that he was related to the Sylannians.

It wasn't long before his thoughts were interrupted by the door opening again, and he learnt what his captor had sent the others for. The collared had returned with pillows, blankets, food, and a drink. Tarkhan had a moment, tensing in anticipation, before his hope was dashed. They didn't open his cage, simply pushed the pillows and blankets through the bars with the tray containing food and drink being slid through the small hatch they unlocked at the bottom of the cage, for just that purpose.

CHAPTER
TWENTY-NINE

Kesha sat in the corner of the common room at a table by herself. Noting the obvious space around her and sideways glances from everyone, she swallowed. The ceiling above did little to mask the sound of someone being sick upstairs. She half stood up, then slumped back down again. It was hard to resist her immediate instinct to assist. She could help ease Damien's suffering, but she'd been told bluntly not to get involved. This was something he had to get through himself. Although he wasn't entirely by himself. The others didn't trust him that much after he succumbed to his addiction.

"He'll recover," Olivia said as she pulled a seat out and joined her at the table. The other woman placed a platter of food in the centre of the table, gesturing for her to help herself.

"So Nathanial said."

"He's not ignoring you on purpose."

"I know," Kesha's said.

Kesha reached for some of the sliced meat, cheese, and some of the bread to avoid the knowing look in Olivia's eyes. Although it wouldn't do any good. Everyone was terribly polite, but they couldn't help but pick up on her emotions.

"How are you?" Michael asked as he sat down with a pitcher and three goblets.

She jumped, looking up wide-eyed. She'd been so intent on paying attention to her food, she hadn't noticed him approaching. With his height, broad shoulders and well-muscled frame, Michael didn't exactly have the body type she would associate with sneaking.

"I'm fine. I promise I won't go off by myself like that again."

"Don't make promises you can't keep." Michael's lips twitched in amusement.

"It's more of a risk in the bigger centres." Olivia picked up her drink and sipped it almost absently before adding. "So, mainly here and Vallantia."

"We all need our own space. If you are going too far afield, though, I'd rather you take an escort with you," Michael said, then traded glances with Olivia.

Kesha swallowed, knowing they were about to ask her about the kidnapping and what happened. She just wished she knew more that could help them track down those responsible. Not for her own sake so much, but for all those the kidnappers had abused.

"The front of the building where they kept you was a pleasure house, if you can call it that, of the worst kind." Olivia leaned forward, her voice low.

Kesha found herself just staring at Olivia. Granted, she'd had other things on her mind that night, but as much as she prodded for details, she couldn't recall anything that even remotely resembled what she imagined a pleasure house would be like.

"Did they force you into their pleasure house?" Michael asked, his voice soft.

Kesha realised why they were being so careful. Why there

was a space around her in the common room as the others gave them some privacy. It wasn't because the others were avoiding her or angry at the trouble she'd caused them all.

She shook her head. "No. Not that. I was stupid. They drugged me when I was in the market and I woke up in a room with the other captives. It had no window, you saw it. Damien was there, chained and drugged. I think they feared him more than the rest of us."

Kesha ducked her head at the relief that came from them. She didn't feel she was as useful as the rest of their unit. Just a constant burden, stumbling into trouble. Her head rose as Olivia laid her hand on her.

"Understand we would have tracked down anyone who'd forced you or used you while kept in such servitude. Everyone, no matter their rank or status, would have paid for it with their lives."

"We will track down those responsible for this trade and they will pay," Michael said.

"If they weren't using us for their pleasure house, what was going to happen to Damien and I?"

"We intend to work that out."

Although she was relieved on one hand, on the other, she doubted she'd wander far in the near future. Despite her assurance that she was fine, the run-in with the kidnappers had shaken her. Not wanting to think about what might have happened to her without Damien to break them free and the Unwanted coming out to rescue them, she pushed her mind away from such thoughts.

"Going through withdrawal this way, well, Damien won't get any freedom any time soon," Kesha said, looking from one to the other.

"No, he won't," Olivia agreed.

"Where tiscan is concerned, he can't be trusted." Michael took a sip of his drink while he regarded her steadily.

"It isn't his fault," Kesha said.

"It isn't, but it doesn't change things," Olivia said.

"I just hate that he's suffering when I can help ease his symptoms." Kesha took a sip of her own drink, frowning. It was more than hate; it was killing a little part of herself that just wanted to help.

"Recovery that way is too easy and not likely to hold him back next time," Michael explained.

"You don't know he'll slip again."

"I hope not, but unfortunately I won't be surprised if he goes through this cycle several times." Michael shrugged.

"This isn't the first time we've helped one of our people get off tiscan," Olivia said, a hint of sadness threaded through her words.

Kesha sighed and took another sip of her drink, then applied herself to her food. She studied those present in the common room and wondered who among the members of the Unwanted had been tiscan addicts. It hadn't occurred to her that any of the others had suffered from the affliction. She paused with her goblet halfway to her mouth, and her eyes widened as she stared across the table at Olivia and Michael.

"Nathanial. That's why he's pulled most of the duty looking after Damien."

"Better than any of us, he understands," Michael said.

"I tried to tell you it is nothing you've done to cause him to ignore you. Right now, Damien just needs him more," Olivia said as she reached for a piece of cheese and bread.

Kesha's cheeks heated and she raised her glass up to drink more of the wine. Not that the action would hide her reaction, she thought, desperately trying to divert the topic away from

Nathanial. Then she remembered the comment Damien had made about Michael knowing how to fight with a chain.

"Who had the audacity to kidnap you?" She frowned as Michael spluttered in reaction, his eyes wide.

"What? Unless you consider getting claimed by the Warlord a kidnapping, no one." Michael's eyebrow rose.

"Whatever gave you the idea Michael had been kidnapped?" Olivia asked, her eyes sparkling.

"Damien. He said he'd never fought with a chain before, but he had the ability because you did," Kesha said, watching as they traded glances with each other.

"When I was going through my last transition phase, the Warlord had me stay at his stronghold in Yalleska for a time," Michael said.

"None of us knew what was happening back then," Olivia added.

"One of his men insisted that anything could be a weapon. I spent some time training with him," Michael said.

"Ah, and one of those things was a chain?" Kesha asked, as she finally understood.

Michael nodded and continued. "He'd been a slave, kept shackled until the Warlord broke him free. What he could do with the chains was phenomenal."

"Oh." Kesha nibbled on a piece of cheese, glancing at them both. "Damien, just before he went to fight, he suffered an attack. He was in so much pain."

Kesha swallowed, brushing at some crumbs on the wooden table, before looking up to see them both watching her, their expressions guarded.

"It is extremely painful when the veil floods back in after being held away," Michael said, obviously choosing his words with care.

"When he was fighting, it was like he wasn't there anymore," Kesha said.

Damien's state had terrified her, but she didn't know now if she'd made it up to be worse in her head than it had been. After all, she'd been drugged, abducted, and had witnessed one horrific death after another. The screaming of those men as they'd died, regardless of how horrible they were, still haunted her sleep.

"For what it's worth, he wouldn't have harmed you. Not even out of his mind the way he was. He was operating out of pure instinct and reacting to what he perceived as a threat," Olivia said.

"While it's not a common reaction, it does happen. When the veil flooded back in, it overwhelmed his mind. He'll probably have nothing but disjointed memories of the fight, if he remembers it at all," Michael said.

Kesha accepted their explanation even though she didn't quite understand. She inspected the men and women around the room that made up the fighting ranks. Not for the first time, it occurred to her how different they all were from the average person. Then she snorted in amusement. Michael's eyebrow rose.

"I was just thinking how different you all are, compared to normal people. Then it occurred to me I couldn't really consider myself normal either," Kesha said.

She was rewarded as Michael's lips twitched in amusement. It was clear he agreed with her assessment.

THIRTY

Damien clutched the bowl as his stomach heaved once more. Time seemed to lose meaning and every part of him ached. His body shook as he sank down, laying his head on the wooden floorboards. It was more comfortable on the bed, but he'd thrown himself to the side to vomit so quickly he'd fallen out. Now he was unwilling, unable to move. As the bowl was removed, he nearly protested, not wanting to be sick on the floor and have to clean it up, but subsided when a fresh one replaced it.

He heard voices murmuring and saw blurred figures in the doorway as the room seemed to spin. No matter how much he tried to concentrate, he couldn't make out the words or who it was. He reached for the veil, but there was simply nothing there. Then, as nausea rose again, he decided he didn't care. His stomach and throat ached as he threw up. Again. He'd lost count of how many times he'd been sick. It left him wondering how he could have anything left to throw up. A brief, sane thought in the chaos of his mind.

Finally, he lay back, pushing the bowl away from him. The

smell was causing his stomach to heave, although this time there didn't seem like there was anything left. Tears tracked down his cheeks, but he didn't have enough ego left to care who observed. He just hurt. His head screamed at him when he moved. Hands gathered him up and he found himself back on the bed. A cool, damp cloth cleaned him up while he lay there, trembling. As they pulled the sheets back over him, he allowed the darkness to take him away from the *wrongness* that settled on him, off to unconsciousness.

Nathanial heard the intake of a shuddering breath that let him know his roommate was finally conscious. He heard a moan and the creak of the bed next to him, and rolled on his side to see Damien fumbling, groping around on the ground next to his bed. Nathanial caught a confused memory from Damien of having a vial of tiscan. He steeled himself as the agitation, the need for more tiscan increased in his friend. Rather than pain and sickness.

"You won't find any," Nathanial said, keeping his tone calm and low.

Damien's eyes flashed up at him and widened as if he hadn't realised anyone else was in the room. His eyes darted to the weapons rack, where there was no sign of his weapons belt. Damien's mind was terrifyingly blank, as if the clamouring of his body had shunted aside all sanity for the product he was addicted to.

"I don't know what you mean."

"Your weapons or any tiscan." Nathanial saw Damien flinch as he mentioned the drug.

"You don't understand. I need some, just a sip will take the edge off." Damien's voice held a note of pleading.

"I understand, probably better than anyone." Nathanial watched Damien, feeling for his friend in his confusion. "We're storing your weapons elsewhere and it's been days since you had vials of tiscan in your room. We checked the room and your belongings to make sure there wasn't any more before we brought you back here."

"You can't possibly know what it feels like!" Damien snarled.

Nathanial sensed the shift in the veil a moment before Damien leapt from the bed, trying to head for the door. The move was predictable. He would have been more surprised if Damien hadn't tried it, given how lost he was in tiscan's grip. Unlike Damien, he wasn't suffering the effects of withdrawal. Nathanial was quickly up, placing himself between Damien and the door. He sensed Damien's momentary confusion as he tried to connect to the veil, which was fluctuating wildly. Right now it had deserted him, and Damien's sense of sickness and agitation would increase the longer he was cut off. Damien was alternating in a void of wrongness, then flipping, with the veil flooding back in and overcharging what he could currently manage. All of this, combined with his addiction to tiscan and withdrawal, meant he didn't know how he felt, or what, or why.

Damien's desperation washed over his mental barriers, on this occasion his need for more tiscan driving him. Nathanial blocked a wild punch thrown at him and grappled with Damien, both of them hitting the floor. Fortunately for him, his landing was softened because of landing on top of his friend, and with the state Damien was in, he doubted his friend would even notice the new set of aches.

Need a hand? Michael asked.

No, he's too drug-addled to fight effectively, Nathanial said.

Nathanial pinned Damien to the floor, easily overpowering him. It wouldn't be long before Damien collapsed again, his surge of activity working to pump what remained of the drug he'd consumed through his system. While Kesha had cleared a great deal of it in the cells, it only made the residue that lingered even more frightening. Even what remained to be flushed out of Damien's system would likely kill a person who'd never used the stuff.

Keeping watch on Damien's mind tipped him off to the moment before he stopped fighting. Nathanial reached out with the veil, and the pillow from the bed flew into his hand as he drew it to himself. He slid it under Damien's head just before convulsions shook his body. Nathanial closed his eyes; Damien had come closer to killing himself than he cared to think about. Nathanial climbed to his feet and reached for a clean bowl from a stack near the door. He placed it on the floor, carefully monitoring Damien's progress, waiting until the convulsions subsided. He released the shield he'd been using to pin Damien to the floor and propped him up, pulling the bowl closer with an adroit use of power—just in time as Damien retched uncontrollably even though there was nothing left to expel. His body knew, even if Damien's head didn't, that it had to get rid of every bit of the poison that had seeped into every cell in his system.

THIRTY-ONE

"Tradition?" The word nearly spat out of Liliana's mouth. "Don't talk to me about tradition."

"Primewife, we need to follow our ways—"

"If we followed the ways of our ancestors, our house wouldn't exist," Liliana said bluntly.

"Please, Primewife—"

"As much as I too would rather be back home in comfort, would our firstwife have sent us here if we would be safe at court?" Liliana tried to remain reasonable.

"There are those who've survived the purge before," the underwife said, a thread of stubbornness in not only her voice but her stance. "Yes, there was that attack, but we proved we could fight them off and these traitors on our doorstep prove we aren't safe here either."

"You would risk all our children in the hope we'd get lucky the second time?" Liliana bit back a curse and said flatly, "All those who've survived that we know of may have been children of the Monarch House but, other than Jaclyn, they did not possess the blood of the Monarch. Our house is a much bigger threat and if some, like Jaclyn, survived in the past, they fled Sylanna to other lands to save themselves."

"Primewife Liliana is correct. We're here because our house shouldn't exist." The head of her security detail interrupted and held up her hand to forestall the underwives' protests. "We are on war footing and, as such, I'm the one who rules on matters regarding the security of us all."

"Our job is to protect Liliana and her child." The underwife glared at the daggerwife. "No one has come in search of us, and we can protect her and her unborn child much better back in our proper place, away from those who are traitors to our whole race."

"We will stay here until our firstwife advises us it is safe to return to court. I will send word to the First; she and our husband need to know what we've found out and the decision about how to deal with the situation is theirs."

Liliana noted with satisfaction that the woman was finally growing into her role. She also noted that while she sent her subordinates off, she remained in position between Liliana and the underwives.

Liliana left the argument in the capable hands of the daggerwife and sank onto a low couch. An underwife scurried forward to rearrange the pillows for her, while another poured a glass of juice from a pitcher on the sideboard. The woman cooled it with a hint of power before handing the chilled beverage to her. Liliana placed her hand on her abdomen.

I promise you, my little one. I will protect our house so you will be safe and can grow to be a husband in your own house one day.

She whispered the words to him alone as she ignored the continuing argument between the underwives and daggerwives. It satisfied her for now that the daggerwives, at least, would follow her orders, and in doing so, pass her message onto Jaclyn.

THIRTY-TWO

Damien slowly became aware he was awake, despite the weight of exhaustion that seemed to pin him to his bed. He had no inclination at all to get up. Not only did tremors run through his body, an overwhelming desire for more tiscan flooded his senses. Sickness washed over him and he swallowed convulsively, feeling an ache in this throat and abdomen. It seemed like an ever-present, unwelcome friend. He groaned, prodding at his memory, trying to remember what had happened. This feeling meant he'd used again. Yet his mind was completely blank.

Sluggishly at first, images, feelings, and sounds flickered in his head. Then they hammered into his brain one after the other. He didn't have a full picture yet, but it was enough to make him wince.

"Powers, what have I done?" he whispered, hearing the roughness in his voice.

"You nearly killed yourself indulging in tiscan." Nathanial's reply lacked judgement despite the words.

Damien turned his head with care, knowing if he moved too

fast, he'd be sick again. His stomach and throat ached with even the thought of vomiting again. He had no idea how many times Nathanial had supported his shaking body as he was sick and cleaned him up after, but it was more times than he cared to think of. His hand shook as he covered his eyes. The filtered light in the room told him that the shutters were drawn, probably to stop him from attempting to jump out of them, but the light still seemed to pierce his head. Moisture tracked from his eyes down his cheeks, but he had no energy left to stop them.

"What am I going to do?" It wasn't really a question, but Nathanial answered anyway.

"Take it a day at a time."

"Michael will never trust me again."

"He will. He's angrier with the people who should have been with you than he is with you. Michael's also taken turns watching over you, along with Olivia and me."

Damien didn't have the energy to feel embarrassed that both Michael and Olivia had taken turns in helping to clean him up and keep him safe.

"The others who were with me that first morning, it wasn't their fault."

"If they'd done the jobs I assigned them to, this mess wouldn't have happened. Even if they couldn't stop you themselves, Michael, Olivia, or I would have been there, we could have."

"When I inhaled that smoke... You don't understand what it's like."

Even at the thought of inhaling more of the drug, he shook in reaction, stomach clenching as need hit him hard enough to make his breath catch in his throat. A deep sense of failure and hopelessness settled on him.

"I know exactly what it's like. It's why, other than needing someone to cover while I get some sleep, I'm your keeper from here on out," Nathanial said.

It took a few moments for those words to sink into his mind, then a few more for them to make sense. Then he shifted slowly onto his side, pinpricks of sweat breaking out and his stomach convulsing as he waited, swallowing, relieved when the sickness passed. Finally, he opened his eyes.

"You?"

"I was a tiscan addict when Michael, Olivia and the Warlord pulled me out of the misery that was my life." Nathanial sat on the bed opposite his own with his back against the wall, watching him calmly.

"Your parents gave you tiscan? Did they know what it would do?" Damien asked.

"No, worse. They sold me to the highest bidder. My new owners fed me tiscan to keep me docile and compliant."

Damien's eyes widened, yet despite the words he'd just uttered, Nathanial still appeared perfectly calm.

"What? Why did they do that?"

"Money, I presume. I never saw them again after they gave me up," Nathanial said.

"What happened?" Damien could hear the horror in his own voice.

"The ones who bought me were a less than reputable family and ran a pleasure house behind the front of a gambling establishment. My handlers made sure they kept me dosed with tiscan to keep me calm. They catered to even the most perverted tastes of those who had the money to afford it. I was quite a popular choice on the menu."

"When I get over this. Tell me who to kill." Damien didn't even try to hide the surge of anger that shook him.

"Michael already did. He, Olivia, and the Warlord cleaned up the whole degenerate den." Nathanial ducked his head. "I was a mess, from more than the drug addiction. If I can recover, so can you."

Damien wanted to believe he'd be fine, but right now, if he'd been physically capable of getting out of the bed, he was afraid he'd run off and get more tiscan. He had to acknowledge, even if it was only to himself, he wanted it that badly. He squeezed his eyes shut and wished fervently for unconsciousness to claim him again. Unfortunately for him his mind didn't seem to want to cooperate and even though he was so exhausted he ached, he couldn't sleep.

DAMIEN STEPPED DOWN from the last stair, leaning against the smooth wooden wall as his skin crawled. He sucked in some deep breaths, keeping the sudden nausea at bay. Nathanial had informed him bluntly it was time he got up. That it would be good for him to spend a few hours in the common room. The thought of getting out of his room excited him, until he realised halfway down the hallway he just wanted to lie down again. He'd decided there was no point in trying to hide the fact he was struggling. Perhaps in his home village he could have disguised it, but not in his current company.

He saw Nathanial, who was sitting with Michael and Olivia in the corner, glance in his direction and the feather-light brush of the veil as Michael assessed his condition. Not that Nathanial had just told him to get out of bed, then gone down to the common room and left him unsupervised. He'd discovered that there were a couple of his squad mates on duty outside his door. They'd taken seriously Nathanial's order before he left to make sure the only place he went was downstairs. As Nathanial's eyes tracked movement, Damien moved his head enough to check over his shoulder and saw Kesha heading in his direction. It told him how far gone he was that he hadn't sensed her approach. His touch on the veil had been fluctuating wildly since he'd woken up. Whereas before his recent lapse he'd almost stabilised. Or at least while his ability to sense and touch the veil fluctuated, he hadn't been losing touch with it entirely. He saw Nathanial's noncommittal expression as Kesha approached and, glancing over, saw both Michael and Olivia were watching as well.

"Damien, please, let me help ease your symptoms," Kesha said.

"Thank you, but no," Damien replied.

"I hate seeing you like this, particularly since I can help."

"My addiction to tiscan isn't my fault, but my current condition is."

"Nonsense, your cravings for the stuff are a symptom of what they did to you. I saw what those people were doing to you."

"As soon as I inhaled the tiscan smoke, I needed it. It clawed at me. The only thing that would make me feel better was more tiscan. I went in and, at first, I just stood there breathing it in. Instead of settling my craving for it, I instantly wanted more. One man held out a smoke to me. I took it and sat down with them. I can't explain but it's like my mind disconnects, pain fades and then... it was so good. They offered me a bottle of a potent brew they make. They didn't hold me down and force me to drink it. I took it. I sculled the whole vial in one hit when I got back here. In the morning, I took the extra vial of the stuff they'd given me to ease the cravings, then snuck out to get more."

Damien spoke softly, aware that it wasn't just Kesha listening but determined to get his confession out. Shame wasn't enough to hold his tongue. It was important his team knew the lengths he'd go to in order to get tiscan. Particularly if they were tasked with keeping a watch on him again.

"Damien, that isn't your—"

"It is my fault. Even in the state I entered that place, I knew I shouldn't. From the moment I inhaled the smoke in the laneway, I didn't have the strength to back away. I could have called out. Michael, Olivia, or Nathanial would have heard. They would have helped me and I knew it. They would've stopped me. Everyone here would have stopped me if I'd asked for help. It's why I didn't call out. Being addicted isn't my fault but what I'm going through now is. I did this to myself."

Feeling sweat break out all over his body and sickness rise, Damien barely had time to collapse to his knees before tremors shook his body. He slumped to the cold wooden floor as he convulsed and a sudden need for tiscan spiked, making him gasp as his body continued to protest his withdrawal from the drug. Heat burned through him, causing sweat to break out from his head to his toes. The heat was replaced with cold so icy feeling it hurt him to his core. Agony and longing radiated through him. He flinched as a hand touched his shoulder, then almost sagged with relief as he realised it was Nathanial. Any ability he had to touch the veil seemed to have deserted him once more with the feeling of wrongness intensifying.

"Everything will be all right, breathe."

"I wish you'd let me die," Damien whispered.

"I know, but you will recover and then you'll be glad I didn't," Nathanial said and helped him to his feet.

"Right now, it doesn't feel like it." Guilt flooded Damien as he noticed Kesha, who still hovered nearby. "I'm sorry I was so short with you, Kesha. But I think the memory of this recovery might prompt me to call for help next time I'm overcome by tiscan. Particularly if there is no one nearby who cares or is strong enough to make me see sense. There will be a next time. Even knowing what's happening to me now, I want more."

"I just hate to see you suffer," Kesha said.

"I have a feeling I'll suffer more in future if I don't do this the hard way." Damien closed his eyes, taking a deep, settling breath before looking back at her. "I need to know I can get through to the other side of this, even if you aren't at hand to brush away the result of my idiocy."

Nathanial helped him over to a corner booth, squeezing his shoulder.

Well done. You're learning, Nathanial said as he sat on the bench opposite.

Damien's brain was too sluggish to respond, so he settled with a nod. Callan crossed the common room, placing a bowl of broth and a plate with some bread down in front of him. He opened his mouth to object that he really didn't have any appetite, then shut it again as Nathanial's eyebrows rose. It was an expression he was familiar with. He either tried to eat by himself or Nathanial would hold down and force him. Instead, he picked up the spoon and took a cautious sip of the broth.

THIRTY-THREE

Khaliun ground her teeth. While what was being said made sense, she didn't want to hear it. The only consolation was that she could feel support coming from some of the other leaders present.

"It makes sense for it to be you," Erden bit out.

"Oh, please. Anyone can go to alert our allies." Khaliun glared at her former lover. "It doesn't have to be me."

"You are the one who has the connection to Michael."

Orghana sent a withering look in Erden's direction before she expelled a breath, clearly unhappy.

"Of all here, you are the best speaker of their language, Khaliun, and you are also our strongest mindspeaker," Orghana said.

"If you think I can reach Michael clear across the Warlord's entire domain, your faith is misplaced." Khaliun threw her fellow clan leaders a disgusted look.

It had taken more time to come to any kind of consensus on a course of action simply because Erden would raise objections to anything she said.

"As much as I hate it, Orghana is correct." Yangir held up his hand as Khaliun glared at him. "You speak the language fluently. You'll be able to explain to the villagers what is happening."

Khaliun wanted to argue, but it was hard to dispute their arguments. As much as she hated it, she was being difficult just because of Erdan's attitude.

"My place is here, fighting."

"It is, but the best chance our people have is if we get help. Besides that, you don't need to do as Erden has suggested." At the last Yangir threw a withering look in Erden's direction. "It isn't necessary."

"You know, the best decision is for her to find the Warleader," Erden snapped.

"If I remember the instructions correctly, we only have to pass word to the village and *they* will relay the message using their own methods," Yangir said.

"I believe Yangir is correct. Word only has to go to the village. Trust the plans we've put in place. That you helped put in place," Orghana said.

"The Sylannians will clear that rockfall, but I suspect we will be back in place long before it occurs," Yangir reasoned.

"We?" Khaliun asked.

"You'll not go alone, I'll accompany you," Yangir said.

"No, you won't, Yangir. You're the strongest healer, one of the few healers we have left. You'll stay here in safety. Khaliun is more than capable of going to fetch the Warleader," Erden said.

He is behaving badly, but it pains him to be the one to send you to fetch his rival, Orghana said.

I do not love Michael. Khaliun allowed the other leader to feel her frustration over Erden's current behaviour.

I know. Even he knows, but jealousy isn't rational. Orghana's exasperation with her co-leader was clear.

Despite herself, that last comment brought a smile to Khaliun's lips. Rational was the last word she'd use to describe Erden's behaviour of late. About the only good thing she could see about being sent away was that it would give them breathing space from each other.

"All right, I'll go—"

"We'll go." Ulagan stepped forward ignoring Erdan's glare. "You'll not do this alone."

"There's no need. It's not far. I know the way." Khaliun's expression was closed. "I'll take some of the warriors from my tribe with me."

"Fine, but I'm still coming with you," Ulagan said, raising his chin as he stared at Erden. "It might save arguments, disbelief and wasting time we do not have on our return. Or do you have objections about me leaving our camp?" Ulagan stared flatly at the other leader until Erden shook his head.

Khaliun opened her mouth to argue, before she finally accepted the offer of assistance. She spun and stalked out of the hut, slamming the door behind her.

THIRTY-FOUR

Jaclyn was suddenly awake, wondering what had disturbed her before she saw the outline of a daggerwife in the doorway.

"What is it?" Jaclyn kept her voice low.

"Sorry to disturb your sleep, First, but a messenger has arrived from Primewife Liliana."

Jaclyn brushed aside the spidersilk sheet with a low pulse from her mind and rose from her bed. The daggerwife stepped forward without further comment and grabbed her robe from a hook on the wall before assisting her into it.

"Where is she?" Jaclyn asked.

"In the small meeting room, First," the daggerwife said, then handed her a sealed message. "This report has also arrived for you from the new territories."

Jaclyn scanned the message as she went down the hallway, noting the daggerwives who stood duty. Ever since the failed attack on her house by her brother's wives, the security of the house had reverted to what they had maintained during the war in the trader lands. As if they were at war and in the heart of enemy territory. Given the early hour, there would be a shift change soon. It would be best to get this meeting done with and the messenger either stashed away or back to Liliana before the change occurred. The fewer people who were aware of the messenger's presence, the better. She also couldn't help the nagging worry that something must have gone wrong. Even if the practical side of her mind said there would have been more than one messenger if anything was wrong, for Liliana to send one at all increased the risk to both her and the children her group protected. Which meant she'd decided the risk was worth the effort.

The daggerwife guarding the small meeting room promptly opened the door and Jaclyn strode into the room, focusing on the messenger as the door closed softly behind her.

"What is pressing enough for Liliana to send you here? Has she had her child?"

"No, First, not yet. The underwives send word both mother and babe are healthy," the daggerwife said.

"That is good to hear." Relief washed over Jaclyn; it was much too early for Liliana to have given birth. Unfortunately, that meant there was more pressing news. "What's happened?"

"Primewife Liliana sends word that traitors from a lower house are trading with the barbarians. They've been trading spidersilk in return for men." The daggerwife kept her tone calm as she spoke.

Jaclyn's anger flared at the audacity of a lower caste house not only having a secret trade in men but in spidersilk. Spidersilk was one commodity that was carefully controlled with only those of the highest station owning garments made from pure spidersilk rather than the commonplace blended variety. They'd found in their explorations that the spiders that spun the spidersilk threads were endemic to their islands.

Uncontrolled breeding with barbarian males was not to her

taste, but it was also forbidden and even more carefully controlled than spidersilk. The preservation of their bloodlines was a priority laid down by the decree of successive Monarch Houses. It dated back generations, when they'd first started exploring and discovered men were not as rare in other lands as they were in their own.

"Is there more?"

"Primewife Liliana tasked us with following the traders and discovering their route back to their homeland. We were success-ful, First. My team leader dropped me off and proceeded straight back to the primewife, but I am tasked with showing the advance scouts the routes. Primewife Liliana thought the information might prove useful to your campaign."

As the woman fell silent, Jaclyn went to the table where the map was laid out and studied it.

"This base the barbarians came from, can you pinpoint it on the map?"

"Yes, First." The woman joined her at the table and, after studying the map, pointed to a place on the opposite end of the barbarian lands. "They appear to be coming from two locations, First. This one here is a big enclave."

"You said two. The other?"

"Here, First. It is of a similar size but on the opposite side of their territory."

"It is closer to the mountains that divide the barbarian lands from our territory in the trader lands," Jaclyn said.

The daggerwife nodded but obviously didn't feel the need to make further comment. Jaclyn was grateful for the woman's silence and continued to stare at the map.

"Where is this island of traitors? Close to your hiding loca-tion, I take it?"

Jaclyn knew it must be, and the fact traitors lived so close to where the children of the house were hidden did not thrill her.

Not only were they traitors to Sylanna, but they were also a risk to her house.

"Yes, First, we can see the island from the shore." The dagger-wife once again pointed out the location on the map.

Jaclyn smiled as a kernel of a plan occurred to her. Handled correctly, they could distract the Warlord and his Warleader while giving the best possibility for the survival of her house. She finally drew her attention back to the messenger, who waited patiently.

"And the rest?"

"Primewife Liliana asked this to be given to you, First."

The woman handed her a small piece of parchment. Jaclyn unsealed the message and scanned its contents. A report on the state of their small outpost and assurances that not only her son and Myra's, but all the children were well. The difficulties with the underwives trying to take on more authority than they would normally have caused her to frown, although Liliana had the situation in hand. Even if she shouldn't be facing such tests of her authority. It seemed her decision to send Liliana's former team of daggerwives with her as the lead guard unit was well made. The last line caused her to smile. Liliana requesting permission to re-join them as soon as she was fit again after giving birth to her child. Jaclyn moved over to the desk and, taking a small piece of paper and fountain pen, she wrote a brief reply. She blew on it gently to dry the ink before folding it and fixing her wax seal on it. Standing, she handed the message back to the daggerwife.

"Give this to Liliana's hand only," Jaclyn said.

"Yes, First," the daggerwife said.

Jaclyn sent a silent signal to those who guarded her doors. The doors opened and the guards ushered their fellow dagger-wife out. There was no need to issue instructions, those who guarded her inner court were trained in their craft well enough.

Jᴀᴄʟʏɴ ᴅʀᴇᴡ her attention from the map she was studying to watch as Ricardo and Myra entered the room, aware of the daggerwives who took station around their meeting place. Even here, in the heart of her own court, it was wise to take precautions. They'd already identified one of the wives who'd betrayed her house by giving her first loyalty to the king. The woman would be dealt with at the appropriate moment, but doing so too early would be pointless. Her brother's firstwife would only replace the traitor with someone else. Jaclyn filled them both in on the information Liliana had sent to them, before going back to the map she'd been staring at. She hadn't seen much use in trying to get back to sleep after Liliana's messenger had left her. Instead, she'd made good use of the time, staring at the maps and adding further details to their battle plans.

"We send the sister houses to launch attacks here"—Jaclyn pointed to the mountains where she suspected the Kallith had disappeared and the city closest to them that the smugglers had been coming from—"and here."

"To what purpose?" Ricardo asked.

"The feint will draw their Warlord and Warleader into those regions to fight," Jaclyn said.

"Where will we be?" Myra asked.

"Once their forces have committed, we will launch our own attack at the other end of their territory," Jaclyn said, her finger tapping on the other city.

"Our people have found a path over those mountains?" Myra asked, her finger tracing the line of the Heights as it stretched in an arch between their new territory and the barbarian lands.

"No, but the report I received today from our agents claims it won't be long now," Jaclyn said.

"As long as they find that mountain pass while they are

distracted fighting the sister houses on two fronts." Myra stared at the map and tapped the habitation marked at the other extreme from the places Jaclyn had marked. "We will take this place?"

Jaclyn nodded, pleased that so far neither had found an obvious flaw she'd missed. Always a possibility with a lack of sleep. "Pressure will be put on the traitor house Liliana uncovered. If they want to live, these barbarians they are trading with will help smuggle our fighters into the walls of the city."

"It will get us past their walls without having to fight. That's a distinct advantage," Myra said.

"We're sending the other houses to their deaths." Ricardo joined them to stare down at the map, his voice soft.

"You disagree?"

"No. Our house comes first," Ricardo said, shaking his head, eyes holding her own. "As long as we all know the consequences. We should never hide from the actions we take."

"It will take time to get all of our people in place, but this is the best chance our house has for survival."

Jaclyn watched her husband and fellow wife as they considered the plan she had laid out. As their eyes scanned the map, she had no doubt they were running through alternative scenarios. At least this time they had the experience of the war in the trader lands to draw on.

"So now we just need to choose which sister houses we send to their death." Ricardo said, his face and emotions calm.

"I'm sure we should be able to slip in some of my brother's staunchest supporters."

"We'll have to be careful, but it should be easy enough to arrange," Myra said.

"As commander you have the right; he must have realised this when he gave you the title," Ricardo said.

"I'm sure he did, but the idea of me dying in the barbarian land was just too tempting."

"He's trying to throw us to our deaths. I see no issue with taking some of his strongest supporters with us," Myra said.

"Particularly given if we do this correctly it will occupy their terribly effective warlord, who will be distracted while we seize control of this place." Ricardo tapped the settlement on the map then his fingers spread out to indicate the surrounding territory. "And reinforce our hold on this territory. Then we can expand."

"We survived the trader lands. We will survive this as well." Jaclyn stared at the piles of paperwork and rolls of maps that surrounded her. "I guess the next step is to put all of this in front of my brother and get his approval."

Ricardo and Myra stared at her in confusion. As her grin widened and they caught a glimpse of what she intended to try, they both chuckled.

CHAPTER

THIRTY-FIVE

Samuel glared out the window, absently chewing on his bottom lip.

"What do you mean, she's coming here?"

His firstwife seemed perfectly calm and pleasant, on the surface, but not only could he see it was insincere, he could feel it. As tied together as their minds were, it was as impossible for his wives to hide from him as it was for him to hide his feelings from them. She was just as suspicious as he was of this latest move from his sister.

"She made the request in her role as Commander of Sylanna. We have no reason to deny her."

"I told you that rank gave her too much power. We'd only just removed it from her, declaring the war with the trader clans over, and you made me give it back to her." Samuel transferred his glare to his wife.

"You know very well why we've done it. We just have to be patient." Chelsie's eyes flashed. Not that he needed that warning regarding her mood. Her irritation pulsed through their bond.

"It's taking her long enough. She and her whole infernal

219

family should have left and died already." Samuel was aware he was sounding petulant, but at this moment, he really didn't care.

It was rather refreshing that his wife hadn't forced him into compliance with her wishes and made him forget his irritation. So, as far as he was concerned, he was going to enjoy the experience. It was a little exhilarating, like he'd returned to that time before he'd bonded with his firstwife and given her control of his mind.

"Perhaps that is what she is coming to tell us."

"She'll have an angle."

"Of course she will. I have every faith, however, that the barbarians will help us with this little problem and kill her. Just like they have others," Chelsie said.

Samuel looked at her sardonically. That explained why she wasn't forcing him to calm down. She was lost, revelling in the impending death of his sister. A flurry at the doors drew his attention and as he'd expected, Jaclyn strode in. His eyes narrowed. Her spidersilk in colours of maroon with the cream woven through in a spiderweb pattern flowed around her, a constant reminder that she had as much claim to the throne as he did. Being loose rather than in armour form also showed she didn't see being in his presence or that of his wives as an immediate threat. He wasn't exactly sure if that should offend him or not. Samuel eyed her silks and found yet another reason to be irritated. Even the spider keepers on her island court excelled, arguably more so than his own. Jaclyn's house produced some of the finest spidersilk found in Sylanna. Although his sister couldn't take all the credit—she didn't specifically tend the spiders, harvest their silk or weave it. How could she? She'd been in the land of the traders for nearly six years. It was yet another little show of competence that caused him irritation.

At least she had a contingent of her daggerwives around her. Yet not as many as he'd expected, and Ricardo wasn't with her, which was surprising. They had advised him that his sister's husband had hardly been allowed out of her sight since he'd recalled her to Sylanna. Then he realised the primewife wasn't with Jaclyn. That explained who she'd left to ensure her husband's safety. Myra had proven to be as deadly as Jaclyn herself. It was a shame the woman had ended up in Jaclyn's house rather than his own. He couldn't help his delight at Chelsie's flush of anger as she caught his thought.

It's not my fault I'm attracted to dangerous women. I accepted you as my firstwife, after all, he whispered.

He was rewarded by a small burst of pleasure, which made him breathe a sigh of relief. It was much more pleasant when his wives were happy with him. Particularly his firstwife.

Jaclyn stopped and half bowed her head, placing her dagger hand on her heart. The silent cue that she was approaching him as commander. As a daughter of the Monarch House, even one who didn't sit on the throne, she did not have to bow to him in that capacity. That they had missed this one younger sibling of his during the purge made him grind his teeth in frustration. It would have been fine if it had been one of his stupid sisters who'd survived.

"Speak, Commander."

"My liege, I have the battle plans for the attack on the barbarian lands drawn up for your approval." Jaclyn gestured to her daggerwives who came forward unfurling a map.

He regarded the oversized map and the frighteningly thick wad of papers clutched in the hands of another of Jaclyn's daggerwives. The woman was in the process of handing the first piece of paper from the stack to Jaclyn. His eyes widened; he had no intention of sitting through the tedium of her explaining a blow-by-blow description of her plans. He'd fall asleep with boredom.

Now, Samuel, be happy, your sister is finally telling us she's ready to die. Just as we want her to, Chelsie purred in his mind.

"I don't need to see your map or hear the battle plan. I trust your skills, Commander, it's why we appointed you."

"If I could draw your attention to the sister houses I'll need —"

"Take them. Whatever you need to do to keep Sylanna safe from this barbarian plague, you have my permission to do."

"Are you sure, Samuel? I have the list here."

Jaclyn gestured to the daggerwife with the overlarge stack of papers, who shuffled through the paperwork. Samuel rolled his eyes in exasperation until, with a look of relief, the woman handed a piece of parchment to Jaclyn. As Jaclyn held out the sheets of papers, he held up his hand.

"I'm sure. I'll even put my directive in writing for you if it will make it easier." Samuel twisted to look at one of his wives. Unable to remember her name he frowned. "You, write that down for my commander."

He gazed back across the courtroom at his sister pleasantly. Chelsie was correct. It was terribly soothing to know she was finally going to die, as she should have done years ago. She'd been here for months. So long, in fact, he'd begun to wonder if she'd been waiting for something else to occur first. Actually, he was certain she had been. Although he found now, he didn't care, as long as whatever it was didn't impede her death. The scuffling behind told him that one of his wives was running to do his bidding.

"I'm sure this occasion deserves a drink to celebrate," Chelsie chimed in, snapping her fingers.

Fortunately, the tray of drinks appeared more promptly than his written consent and orders for his commander. He didn't miss the fact that Jaclyn tested her drink for impurities before she took a sip. As Chelsie's free hand moved to rest on his shoulder, he ignored the insult. After all, if he'd thought poisoning her was going to work, he would have sent someone to try it long ago.

We have tried poisoning, several times.

Samuel sighed. If his wives had bothered to consult with him, he could have told them Jaclyn wouldn't be taken down with that one. It was one of the lessons that had been ingrained in them as children of the Monarch House. Their mother had been paranoid, particularly towards the end. Jaclyn had always been an extremely clever child. He had no doubt she'd passed those strict lessons to her fellow wives. And Ricardo wouldn't have needed to be told that one. He was raised as a son in one of the oldest houses of Sylanna that stretched, unbroken, as far back in their history as the Monarch House.

Finally, one of his wives—he assumed she was a wife even though he could swear he'd never set eyes on her before—rushed forward, holding out a rolled parchment to Jaclyn. Samuel nearly forgot himself repressing the groan in embarrassment as his sister's eyes flicked to his own. One of her daggerwives stepped forward and intercepted the woman before she got too close to Jaclyn. He could almost see the confusion in his very junior wife as the daggerwife of Jaclyn's house accepted the orders that bore his seal. This wife of his still didn't seem to understand her error and did not step back. Which caused Jaclyn's daggerwives to step forward, placing their own bodies between this low-level wife and their firstwife.

"That will be all. Jaclyn is a daughter of the Monarch House and the Commander of Sylanna," he explained, trying to stay patient. "Request the underwives to give you lessons in protocol."

He was amazed his voice remained steady, trying to throttle his irritation as he realised how young this wife was. This was likely her first season away from the house of her birth. Since it was such an auspicious day, he could let this breach of protocol, and embarrassment to his house this junior wife caused, slide. After all, if his commander was willing to let the insult go, which since his wife was still alive she obviously was, he could afford to be forgiving.

THIRTY-SIX

Michael repressed the sigh he wanted to let past his lips as the man he'd been told wanted to speak with him entered the common room of their accommodation. The guards on the door confirmed the person was someone they'd rescued from the back of the warehouse, along with Damien and Kesha. Only years of practice stopped him from reacting as one of his childhood friends, Lukas, strolled into the bar.

Did you know Lukas was involved in that mess? Olivia asked.

No, he must have slipped out when we were dealing with Damien and Kesha, Michael said.

Tension increased noticeably among the Unwanted as Kesha flew over to hug the man. After recent events, none of them were happy about anyone they didn't know getting close to her at all. Michael saw Lukas look at him, his eyes flicking around the room as he hesitated before hugging her gently back.

"It's good to see you, healer, but I think you are making the Unwanted nervous," Lukas said.

"They won't hurt me."

"No, but they might hurt me," Lukas said and took a step back, showing his palms were empty as he did so.

"But to do that while I was hugging you, well, they'd hurt me while trying to get at you."

Michael shook his head as Lukas's lips twitched.

"Not precisely, healer, the Warleader could still kill me without harming a single hair on your head," Lukas said, his eyes dancing with amusement.

Michael snorted softly but didn't deny Lukas's assertion. Olivia shrugged and gestured to the seat opposite them at the table.

"He's correct, Kesha, but it would probably be just a little impolite. Particularly since we know you mean her no harm and we let you in," Olivia said.

As the noise from Damien's room filtered down, Lukas paused, one hand on the chair to pull it out from the table, looking up with a hint of concern on his face before his expression cleared.

"Ah, he's still alive then? I think I owe him my life," Lukas said.

"You thought he would die?" Olivia asked.

"No offence, ma'am, but I did. With the amount of tiscan they were pouring into him, even with one like her"—he gestured to Kesha as he sat down—"at that level, an addict is more likely to die coming off the drug than staying on it."

He's obviously going to keep pretending that he doesn't know us, Olivia said.

Probably for the best. The fewer people who know the connection between us, the better, Michael said.

"You know he's an addict?"

"To put it bluntly, if he hadn't been, he would have overdosed and died before they threw your healer in the cell with us all." Lukas shrugged. "Besides that, he admitted he was."

Michael reminded himself not to get up and hug his friend outright. Lukas was immaculate, yet nondescript, and armed to the teeth, even if the weapons weren't externally visible.

You're not treating your recruit too harshly, I hope? There is nothing he could have done once they got that stuff into him, Lukas said.

I know, my friend. Your guess was correct. He's a full addict. Damien's is one of the usual stories—well-meaning but ill-informed people dosed him with the stuff from childhood. We were expecting him to relapse again. It's only Kesha's healing abilities that kept him balanced.

It was the kidnapping of both him and our healer that threw us, Olivia added.

"It was strong, high-quality tiscan they were pushing. Damien obviously dealt with the ones in the warehouse, which was good, but unfortunately that means we are back at square one since I can't question them," Michael said.

"Do you know who was making the stuff?" Olivia asked.

"I was trying to find out when I got sloppy, and they found me poking around." Lukas had more than a hint of disgust in his tone. *I was following up on the Warlord's request about the slave trade.*

"I was wondering how you ended up in your predicament," Michael said. *I didn't mean for you to get yourself captured.*

"It's concealed by several layers of misdirection, but that warehouse is owned by the Kastler Consortium. In the past they used it for some of their less honest ventures," Lukas stared at him steadily, a glint in his eyes. *I decided it might be worthwhile to find out who they were trading with before I freed myself. Your problem child, however, intervened in that strategy.*

"It seems they are still engaged in business dealings in the shadows," Michael said. *For the best, if information is correct—you would have found yourself in Sylanna.*

Michael watched Lukas, who was too adept to give anything away other than a glimmer of amusement in his eyes at the comment. Michael mostly ignored those who engaged in less than honourable dealings, unless they brought attention to themselves. Of course, it helped that he didn't have to sort them out since, if they stepped too far out of line, Lukas and his people took care of them. Lukas ran the dealings in the shadows and crossing him was not a good idea. What most people didn't know was that Lukas worked for him, just as Ben and the twins did.

If I find out more, I'll pass the information to you and I'll clean up some of the smaller players in this mess. A hard glint flashed in his friend's eyes.

It would be appreciated, Michael said.

Lukas probably had more valuable commodities stashed away than Michael did, but in keeping with the role his friend was playing, Michael reached into his belt for coins to pay for the information.

"No need. The way I see it I'm still in Damien's debt." Lukas stood and took a step before looking back. "For what it is worth, I hope he lives."

"He will. He just wishes we'd let him die right now," Michael said.

"I can imagine." Lukas regarded Kesha, genuine warmth in his expression. "Stay safe, healer, and listen to the Warleader. People like me aren't nice to run into, but you have a friend in this one."

Lukas strode out through the front doors of the inn without a backwards glance. Michael transferred his gaze to Kesha, who stood frowning at the door as it closed.

"What did he mean? What type of person is he?" Kesha asked.

"Dagger for hire, I'd say, given the weapons he was carrying and probably similar other dealings that neither Olivia nor I care to look into."

"I didn't see a sword," Kesha said.

"Because he wasn't wearing one," Michael said.

"He was extremely well armed, though, with a variety of weapons on his person," Olivia explained. "It was why he was careful to keep his hands where we could see them."

"Also likely why he was the only other person in that cell besides Damien who was shackled." Michael shrugged.

"Oh, I didn't notice any of that." Kesha went and sat quietly in the corner.

"What's wrong, Kesha?" Michael asked.

"I really am a poor judge of character, aren't I?"

"Don't judge yourself so harshly. I think your senses are pretty good in that regard," Michael said.

"He means you no harm, and you were perfectly aware of it. I think it's something your gift as a healer lets you sense more than our own. That man is very good at disguising what he is," Olivia said.

"He's a dangerous man but, if anything, in the future I think he'll go out of his way to protect you to the best of his abilities," Michael said.

"I think you've made a friend," Olivia said.

"That is a rare thing with a man like him," Michael said.

Kesha still did not seem completely convinced. Michael sent a wave of reassurance at her. She knew he'd done so, but allowed her unhappiness to be soothed away.

"The Kastler Consortium really seems to keep coming up tied to all kinds of endeavours they shouldn't be."

"They do; first that mess in Vallantia, now this one as well? At least they will be easy enough to find."

"The local head will be at your father's ball, I'm sure," Michael said.

"Just as well I let you talk me into attending," Olivia said.

Michael relaxed into his chair, and picked up his forgotten mug to take a sip. Then rolled his eyes as he realised it was empty. Olivia chuckled and filled it up for him from the bottle on the table between them.

THIRTY-SEVEN

Nathanial swung his gaze back to Damien as he heard a crack and a surge in the veil. He winced at Damien's ragged, indrawn breath. The veil flickered like lightning all over him as it rushed back in. He, Michael, and Olivia had discussed this strategy, knowing it was a double-edged sword. If they shielded Damien fully from these veil attacks, it might save him some pain, but it would prolong his recovery. It wasn't just tiscan abuse that caused the frightening gaps in Damien's mind—the level and frequency of the veil attacks he was suffering could cause blackout periods as well. It was a sign he was getting closer to his final transition. That meant the longer Damien spent cut off from the veil, the sicker he'd feel. Allowing the veil to rush back into him again this way would hurt but along with the pain of it racing through his body would come healing. If it worked, it would probably take several cycles. Unfortunately it wasn't something that they could predict with certainty, but it would still be quicker than the alternative.

Nathanial rose from where he'd been lying on the bed closer to the door, then froze as a second volley of lightning danced over Damien's body. Damien threw back his head and screamed, physically and mentally in agony. This time Nathanial gasped, as Damien was suddenly up in front of him, flames dancing in his eyes but no signs of recognition. He hadn't even seen Damien move. It was a phenomenon Nathanial filed away to explore later when things were a little calmer.

Olivia, Michael, could you come here. Carefully, Nathanial whispered.

He's flipped out again? Olivia asked.

He has.

Nathanial tried to remain calm and unthreatening. Damien, or what had been Damien, was reacting on instinct, fuelled by pain. In this state, he'd kill anyone or anything he perceived as a threat.

Damien's lips peeled back in a snarl as the door opened, his blade in his hand as Michael and Olivia eased in. Nathanial's eyes widened at that feat. The blades hadn't even been in this room. It took a considerable amount of power to pull an object that wasn't even in the direct line of sight. Not to mention a knowledge of where the object was stored.

Is that what I was like? Michael asked.

Nathanial glanced across at Olivia and saw that shared memory of the time when Michael had been out of his head this way and suffering from blackouts. He'd killed more than one person who'd made the mistake of trying to restrain him before they'd learnt.

Exactly what you were like, Olivia said.

Sorry. Had no control over it and still have very little memory of what I did. Michael sounded embarrassed. *Except I remember the pain. It was like the veil was tearing me apart. Then nothing. Like it kicked me out of my head while something else took over.*

We could tell the moment you came back, Nathanial said.

There was always confusion; you didn't know what you'd done other than a few disjointed memories, Olivia said.

Nathanial was aware they were all subconsciously using the mindspeech equivalent of whispering. Not that it would make any difference to Damien. Talking loudly wasn't something that would trigger him. While they may have sounded to anyone else like were just reminiscing, in reality, they had focused all their attention on Damien while they slowly, gently, gathered in the veil.

As the veil intensified and danced around the room, Nathanial held his breath.

Oh, this isn't good.

It was that moment between one breath and the next when his intuition screamed. His own mental barriers flared on instinct, as did Michael's and Olivia's. Damien's knees buckled as more power charged into him. He collapsed to the ground, shrieking in agony, but this time it held a note that signalled he was back in his own head again. As suddenly as the excess power had appeared in the room, seeming to seek Damien, it faded. Nathanial breathed a sigh of relief that became a gasp as one moment Damien was curled up in a ball, radiating agony. The next, there was an empty space where he'd lain.

"Where the Powers did he go?" Olivia stared around the room, eyes wide.

"How...?"

"Wait," Michael ordered, holding up his hand.

Nathanial was relieved to see Olivia was equally disbelieving and suspicious, as they both regarded Michael.

"We need to find him..." Olivia said.

A look of relief washed over Michael's face and he reached out to grab each of them on the arm.

"I have, don't panic. As Damien said to me, it's easier to show you than tell you."

Michael's power flared. A blast of cold from the veil, greater than any he'd felt, brushed Nathanial's skin and everything went grey. He swallowed and scanned his surroundings, reassured to see Damien off to one side, with wisps of grey fog swirling around him.

This place, it's...

The veil, Olivia said.

As far as I've been able to work out, we're still right where we were standing, but not. If you concentrate, the grey fog will thin and you'll see the room.

Ah. I take it no one else can see us, though, Nathanial said.

Except Damien, Olivia said.

I think others like us could perceive us, but they'd have to know where and how to look, Michael said.

Olivia sank to her knees at Damien's side. Nathanial tensed until he saw Damien didn't resist as she pulled him into her arms. Damien clung to Olivia like a lifeline. Nathanial frowned as he saw the grey mist ripple and a soothing forest with a river burbling and rushing through appeared, replacing the grey mist. Like a small oasis in the middle of madness, the veil flickered between the soothing image and the nondescript grey mist.

What's happening to me? Damien asked.

Everything will be all right. I'm here. Olivia stroked Damien's temple with her fingertips as she spoke, waves of reassurance flowing between them.

Michael went to Damien's other side and sank down next to them. It fascinated Nathanial as a path seemed to form out of the greyness ahead of each step he took and the image of a forest complete with river rushing nearby solidified.

If it helps, I apparently went through the same thing. Not that I remember much about it, Michael said.

Nathanial was exasperated but stopped what he'd been

about to say. Somehow the distress from Damien's mind seemed to lessen.

Michael, we need to get him back. I would, but I don't know how, Olivia said.

Nathanial swore as, this time, both Olivia and Damien disappeared. Michael looked back to where the others had been and closed his eyes briefly.

It's all right, Damien just took them both back.

Michael grabbed his arm and once more the power rolled around him, and between one breath and the next, they ended up back in the room where they started.

"What's happening to me?" Damien asked.

"As far as we've been able to work out, the veil is overloading your body and brain. It knocks your conscious self to sleep. Then you run on survival instinct until something kicks you out of it," Olivia said.

"Let me guess, between those two moments I remember, I might end up killing everyone," Damien said.

"The only ones you've killed were those who drugged and imprisoned you, Kesha and the others," Nathanial said.

"They tell me the only people I killed when I went through this was anyone who was stupid enough to present as a threat," Michael said.

"So we all go through this? Why didn't you warn me?"

Damien turned his head to look at them both as he rested in Olivia's arms, exhausted.

"No, not all of us. Michael here is the only other one we've encountered who had these symptoms." Olivia's hand gently stroked his temple as she held him.

"So I'm in good company?" Damien laughed weakly.

"You need sleep," Olivia said.

"I always seem to need sleep."

"In this case, it's not the other problems, but the veil rushing back in after your tiscan overdose. It can hurt when it fluctuates like this, but your powers will settle again."

"It may not feel like it right now, but this is a good thing. You're on the road to recovery."

"We can do much more than the regular person, but I'm sure you've noticed we also sleep more."

"It's one reason, when we engage in bigger actions, that the Warlord has us camp in the middle of the other warbands."

Damien, who'd made it to his bed despite his protest about having to sleep all the time, paused, his brow furrowed.

"We do our best to protect the others riding into action and then they protect us when we're forced to sleep it off?" Damien asked.

"Pretty much."

"We can usually keep going if we need to, to a point, but it's best not to push it too far. You don't want to collapse into veil-fuelled sleep in the middle of a fight."

Damien laughed weakly as he lay back.

"That doesn't sound very healthy."

"It's not recommended. Now, sleep."

Nathanial watched on as Olivia once again pushed Damien down into sleep. As much as he complained, it was the best thing for Damien right now. It would also hopefully mean their problem child stayed right where they could see him. This disappearing act complicated the job of protecting Damien from himself even more.

THIRTY-EIGHT

Jaclyn returned to her own domain and couldn't help but throw her head back and laugh. Not even she had truly thought her brother and his wives would be that stupid. Yet in their haste to have her gone from the court, they'd given her everything she needed and more.

Her family stood, smiling uncertainly as she laughed.

Ricardo finally approached her, satisfaction and delight radiating from him as he caught her mood. She wrapped her arms around him and kissed him. As she expected, he responded enthusiastically. He always did and rarely needed prompting in other ways. At least not with her. Some of the other wives might have to work harder occasionally. Particularly since she wouldn't allow any of them to take his mind, the way her brother's wives had taken their husband's mind. That way, she was certain, led to madness.

"I take it that things went according to plan?" Ricardo's voice was low.

Jaclyn knew the last thing on his mind was really the attack they were about to launch. What he was imagining was dragging her off to bed, although he was doing an impressive job of trying to stay focused.

"It did. The idea of having the battle plans explained to him was something that didn't thrill him. He approved everything and even put it in writing with his seal."

"His wives let him do that?" Myra's eyes widened as she joined them.

"They did. They were too pleased with themselves." Jaclyn held up the rolled parchment, unfurling it as she handed it to Myra.

Myra's breath caught as she read the decree, eyes rising to meet Jaclyn's, and she laughed, handing the document to Ricardo.

"Now all we need to do is survive," Ricardo said.

"Come, it's time to discuss the rest of my plan," Jaclyn said.

She didn't relinquish her hold on Ricardo—she had plans with him later that had nothing to do with war—but led the way to her inner office. The squad of daggerwives formed up around them as she led the way back into the inner sanctum and the small private meeting room she favoured.

CHAPTER

THIRTY-NINE

Damien sat on the window seat, leaning against the wall, his head resting against the cool window as he gazed at the life passing by down on the streets below. While he slept, they'd relocated him. It told him more than anything how bad a state he was in that not only had he slept through the move, but he also hadn't even been confused about waking up somewhere different to where he'd fallen asleep. At least this time, he was still in the quarters of the Unwanted. Except they'd moved him to the room Michael had been using. He'd guessed the leadership had bigger rooms, particularly since they disappeared to them when they were having meetings. Right now, all three of them were sitting around discussing business.

Under normal circumstances, he'd have found the conversations between the leaders fascinating. They discussed everything, right down to the finer details, and then ran through the consequences. It certainly didn't hold with the commonly held belief he'd had from his childhood that their number just rode in and destroyed everyone and everything. Right now, it was hard for him to ignore the fact that the current problem they were discussing was him. Not that they were being rude. Since he'd gone out of his head, one of them always remained with him. When all three of them needed to be somewhere, that meant he had to be where they were. They just weren't sure if he was stable enough and if he was being honest, he didn't blame them. He didn't trust himself if they weren't present. He closed his eyes as they spoke, allowing the words to almost drift into the background.

"He needs to build up his confidence again," Olivia said.

"It's too soon to put that pressure on him. He can't care for himself right now, let alone anyone else. He's still blacking out and struggling to remember things from moment to moment," Nathanial said.

"It was the worst timing to lapse into using again with his powers surging on him," Michael said. "Although I trust him in everything except tiscan."

"Unfortunately, that stuff can be found just about everywhere in these parts without too much effort. I don't doubt there will be vials of the stuff in the castle, it's commonly used," Olivia said.

"At the moment he's too raw; if he encounters it again, without one of us there..." Nathanial trailed off.

"I'll use again. I wish I could say I wouldn't but, I can't." Damien didn't even turn from his observation of the street below as he spoke. "Right now, if there was a bottle of tiscan here on the table, all it would take would be for something else to draw your attention elsewhere. I'd drink it, probably all in one hit." Damien shuddered.

His body reacted to him even thinking about tiscan. Every part of his body was screaming as pain shot through him. His shielding was so bad they couldn't help but be aware of his reaction. Damien gritted his teeth and resisted doubling over as his stomach cramped. Before he'd had his relapse, he hadn't thought he really had a problem. It was under control. He could choose not to use the drug and, even when he had consumed it, he'd just had a sip here and there. He controlled his use. It didn't control him. Or so he'd told himself. Now he knew without a doubt he was wrong. He didn't control the drug. The drug controlled him.

"Not sure if it helps, but it took me several relapses to come to that conclusion," Nathanial said in response to thoughts he hadn't verbalised. "How in the Powers are we meant to go to the ball to sort out this mess? We can't exactly leave him behind."

"We bring him with us." Michael shrugged.

"What if he loses it in the middle of the court?" Nathanial asked.

"Then I guess my family might just finally learn to fear us. Don't look so concerned, Damien. I won't be worried if you dispose of a few of them," Olivia said, her tone overly cheery given the subject matter.

Despite himself, her comment caused him to laugh, particularly since she was being absolutely sincere. He had to admit that while his cravings for tiscan hadn't eased, after sleeping like the dead, he was feeling better. Which was saying something. It seemed their theory of letting the veil overload his body and mind was working. Even if he potentially became homicidal and left another terrifyingly blank space in his memory. Damien went back to watching the teeming life in the street below his vantage point, and let their conversation fade to the background again. He was here because they didn't trust him not to disappear on them and use again. Not because they needed his input.

As exhaustion seeped into him again, he rested his head back against the window, closing his eyes. At a hand on his shoulder, he opened them again to see Olivia.

"If you fall asleep here you'll only collect another set of

bruises when you fall off the window seat. Go to bed, sleep, you'll be more comfortable," Olivia said.

Damien contemplated the enormous four-poster bed on the other side of the room. There was a certain amount of guilt that plagued him, knowing he'd kicked Michael out of his bed. Even if he hadn't been a part of the decision-making process that had caused the move. It was an amusing mental image to think of all three of them trying to squeeze into the room that had been assigned him to have a meeting. Olivia had commented to him they'd tried it and it had proven to be a frustrating exercise, particularly when they needed to look at maps.

He half rolled off the seat, Olivia steadying him as he stood. Damien made his way across the room, aware they all watched his progress. He took it as a small victory that he made it the entire way without incident. He climbed up onto the bed and sank into it the soft mattress without even bothering with the covers. When he woke, they'd probably be over him anyway, since his keepers took much better care of him than he thought he'd earned.

FORTY

At the sound of the door, thinking a servant was bringing him food, Steven walked towards the small circular table on the far side of the room. It was amazing really. Once he'd settled some issues with his parents, they'd started serving him again. He'd been treating them like spun glass, fearing that with the smallest slight they'd disappear again. A couple of weeks without them had proven to be enough as far as he was concerned. As the face of the person who'd entered registered, and not that of a servant, he sprung up from his chair. Rushing forward, he hugged the other to him.

"Evan, damn it, how did you get in here?" Steven asked.

"Used the servants' entrance." Evan shrugged.

"They just let you do that?"

"I took a box of kitchen supplies from one of the delivery carts and just walked in. Their guards didn't so much as blink."

Steven was astonished and dragged his friend over to the sitting area. Pushing him down onto a chair, he rushed over to the sideboard where a collection of his favourite drinks were kept and poured a drink for each of them. He handed one to Evan, and they clinked goblets before taking the mandatory sip.

"How has it been outside these walls?" Steven asked.

"The Kastlers have their thugs all over the town. People have taken to staying indoors after dark."

"Why? Is it worse at night?"

"Rumour has it people keep going missing off the streets. No one knows where they've gone or what happened to them."

"They think the Kastlers are behind it?"

"Who else? It got worse after they took over. I was going to ask what action you were going to take, but I see that is pointless."

"Our guards are dead or locked up in the cells. We're virtually prisoners in our own estate," Steven said.

"I worked that part out. There is another part to that rumour."

Steven stared at his friend wondering how everything had deteriorated so rapidly.

"I take it I'm not going to like this part?"

"You know how the Kastlers were trading with Sylanna?"

"Don't remind me about my part in that little venture."

"It's rumoured the coin they are using is *people*. Mostly men."

Steven's eyes widened. To engage in the flesh trade was a death sentence.

"That's who's going missing? Men? And they're being sold to Sylanna?"

Steven felt like someone had just thrown him in the river in the middle of winter. He'd never thought it could be worse than life under the Warlord's rule. Apparently, that was another thing he'd been wrong about. Steven rubbed his face and almost groaned at what he was about to ask his friend to do.

"I don't believe I'm saying this, but do you know anyone that can get out of Vallantia and go to Michael?"

Evan shrugged and ambled over to the drink cart to help himself to the bottle, bringing it back to refill his glass and waggling it in offer to Steven, who accepted a refill.

"We can't trust any of the traders, the Kastler Consortium have links to them all."

"Even I'm not that stupid."

"Not sure if they'll do it, but the most likely to get through, that Michael will trust, would be the twins. I'm not sure they'll want to leave their father alone here given the situation, but I can ask."

"I'd say their father could stay here while they're gone, but I don't think that would be safe given the Kastlers have taken over my home," Steven said.

"I can offer him a place at mine, I guess. I doubt Father will mind and so far, Kastler's thugs have left me alone."

"They probably still think we're onside with them."

"Trust me, I will not go out of my way to disillusion them of that."

"Me neither. What they don't know can't hurt us." Steven gazed out the window, troubled. "Do you think Michael will come and help? I mean, I've been an idiot."

Steven looked at Evan as his friend leant back into his chair, laughing weakly. He would be indignant, but he was used to Evan pointing out he was being stupid.

"Of course he will. The Warlord is not just going to sit back and allow the Kastlers to claim his territory."

"The Kastlers say the Sylannians are going to launch an attack, which will keep the Warlord and Michael too busy to notice until it is too late," Steven said.

"For them to be that certain they must think the attack is going to happen over the other side, towards Callenhain. I'll pass that on to the twins."

Steven was pleased he'd at least partly redeemed himself

with that tiny piece of information. Although he guessed the twins would have a way to track down his brother's whereabouts, regardless. He sat back and sipped his drink, not at ease but at least more confident about the situation smoothing out in the end. Evan was correct. Michael would come, probably with all the Warlord's fighting warbands at his back. All they had to do was stay alive long enough for his brother to get here. For the first time he could remember, he was actually looking forward to the Warleader, his brother, and the warbands he led paying a visit.

STEVEN ENTERED HIS PARENTS' outer rooms without fanfare. He'd made this a habit, so much so Kastler's people didn't pay any attention to him at all. Seeing them sitting in their usual chairs by the window, he paused, giving them both a half bow. They welcomed him and gestured to a chair, he hesitated a half step before continuing. That was a recent development. He couldn't remember the last time his parents had been genuinely pleased to see him. He took the seat they'd indicated; it was his usual one as well, although on this occasion the side table beside the chair had reappeared.

"What did Evan have to report?" his father asked.

Steven opened his mouth to ask how his father had known his friend had managed to sneak into the estate, then closed it again. He contemplated at them both, eyes narrowing.

"The servants."

"Of course. Very little happens that they don't see and hear," his mother said.

Steven processed that little piece of information and decided Evan wasn't as clever as he'd thought at being able to sneak in. The servants probably recognised him instantly and did their best to make sure he was hidden in their midst. He ducked his head. It was a brave thing they'd done. If the mercenaries had realised who Evan was they would have killed the servants, even though Evan himself, as the child of one of the wealthy elite of Vallantia, might have survived.

"He said the townspeople are scared, rumours of many of them, mostly men, disappearing in the night." He took a breath, not wanting to admit the next part, but he had to. "Whispers around the city say the coin the Kastlers have been using to trade with the Sylannians for silk... is people."

As the silence stretched, he looked up to see the horrified expressions on his parents' faces. For once, it seemed he'd shocked them.

"They dare..." his father said.

"It's what people think. Not so shocking when you consider that before the Warlord came, we had indentured as well," Steven said.

He swallowed and closed his mouth abruptly; he wasn't sure what had possessed him to mention that little blight in their past.

"We did. It was what was done at the time," his mother said.

"We didn't take new slaves after your grandfather died, but I admit I didn't free the ones we had when I took over," his father said.

"It was common practice, and many believe why the Warlord embarked on wide-scale conquest," his mother said.

"Did you know this when you helped them?" his father asked.

"They mentioned trade with Sylanna after they took me out into the tributaries, but no, I didn't know what they were trading."

"Are you sure?"

"Even I would have come to you if I'd known what they were really doing," Steven said.

Steven tried not to take the question personally. Before recent times, even he would have suspected himself of ignoring that little detail for his own self-interest.

"I'm glad that as self-involved as you were back then, there was a line," his mother said.

"I asked Evan to send someone to Michael, to tell him what is happening here."

"That is a risk to him if the Kastlers' people find out," his mother said.

"I know. He knows. He suggested the twins."

"They're a good choice."

Steven stared at them for a moment. He shouldn't have been surprised his parents were already aware of the connection between his brother and his childhood friends.

"We thought so. Evan thinks they might hesitate, fearing for their father in their absence. So, he's going to invite the Smith to go to his family estate for the duration."

"You think he'll be safe there?"

"Evan tells me even the Kastlers haven't really touched the major houses too much. They're mostly barricading themselves in their homes, particularly at night, but they are intact."

Steven froze as a servant placed a drink on the side table for him, while another did the same for his parents. He wondered how he'd missed them entering the room. Then he dismissed the instant fear. If their servants were traitors, it was highly likely they'd all be under further restrictions than they currently were. He picked up the glass and sipped it. Waiting. His parents were considering options, probably even having a private conversation he wasn't party to. So, he contented himself with staring out of the window and the glorious colours that lit up the sky as the sun fell. It seemed so cruel that it could look so stunning when life had spiralled out of control. Of course, he realised this was a new pastime. He'd never paid it much attention before. It was a consequence of being mostly restricted to his room or his parents' room, and perhaps finally growing up.

"In the morning, you'll revert to your former arrogant self," his mother ordered.

"To what purpose?" Steven didn't bother to protest. His mother was much smarter than he was. It was probably why his father would often lapse into silence, allowing his mother to guide the conversation.

"Make them believe you will allow them to use you as their figurehead. In return for certain favours," his mother said. "I doubt they will completely trust you, but it may put you close enough to hear some of their plans."

Steven took a moment to breathe in an attempt to calm the nerves that rose in him.

"As you wish." Steven regarded the servants, before shifting his attention back to his parents. "It would probably be best if the servants mostly deserted me again, to show their displeasure in my actions."

"It will appear they have done so, but you will know they have not. It will be a carefully disguised ruse to hide the truth," his mother said.

His mother focused on the servants, who stood quietly to one side. Both bowed in acknowledgment without saying a word. Steven stared at his parents as if seeing them for the first time. What the Kastlers saw, what most people saw, were two old people—one of them a useless cripple, the other a disfigured old woman. They couldn't be more wrong.

There was power in Vallantia and it was only just awakening after a long hibernation.

CHAPTER
FORTY-ONE

Olivia poked her tongue out at Michael and Nathanial as they grinned at her from their lounging position on the couch. Each of them was perfectly at ease. Even Damien simply sat in what had become his accustomed perch on the window seat, without a hint of concern. She was the one pacing with nervous energy.

"Calm down," Nathanial said.

"Seriously, you display fewer nerves going into battle," Michael said.

"Killing invaders and terrorising new conquests is something I'm well equipped to do," Olivia replied without pausing in her path across the room.

"You've been to more than one ball in your life," Michael said, his lips twitching.

"We're not all stepping off into the void," Nathanial said.

"It's all right for you two. You aren't the ones who have to wear a dress," Olivia grumbled.

"Either the people you are expecting are here or we're being besieged by a very unlikely lot of people," Damien said.

Olivia stopped and regarded Damien, who sat peering down at the street below. His word choice gave her pause.

"What do you mean, besieged?"

"There's a lot of them. More than just one woman and her husband, which I gather was what you were all expecting," Damien said.

Olivia's eyes widened and she crossed over to the window. Placing a hand on Damien's shoulder, she leaned forward to peer out, before pressing her face against his shoulder to block out the view and groaning dramatically. She swung around to glare at Michael.

"What have you got me into? Damien is not overstating this. There's a virtual horde out there." Olivia glared at Michael, who simply chuckled at her reaction.

"Between us and the rest of our people, there are quite a few of us." Nathanial didn't quite laugh but his lips twitched suspiciously like he wanted to but was restraining himself.

"Why do I feel you're going to make this more than a one-time thing?" Olivia's eyes narrowed as she switched her gaze between both Michael and Nathanial.

A knock at the door forestalled any answer the two might make, and Michael granted entrance. Olivia tried to plaster a pleasant expression on her face as the Smith's daughter, Jenna, her husband, and what seemed like a veritable army of helpers bearing fabrics, pins, measures and notepads entered the room. She was perfectly aware she must have failed miserably at her attempt at grace when Jenna's eyes sparkled, dimples showing in her cheeks as she traded knowing smiles with both Michael and Nathanial. Olivia backed up as Michael rose and, without a word, wrapped his arms around Jenna in a fierce hug.

"It's so good to see you. It's been far too long," Jenna said.

"It has, but I'd rather not have anyone go after you to get at me." Michael nodded a greeting at her husband, Theo.

"Oh, please. Who would dare?"

"I'd rather not find out. The sheer number of stupid people out there in the world would surprise you," Michael said.

It never ceased to amaze Olivia how much tension drained out of Michael when he was reunited with one of the few who he counted as a friend from his old life. No matter how many years stretched between those occasions, it was like they'd never been separated at all. Jenna had been Michael's first childhood love. It had been a childish affair between the two, but Olivia couldn't help but wonder what would have occurred had the Warlord not appeared. Olivia observed that Theo just smiled indulgently, without even a hint of jealousy, even though he knew the history between the two as well as she did.

"So, your message indicated you needed suitable but elegant attire to attend a ball at the Strafford estate?" Jenna stepped back, her head cocked slightly as she looked up at Michael.

"We do," Michael said.

"Preferably not hideous," Olivia muttered.

"I would also appreciate functional if the bounds of the height of current fashion can accommodate it," Nathanial said.

"They don't, but we'll make it work," Jenna said then waved one of the women forward. "This is Shana, she's a talented dressmaker and a friend. I thought the assistance of someone who knows a little more about fashion than we do would be useful," Jenna said.

"Easily done for you men," Shana said absently as she stared at Olivia. "You, however, will be a welcome challenge. Current women's fashion in Callenhain is terrible."

"What do you think? Should we start with the men since their attire will prove to be easier?" Jenna asked.

"Measuring is the same, regardless, but more time with Olivia, particularly with the colour swatches..." Shana trailed off as she continued to stare.

Olivia shifted uneasily. "Black…"

"With the symbol of the Unwanted stitched into it." Michael added.

"Of course, but even the Warlord allows himself some colour occasionally when he's out of his armour," Jenna said firmly. "The Rathadon colour is blue, I believe."

"I'll not be seen in my house colours," Olivia said.

"I also don't have a house colour." Nathanial shrugged.

"Hmmm… We'll come up with something," the woman said, and pulled out a tape measure, gesturing for Nathanial to step forward.

Olivia sighed and slumped into the lounge, guessing she had no choice but to give into the inevitable.

Olivia stood as the women and men fussed around her, trying to at least pretend she wasn't irritated by this whole production. Her attempts to not show her frustration weren't helped by the clear amusement on display by both Michael and Nathanial, who'd gone through their own fittings with much more grace.

Even Damien had taken the poking and prodding without complaint. He'd simply endured the experience, then put himself back to bed when they dismissed him. At first, Jenna and her crew had tiptoed around and spoke in hushed tones. Until they reassured them that the building could probably fall down and Damien would sleep through it.

Jenna, her husband, and indeed their whole extended family fell onto the project with frightening glee. Olivia had been measured and bossed around, different types and colours of fabric held up against her skin with conversations about light, shade and drape. She didn't even attempt to make a pretence of understanding.

"Don't look so depressed, Olivia. Trust me, you won't recognise yourself," Jenna said as she caught her gaze in the mirror.

"That's what I'm afraid of," Olivia muttered.

"Come on, it's not that bad," Michael said.

Olivia contemplated responding but decided both Michael and Nathanial would get far too much amusement out of the exchange. Instead, she ignored them both and focused on Jenna.

"Are you sure I'll be able to fight in whatever you come up with if I need to?" Olivia asked.

"It's a ball, Olivia, not a full pitched battle, but yes," Jenna said.

"You know my family. The possibilities for mistakes are endless."

"It could be worse," Michael said.

"How?"

"We could have left the dress selection to your mother." Michael's eyebrows rose as he met her eyes in the mirror.

Olivia shuddered, remembering the last monstrosity that had been left in her room on a previous visit to the estate.

"I would never inflict that on you. Your mother has appalling taste," Jenna said.

"That is an understatement." Theo chuckled.

Olivia sighed and held her arm up obligingly as Shana measured it again. She was sure they had repeated this procedure several times over.

Finally, the fussing horde stepped back.

"Your suffering is over, for now." Jenna chuckled at Olivia, not taking offence at all as she sighed dramatically. "We'll check that our staff downstairs has finished measuring up your people and be back in a couple of days with your clothes."

"Thank you. We appreciate your help," Nathanial said.

He at least sounded sincere.

"Thank you. I'm grateful, honestly. I just hate being fussed over and being dressed up like a child's toy," Olivia said.

"Don't worry, I swear you will love it."

Much to Olivia's shock, Jenna stepped forward and hugged her, then ushered her people out of the rooms. Relief flooded her that the ordeal was over and Olivia half contemplated collapsing onto the other half of Damien's bed. Then, thinking better of it, she flopped on the long couch instead.

"Granted, he was up all morning, but do you think he'll be well enough for this drama, or will one of us have to stay behind?" Olivia asked.

"He'll be fine as long as he rests during the day," Nathanial said.

"I'll wager we can move on after we've sorted this mess out as well," Michael said.

"I guess he can be relieved of any camp duties. So, all he has to do is ride and sleep," Olivia said.

"He should be able to manage that, and he's not to go off hunting either. It's too soon," Michael said.

"Beginning to use the veil again will help to speed his recovery."

"Keeping occupied with an activity, even if it's only riding, will help take his mind off tiscan as well," Nathanial said.

Olivia wished she had some way to smooth Damien's path through his addiction issues. Unfortunately, she agreed with both Michael and Nathanial. Short of the hope that getting strong enough in his powers would counteract the poison as it had with Nathanial, there wasn't much they could do.

FORTY-TWO

Samuel lay with the breeze wafting through the open shutters as several of his wives massaged him. The fragrance from the oil they used and the play of their hands, working out the knots in his muscles, should have been relaxing. Yet in his head he could hear whispers filled with pain that remained meaningless and without context.

My son, why?

No!

Brother, please...

Traitor...

Images flickered through his brain. Lifeless bodies strewn everywhere. Blood dripping from blades onto the polished wooden floorboards. They were images that both confused him and yet seemed oddly familiar. Like he was looking through a lens that distorted everything. These were things his wives bade him to forget.

Yet increasingly they haunted him, both waking and sleeping.

He'd done those things, invaded this house of his queen, his mother. He and his wives had killed her, her husband, all the wives and his sisters. Or so he'd thought. They'd missed one.

Jaclyn.

His wives thought that was what ultimately distressed him. They routinely cleansed the images, and sounds from his mind, making him forget. It even worked. For a time. When the fragments of memories broke through the cracks of their control, he feared they were descending the path to madness. He wasn't even sure who it was among them that was cracking first. He had no way to tell if it was him sliding into madness and dragging his wives with him, or if it was it one of his wives dragging him and all of them into the spiral of madness. Connected as they all were, it was hard—if not impossible—to work out. It was possible it was the fault of all of them rather than one of them.

Please, not now. I'm not ready to die yet, Samuel whispered. It was only a quiet plea. In the back corner of his mind, whispered so none of his wives would notice.

He shuddered, thinking what they'd do if they discovered what he was thinking. It might just cause them to cleanse his mind once more. Or this time it might trigger them to cleanse the court. It had happened so many times before. After all, it was what had prompted his own belief that it was time for him to ascend the throne. He remembered that distinctly. Yet the act itself, that horrible nightmare, remained mostly obscured.

As he heard the doors to his chambers open, he almost breathed a sigh of relief as the whispering and images were banished from his mind. Not through any action of his wives, but simply because he had something to focus on. Sometimes, like now, that even worked.

Soon.

His own quiet inner voice mocked him. Soon, that would not be the case. He rolled off the bed, raising his arms as his wives pulled his robe on for him. Walking over to the couches, he sat, a flurry of activity behind him ensuring the cushions were arranged perfectly as he eased back. The one in front of him waiting for his pleasure was one of his wives. In name. He'd never slept with her, and he doubted he ever would. That really wasn't her function. She was one of his spies and as such she gained the instant attention of him and his firstwife as soon as she made an appearance. Samuel didn't bother to call for Chelsie to join him. One of the other wives would have done so as soon as the spy had shown up in the inner court requesting an audience. Samuel was just starting to get impatient when the doors to his inner private rooms opened and his firstwife joined them.

For appearance's sake, he held out his hand to her. Even though he really wasn't in any kind of mood today. She accepted it, smiling at him as she slipped onto the couch and into his arms. His firstwife played this game of pretending there was nothing wrong extremely well. Not that anyone else would be able to tell by looking at her, but Chelsie was out of sorts, even though she appeared relaxed and happy to be disturbed from whatever she'd been up to. Still, she could turn his mind away from his troubles and make him interested if she chose. Sometimes she allowed him the dignity of wallowing, for a small space of time.

"What is it?" Samuel asked.

"There is unease and whispers in the lower caste, my husband," the spy said.

"What whispers?" Chelsie asked, stirring in his arms, suddenly seeming to pay attention. The whispers wouldn't be good or else this report wouldn't be happening. For this to be something springing from the lower caste was unusual.

"There is a house somewhere in the outer island. Many men have been seen, in the beds of the lesser. It is said they are barbarian men. That the house is flouting the law and engaging in undisciplined breeding with the barbarians, without sanction or control."

Samuel's anger flared and he surged to his feet. Crashing glass suggested Chelsie had thrown the glass she'd been drinking from as she stood too.

"We are at war with the barbarians and this house dares to consort with them without our approval?" Samuel snarled.

"It is what is being whispered, my king. I don't know this from anything I have seen myself," the spy said.

"I'm sure there's an explanation—"

The words halted in the throat of the lesser wife who moments before had been massaging him, as Chelsie's daggers flashed, silencing her forever. Samuel stared at her as she crumpled to the floor, a pool of red blood spreading out around her. He felt nothing for the woman. She was his wife, but there were so many of them and he didn't really know her. As he stared at her, half-remembered images flickered in his mind, confusing his reality between the past and now. He probed his own mind, trying to work out how he felt about her death. Or the death of his mother so long ago. He reached the rather stark conclusion that he didn't really care at all. Samuel tried to push back the anger that assaulted him. He couldn't tell if it was his own, or his wife's, or both. Samuel's eyes narrowed as he thought of anyone disobeying him. Even those of an insignificant lower caste house.

"Send for my commander. I have a task for her before she departs for the barbarian lands," Samuel snarled.

The anger crashed over his attempts to keep it at bay, flooding his mind until he didn't care anymore whose it really was.

FORTY-THREE

Olivia shifted in her seat, then settled with a sigh as the man in front of her swatted her on the shoulder. As far as she was concerned, he was engaged in arcane arts with pots of powders and slathering pastes on her face, while someone else was working on her hair. Apparently, from the horrified look they'd given her, a simple braid just would not do. So she'd sat as directed while they all buzzed about her. Others fussed over her nails, smoothing out the chipped, rough edges and painting colour on them.

Finally, they all stood back, admiring their handiwork. After a few more touches to her hair, they had her stand while Shana stepped forward with black and deep-green fabric spilling over their arms. Two of the women removed the simple robe they had given her to wear while they messed around with her hair and make-up. She only hoped she didn't look as hideous as some women she'd seen wearing the stuff. Shana bustled around her, buttoned, and tied her into her gown. Given how many people fussed around her to get her ready for the function tonight, she found herself grateful this was a rarity. The thought of having to go through a production like this every day made her shudder.

The upper bodice fit like a glove, but it was soft and pliable instead of the tight restrictive fabrics of current fashion that made it hard to do anything more strenuous than sip a beverage from a glass or eat a few mouthfuls of superb food at a banquet. In this dress, she had a full range of movement, meaning she could wield her weapons. Better yet, the bodice was flexible and allowed her to breathe. From the waist down, the fabric spilled, seeming to flow to ankle length. There was room in the skirts of the dress to lunge and, because they weren't floor length, she would not trip over them.

"Trust me, Olivia, you'll be able to fight in this and the skirts won't tangle around your legs. You'll also have full range of motion if you need it in your upper body, so you won't have to modify your fighting style." Jenna's green eyes sparkled in clear amusement.

"I'll have to take your word for it," Olivia said. "Although hopefully I won't have to find out."

Gesturing for the others to step back, Jenna stepped forward and strapped the new weapon's belt around Olivia's waist. An ornate affair of fine interlinking chain. One by one, Jenna carefully presented Olivia with her weapons, which she slipped into their appropriate sheaths. Olivia knew she shouldn't be surprised that the fragile-looking weapons belt was strong enough to hold her weapons: this was Jenna's work. The woman was her father's daughter, after all. Finally, Jenna stepped back with an air of satisfaction.

At a gesture from Shana, Olivia let out a slow breath. She'd been steadfastly ignoring the large mirror on one side of the room. She stopped mid-step. The woman who looked back at her didn't look foolish or out of place. Not like she'd feared, anyway. Olivia realised that somehow in her mind, she'd thought she would look like the little girl she'd once been, fussed over and dressed like a doll. The elegant woman who gazed out at her was as far away from that as it was possible to be. Black with deep green, threaded with silver, culminating in the sword and flame emblazoned on her chest. Olivia watched as power passed from her to the silver woven into her garments. The silver-blue stream of power sparkled as it flared, racing its way along the threads in her gown until it reached the insignia of the Unwanted. The small silver sword flared blue, buried in the stylised flames that glowed red and seemed to flicker with a life of its own. While it must be her own mind that controlled it, the action hadn't been a conscious one. Aware that those around her were staring at her, eyes wide at her display of energy, she reined in her wayward powers.

"My thanks to you all. You've outdone yourselves," Olivia said.

As several of those around her blushed at the compliment, she straightened her shoulders, taking a settling breath. Now to see how everyone else reacted. Olivia was certain they had been outfitted hours ago and were down in the sitting room waiting for her to make an appearance. Although she was certain even they had taken more time to dress than they normally would have.

She went down the hallway, hand resting on the banister, appreciating that she didn't have to hike up the skirts to negotiate her way down the stairs. Reaching the bottom, she entered the sitting room off to one side, where the team waited for her.

As she entered, all noise in the room stopped abruptly and eyes stared at her. Olivia kept herself still and hoped her blush didn't show through the pastes and powders that had been applied to her face. Perhaps they were good for something after all. Michael stood and wordlessly swept a bow in her direction, followed closely by Nathanial, who mimicked the move expertly.

Michael's clothing mirrored his family colours, a deep blue with the Unwanted's colours of black and the same silver strands threaded through it as her own. Nathanial didn't have a house colour, but she saw they'd selected a greyish blue colour, which offset the black and silver of his attire. The others of the Unwanted who would accompany them all wore the black and silver with woven threads of blue, green, and grey to show their allegiance. The cleverness of Jenna and her partner was apparent in the design and colours they chose. She stood with Michael and Nathanial and on either side of her, their individual colours showing they had leadership roles without having to say it.

"Elegant and deadly. Just as we ordered," Michael said.

"Beautiful, you forgot beautiful," Nathanial added.

"All right, I admit it I was wrong; we don't look half bad." Hearing a huff of indignation, Olivia turned to see Jenna behind her.

"I predict you will all stun the ball and start a new wave of fashion," Jenna said.

"Ah, and not so coincidentally prompt calls for your services and fabrics from the wealthy?" Olivia asked.

"Perhaps, but theirs won't quite be like yours," Jenna said.

"In what way?" Nathanial asked.

"You probably don't realise it's not a common addition in the clothing of the wealthy, but yours has fine mesh in the bodice. Just like Father works into your fighting leathers," Jenna said.

"The placement of the sword and flame covers the heart," Olivia said, the sword and flame sparkling as she brushed her fingers over them.

"Correct, with more layered beneath," Jenna said.

"So, not as good protection wise as our actual fighting leathers, but substantially better than normal formal wear," Nathanial said.

"I have a little of my father's talent at weaving metals," Jenna said.

"Your ability to weave the metal just like your father and brothers will remain a closely guarded secret," Michael said.

"It's the veil. Can't explain, really, but it is in the metal if you know how to listen. It responds to manipulation." Jenna blushed and her fingers fluttered, as if she were pushing away the compliment.

"I'll take your word for it, as I do your father's and brother's," Michael conceded, clearly amused. "I also think your idea of 'little talent' is everyone else's idea of being extremely gifted."

"Enough of this stalling. We need to get moving." Nathanial presented his arm to Olivia. "If you will allow me to escort you, my lady?"

Olivia rolled her eyes, but couldn't help responding to Nathanial's infectious grin. She laid her hand on his forearm. Michael stepped up to her other side and the three of them walked from the inn to the carriages that awaited them in the courtyard. It was one advantage of being the ranking member of the family here in Callenhain. She could commandeer carriages. While she might have agreed to wear a dress, she wasn't even going to bother trying to ride her horse in one.

CHAPTER

FORTY-FOUR

Liliana tuned out the ongoing argument. The spats between the daggerwives and underwives as both groups jostled for supremacy had been going on ever since the nearby house dealing with the barbarians had been uncovered. Liliana was relieved as she read Jaclyn's response to her report. The First's words were the only authority she needed.

"Enough!"

The silks hissed as they slithered and snapped into place around her, forming her armour, with a faint mental hum. Her eyes glittered as she regarded the underwives. Little did these underwives know, but she could control their silks as well, if she wished it. It was a trait she shared with Myra, and a skill that helped to keep them all alive.

"Primewife…" The senior underwife's eyes darted around her fellow underwives as she swallowed.

"The First has made her decision. Our house will deal with the traitors, and we will stay put until advised otherwise."

"But the safety of the children," the woman protested.

"The care and protection of the children of the house remains

267

with those of us here and hinges on our whereabouts remaining hidden."

"The traitor house has drawn attention here..."

"Which Firstwife Jaclyn will deal with before she proceeds with the campaign against the barbarians." Liliana gazed around those present. "I remind you I am primewife. We will follow the direction of our firstwife. Any who seek to disobey, who put the lives of the children in our care at risk, will be put to the blade by my orders."

One and all they were uneasy, their shock and resistance holding for but a moment before it crumbled in the face of her threat. Liliana forced herself to calm down, reminding herself that despite the bickering and separate camps, they all feared for the safety of their family. The underwife finished reading the orders from their First, before nodding at Liliana, her eyes troubled.

"Yes, Primewife."

The woman's concession was barely a whisper, but Liliana had won.

"I wish to be reunited with the rest of our family as much as the rest of you, but when the attack on the nearby island launches, we will stay well clear. Not even a hint of us being here must be seen. By anyone. Not even our own." Liliana dismissed the underwives, and her attention then shifted to the head of the daggerwives. "Keep a careful watch on proceedings at the traitor house. If you believe there is anything that may hinder or harm our firstwife when she launches her attack, you will inform me immediately."

"Yes, Primewife."

Liliana pushed the argument from her mind and went back to the outer room to continue her exercises. She wondered how long the peace here in their court in exile would last this time.

FORTY-FIVE

Olivia gazed out of the window of the carriage. She had to admit it was a novelty to ride in such a fashion, but she found it tedious just sitting in the close confines of the cabin. While in normal circumstances she'd have preferred riding her horse, at least she wasn't in exile in the confines of the carriage by herself. Michael, Nathanial, and Damien had joined her, while the squad of members who'd drawn protection detail tonight rode around them. They didn't normally take a protection detail with them, but Michael had explained it was all about appearances. On this, she'd trust his instinct. Somehow, even though he'd been torn from his family the same as she had been, he'd retained the ability to blend in with the rich and powerful in their world much better than she had.

The carriages were clearly identifiable as belonging to the Strafford family, but the occupants were just as easily identifiable as the Unwanted. Particularly since they hadn't drawn the curtains on the windows of the carriage. Their passing had attracted the curious stares of those still in the streets at this hour. A combination of the strangeness of seeing some of them riding in the Strafford carriages and the fine gear they were all wearing made the commoners forget their usual fear despite the insignia of the Unwanted, clearly on display.

Damien, alone out of the four of them, seemed to be enjoying the ride. Olivia traded amused glances with both Michael and Nathanial. Of course, it was the first time he'd been out of the confines of their accommodation in a couple of weeks.

It's the first time he's ridden in a carriage like this in his whole life, Nathanial said.

The clattering of the hooves on the cobblestones as they drew into the courtyard, their guard taking point, and the flare of lamps in the outer courtyard caused her to draw in a breath.

"This is just a different type of battle," Michael said.

Olivia closed her eyes, allowing the wave of reassurance he sent to calm her nerves, and took another breath as the carriage drew to a halt. As the doors opened, Nathanial and Michael preceded her out before Michael held out a hand to her. Sudden amusement flooded her, and she placed her hand in his, allowing him to assist her out of the carriage.

Careful to keep her gaze ahead, she ignored the stillness of her family's guards in the courtyard. She could feel their shock as their party crossed the intervening space and made their way up the stairs to the ornate double wooden doors. A light application of the veil from Nathanial opened the doors before the guards stationed on them could do so. With a barely perceptible hesitation the guards snapped to attention as they sailed through.

As they strode across the large foyer to the ballroom, those on the ballroom doors pushed them open. The herald rapped on the floor announcing her arrival as they entered the room. Olivia ignored the sudden silence that spread around the clustered rich merchant families. One and all turning to stare at them. With Michael and Nathanial on either side a half step behind her but keeping pace, she walked towards the centre of the grand hall, their booted feet overloud on the stone floors, to where her parents and brother stood. Prior to her arrival disrupting the proceedings, she was sure all of them had been basking in the adoration of their guests.

"Olivia, gentlemen, I'm so glad you joined us." Her father fixed a pleasant expression on his face.

It was a greeting empty of any genuine warmth. Their presence here was calculated by her family to increase their own standing and security. If the Warlord's most trusted Warleader and his two second-in-command warriors graced their halls, it added to the prestige and safety of the family. The fact that one of those seconds was their own daughter was a situation they didn't quite know how to handle. They flip-flopped between trying to ingratiate themselves with her to doing their level best to ignore her entirely. It was Michael's presence that her father cared for. Her mother pursed her lips, eyes cast down before she looked demurely back up. Olivia couldn't work out if the woman was batting her eyelashes at Michael or Nathanial.

Both of us. Michael kept his amusement from showing on his face although his eyes sparkled.

She's confused which of us she should pick as her quarry. Nathanial's own tone was dry. *Huh, I was right. She just noticed Damien as well. Now she's really in a quandary.*

Olivia choked back her amusement. How her mother possibly thought any of the men would take her seriously was beyond her. Her mother had to know by now that both men were aware she was only thinking of the influence she imagined she could wield, if she was having a liaison with one of them. Steeling herself, Olivia gazed at her father coolly and presented her hand, the silver ring with the Strafford crest glinting on her finger. She rarely wore it, but the family title was hers by the Warlord's decree. It was an old gesture. The demand of an apology from a subordinate for wrongs committed. A collective gasp rippled around the room before settling into shocked silence. Her father froze, eyes darting from her to Michael and Nathanial. Swallowing, he bowed slowly over her hand to kiss the ring on her finger, his neck exposed, giving the opportunity for his life to be ended to expunge the honour debt she demanded. His lips brushed the family crest, signifying a subordinate requesting the forgiveness of his liege.

"There is much I'd overlook for the sake of the family bond between us, but not what we uncovered on this occasion." Olivia gazed steadily into her father's eyes as he straightened.

"Really, Olivia, I don't know what—"

"Don't play games. You know I ordered the city locked down and I'm sure the reports of those we rescued from bondage have reached you." Olivia marvelled that her voice remained steady.

"Oh, come now, Olivia. While I'm sure pleasure houses offend your sensibilities, they serve their function—"

Her brother's words froze in his throat, colour draining from his face as Damien's blade lashed out to hold a hairsbreadth from the artery in the side of his neck. Damien paced forward, his blade pressing against Baren's skin. The keen edge caused a trickle of blood to trace its way down his throat into the lacy collar of his shirt.

"There is a big difference between those who choose to work in reputable pleasure houses and those who are bound in servitude." Nathanial's voice was low, with a slight tremor giving away the anger he was barely holding in check.

"Please, Olivia, there's no need for such unpleasantness..." Her mother tittered and glanced around at her contemporaries.

Olivia stared at her mother, seeing her wilt as her attempt to garner support fell flat and the room remained still.

"You have no idea how unpleasant things will become if you don't cooperate." Despite his words, Michael sounded as pleasant as if he were commenting on the weather.

Can I kill him yet? Damien whispered.

Unable to help herself, Olivia's eyes slid across to Damien who still stood, his blade pressed against Baren's trembling throat. Damien hadn't even bothered to restrict his mindspeech to them alone. She opened her mouth to almost regretfully say no, then closed it again. Her eyes narrowed.

No. We need information, remember? Michael's voice was firm.

Olivia's eyes slid across to Michael and saw the exasperated expression on his face. A chuckle escaped her lips that unaccountably caused the eyes of her family to focus back on her.

He knows those responsible. I can feel his sudden fear and guilt, Damien whispered.

"Such a tempting request." Olivia smiled sweetly at her brother, who blanched.

"Please, Olivia, I had nothing to do with the Kastlers' operation—" Her brother stopped speaking abruptly, his eyes widening as he realised what he'd just admitted.

Kastler? Nathanial swore. *The Kastlers are behind this as well as the problems we had in Vallantia?*

Sorry, you were busy looking after Damien and we forgot to pass that on, Michael said.

Someone already confirmed the Kastlers were behind all this? Nathanial asked.

One of the men we rescued, or rather that Damien rescued, was Lukas. He dropped by to let us know the Kastler Consortium owned that place, Michael said.

I guess it's refreshing that Baren didn't ask which *pleasure house.* Olivia traded glances with Michael.

It also neatly confirms what Lukas told us, Michael said.

Which allows us to hide his involvement. Since now no one will wonder how we came by that knowledge, Nathanial said.

"How much did you know about the Kastlers' *trade*?" Olivia spat out the word.

She didn't think it was possible for her brother to pale more than he already had, but somehow he managed it. Olivia transferred her regard to her father and his eyes shadowed.

"I don't know what—"

"Don't play games, Father, or I'll happily take your life myself as payment," Olivia snapped.

Her father's eyes slid to Michael.

"Oh, don't look at me. By the Warlord's decree, any messes in Callenhain are Olivia's to fix," Michael said.

Olivia marvelled that somehow, despite Michael's positively cheery tone, her father's eyes widened in fear.

How do you manage that trick? Olivia asked.

He believes he is too valuable to the Warlord. Michael's mind voice held amusement.

It's you he fears, Olivia. He thought Michael would intervene, Nathanial added.

Olivia caught her brother trembling. Damien's blade still hadn't moved from his throat.

"I wouldn't test Damien's patience if I were you, brother. He's a little on edge since some of your friends tried to drug him." Her brother's eyes widened at that piece of information.

A palpable hit. He's even more terrified now, Nathanial said.

"I... I don't know what you mean," Baren said.

"Of course you do. I think it's time we finished this conversation in private." Olivia caught the eyes of Gavrel and Shallan, the senior members of their protection detail. "No one is to leave this room. I'm not done yet. Damien, you're with us."

The squad of Unwanted spread out, each of them taking a

position at the exits of the great hall. Olivia gestured to Damien, who withdrew his blade, although he kept it drawn as she led the way to a discreet door in the far corner of the room. Tension and fear from her family flared. She knew without having to look that Damien had fallen in as tail guard behind her parents and brother.

CHAPTER

FORTY-SIX

S amuel paced, growing more infuriated as he waited for his commander to show up. He went to grasp the blade at his waist and froze mid-step as he realised he wasn't wearing one because he'd been getting a massage, or at least he had the distinct impression he had been. His confusion over the detail caused him to stop altogether. He should be able to remember something that had happened moments before.

What will you do?

A voice whispered in his head along with an image of a young girl looking at him with a pent-up intensity.

Go to Ricardo. He'll accept you. Bind yourselves and do not come back.

Samuel's breath caught. He recognised that voice. It was his own and the young girl had been Jaclyn. He was grateful his wives were too lost in their own world to notice him. Samuel began to pace again, unable to stop the shaky breath that would give away his distress if Chelsie was paying attention to him. He carefully reached down the bond between them and winced at the turmoil. It beat at his mind with such intensity he was surprised he hadn't noticed before now.

He closed his eyes and took another breath to calm himself. These moments where he was back in his head again were rare. The disconnect between who he'd been, who they'd been, and what they were now was confusing. He stared at his firstwife, swallowing against the lump that rose in his throat. Chelsie hadn't always been like this. They'd had such good intentions to hold back. Not to go down the path of madness. She'd known back then that they were allowing Jaclyn to flee the purge. Samuel blinked. They'd allowed Jaclyn to live. He prodded at the memory. Absurd though it sounded, it rang true. This was something *he'd* done, something his wives bade him to forget. A worry nagged at him that he and his wives shouldn't still be here in the Monarch House, but he couldn't tease out why. It made no sense. He was the king, so this was exactly where he belonged. Shaking his head, he caught sight of the body on the ground in the pool of blood. The person he had been retreated, as if his own head was fragmented with multiple versions of himself.

"Someone get rid of the body," Samuel snapped, irritated all over again—but this time because no one had even bothered to act. With his commander on her way, it's not like he wanted her to see the body lying there on the floor.

Samuel paused; it was like someone had thrown an ice-cold bucket of water over him. That other part of him was horrified that Jaclyn was coming here. He wanted her safe. The further away she was from him and his wives, the safer she and her family would be. It seemed keeping Jaclyn away was something both his past and present selves now could agree on, even if for entirely different reasons.

"Why didn't any of you stop me from calling her here?" Samuel groaned.

"We need her to deal with the traitors. Who else were we going to call for?" Chelsie snapped.

Samuel swallowed as he regarded his firstwife who was clearly not thinking straight. He guessed the thread of insanity that threatened to topple them all was coming from her. At least today. Otherwise, she'd realise his commander, his sister Jaclyn, was the last person who should see that body on the ground. She would *know*. Chelsie would also have noticed the internal conflict he was struggling with and soothed away his independent mind and concerns if she hadn't been a little lost herself. As someone rapped on the door and it opened, he hissed.

"At least drag the body behind the couch where she can't see it."

Irritation and anger rolled over him again from several sources. He gasped, feeling like he was drowning, and struggled to push it back. He could almost work out that it was separate from himself.

"My king, you sent for me?" Jaclyn said.

No matter how he tried to cling to that brief understanding, anger surged over his mind as he faced Jaclyn and it was washed away.

"Deal with the traitors," Samuel said.

Samuel saw a flicker of emotion play across her face; it was only a moment before it was wiped away.

"Of course, my king. Who precisely are the traitors you need me to deal with?" Jaclyn asked.

"Whispers reach our ears of a lower-caste family hoarding men, forgetting who they are and becoming no better than savages," Chelsie said.

"I'm told they are trading with our enemies," Samuel said.

"I will attempt to identify the traitor house and will deal with them, my king."

Samuel watched as she bowed her head. He seethed as he

thought of someone disobeying him. Then a tiny part of him felt a glimmer of satisfaction that the most able commander his people had known would track the traitors down and deal with their betrayal. As Jaclyn bowed and excused herself, he saw her eyes track to the side of the lounge before flicking up to his own. As he watched her retreating back, an image struck him through that distorted lens of his memory. Bodies on the ground, pooling blood, then a whispered voice.

Save us, my son, before we destroy everyone.

That small part of him that lay in the back of his mind surged forward, blocking the clamouring insanity of his wives. Samuel shook his head, trying to push away the haunting images and words that he half-remembered. He'd never before jumped this frequently between the self he'd been and the imprint his wives had constructed. He rubbed his temple as a splitting headache reared. Then he saw what Jaclyn had obviously seen. The pool of blood smeared along the floor and the foot of his dead wife extending beyond the edge of the couch.

I'm not lost yet, sister, but I fear my wives are succumbing, sinking in the multitude, and you may need to act before any child of mine is old enough. Deal with the traitors and the barbarians as you see fit. Then save our people.

Samuel saw her back stiffen as she heard his plea.

Stay strong, brother, I had feared you lost already. I will save you.

No. Go deal with the traitors and the barbarians. Let me deal with my wives. I can last a little longer.

Yes, Samuel.

Jaclyn?

Yes, brother?

Did you do as we promised? When we were children in the inner sanctum?

As the doors closed her voice floated back to him.

Yes, my king. I did not forget what you made me promise.

Relief flooded that little corner of his mind that he resided in. There was hope, a very slim one. Even if there was none for him or his wives. She would succeed where he had failed. His little sister always had been frighteningly competent. There would come the day that Jaclyn and her house would rise to take the Monarch House. In doing so, this nightmare would end and perhaps forge a new path for Sylanna, away from the insanity they courted.

FORTY-SEVEN

Olivia pretended to look out of the large windows into the courtyard garden. She heard the door close and stood for a moment longer with her back to them all. A rush of power that had Damien's signature threaded through it heralded the flaring of the lamps out in the garden. If it wasn't for the circumstances they found themselves in, she'd find this almost neglected, half wild courtyard garden soothing. The spurt of fear that came from the members of her family at the casual display of power from Damien amused her. Almost regretfully, she faced them all.

Her father was transferring his weight from one foot to the other, his hand straying halfway to his sword before he'd remember himself and stop the action. Her mother glanced around from one to the other of them, a smile plastered on her face with a slight frown marring her forehead. Baren stood, hand pressed against his bleeding throat, as he kept a wary eye on Damien. Awkward silence filled the room. At least, her family seemed to find it disconcerting. Michael and Nathanial were perfectly at ease. She could feel Damien was on edge, but that was more to do with recent events than the current situation. Olivia shifted her attention back to her family.

"Tell me about the Kastlers," Olivia demanded.

"I don't know, I swear—"

"Stop lying!" Olivia snapped.

"They didn't mean any harm. They thought opening the trading lines with Sylanna might stop all the raids." The words tumbled out of Baren's mouth in a rush.

"I don't understand what the Kastlers' trading exploits have to do with the pleasure house you were going on about," her mother grumbled.

Olivia gazed at her mother in disbelief, taking in her perplexed expression.

She's not putting on an act. She doesn't know, Nathanial whispered.

"Do you want to admit what they are up to, Father?" Olivia asked.

"I've never asked." Her father's face was blank as he looked at Michael, then back at her. "I admit I was aware they had a less than reputable pleasure house and were trading with Sylanna. I didn't ask what tastes they catered to at the pleasure house. The specific goods or services a trader offers is not something I usually bother to ask about when I approve their trader status in Callenhain."

"I heard a rumour, but I dismissed it..." her brother whispered.

"Did you even think to advise Father of this rumour?" Olivia asked.

"No, it was ludicrous. I just thought the others were jealous of the Kastlers' success," Baren said.

"How about you tell them now? Just so we're all on the same page," Olivia said.

Baren's eyes widened, then slid over to their parents. He

swallowed as he realised that everyone in the room, including their parents, was staring at him.

"People…" Baren said.

Olivia heard Damien gasp and saw the colour drain from his face.

I… I remember. They said they were going to sell me to Sylanna. That the women would pay well for me, Damien whispered.

Olivia caught the half-remembered fragment of conversation from the confusion and blankness in the memory that he shared. His kidnappers hadn't been intending to use him in their pleasure house. They'd planned to sell him to Sylanna. Olivia spared a moment to send reassurance to Damien. She couldn't imagine how difficult it must be for him to realise his lapse had nearly resulted in him being sold into slavery.

She traded looks with Michael and Nathanial as her parents swung horrified glances at her brother. Oh, they had no real moral objections to selling people. Not really. After all, they'd thrown her at the Warlord's feet promptly enough, and she was their own flesh and blood. Yet all knew the Warlord's stance on trading in people. Servants that you paid in some fashion or the punishment of those who'd broken bond with their village or community were one thing. Trading another person as if they were a fine blade, leather, or some type of commodity was punishable by death.

Calm settled on Olivia. The choice was now undeniable. There were many things they could overlook. Selling off people as trade goods was not one of them. The Warlord was very clear on this subject. Even though her own experience was nothing like his own, it was a position she agreed with. They all did. Each of them had their own stories, the life he'd saved them from.

"You can't own people. You can't trade them just to make your own life that little bit easier. Is the Kastler family representative here tonight?" Olivia asked.

"Sebastian Kastler? Yes he's here, he's the nephew of Peter and Constance Kastler from Vallantia and represents the family interests here in Callenhain," Baren said.

The coldness wasn't just in her voice. It was the very real manifestation of the rupture in the veil as she ripped the thin barrier wide. Frost tracked across a mirror on the wall and the glass froze, then shattered. Not even that explosion in the relative silence stopped the veil flooding into the real world as it responded to her anger.

The doors to the anteroom blasted open, shattering with the force thrown and she stalked back into the ballroom flanked by Michael and Nathanial with Damien but a step behind. Not even the shrieks of terror that sounded from the ballroom stopped the spread of their power. The Unwanted standing guard on the doors all turned to look at them, their own abilities flaring in response. As their band members' power joined with their own, the sword and flame crest on their chests and the threads of silver in their clothing blazed with a life of its own. Olivia drew her sword as she strode across the space, only absently noticing those who pressed back, leaving her in a clear space in the centre of the room. She could ask one of the others to carry out the Warlord's justice on the head of the Kastler trading house. But this duty was hers.

"Sebastian Kastler, present yourself."

Fear flooded the room as people edged back, leaving one person standing by himself. As Olivia transferred her gaze to him, the glass fell from his hand and the sound caused more than one person to jump and a few others to shriek. His eyes widened as even his peers pressed back, deserting him.

"That's him..." Damien's face was pale as he stared fixedly at Sebastian.

"You've met Sebastian before?" Olivia asked.

"When the kidnappers drugged me at the warehouse, he came and inspected me," Damien said.

"Sebastian Kastler, you stand accused of engaging in the flesh trade. By decree of the Warlord, the punishment for engaging in such trade is death," Olivia said, her voice as cold as the veil that flowed through her.

"But it's my uncle and aunt's fault. I'm only following their orders…"

"Don't worry. It's my job to deal with them," Michael said. "But thank you for your admission of their involvement. It will make my job easier."

If anything, the room went even more silent before a rumble sounded. A tracery of veil-fuelled lightning danced around the edges of the ballroom, throwing its eerie blue light on everybody.

"You traded people for your own personal gain," Olivia said.

The room grew still, the only movement heads adjusting slightly to look at Sebastian Kastler who stood in their midst.

"Well, you could hardly call them people, just those from the street—"

His words froze in his throat as Damien was suddenly there, his blade against Sebastian's throat. Sebastian's eyes widened, as a spurt of horrified recognition came from him, as he stared at Damien.

"How does it feel to face me now that I'm not drugged and bound?" Damien hissed, loathing rolling from him.

Olivia paced forward. Somehow, that pool of calm remained. It wrapped around her, filaments of the veil brushing over her skin and singing in her mind.

"Damien."

Damien's knuckles whitened, and then he ducked his head before finally withdrawing his blade and stepping back. Sebastian breathed a sigh of relief, a chuckle escaping from his lips. He looked around at his peers, relief evident as his body sagged.

Sebastian didn't even see it as Olivia's blade cut through the air. The trace work of metal in her garments flared to life, the blade and flame of the Unwanted flickering and pulsing. Power ran through her arm and blade as it swept across his neck. The smile on Sebastian's face faltered as he stared at her, his eyes going blank as the spark of life within them vanished and his head toppled, a moment before his body did.

FORTY-EIGHT

Jaclyn kept control over her outward appearance with a firm will. Every step killed a little piece of her, but every step also drew her closer to her own sanctuary. She tilted her head back and chuckled, hearing the despair. Those who encountered her as she strode the walkways blanched and plastered themselves against the rails. Not that she blamed them; she was emoting, and they weren't pleasant feelings or memories. That alone would have caused anyone with any perception to back off. The fact that her daggerwives bristled with hands on daggers, glaring at anyone who might even conceivably be a threat, probably didn't help either.

They'd seen what she had seen: the pool of blood, the drag marks and the foot not quite hidden by the lounge. They feared what it meant. After all, the king would have had no reason to try and hide the body if the death had been legitimate.

As she crossed the last bridge that led to her own court, she blinked rapidly, trying to hold back the visible signs of her distress, but increased her stride. When she entered the doors of her court, she burst into a run, ignoring the daggerwives that chased after her. They needn't have worried—she was only going to her rooms. She was aware of the shocked reaction of her household as she ran through it, a whirlwind of emotions she could barely keep contained. It wasn't a side of her they were used to seeing. Perhaps they'd understand better if they'd met that young girl who'd run from the inner sanctum of the Monarch's House to Ricardo.

Jaclyn flung herself into her rooms, slamming the door shut behind her with a thrust of power. Ignoring the bed, she curled into herself in the corner of the room, biting back the sobs that wanted to escape her throat. She might be in her rooms, but the walls weren't very thick. Everyone would hear her distress. That they would feel it anyway wasn't lost on her. Somehow, that seemed different. Most people tried to ignore it when they caught the leaked emotions from others or simply strengthened their mental barriers to block it out. Physically hearing raw emotion, or seeing it, had far more impact than sensing them, if for no other reason than there was no way to not hear or see it.

"Go!"

She flinched as she heard Ricardo's command, although it wasn't directed at her.

"But, husband..."

"I won't tell you again, go. Guard the outer perimeter of the court if you must but clear the inner sanctum. Now."

The last came out as a snarl and the presence of her fellow wives retreated as Ricardo entered her room, closing the door firmly behind him. She didn't resist as his arms gathered her to him. They didn't speak. He simply offered her his strength and comfort, his own powers enveloping her in a bubble of shimmering power.

She remembered all those years ago, when her big brother had sat and talked with her, played children's games in the inner sanctum, and taught her the finer points of fighting and strategy. The wives of the house had found it strange. Yet it had been Samuel who shown her how to shelter her mind from the early onset of madness in the Monarch House. He'd been the one to disturb her sleep and warn her to get out and go to Ricardo. Made her promise not to control Ricardo's mind, to make her house different from all those that had come before it. Or at least, that is what her memories told her. In the intervening years she'd almost begun to think she'd rewritten her own history. Even if only to give herself something positive about her childhood to hold on to.

He's still there.

She didn't even try to hide her pain. It would be so much easier if Samuel was the monster she'd thought he'd become.

There may be glimmers of the brother you grew up with, but he is losing himself.

I don't know how he's done it, but he's kept a part of himself away from them.

It's not possible, Jaclyn.

It shouldn't be, but he's done it.

Jaclyn reached up, placing her hand on the side of his head, fingers brushing his temples and shared what she'd sensed from her brother. She heard Ricardo's breath catch.

Do you think we've been wrong? Ricardo asked.

About what?

They, the Monarch House, are trying to kill us. But Samuel, or the part of himself he's locked away—is he trying to protect us in the only way he can?

What do you mean?

Sending us to fight the barbarians. They hoped we'd die. Including that part of your brother they control, but...

But?

That part of him that is separate from them. He knew you'd survive. He's the one who helped train you to fight and strategise. By getting you out of reach of the Monarch House...

It's kept us alive, Jaclyn said, before continuing to the part that was really upsetting her. *He's not certain they can last long enough for their children to come of age.*

If we have to cleanse the Monarch House for the good of all our people, then we'll tackle the problem when the time comes, Ricardo said.

Not the children. We must find a way to at least save them or we're no better than any of my ancestors who came before me, Jaclyn said.

The agitation in Jaclyn's mind calmed under the steady stream of support and comfort from her husband.

We'll work it out. What is it he asked you to promise? Ricardo asked.

Jaclyn stirred and smiled up at him.

He made me promise we wouldn't all link minds, that I wouldn't control you so completely the way our entire culture demands.

It was too late for him and his wives. Sadness coloured Ricardo's mindvoice.

But not for us.

Not that I'm complaining, but I'm not sure he meant you to forgo the positive benefits of the mate bond entirely.

Jaclyn could hear the amusement in his tone and frowned as she thought through the position they were in.

Perhaps, but forcing you to forget, to comply with what I wanted —for your safety, of course—is an insidious sickness of the mind.

It took some adjusting to. I was raised my whole life to submit to the dominance of my firstwife.

I think we are stronger without it, you and I. Our house is stronger for it.

We don't have the single-minded focus the way houses who link their minds together do, but the trade-off, not losing ourselves in each other, has been worth it.

I almost forgot. They've heard rumours about the house that is trading with the barbarians. The king ordered us to deal with them.

Ricardo stirred at that one as he thought it through. Like her, she was sure he was seeing the inherent risks of leaving the house be.

We cannot afford to leave them alone. Not with their proximity to our hidden children and the Monarch House's awareness of their presence.

The choice of whether to sacrifice them for the good of our own house has effectively been taken out of our hands. If the king has ordered us to deal with them, then we must do so. The risk would be too high if we refused.

Now that her mind had focused back onto the coming attack in the barbarian lands and how their house might survive it, she found calmness settled on her. That small kernel of self that remained of her brother and the signs the Monarch House was disintegrating could wait.

CHAPTER

FORTY-NINE

Michael glared at the offending paperwork on the table. The reports were seemingly endless. He swore people must hold on to the petitions or requests for help waiting for him to come to town.

Warleader, there's a woman here to see you. Says she has a message from the Heights.

Michael sighed, almost with relief at the distraction, and pushed the paperwork aside. Damien wandered across the room and sat at what had become his regular spot on the window seat, and peered out at the streets below. Olivia and Nathanial shrugged and happily pushed their own piles of paperwork away.

"She doesn't look like a city dweller and she seems concerned," Damien said.

I'll see her, Michael said.

"To be truthful, I'm glad for the excuse to stop looking at this stuff. Why do they think we'll care that they paid extra tithe?" Olivia grumbled.

"If we're lucky, this will be important enough to draw us

away and we can simply package all this up and leave it until our next visit." Nathanial didn't quite manage to disguise the satisfaction that possibility gave him.

"I don't know how we ended up with half this stuff. We never used to," Michael said.

"Delegation is what the Warlord decided it was called."

Michael snorted in amusement. More like the Warlord found most of this administration work as tedious as they did. As the door opened he barely repressed his relief.

"Warleader, your visitor."

The guard gestured for the woman to enter. Michael thanked them and waved dismissal, although the guards would remain outside the door in case they were needed. He frowned at the woman.

It's that woman, Kara, that you recruited from Bergan, Olivia prompted.

Where we got saddled with Aiden, Nathanial said.

Michael nearly groaned. If she was here, it meant something was wrong. Those in his relay network mostly stayed put, unless there was an emergency that drew them out to seek either him or the nearest of the Warlord's warbands. The woman scanned the room, pausing as she saw Damien over by the window. For his part, Damien paid her no attention at all. He'd almost perfected the art of sitting quietly, trying not to intervene in their business, although Michael had no doubt he listened in.

"You have something to tell me?" Michael asked.

"Yes, Warleader, sorry. Word came down from the Heights. The Kallith have requested your presence. They say the Sylannians gather in great numbers at the base on the other side of the mountains," Kara said.

Michael could see the small frown on her forehead as she repeated what had been relayed to her.

"You couldn't just pass that on? You had to come here?"

"Oh, I was here already with the tithe from Bergan. I figured I might as well pass it on to you myself," Kara said.

"Very well. Anything else?"

"No, that's all I was told. I passed back that you were here in Callenhain, and I'd let you know," Kara added.

"Will you be heading straight back to Bergan?" Olivia asked.

"No, ma'am. We're in the markets with trade goods as well and we'll take back commodities we can't get readily when we're done. Probably be here a couple of weeks," Kara said.

"Don't let those in the market rip you off. I'm advised they come out on top of any exchange," Olivia said.

"We'll try, ma'am, I'll leave the bargaining to those better at it. I'm just part of the guard detail," Kara said.

Nathanial took a small pile of coins from a leather purse on the table and handed it over without comment.

"Thank you for seeing the message got to us," Michael said, sending a mental prod to the guard outside the door.

"Thank you, Warleader, ma'am, sir." Kara checked the coins in her hand before she stuffed them into her belt pouch.

The guard promptly opened the door and ushered Kara out.

"I'll get everyone packing, then pack your gear after mine," Nathanial said.

"Thanks. Damien, just get ready and pack your personal gear. You'll walk out when we do. One of the others will collect your gear and saddle up for you."

He watched as Damien wandered around the room and gathered his few possessions, folded into a neat little pile on the bed, then stuffed them back into his bags. When he was done, he placed them near the door. Nathanial appeared and handed Damien his weapons belt and then picked up the bag and took it with him. Damien held his weapons belt waiting until Michael nodded his consent. To Damien's credit, he hadn't argued at all about being denied his weapons. He'd given them back again after the visit they'd paid to Olivia's family estate without having to be asked. Damien strapped on his weapons before giving the room one last check. Satisfied, he went back over to his accustomed window seat and settled in to wait until it was time to leave.

J aclyn and her fellow wives scaled the pylons of the stilt houses. This house was overflowing their island and instead of building up or moving off the island entirely, they'd expanded and built a series of houses on stilts in concentric rings around the island that was their ancestral home. If anything, that told her how long this house had been out here in the outermost rim of the islands. These were their ancient lands, where their people had been born. She could admire their desire to stay on their island, refusing to admit defeat and resettle elsewhere in the new lands claimed by Sylanna to allow their people to spread out and flourish. It was almost a pity they had become traitors and started dealing with the enemy barbarians. Such a thing could not go unpunished. Yet even for such crimes, there could be redemption—if they accepted the path she offered.

Reaching the top, she paused, looking to either side to see the progress her fellow wives were making. Satisfied, she checked on Myra and Ricardo on either side of her, then scaled the final wooden railing to step on the walkway. Her silks clung to her, waterlogged. She flicked a small burst of power through the silk and the water streamed from them, pooling at her feet on the wooden walkway. With an almost inaudible hum, the silk reformed around her, wrapping around her legs, arms, and torso in a hard shell.

Let's do this, Jaclyn said.

The head of her daggerwives, Arianne, acknowledged her order and with a few orders of her own, her teams leapt into action. Jaclyn drew her daggers and followed in their wake, following a trail of blood and wailing as the unsuspecting traitors filling the very outer ramshackle huts went down, mostly uncomprehending they were under attack. By the time they reached the centre of the island, where the firstwife resided, they would no doubt meet some resistance.

A man with the pale skin of the barbarians lurched up, clutching a dagger wound in his abdomen; Ricardo lunged and lashed out with his knives and the man crumpled to the ground, motionless as they passed. As the numbers of barbarian men started to add up, Jaclyn found her anger mounting.

This bloodline is polluted beyond redemption, Ricardo spat as he dispatched another of the foreign men.

Selective breeding with some of the strongest outsider males is one thing, but this...

The disgust in Myra's tone was clear. Of course, selective breeding occurred under careful supervision in the middle caste houses. They chose only a few—those with exceptional power or skills—to use as breeding stock. To make sure their blood wasn't watered down with outsider blood to the point they became unrecognisable. To breed so wantonly with those who were lesser defied belief.

Remember, we need enough of them to live. Even ones as depraved as this house will serve their purpose, Jaclyn said.

Jaclyn hauled the head of a barbarian back and slit his throat.

The woman he'd been rutting with before their world exploded screamed, lurching up, but it was only moments before Jaclyn's other blade silenced her, too. If anything, it was a mercy to the woman—she had mate-bonded to the male and her mind had broken when he died.

They continued to wade through the house. Whatever these people were, they were clearly unprepared for fighting. Most seemed to barely be able to find a weapon, let alone use their daggers expertly. Then again, as remote as this island was from the Court of a Thousand Islands and the heart of their people, it was unlikely anyone had bothered them before. It seemed they were far enough removed from the ideals of the elite of their own people they scarcely resembled Sylannians at all. At least those of the middle caste aspired to improve the station of their house and bloodlines. As did hardworking low-caste families. Unlike these people, who seemed to have regressed to unthinking animals.

With effort Jaclyn kept her disgust under control. Instead, she focused on the progress they were making, conscious they had made their way through layer upon layer of wooden shacks to get to the island itself. She breathed an unconscious sigh of relief as they finally reached land. It at least bore more resemblance to one of their home islands. Unlike the rings of hovels that surrounded the island, here the tall trees stretched out as they should. Jaclyn had feared the firstwife who ruled here had the audacity to clear the island of trees when she'd first seen the ring of wooden huts. She jumped lightly to the ground and ran over what appeared to be a buffer between those who actually lived on the island and those who lived in the shacks that circled the island. Communal longhouses stretched out at ground level among the trees where the serving class lived. Above, disappearing from view in the heights of the giant trees, was the housing of the ruling class. Using the veil to assist, she leapt up, catching the edge of a covered walkway. Her daggerwives picked up their pace, leaping from bridge to bridge as they converged on the sprawling, multi-layered tree home. With its peaked roofs and flowing designs, it finally resembled something she recognised.

As light spread over the treetops, a holler went out as the house belatedly woke up and realised it was under attack. Women from the traitor house streamed out to engage with Jaclyn's daggerwives. The ring of steel on steel resounded in the early morning. While under normal circumstances Jaclyn knew her daggerwives would be at a disadvantage, since they were trying to keep as many of their opponents alive as possible, it was sad how little difference it made. Either these women were appalling at fighting, or her own people were really that much better.

FIFTY-ONE

Damien hadn't even had to be told that he'd be relegated to riding in the centre of the warband as they finally left Callenhain. Even when they were out on the road with their formation a little looser, he still rode towards the centre and Nathanial was nearby. He wouldn't test Michael's patience by trying to be anywhere else. That bridge was well and truly burned until he proved himself again.

His recovery was taking far longer than he cared to think and even now fatigue hit him sooner than it would have before. Looking around their camp for the night, he contemplated helping with something, but realised he wasn't suited to many of the camp duties. There was no way Nathanial would let him out of the camp by himself to hunt—tiscan vines were everywhere in these parts. Besides that, since they'd just come from Callenhain, they were fully stocked. It was also no favour to his squad mates if he tried to cook. Seeing his hand shaking, practicing his sword work probably wasn't a good idea either.

Sighing, he gave up and climbed into his hammock, hoping he wouldn't forget and roll out of it after all the time he'd spent in a bed. He closed his eyes, only intending to relax until dinner was ready. But when a hand gripped his shoulder, his eyes flared open and he realised with shock that it was full dark and he could smell the food. That meant hours had passed, and he'd been dead to the world in a dreamless sleep.

"Easy, you're safe. Come and get some food. Then you can sleep again," Nathanial said.

Damien groaned. He still didn't have his appetite back, but the ritual of eating was something Nathanial insisted on.

"All right. I know I brought this on myself, but I'm sick of feeling exhausted and unwell," Damien grumbled.

He rolled out of his hammock, accepting the assistance as Nathanial steadied him. There was a time he would have been embarrassed; it was an emotion he'd run out of now. All of his band mates had seen him at his worst. Or at least he hoped they had.

"Your fatigue is normal. The ride today is the longest you've been active and channelling the veil since you started using again."

"I'll have to trust you on this one, since I'm finding it hard to tell. I still don't feel like eating either."

"You'll get your appetite back eventually, around the time you stop feeling sick all the time, but you still have to eat," Nathanial said.

"Sorry, I don't mean to whine." Damien closed his eyes and took a steadying breath. "Seems to have come out naturally."

At least Nathanial didn't seem to be all that annoyed or concerned about his whining. Damien acknowledged both Michael and Olivia, who waved at him to join them.

"You've actually been a good patient, as far as it goes," Michael said.

"Believe it or not, right now, even though being connected to and using the veil again is a part of what is exhausting you, it is also what will help get you up to strength again," Olivia said.

Damien ducked his head and decided he'd have to take her at her word. She was, however, correct that right now he felt terrible. Easing himself down onto a log, he thanked Callan for the bowl of broth. While the others ate something more substantial, those on cook duty were still making him soup, knowing he wouldn't be able to stomach much else. He finished the bowl under the watchful gaze of his band and as he ate, he prodded his memory. Even the days of his recovery were fragmented and unreliable.

"Did you all take me with you to a ball, or did I just dream that up?" Damien asked.

"We assessed we couldn't afford to leave you alone, so yes, you came with us to the ball," Nathanial said, seemingly unconcerned with the evidence of his memory loss.

Damien shook his head and laughed; Nathanial just raised his eyebrow at him.

"You all know my memory is shot and I'm a little unstable right now, but you let me loose on Olivia's family and guests." Damien wiped the tears from his eyes.

"Well, Olivia doesn't care for her family all that much. More importantly, you don't feel safe unless one of us is watching over you. So, since we had to sort out the mess, you had to come with us." Nathanial shrugged as if it all made perfect sense. "Do you remember anything that happened at the estate?"

Damien swallowed as he probed his memory, then shook his head. He had a fleeting memory of the streets passing by and remembered blood and a dead body, but not much else.

"No, not really. Someone died. Did I...?" He couldn't finish the sentence and ducked his head.

"No. I ordered you to hold your blade, and you did. I killed Sebastian, the representative of the Kastler Consortium, for engaging in the flesh trade. We shut down their operation in Callenhain," Olivia said.

"I'll deal with the heads of the Kastler family when we make it back to Vallantia," Michael added.

Relief flooded Damien. Not that he really cared that the man responsible for his kidnapping was dead. It was just that if he was going to kill someone, he'd rather do it in his right mind and know he was doing it.

"Is it because of the tiscan that I keep blacking out this way?" Damien asked.

"Some of it, particularly while you were being fed so much of it. It's also the veil. It's been surging back into your body and as best we can work out, it knocks you out of your own head for a bit. On those occasions, you're up and functioning, but there is no sign that you are actually present in your own head."

"Wonderful. Now I'm going out of my head crazy." Damien's face flushed. "You've told me all of this before, haven't you?"

"If it helps, you are getting better, even if it doesn't feel like it."

"If you weren't, we'd still be back at Callenhain," Michael added. "You remember more each time we go through it."

"Unless someone threatens you when you're in that state, you don't hurt anyone. At least, not yet."

"Michael, you went through this as well? The blackouts, that is, not tiscan addiction."

Damien could hear the undertone of uncertainty in his own voice as he looked across at his Warleader, who nodded at him gravely.

"So these two tell me. I still have gaps in my memory from that time. It was one of the more disturbing things I've ever been through."

Damien appreciated the candour in Michael's tone. It relieved him a little.

"So now that we have a little time, perhaps you'd both like to fill us in on that veiled place that Damien took us to?" Olivia asked, her eyebrow rising.

Damien heard the dryness in her tone and tried not to show his amusement as both she and Nathanial fixed Michael with twin glares.

"I found it by accident one time. I worked out no one could see or sense me, so I used to hide there." Damien shrugged.

"It's useful for hiding. Which is something we don't spend much time doing. I didn't think about it until Damien disappeared." Michael echoed his earlier shrug.

"I could keep experimenting with it but..."

"No."

The three of them echoed each other with that negative.

"Got it." Damien held his hands up. "Tiscan addict pulling disappearing acts. Not a good idea."

"When we get further up, closer to the Heights, it's cooler, so the stuff doesn't grow. Perhaps we can both experiment then," Nathanial said.

"We might be able to integrate it with our fighting techniques somehow," Olivia said.

"How?" Damien said, startled.

"No idea. I'm just thinking out loud," Olivia said.

"We'll work on it. You go and rest. It will be a long day of hard riding tomorrow," Michael said.

Damien took a deep breath and stood, keeping his gaze averted as a lump rose in his throat.

"You're doing well," Olivia said, reaching out and squeezing his hand gently.

"I'm not trying to be hard on you or exclude you. Tiscan cravings get worse when you're tired. We know this from helping Nathanial." Michael reinforced his words with a wave of reassurance.

"He's right, it makes it worse, and you know it," Nathanial said.

"Besides that, I'd like you functional when we get up to the Heights. The only way you won't fall over and collapse is if you do as you're told. Go rest," Michael said.

"You're right, and if I wasn't tired and wanting tiscan to wash me away into oblivion, I wouldn't have taken that the wrong way."

Damien returned to the sleeping area and sank into his hammock with a sigh. He figured he wouldn't be able to sleep so soon after waking up, but he could rest until he did. He wished, not for the first time, that he hadn't been weak and succumbed to his drug of choice.

CHAPTER

FIFTY-TWO

Tarkhan leant against the bars of the cage as they carried him through the bustling streets, watching the world that passed by. Sylannians and collared clansmen threw a few curious stares in his direction, but none of his former countrymen seemed even remotely inclined to assist him. The air was heavy and oppressive with the rushing sound of water telling him the river was nearby. Sweat rolled down his face and he swiped at it with the back of one grimy hand. He couldn't tell if the rank smell that assaulted his senses was coming from the teeming press of people in the street, or him, or his clothes. His captor had kept him caged other than a few occasions along their journey. But he certainly hadn't been given the freedom to bathe and when he was allowed to venture beyond the confines of his cell, he couldn't pull himself free from the constant stream of soothing that she sent him. The disjointed song of his bindings didn't change, no matter how much he tried to prod at them. He'd had many sleepless nights waiting for the Sylannian to attempt to break into his mind, to assert her control of him, but she hadn't even tried. This restraint confused him, although he suspected the discordant hum of his bindings aided in pacifying him. It seemed his captor had been correct: these bindings were different to the ones they'd first used on him.

The rhythmic thump of the boots of those who carried his cage changed in tone as they left the hard baked dirt road for the wooden pier. Giant boats docked in a line told him he was near the end of this journey and despair hit him as he realised any chance he'd had of escape had vanished. Soft laughter caused him to adjust his position to bring the woman into his field of vision. As always, she was nearby. Her lips curved into a smile that didn't reach her eyes.

"I would never allow you to escape. The women of this place have done you no favours by allowing you so much freedom. It's not good for you. You'll be on the boat and shipped to the Thousand Islands, where you'll be safe, soon enough."

"I'll never submit."

"Once you are in the hands of those who run the breeding house, you won't have a choice. Your life has changed now. The sooner you accept this, the happier you will be."

"I'm no traitor to my people."

"Good, keep that in mind. You are simply returning to where you belong. All those with Sylannian blood, particularly males, belong to Sylanna."

"I'm not Sylannian."

"The only way you could possess the ability to sing to the spidersilk the way you can, is if you have Sylannian blood flowing through your veins." Her voice was calm, as if she was explaining things to a child. "The silk spiders aren't found anywhere else. No blood but ours can command them."

"I was born here. My parents..."

"Somewhere in your family's past there is someone with Sylannian heritage. At a guess, a female fleeing a cleansing of her house. That suggests a daughter of one of the high caste houses.

It's the only explanation for your talent. That bloodline, along with your strength with the veil, makes you extremely valuable. We have many of the collared but not so many men with Sylannian blood." A gentle hand brushed the side of his face and he shuddered, unable to help leaning into her touch, which amplified the comfort she sent to him. "Now, hush, you'll soon be loaded onto the boat and on your way home to Sylanna, where you belong."

Despite his intentions, Tarkhan relaxed. If only she'd tried to break into his mind as the others had, it would be much easier to fight against. Somehow this woman seemed to know this, and he subsided just as she ordered. While he'd kept trying to fight her and the silken bonds that she controlled, it had proven futile. At another brush of her fingers his bindings shifted, pulling him against the bars of the cage and holding him in place. At a noise above, he craned his head to see ropes being tied to the top of his cage. Panic hit him as his cage lurched into the air, swaying as a series of ropes and pulleys operated by his former countrymen winched him from the pier to the boat. With one final lurch and a thump, his cage settled onto the deck. Tarkhan took in his surroundings, his mouth dry as his captor stepped onto the boat and stood talking with another. The way they both kept looking over at him as they spoke told him he was the subject of the conversation. If he could have backed away when they strode towards him, he was ashamed to admit he would have.

The door to his cage was unlocked and his captor, along with the other Sylannian she'd been talking to, came in. He took in the other Sylannian. She was older than any of the others he'd encountered. As she closed the distance between them, in one last act of defiance, he yelled and tried to throw himself at her, only to find he was still fastened to the bars. The older Sylannian ignored his outburst and hummed to some silk she carried. The stuff slithered around his neck, arms, waist, and legs. Where the older Sylannian's silk went, the bindings from his original captor retreated.

"Hush, Tarkhan, you'll only hurt yourself. I know you don't believe me right now, but this is for the best. You'll have a much better life where you are going."

With that, his original captor spun and went back the way she'd come, disappearing from sight. Somewhat reluctantly he regarded the older woman who now held his bindings.

"Come, Tarkhan, you're in a fine state, although it's not your fault with the women of this place allowing you to run around uncontrolled the way they do. Such an unnatural way for a man to live," the Sylannian said.

She walked away from him, the end of one of the silks that bound him in hand. He gasped as the band around his neck tightened and he lurched to his feet to follow her. Tarkhan attempted to throw himself at her again, only to find the length she carried was as hard as steel between them and he couldn't close the distance. His new captor seemed to ignore his futile escape attempts, simply leading him into a cabin with large double doors at the far end of the boat. As the door thumped closed behind him, Tarkhan jumped.

"What are you going to do to me?" Tarkhan asked.

"I'm going to remove those filthy clothes you are wearing, and I am going to help you bathe. Then I'll dress you as befits a male with Sylannian blood. When I have you settled I will get you some food and you can rest while we depart. I was told you fretted most of the way here and didn't get much sleep. That will never do."

His bindings snaked up to the beams in the rafters, holding him in place as the older woman stepped forward, using her sharp blades to cut him free of his jerkin and trousers, discarding the rags his clothes had become in the corner. He'd been determined to fight her will but somehow, Tarkhan found himself standing in a basin as the woman bathed him, simply because her whispering voice in his head urged him to. Every time he tried to so much as twitch in a way the older Sylannian didn't like, she'd make a disproving tutting noise and his bindings would tighten until he desisted. Finally, Tarkhan stood trembling under the woman's ministrations as she sent pulses urging him to calm and made soothing noises in her throat as she bathed him as if she was trying to gentle a spooked horse. For the first time, he understood how his people living in the lands conquered by the Sylannians must have felt. Bound with bonds he could not fight, abandoned, alone, and without any hope of the situation changing. He tried to convince himself that it wasn't tears streaking down his face, simply water from the sponge she used to gently, methodically cleanse his skin. Wiping away who he'd been with each stoke.

FIFTY-THREE

No sooner had Isabella wondered what time it was than the protective gossamer-grey lace that wove around her thinned, bringing her surroundings into focus. With a start, she realised that despite her assumption that she would never be able to sleep after her visions, it was morning —albeit barely—and the villagers would be going about the rituals they performed every day. Despite the nightmares that plagued her, Isabella found she'd been sleeping much more than she used to. Her parents and the elders had begun muttering about veil sickness. It was a pattern she at least recognised as one Damien had gone through. That gave her some comfort. After all, he might be suffering, but he was still alive. As tempting as it was to stay in the veil's comforting embrace, Isabella pushed aside the curtain that stood between her and the real world.

Glancing around, she realised she wasn't far from her intended destination for the day. She strolled through the forest towards Owen's hut, soaking in the sun's warmth. She was far enough away from the village that all she could hear was the call of the birds and insects. Owen lived on the outskirts of the territory claimed by the village, saying he preferred things that way. Isabella was beginning to appreciate why. It was so peaceful.

Isabella paused where the small trail that wound between the trees ended in a clearing. She'd known where Owen lived. Ranlith wasn't that big a village, but she'd never had cause to come here before. What she saw startled her. She had been expecting to see a neglected, run-down hut with an overgrown vegetable garden—if he'd a garden at all. Instead, there was a small, well-made wooden hut with a veranda. A quick glance at the garden bed revealed thriving vegetables and herbs. Looking with her othersight she could see the residual traces of power he'd used to reinforce the structural integrity of his hut and the light traces on his plants, helping them grow. Now that Damien was gone, Owen's were the strongest abilities in the village. Aside from her own. It surprised her the villagers didn't seem to be aware of that fact.

"You don't need to hide, Isabella. You're always welcome."

Isabella felt her cheeks heat as she realised Owen was standing on the other side of the small clearing.

"Sorry, Owen, I was just startled." Isabella moved from the sheltering trees towards the hut.

"What, that it wasn't a neglected, sorry excuse of a hut?" Owen asked, his eyes sparkling in amusement.

"No!" Isabella bit her lip as his grin widened. "Well, yes, I guess that is what I expected."

"To be honest, some of the other villages come out a couple of days a week to help, in trade for some of my herbs, vegetables and a share of the game I've hunted," Owen said.

"I heard you came back from your journey a few days ago, but I didn't want to intrude."

"As I said, you are always welcome here. Even if I'm out hunting—if someone is hassling you or you just need some space, you can come here." Owen's voice was soft as he stared at her. "What has brought you here? Has someone tried to hurt you?"

"Oh, no! Nothing like that, not since, well, you know. Damien said to come to you. He said I needed to know how to fight." Isabella closed her eyes. Making that admission brought back that horrible moment when she'd realised she'd put Damien's life and her own life at risk.

Owen stared at her for the longest time. Defeat settled on her and she went to walk away.

"Wait. I'm sorry, Isabella. You just surprised me." Owen reached out to her.

Isabella hesitated as she contemplated his outreached hand, then went towards him. His hand rested lightly on her back and he guided her towards his hut. She stood looking around, feeling a little uncomfortable as he took off his pack, leaving it by the door.

"I'm afraid I won't make a very good student," she whispered.

Owen sat back in a chair, gesturing for her to take the other. After a slight hesitation, she perched on the edge of the well maintained but worn wooden bench, eyes fixed on the floorboards of the deck.

"Yet you are here anyway. Why?" Owen asked.

"Damien is worried he'll fail and the Warlord will come back to claim me. That I'll die like his warleader's sister." The image of the dead girl that Damien had shared flashed in her mind.

"You will not be Damien's equal in the time I fear we have, but we can work on your skills to give you a little more confidence," Owen said, waiting for her approval.

"Unlike my brother, I've never had any interest in learning to fight. I don't expect you to work miracles."

"Very well. Wait here a moment."

Owen stooped to pick up his bag and went inside. Isabella

swallowed, suddenly nervous, wondering what he'd make her do. When he reappeared, he was carrying what seemed to be two swords. As he held one out to her, she stared at it, then back up at him before reaching out to grab it. He chuckled softly, and she blushed. On closer inspection, she realised it wasn't a proper sword at all. It was made of wood instead of metal. Isabella sighed, feeling like her heart descended from her throat where she was certain it had lodged as soon as she saw it. Isabella noticed Owen had reached the corner of the house and realised time had passed as he stood waiting for her, clearly amused by her reaction. Feeling her face heat again, she hurried to follow him.

"Sorry. I've never handled a pretend sword. I've seen some of the younger boys hit each other with sticks, but not one of these." Isabella realised she was babbling.

"It's a practice sword. It is the approximate weight of a real sword of that length. At least with that one you won't cut yourself," Owen explained as he led her around to the back of the hut.

"Did Damien use one of these?" Isabella asked.

"He did. That one, actually, when he was younger. He grew out of it, but it should be about the right size for you."

Isabella looked up at Owen's broad back. She could hear the amusement in his voice, even if she couldn't see it. She'd been prepared to be offended so she could storm off, but he'd neatly deflected her outrage. As they rounded the corner of the hut, Isabella stared at the unexpected open space. To one side, there was a large wooden pole stuck in the ground, with other bits of wood attached to it so it resembled a person. Towards the back, a large bag hung from a tree. Owen had stopped in the centre of the space, facing her, his head cocked to one side. She swallowed and took a few small steps forward until she was inside the grounds. He held up his wooden sword so she could see it, pointing to the various parts of it as he spoke.

"This is the grip, the guard, the blade and the point."

Isabella held the wooden sword she carried up in front of her. She frowned, moving it from side to side. It was much heavier than she'd thought it would be.

"Please don't wave your sword around like that," Owen said, a pained expression on his face.

"Sorry. Grip, guard, blade, and point," she repeated, pointing to each part of the wooden blade.

"Here, move your hand until it is near the guard. Hold it out. Do you feel the difference in the weight?"

"Yes. Why?"

"A good blade is balanced. You will have more strength holding it this way and the guard will protect your hand. If you try to hold it too far up the grip it becomes unwieldy and in a fight against an opponent, you will lose your blade."

Isabella adjusted her grip as Owen demonstrated. He nodded in approval, then sheathed his sword. Isabella checked her own hip and then felt her face heat. While she'd managed to get some more appropriate clothing and a belt, she hadn't thought about a scabbard.

"I'll look in Damien's room. He might have an old one."

"No need, I have one for you."

Isabella blinked as Owen stooped and retrieved it from its position near his feet. She hadn't even noticed he'd been carrying it when they'd come into the training ring. She went to unbuckle her belt but the wooden sword she held made it difficult. Not looking at Owen's face, guessing she'd see that pained expression again, she stuffed the sword under her arm, then unbuckled her belt. Isabella held out her hand. This time, she chuckled. She was correct about the expression she'd see on his face. He shook his head at her and handed the scabbard to her. Turning it over, she slid her belt through the loops, tightening the fastenings to make it secure, then buckled her belt once more. Taking the sword from under her arm, she slid it into the scabbard.

"All right, don't say it. I know. Don't do that again, either." Isabella grinned at him, unaccountably relaxing.

"Now, widen your stance, feet about shoulder-width apart." Owen waited, nodding as she mirrored his position. "Move one foot forward, like this, bend your knees, making sure your weight is balanced on the balls of your feet."

Isabella copied his instructions, feeling awkward and clumsy at first. She'd expected that they'd be hitting at each other with the swords. Like she'd seen some of the other children do while playing. Instead, they spent what seemed like hours practicing her stance and moving in a series of steps as she tried to keep her weight balanced and stay on the balls of her feet. It didn't seem long at all before her thighs protested, even though it had seemed a ridiculously easy task to start with.

Owen didn't have to say anything. She could tell he was pleased, even though all she'd done was practice standing and walking, one careful shuffling step at a time. In a stark counter to how she'd felt to start with, her excitement surged as his hand gripped the hilt of his practice sword. Owen drew it up in a sweeping motion before twisting and slashing back across again at an unseen opponent. Then he paused and waited expectantly.

Isabella did her best to draw the blade and copy the series of motions he'd made with it. Owen corrected her stance, then reached around, his hand overlaying hers as he guided her slowly through the sword strokes he wanted her to perform. He kept her working, performing the same series of movements over and over again. It wasn't until her arms, back, abdomen, and legs were screaming at her that he finally called a halt to their session.

"Well done. I'll talk to the taskmaster to have your chores adjusted to help build your strength. I'll expect you here to train every morning…" Owen paused and shook his head. "Or rather, when you wake. You are starting to sleep late, I hear, much like Damien used to?"

"Sorry, I can get my parents to make sure I get up," Isabella muttered.

"No, it's the onset of veil sickness. Your brother was always better for a little more sleep. About the time you showed up today is fine. I can get my hunting done as usual, then help you train."

"Thank you, Owen."

"Go. Keep the training sword and scabbard. You need to get used to it," Owen said in a clear dismissal.

Isabella walked from the training grounds to head back to the main village. She had no idea how her brother had managed to complete all his daily chores on top of training every day with Owen. All she wanted to do right now was curl up in a bed and sleep. That thought made her face heat since, unlike the rest of the village, she'd only really been up for a few hours. Her shoulders straightened. Somehow Damien had managed, even with sleeping until nearly midday. So that meant she could, too.

FIFTY-FOUR

Jaclyn crossed the open floor of the house. She had to admit if the circumstances had been different, this home would be quite pleasant. At least, it would be if the wooden shacks that surrounded it were destroyed. As it was, her daggerwives were holding the firstwife, her husband, and her entire inner circle at knife point. With a hum, Jaclyn's armour changed to flow and ripple around her, caressing her skin and fluttering in the slight breeze that wafted through the open shutters. The woman kneeling at the centre of the room had a slightly dazed look in her eyes, giving away that she'd at least tried to fight before she'd inevitably lost. It gave Jaclyn some hope this firstwife would try to complete the task Jaclyn had for her, if only to survive herself. At least her daggerwives had shown restraint and followed orders once they'd reached this place. Keeping as many of these women alive as they could without risking their own safety. The woman's eyes widened as she registered the colour of Jaclyn's silks, and her breath caught. Even here at the edge of the Thousand Islands, the head of this house recognised the royal silks.

"Your name?" Myra asked.

It took a moment before the dazed firstwife responded. "Allani. Why... why would you bother with such as us? We are no threat to the throne," Allani said.

"You are a threat to our entire people," Myra said.

"We don't engage in the politics of the inner courts," Allani said with an air of desperation.

"Perhaps not, but you not only deal with the barbarians, who are the enemy of Sylanna, you allow your family to engage in uncontrolled breeding with them, like animals," Jaclyn said.

"Please, it harms no one and gives the women of the outer circle happiness. They're not forced to take the barbarian men to their beds—"

A daggerwife lashed out, striking Allani, and she doubled over in pain. Jaclyn held up her hand to prevent a second blow from being aimed at the woman.

"I should kill you all for sinking to barbarian customs and treason. Luckily for you, as Commander of Sylanna for the assault on the barbarian lands, I have a certain amount of latitude," Jaclyn said.

She saw the hope kindle in Allani's eyes, along with a healthy dose of caution. So, despite what Jaclyn had seen here of the depths they'd sunk to, the woman wasn't entirely stupid. Either way, it didn't matter. As long as this house did as she wanted.

"What compensation is required of my house, Commander?" Allani asked.

"The barbarians you trade with. They run from two different habitations," Jaclyn said.

"Yes." Allani's eyes widened.

"You'll have them smuggle you into one of them—the one I'll show you. You'll lead the Sylannian attack on that region. I have selected some other families to join you," Jaclyn said.

"I... my house isn't much good at strategy or war, Commander." Allani flinched as if expecting another blow.

"You don't have to win. Just cause as much disruption on that side of the barbarian lands as you can," Myra said.

"What will my house gain?" As the words left her mouth Allani's face drained of colour.

Jaclyn held up her hand again, stopping the blow before it landed. It was good to see this woman at least had some drive to live. She might even make a better job of causing disruption than they'd estimated.

"You might surprise me and live. Given you and yours seem so taken by the barbarian ways, should you chose to remain in those lands, well, I won't hunt you down and kill you."

"When you conquer the barbarian lands, my house will be allowed to hold land and move there permanently?" Allani persisted, looking at her desperately.

"If you live and do well, as commander this is something I can grant you." Jaclyn paused, waiting while the other woman processed the possibilities contained in the promise. "The other houses that go with you don't need to survive."

"I pledge my house will serve you so we might live, Commander," Allani said. Hope had dawned in her eyes, although it was tempered with fear. She was smart enough to know there wasn't much hope in her survival. As remote as this island was from their centre and the intrigue of the high-caste families, Allani could hardly be unknowledgeable about all the politics at play.

"Very well. Now, which of your people speaks the barbarian language?" Jaclyn frowned and added, almost absently, "It would probably be better for you if they were disposable. I don't have the time or patience to do this the soft way."

"We can select someone from the outer ring, if any still live, Commander." Allani swallowed.

"Escort one of them to fetch a few, or even some barbarians,"

Jaclyn said to the daggerwives before turning her attention back to Allani. "Of course some still live. We merely cleared a path to you. The rest are being detained. I know you will still need a fighting force," Jaclyn said.

Jaclyn walked over to the breezeway and gazed out over the treetops. It would almost seem a pleasant place if she hadn't had to wade through the filth to get here. As scuffling sounded behind her, she turned to see a small group being herded into her presence. Some women and a male.

Her eyes narrowed as she approached the male. As her people held him, Jaclyn placed her hands on either side of his temples and stared into his eyes.

Hush, the pain will end soon and you will have served your purpose in this life. Jaclyn whispered to him.

The man breathed rapidly, then screamed as she sent a lance into his mind. She didn't bother with niceties; his mind didn't have to be intact when she was done. Ruthlessly, she sucked up as much as she could of his language, channelling the knowledge from his mind to her own, ignoring his agonised screams as she did so. When she was done, she wrenched her mind free of his, the bond she'd used to tie their minds together snapping back into his unprotected mind. One of the women screamed in tandem with him. She guessed she'd just identified the woman who had been copulating with this one.

"End his racket," Jaclyn snapped.

Forcing her way into another mind in such a way always left her with a headache and she tensed in irritation until the blades of the daggerwives flashed, ending his noise with admirable efficiency. Myra stepped forward, selecting her victim without prompting, as did her senior-most daggerwife, Arianne.

Allani was pale as she watched, but Jaclyn was certain the woman and her people had done something similar themselves to learn the barbarian tongue. There was no way they would have left themselves at a disadvantage.

As the low trader barges pulled up to the wooden piers and the sailors lashed the boats to the tie points, the daggerwives leapt. A few of the crew drew their weapons but found themselves disarmed and face-down on the deck in short order. Not having the inclination to deal with the barbarians—there were plenty more where these came from—the remaining daggerwives went through the barge, dispatching the prisoners with brutal efficiency. All the men and boys in the hold were bound and they'd even drugged some, so they posed no threat to her people. The daggerwives dumped the bodies over the edge, trusting the current to sweep the bodies out to deeper waters where the flesh-eating fish of the ocean would make short work of the bodies.

At Arianne's signal that the vessel was secure, Jaclyn jumped lightly onboard, wrinkling her nose at the rank, unwashed smell of bodies. She gestured at the firstwife of this house who, after a slight hesitation, joined her on the boat. The captives were hauled upright but still restrained and on their knees. As they approached one of them, he paled and tried to shrink back.

"Calm down. If I was going to send you down into the depths to feed the giant fish, my people would have ensured you joined your unfortunate cargo," Jaclyn said.

He didn't even blink in shock as she spoke his own language to him. It confirmed her suspicion that the firstwife of this island and her people spoke their language as well.

"Please, we were here to trade. If we're no longer welcome, we'll head on our way," the man said.

"You will, indeed, but you'll do so with my people. Which of your habitations do you come from?" Jaclyn asked.

The man opened his mouth, then closed it again as a map was unfurled in front of him.

"Callenhain, that one there on the right, near where the multiple rivers meet," the man said.

"Do you wish to live?" Jaclyn asked pleasantly.

"I've no wish to die."

"Then, just as you smuggle slaves out of your city, you will smuggle my people in."

He swallowed, looking up at her, his face pale. "The Warleader will kill me if he finds out."

"You will serve me, or you won't survive long enough for your Warleader to kill you."

"That's a valid point," he said.

She returned her attention to the map and pointed to the other habitation.

"What about this one? Can you get us into this one as well?" Jacklyn asked, trying to be sincere and kind, although given how he flinched, she gathered he didn't find it so.

"Vallantia? Yes, I can get you into Vallantia. The head of our trading consortium lives in the city. But..." He paused, looking half panicked.

"But what?"

"You don't want to take Vallantia." He shook his head.

"Ah, but I do. Why do you think I don't?"

"That place is the Warleader's ancestral home. His family still live there," he whispered, sweat breaking out on his forehead.

Jaclyn found it interesting that the man persisted in being more terrified of the threat posed by the barbarian warleader than he was of her. If anything, it intrigued her even more to finally meet this new opponent.

"It's all right. He'll be tied up elsewhere, and by the time he finds out, it will be too late." Jaclyn turned on that last and walked away from the man.

As she jumped out of the barge and back onto the pier, Jaclyn decided she needed a bath. A long, hot, soaking bath to wash away the filth she'd been forced to consort with. Unfortunately, in the weeks, months, and possibly years to come she'd be in the barbarian homeland surrounded by all of them. So she'd only feel clean for a brief period of time.

FIFTY-FIVE

Steven tugged at his jacket as he stood in front of the mirror. It was much easier to get ready and look presentable when the servants were around to help. He'd taken care to choose the house colours. He normally left that to his father, but since he was going to be playing 'arrogant wannabe warlord' he thought it was appropriate. The door opened to admit a servant, who came over and fussed at his jacket and vest. Brushing what he was sure was imaginary specks off the jacket.

"One moment, sir. If you are going to go in the formal house colours, I think the half cloak would be most appropriate."

Steven waited patiently as the man bustled off and rummaged in his closet. It didn't take too long before he came back and threw the deep-blue half cloak over his shoulders, fixing it in place with the ties.

"Thank you," Steven said.

"Just take care, sir. I've heard bad things about the way they treat their serving staff."

Steven couldn't help but stare as the man went off and

fetched his weapons belt. He'd caught the distinct hint of concern in the servant's tone. While the servants had always done their jobs, they didn't exactly seem to care for him. Which was fine, they were servants, not one of his contemporaries, but somehow, it made his day a little more bearable.

Steven stood patiently as the servant helped him arm. He'd been astonished that the Kastlers had left him with his weapons. Then he'd realised it was probably because they didn't think he was any good with them. Of course, he had to concede they might have a point. He wore them and had trained, but after the debacle out in the tributaries where all his training had fled out of his head at the first confrontation, he had to admit to himself he wasn't very good, though in his head he'd always believed he was equal to or better than his brother. The only other possibility he could think of for why they left him his weapons was if they already believed he was on their side.

With one final look in the mirror, he conceded he was the epitome of a Rathadon scion and hoped those he faced went on appearances alone. He took a breath, not that it helped to settle his nerves and, holding his head up, strode to his outer doors and out into the hallway. He kept in character even though there were no guards in the hallway to see him, and continued to the other end and down the stairs to the first floor. Some guards, if they could really be called that, were leaning lazily against the wall near the main ballroom. He guessed that was where the Kastlers were having their meetings. He hadn't bothered to attend before. With a sigh, he pushed open the doors and breezed inside. All conversation stopped and the Kastlers and their people, one and all, stared at him. He couldn't help but notice the consternation on Peter Kastler's face.

"Did you need something, Warlord?" Peter asked.

"No, not at all, but I decided if I'm to be Warlord I should be involved in the decisions," Steven said.

Choosing to ignore their irritated looks, he took a seat at the head of the table. He'd concluded they'd intended to use him as a figurehead while they ran everything. If they pulled it off, that was. Steven almost forgot himself and chuckled at the thought of seeing someone else come up in second place to Michael.

"There's no need to bother yourself with these trivial matters, Warlord," Constance said.

"Oh, it's no bother, please, continue." Steven kept a vacuous smile plastered on his lips.

He waited expectantly as they looked at each other, then, after throwing him another irritated glance, Peter finally shrugged and returned his attention to the man he'd been talking to.

"What do you mean, we lost the shipment?" Peter asked.

"All of our stock?" Constance asked.

The man swallowed, looking anywhere but at them, clearly wishing he were somewhere else. Steven could sympathise.

"All of it, and there's more," the messenger said.

"Well, what else?" Peter snapped.

"Olivia Strafford had your nephew, Sebastian, put to death." A fine beading of sweat sprung up on the messenger's forehead. "Right in the middle of the ballroom at Callenhain."

Steven tried not to let his eyes widen at the mention of Olivia Strafford, one of his brother's most trusted people.

"What, why?" Constance asked.

"Orders are to keep their heads down when the Warleader and his people are in town. What did he do that drew Olivia Strafford's attention?" Peter asked.

"Rumour is one of the men they took was one of the Unwanted. He killed the guards and escaped with the rest of the stock."

"What possessed that imbecile to take one of the Unwanted?" Constance asked.

"How would I know? I wasn't there, but I'm told that's how we lost the shipment."

"We're going to have to get more stock," Peter grumbled.

Steven leaned forward, compelled to ask, although he had the sinking feeling he didn't want to know. "When you all say stock. What do you mean? What type of stock?"

"Men, and those with healing talent. Not only will Sylanna trade for it, but they pay well." Constance threw a distracted look in his direction.

"It costs us very little to round up strays from the street, so we come out with a big profit," Peter said.

"Why would anyone consider one of Michael's men strays? If they killed your nephew for it, they'll come here." Steven swallowed when he realised there was an underlying hint of satisfaction in his tone.

"They'll be too busy shortly. Besides, according to what we've been told, it was Olivia, not your brother, who did it," Constance added.

Steven pressed his lips together. He didn't need to point out the flaw in the Kastlers' argument to them. He'd encountered Olivia more often than he'd been comfortable with over the years. His face heated as he remembered all the times she'd rejected his advances. When he'd been drunk, he'd thought it was a great idea to try to talk her into his bed. His drunken self had thought she must hate his brother as much as he did. After all, she was stuck playing second to him as well. She'd proven, forcibly, that she didn't need his brother to fight her battles for her. Cold sober after one such incident, the idea terrified him. He'd seen her training with some of their warband. The woman was frighteningly competent, both with her weapons and the veil. If his brother hadn't proven himself to be so disgustingly competent and been made the Warleader, he suspected she would have. She was Michael's second-in-command, his shadow. Where one was, generally the other wasn't far behind. Logically, it meant if Olivia had ordered the death of the Kastlar nephew for engaging in the flesh trade, then Michael knew all about it and he would come here. They all would.

For the first time in his life, that particular thought cheered Steven up.

Then he frowned. "What do you mean? That he'll be too busy?"

"On our last shipment, our trading partners warned us there was about to be a big attack," Constance said.

"The Sylannians have recalled their commander from another battle. She's apparently brilliant," Peter said.

"What if she attacks here?" Steven asked.

"We've taken steps. Our people in Callenhain took out a few of the Warlord's sentries." Peter was smug.

"That is why you think they will launch their attack down that way?" Steven asked. He didn't feel the particular need to point out to the Kastlers, that he knew all about their efforts to kill off the Warlord's sentries, since he'd killed one himself.

"Makes sense for them to take the easy path. Besides, Callenhain is closer to their homeland than Vallantia." Constance shrugged.

"Wherever my brother is, he will hear about it and ride there to fight along with the rest of the Warlord's people." Steven's mood deflated a little at the thought it would take a long time for his brother to get back here.

"Cheer up. This new commander might even kill your brother for you." Peter seemed positively cheerful about the prospect.

"You'd best hope so," Steven muttered under his breath.

"What?" Peter asked.

"I said I hope so." Steven said blandly.

Steven had to force himself to sit through the rest of their meeting and pretend to take an interest. It wouldn't do for him to excuse himself and go running straight to his parents on the back of hearing that information. It appeared the rumours Evan had heard had been correct. The Kastlers were engaged in the flesh trade.

FIFTY-SIX

Allani stared around at her fellow wives. She wanted to wallow in self-pity, to roll up and die. After all, it was what her king had decreed in sending his commander to come after her house. Yet in that moment of complete devastation, seeing the death of all she cared about, a small glimmer of hope was offered to her.

"Get the wives ready to travel to the barbarian lands," Allani said.

As her words sounded in the silence her fellow wives in her inner circle looked at her startled, their eyes red and puffy from their weeping.

"Why, why should we help this king who ordered the death of our house?"

"I'd rather die here in our home than in a foreign land."

"Because she offers us a chance of survival," Allani snapped, glaring around the clustered wives. "Did none of you listen to her words?"

"She came here and killed our men," one of the wives wailed.

"As she was ordered to. At the end, she threw us a lifeline. She can do very little here to thwart the king's decree. That changes once the war begins in the barbarian lands; she will be the one who has the power."

"Jaclyn is the sister of our king. She survived the purge when he ascended the throne. Rumour has it he's been trying to orchestrate her death since then," a wife said, her voice soft.

Allani saw her fellow wife still had her head bowed. She could feel the woman was distraught, but it impressed her that she could at least still think her way through a problem.

"That old rumour. She wields the king's daggers. Everyone knows that." Another wife spat.

Allani sat back as arguments rose between the wives, all of them highly emotional. Very few making valid points. She sat, allowing them to run out of energy. After what they'd all been through, they could hardly continue at such a high emotional level. It was exhausting. Finally, everyone settled, resentment seething among them.

"It is an old rumour, but it is true. Those of the outer circles are free to flee to other houses but for us, the core of the inner circle of this house, there are only two choices. We can accept the duty given to us by the commander, or we can sit here and die. I know which one I'm going to choose," Allani said, sitting back to regard her fellow wives.

Her heart broke as she could see they clearly did not want to accept the situation they found themselves in. As firstwife it was her job to protect her house and she'd failed them all.

"Surely other houses will take us in?" one wives said.

"What, and face the king's decree they die for sheltering us?" Allani asked.

"I think not. I will accept the challenge the commander has given us," a wife said.

"To die on foreign soil?" objected another.

"No, to orchestrate the death of the sister houses she sends with us. If we succeed, we have the chance at a new life in a new land," Allani said, calmer now that she had made her choice.

"Why, why does Jaclyn seek the death of the sister houses?"

Allani's expression hardened. "I did not ask, but what other reason could a daughter of the Monarch House, a claimant to the Throne of a Thousand Islands, have to kill off some of her brother's strongest supporters?"

The other wives stared at her, stunned. She didn't add that there was the distinct possibility of settling back here in Sylanna if Jaclyn succeeded and then made a play for the Monarch House. To even utter the sentiment that the Monarch House was showing signs of madness could result in the order for their house to be killed. Again. Despite what some of the wives might believe, she and what remained of her house were alive because Jaclyn allowed it. No one born of the Monarch House did anything for anyone that wasn't driven out of pure self-interest.

"We can die here or die there, except there we have a chance of survival," one of the others said.

She regarded the inner circle of wives. They would do as she asked. They didn't have a choice. As soon as they stopped long enough to think, they would realise there was only one path forward that lead to a potential future for them all. Despite how small a chance that possibility was. The men they had taken had filled their ears with stories about their Warlord and his feared Warleader, but she would take some chance over no chance.

FIFTY-SEVEN

Michael dismounted outside the meeting hut. Khaliun was inside. That he didn't even have to check to know where Khaliun was was problematic in itself. Michael groaned, resting his forehead against his mount.

"What?" Olivia asked.

"We haven't been apart long enough," Michael said.

"Ah. Need me to stop you from doing something stupid?"

He glanced at her and, as he suspected, she couldn't quite hide the quirk on her lips. Of course, he could also sense the amusement. It was both a blessing and a curse. Although he didn't really know what life was like for people who couldn't sense what those around them were feeling.

"Please. It would be wrong."

"The woman is going to glare at me," Olivia muttered then turned to Nathanial. "Michael will bunk in with me."

Nathanial glanced at him, then Olivia, before he snorted in amusement as communication obviously passed between the pair.

"It's not funny." Michael threw her a disgusted look before his irritation crumbled. "Oh, all right, it is."

"Not for you, it's not. I'm sorry, I shouldn't laugh. You realise most would just roll with the situation until the effect wore off?"

"What about when reality hits and they discover they don't really like each other?" Michael raised his eyebrows at her.

"See, you know already, it's just that effect of sharing minds with the woman. It will wear off," Olivia said.

"I'd rather actually know I like someone if I sleep with them. Not just do so because our heads are messed up and fooling us."

Michael shook his head and stopped abruptly as Khaliun appeared outside the meeting hut. He closed his eyes briefly and reinforced his mental shield. Olivia squeezed his arm in warning as he continued to close the distance between them.

"You came," Khaliun said.

"Of course we came. We said we would," Olivia said.

Khaliun wrenched her gaze away from him to Olivia. Then she blushed. Khaliun's words had been meant for him alone, not his second-in-command.

"The messenger said the Sylannians have found the trail on their side of the mountain?" Michael asked.

"They have," Khaliun said and gestured for them to enter the meeting hut.

As he closed the distance between them, Khaliun reached out and, against his better judgement, he hugged her.

"How have you been?" Michael asked.

"It's complicated, I'm sorry." Khaliun ducked her head.

"Don't be. You know it's not real, right?" Michael said that last as gently as he could.

"I do. It doesn't make it easier," Khaliun said.

Michael was relieved that at least he didn't have to explain the situation between them to her. He drew away and moved across the room to put himself near Olivia, even though his emotions were screaming at him to stay close to Khaliun.

"I take it they haven't made it up the trail yet or we wouldn't be sitting here so calmly," Olivia said.

"They wouldn't have found us at all if it wasn't for Khaliun and her late co-leader." Erden spat, glowering at his fellow clan leader the entire time.

That one reeks of jealousy, Olivia said.

Erden; he was Khaliun's lover.

Well, it seems I was wrong. It isn't Khaliun glaring at me, but Erden glaring at you.

I guess that's not exactly a new occurrence, either.

Michael drew his attention to Erden, who glared not at him but at Khaliun. Michael shook his head at the situation. It was ludicrous. It wasn't like Michael had been here these last few months sneaking into Khaliun's bed behind her lover's back. Michael pushed the matter aside and scanned the meeting tent. His eyes slid from Erden to Khaliun to the empty spot where her co-leader would normally sit.

"What happened?"

Khaliun took a shaky breath and rubbed her face with her hand before she finally cleared her throat and detailed their fateful run back to their former homeland. She told it all, not sparing her own role in their mission. Guilt and anguish were a tight ball within her.

"I fear there were too many of us to hide the trail of our passing completely. The Sylannians that are below followed us. I don't understand their delayed response in following the rest of us, unless they wanted to fully secure Tarkhan and his small group."

"Or perhaps they were waiting for reinforcements before running off foolishly against an unknown number of enemy forces?" Olivia said. "I don't have to tell you trying to go after

Tarkhan, even if he is alive, is not a course of action I would recommend."

Khaliun shook her head mutely.

"It should have been obvious to the pair of you that returning to Hallaran was idiocy," Erden said.

"Correct me if I'm wrong, but there weren't many directions you could have gone undetected from your home at Kallith. So, the Sylannians had probably already guessed there must be a trail over the mountains," Michael said, doing his best to ignore the strained atmosphere in the tent and not react to Erden's open antagonism. "I doubt the Sylannians failed to notice the disappearance of the entire Kallith Clan."

Khaliun stared at him at the last, her expression clearing as if she'd expected a much different reaction from him. "We of Kallith weren't the only clan who used the old trade route over the Heights. It surprises me it's taken them this long."

"Have they found the trail? Or are they just guessing the approximate location?"

"They have, but we sent boulders down the trail, as if there'd been an avalanche. It should delay them a bit," Khaliun replied.

"You think they'll clear it?" Michael asked.

"Without a doubt. Our scouts tell us they are already doing so," Khaliun said.

"They—"

"They are also amassing a lot of people," Orghana said, cutting off whatever her co-leader had been about to contribute. "Too many for us to fight alone."

"We'll sleep the night, then perhaps you can take us to check it out?" Michael said.

"Unless you think it wise we travel there straight away?" Olivia asked.

"Tomorrow will be fine. Our scouts said it will take them a few more days yet to clear the rockfall." Khaliun shook her head.

Cushions scattered as Michael stood and left the meeting tent and, sighing, he went to ask where his people could camp for the night, only to find Erden in front of him. The other man's chest was puffed out, his lips pressed into a thin line. Michael also noted the man's clenched fists, although wisely they stayed down at his sides and didn't contain a weapon. Although he shook as if he was barely containing himself.

"Erden, don't be foolish. Haven't you caused enough trouble?" Orghana said.

"I don't know what has gotten into your head, but I suggest you get over it." Michael's voice dropped, flat and cold as he spoke to the other man, and he took a step forward leaning in to whisper the last. "If you attack me, your tribe will need a new co-leader opposite Orghana."

Olivia stepped up to his side. "I think perhaps when we go to check out the situation in the Heights, it's best if Erden stays here. I don't think we want an incident between our people."

Michael kept his gaze steady as two other leaders took hold of Erden and hauled him back. Michael showed his back to the leaders of the clan and strode towards his warband, leaving Olivia and her much cooler head to deal with them.

Michael stood in the shadows thrown by the mountain around him, his gaze focused on those below. He drew in a breath of the veil and sharpened his focus. Those of the clan had been correct. The mass of people gathering below were mostly Sylannian. There were those that were obviously originally of the clans, but he trusted the word of his allies that they'd been under the rule of Sylanna long enough that they were probably the ones most trusted by their conquers.

"They've definitely cleared the trail?" Michael asked.

Michael waited patiently as the scout checked with Khaliun, who nodded at her before she answered. It wasn't because the woman didn't understand him. It was one of the few advantages of having merged his mind with Khaliun's. His command of their language was flawless.

"Yes, as of this morning," the scout said.

"Why do you think they haven't started up?" Michael asked.

"They've been amassing more people. Hundreds of them arrived just yesterday. It wouldn't surprise me if more come today."

With Olivia and Nathanial, who stood at his side, Michael contemplated what they faced. It would be easier if they could somehow stop those below from making their way up the side of the mountain to the top. Once they got up here, it would be reasonably easy for the Sylannians to traverse across and descend on them down on the plateau.

Suggestions?

Find places to launch an ambush as they come up the trail? Nathanial said.

Michael waited as Olivia's eyes narrowed as she caught sight of the top of the trail. It resembled a corridor with rocky outcrops on either side.

We won't be able to stop them all. There's too many down there already, but another rockfall would be helpful. The clans could prepare it while we fight them down at a likely spot, Olivia said.

Then we retreat when we have to and the clans unleash the rocks, Nathanial said.

Best-case scenario, it will give us a chance to rest before having to fight again, Olivia said.

Michael crossed to the trailhead, gazing up at each edge and down the trail. He could see the last stretch was steep. The Unwanted could account for many of their enemy before they would be forced to retreat. Then those coming up would be crushed by the boulders crashing down on them. The strategy had possibilities. Particularly if they had time to set up such rockfalls further down the trail, which they could release as they retreated. If they did it correctly, they could block the trail entirely. He retraced his steps to where everyone stood watching him.

"Do you think your people could rig something to kick off another of those rockfalls down the trail?"

Khaliun conferred with the group of clansmen, then shrugged and nodded thoughtfully.

"We should be able to manage that. There are certainly enough rocks—although it will probably take more time than we have," Khaliun said, a frown appearing on her forehead. "I doubt we can get it done before the Sylannians can get up here."

"We will run interference and slow them down. A couple of rockfalls at suitable points down that trail could be an advantage," Michael said.

This is going to hurt, Nathanial said quietly to them both.

"We'll do the fighting. Your people will need to release the rockfalls once we clear the checkpoints," Olivia said, before adding to Michael and Nathanial, *There'll be no way we can hide our secret.*

I don't know how much about us Khaliun learnt when we joined minds. She might know our weakness anyway. Even if she doesn't, I judge it will be a whole lot worse if we allow those Sylannians to get up here.

As soon as the Sylannians get up here, we'll have to fight anyway, Nathanial said.

Then we'd collapse at an even worse time, at which point both the Sylannians and the Kallith would know our secret, Olivia said.

The Sylannians would wash down the mountain, the Kallith would collapse. Nathanial inspected the mostly barren mountains as he spoke. They offered very little protection and few good vantage points to mount a defence. *Then they'd be free to attack our people from behind.*

I agree, we fight now, Olivia said.

"Can a couple of your scouts show us some of the trail? If we have to ambush the Sylannians to give you time, I'd rather we pick the best locations for that now."

"Of course, we'll come with you," Khaliun said.

Khaliun issued instructions to some of her own people to fetch more workers, crafters, and supplies. When she was done, she gestured to a couple of their scouts to join them and led the way to the trail.

MICHAEL TENSED. He didn't need his other abilities to know their enemy approached. It was the crunch of rock against rock and the skittering of shale that gave away that the Sylannians had finally made their way up the trail. They'd picked this narrow section of the trail on purpose. Those ascending could only be three abreast at the most. Whereas for them it was a little wider, allowing them the higher ground as well as several ranks to help with the assault. Not that he figured they'd need help this first time. As far as he could tell, the approaching Sylannians did not know they'd been under observation, or that their luck had just run out. As two of the Sylannians came around the bend, they stumbled to a halt. Frozen in that spilt second in shock, those ascending behind them stumbling into them. It was the only warning he needed.

Michael launched himself at the first rank of the enemy. He had one of the Unwanted on either side of him and all of them reacted together. While this wasn't a fighting style they commonly used, it was something they'd practiced for. Their blades lashed out and the enemy fighters tumbled before they could even draw their weapons. The second rank of Sylannians did no better than the first, other than to yell a warning to those behind them as they fell. Michael gritted his teeth and paid attention to the play of the wicked curved blades in front of him, careful to hold the line and not get drawn further down the trail. From experience, the Sylannians did not give up easily. From their observations above, their enemy had thousands to draw on. His own group was vastly outnumbered, but the other warbands would head this way when they received word. They just had to delay and kill as many of the Sylannians as they could while they were at it.

Fall back.

At Olivia's order, he and those on each side of him fell back, with Olivia and two others stepping forward to take his place. Michael wiped sweat from his forehead, only now realising he was breathing heavily. He checked on those he fought with and frowned, tapping the man on his left on the arm to gain his attention.

You're injured. Drop back.

The man was rebellious at first, but did as he was told. Damien stepped forward as anchor point with his squad mates on either side of him. He could feel Damien's pent-up energy as he watched their companions fight in the narrow confines the trail allowed them, waiting to take their own turn. Nathanial took to the front as Olivia and her crew dropped back. She plastered herself against the rocky outcrop, giving them some cover, and gazed up at the sky as she sucked in air.

It's going to be a long day, Michael said.

Hopefully, at some point, they'll drop back to consolidate and consider their options, Olivia said.

Only if they're smart. It should occur to them at some point that shields would be a great start, Michael said.

Just as well you're not on their side, Olivia said.

Do you think Damien will hold? Michael asked.

He's stable right now and one of our strongest, or we wouldn't have put him as the focus. Olivia shrugged. *Besides, if he doesn't, he's got a level-headed team. It will be no different from when any of us go down.*

He'll be pulled back and others will take his place.

Michael nodded, then motioned to his team and stepped forward, taking their place several ranks behind, ready to slip forward to re-join the fight.

FIFTY-EIGHT

Myra sat with Jaclyn and Ricardo in the rooms they'd taken over in what would become an abandoned island. She'd disabused the wives of this island of the notion that there was any choice at all for any of them, other than to die here by the blades of Jaclyn's daggerwives, or travel to fight in the barbarian lands. Some of them had apparently thought they could go to other houses. Now it was just a tedious delay to give time for their forces to amass at one of the muster points, depending on which attack their houses were designated to. Still, despite the appalling wooden hovels that ringed the island, the old heart of the place was rather pleasant.

"We can't afford to have a viper in our midst when we enter the barbarian lands," Myra said.

"It will be easier to arrange her death over there, unnoticed, than here," Jaclyn said.

"Only if you want it discreet," Myra said.

Myra shrugged as the other two stared at her. They'd talked over this topic before and gotten exactly nowhere.

"You don't think it's a risk?" Ricardo asked.

"Not particularly. The only reason we allowed her to live was because we were better off knowing who the spy was. If we kill her, the king's wives would just replace her with another that we didn't know," Myra said.

"The same applies, if he hears we've killed her..." Jaclyn shrugged.

"How? Everyone here is joining us in the barbarian lands. We aren't going back to the court. The other houses joining us in battle have their muster points and should already be on their way to them. We're going into the barbarian lands for an unspecified length of time, but I doubt this fight will be shorter than the last." Myra raised her eyebrow at them as Ricardo and Jaclyn looked at each other, seeming faintly embarrassed. "Correct me if I'm missing something, but we are going to kill her? Either here or there. I vote here. I'd rather we didn't have a traitor with us when we take the barbarian city."

A silence settled on the room as they considered her words. Only long practice stopped Myra from fidgeting. Unlike Jaclyn and Ricardo, she hadn't been born to a high-caste house. She'd gained a place in Jaclyn's house due to showing early potential with the blade, and her abilities with the veil. Then she'd birthed a son to the house, which tied the three of them mind to mind. Thankfully, in those early years, while their bonds settled into place, they all mostly got on with each other. There were times the mind bonds could be exceedingly difficult when people ended up hating each other. That Jaclyn, a daughter with the blood of the Monarch House, had accepted her had astonished her. It was almost unheard of. The house—her house—had given her, a daughter of a low-caste family, an opportunity. As far as some of the others were concerned, her lot in life was to go from daggerwife to underwife, if she lived that long, then die without ever seeing their husband's bed. She'd made her pledge long ago that she would defend them all with her life.

"You're right. She might as well die now. I'll make arrangements," Jaclyn said.

"No bother. I'll do it." Myra stood smoothly, rising from the pile of cushions she'd been sitting in. This time, it was Jaclyn's eyebrows that rose. "I've never liked the woman, even if I understand why we left her alive. She's a traitor to all of us and to her culture."

Myra had no need to steel herself for the task ahead, as she walked towards the door. She slid it closed behind her as she stepped out, nodding to the daggerwives who stood duty at the door. She held her hand up as they went to split and follow her.

"No need, I'm not going far and our own people are everywhere," Myra said.

They shifted, one foot to the other, before two of them shook their heads.

"No, Primewife. It's our duty to go with you," one of the daggerwives said.

Myra sighed. She'd thought it worth a shot, but the daggerwives had a duty to go with her even if she'd rather they didn't. She should have been used to the arrangement by now. They were, after all, away from their court and back to a war footing. Myra waved one hand absently in consent and continued down the hallway, a handful of daggerwives falling in around her. Myra kept her pace steady, heading for the outer cross island pathways. The woman she was looking for should be right where she'd been assigned at the outer edge of the island, looking out to sea. Where she could do the minimum of harm if she betrayed them all.

Myra opened her mind, questing out. The large glowing mass was the wives of the traitor house. They may have agreed to Jaclyn's terms, but Allani and her inner cohort were still being kept under guard. Myra filtered that group out, concentrating on the members of her own house. Not that it was as useful as it had been in the early days. Jaclyn's house had grown from its modest beginning to number in the hundreds. Some of the mental signatures she recognised. She'd led some of them in battle after all. Others she didn't know, but a quick, light touch on their minds before moving on showed them to be the daggerwives of Jaclyn's house.

In short order, Myra detected the daggerwife she was after and altered her path, taking a wooden pathway that hung between the great trees and spanned the forest. She could see other bridges spearing off to other structures that wound their way up the giant trees and spread out along the supporting branches. Mostly, she ignored them and kept to her path. Feeling a vibration that seemed to pulse through her with a faint hum on the edge of her awareness, she turned towards where the sound was coming from. Sure enough, a colony of the giant silk-spiders were being herded from their giant webs by the spider keepers. Nostalgic pleasure settled on her at the sight. That had been her life once. It was a skill she and Liliana shared. One of the reasons Jaclyn's house produced the finest spidersilk in Sylanna was that they actively sought and accepted those with an affinity for the silkspiders. Much like any spiders, these had eight legs, but they were half the size of a person and they glowed. Unlike any other creature they'd encountered, the spiders seemed to channel the veil, storing it somehow in their bulbous abdomen, where it combined with the silk they spun. That almost living silk, which the Sylannians harvested, remained viable for years before it lost its responsiveness. Their silk weavers spun it into everything from their clothes to their sheets. Jaclyn had ordered the spiders to be herded up and transported to her house's home island. They were far too valuable to be left untended on this island once everyone left for the battlefront. Everyone, right down to the spider-keepers, weavers and servitors of the traitor house would go to live or die in the barbarian lands with the firstwife, or die here on their former home island if they so choose.

"Primewife."

It was just one word of warning from the head of the dagger-wives that drew her attention back to the task at hand. She was closing in on Tracy. As she went around a sweeping bend in the walkway, she found herself on the outer perimeter of the island. The traitor stood, leaning against the rail, seemingly inspecting the inner island and buildings, her back to the approach she was tasked with watching. Myra's eyes narrowed and a spark of anger flared. It might seem like a useless lookout post, gazing out at the open sea. Any reasonable person would expect that any threat would come from the other side of the island that faced back towards the Thousand Islands that formed the heart of their homeland. Yet this approach was of no less importance and, given the lookout wasn't even watching, likely to be the most successful attack point should attackers come this way.

Myra's anger flared as Tracy finally noticed her approach. She couldn't even keep watch properly. It had taken the traitor too long to become aware she had people walking up on her. Myra relaxed her control just a little to allow the low burning anger to filter through. Tracy still didn't bother to watch the approach to the island she was meant to be covering. It seemed the woman was a failure on multiple levels.

"Do you really think your current position is the most suitable to keep watch for enemies that may fall on us?" Myra asked.

Tracy shrugged. A look of disdain passed fleetingly over her face before she retained control and smiled. Myra guess they should all be grateful the women the Monarch House inserted into their house had mostly, with a few exceptions, proven incapable of hiding their true natures. At least, in this house, in which talent in the veil ran strong.

"Who precisely are we expecting to fall on us?"

"We're expecting the barbarians any day now, for one."

"From this direction?" Tracy rolled her eyes.

"We're on war footing. Your job is to do your duty…"

"I am."

"To Chelsie?" Myra saw Tracy stiffen and her face flush, eyes darting from Myra to the daggerwives who accompanied her. "You're a traitor to your house and a disgrace to your people."

"No. I'm loyal to our king and his wives. It's the duty of all of us to be loyal."

"It is your duty to be loyal to your husband and firstwife."

"She should have had the grace to die in the purge!"

Myra drew her daggers and, as she lunged with a subtle modulated hum, she manipulated Tracy's silks. Tracy's eyes widened as she discovered her armour shell stayed in its floaty silken form no matter how hard she tried to control it. Myra's ability to control spidersilk keyed to another was rare and something she, Jaclyn and Ricardo kept to themselves.

"How?" Tracy asked.

"We all have our secrets. I am just better at keeping mine."

Tracy's stumbled back, belatedly drawing her own blades. Myra's blade sliced across her opponent's forearm and red burst forth. Myra continued her discordant hum as Tracy desperately tried to control her silks, which distracted her even further. Metal clashed as her second blade was deflected.

Myra was aware the daggerwives had drawn their own weapons and bracketed her but she raised her blade to deflect Tracy's strike for her throat, then blocked the second blade as she lunged in past Tracy's guard.

Without the spidersilk in armour form to resist it, Myra's blade slid into Tracy's abdomen. A blade fell from Tracy's hand as she pressed it against her wound, trying to stem the flow of blood. As Tracy gazed up at her, eyes wide, Myra slashed her throat, watching dispassionately as she slumped to the ground.

"Make sure she dies, then dispose of the body and clean up."

"Yes, Primewife."

"Find another to take this post."

"Yes, Primewife."

Myra paused and considered each of the daggerwives. These who guarded the heart of the house were loyal, beyond any doubt. Opening their minds to inspection by both herself and Jaclyn.

"There will be no need to mention my ability with the spidersilk to anyone. Not even your fellow daggerwives. The lives of our husband and First may one day depend on the advantage it gives." Myra glanced from one to the other, pausing on each until they acknowledged her order.

She ignored the blood splattered on her hands, face, and clothes. She also ignored the daggerwives who peeled off to dutifully follow her, while the others stayed to follow her orders. As she retraced her steps, she decided a bath and a fresh set of silks were in order before she reported back to Ricardo and Jaclyn.

Myra breezed back into the room as the daggerwives opened the doors for her to see Jaclyn and Ricardo relaxing back in each other's arms on the low couches.

"It's done." Myra frowned as she took in Jaclyn's distracted nod and settled on the couch with them. "What else is wrong?"

Jaclyn shook her head. "I never could hide anything from you. I've been thinking about that lookout we found on our first raid."

Myra expelled a breath. "You think there are more than we found?"

"It makes sense they'd be stationed all along the river

between the two major cities. Our scouts mainly concentrated on those closer to Vallantia."

"If there is, and they catch our attack forces getting into position, the whole element of surprise is up," Ricardo said.

Myra had to concede it was an issue. "I'll lead a team. If those barbarian lookouts are there, we'll locate them and take them out."

"I think we should ask the smuggler to pinpoint the locations he knows about," Ricardo said.

"You're right. If they have been coming to and from Callenhain and Vallantia, it makes sense they'd know the locations of at least some lookouts," Myra said.

"Choose some good mindspeakers to take with you. Travel ahead of the traitor house and replace the lookouts with our own. When you're done, the traitors can launch their attack on Callenhain," Jaclyn said as she stood and went to the map table, tapping with one long finger at the location where they'd found the dead lookout on their first raid. "Wait for us here and we'll pick you up on the way to launch our own attack."

"I'll make arrangements." Myra hugged Jaclyn and Ricardo. "The pair of you stay safe."

Myra straightened and strode from the room. She didn't give herself the luxury of looking back at the two people who mattered more to her than anyone else. She had a job to do. If she was successful, it was one small thing that might help her house survive.

FIFTY-NINE

There were a number of fail points in their battle plan to take the barbarian lands and this was the first. If the barbarian warlord was alerted of their attack by any of his watchers in the tributaries the risk of failure was high. Myra fixed her gaze on Allani. In the month that it had taken to mobilise the houses that would join Allani's in the first assault on the barbarian lands, Allani had grown more confident.

"You and your forces will wait here until I give permission for you to get into position and launch your attack," Myra said.

"As you command, Primewife Myra. We'll await your orders," Allan said.

"In the meantime, get the rest of the forces unloaded here. Remember, only smuggle in one team at a time. The goal is to get into the city undetected, before launching your assault."

"I assure you I haven't forgotten Commander Jaclyn's instructions. I'll do exactly as I've been ordered," Allani said.

Myra took in all the boats arrayed behind them, filled with the forces Jaclyn commanded. Those from the traitor house were joined by the houses from the central islands of Sylanna. Houses who'd sent some of their own to infiltrate Jaclyn's house and try to kill Jaclyn and Ricardo while they'd been in the lands of the People. One and all they were loyal to the Monarch House. Or more precisely to the firstwife of the Monarch House. The very houses that Jaclyn had tricked Samuel into sacrificing. Yet she caught no uncertainty or distrust from any of those who filled the boats, only a sense of anticipation. Myra signalled the daggerwife team detailed to accompany her and they made their way overland as quickly as they could to get into position. She paused, a pang of worry striking her, only to have her scout step out from the concealing bushes. Myra closed the distance between them and settled into the hideout, with a view of the small hut on the water's edge below. Jaclyn had studied the barbarian warlord, his warleader and their tactics even before Samuel had tasked her to defeat the barbarian lands for Sylanna. More to safeguard their own against discovery during their initial raids than anything else. As soon as the king had conferred the rank of commander on Jaclyn they'd sent out their scouts to learn the location of those who formed the barbarian communication network along the tributaries. The barbarian smugglers had been able to pinpoint some of the lookout locations they'd missed. They'd scoured their own house for strong mindspeakers to replace the barbarians. Even some of the serving class had been given higher status to gain the numbers they needed. Myra turned to the daggerwife who was charged with remaining here, replacing the barbarian communication network with their own.

"Is everyone ready?" Myra asked.

"The others advise they'll strike when you command, Primewife Myra," the daggerwife said.

"Attack," Myra said.

As she spoke, Myra rose with her team of daggerwives around her and converged on the small hut below. She'd just reached the hut when the door opened, the barbarian stepping out, a frown on her face. Myra's blades struck out at the barbarian lookout. The woman stiffened, a cry of pain escaping her lips as she went down without a fight. Myra's team went through the door of the hut. She only had a moment to wait before the daggerwives reappeared.

"All clear, Primewife Myra," a daggerwife said.

Myra waited as the daggerwife who would remain held up her hand, head cocked to one side listening for the reports from the other strong mindspeakers attached to the other assault teams. Each of the assault teams had been tasked to take out the barbarian lookouts, replacing the barbarians with their own teams along the river. The moments that passed seemed like an eternity, with the sun beginning to set as they waited. So much of their success rode on this moment and the elimination of the communications network that would alert the barbarian warlord of their attack if they failed. The daggerwife took a deep breath, excitement thrumming through her.

"It's done, Primewife. The relay is in place, the first stage of our attack is complete," the daggerwife said.

SIXTY

Tarkhan lay on his bed. The rocking of the boat, combined with the flowing water, was oddly soothing. His eyes flared open, lips pressing together in a thin line as he realised he'd fallen prey to the whispers in his mind telling him to submit to his fate. The muscles in his abdomen and arms bunched as he strained against the silken bonds and he sank into his pillows once more, panting as his efforts, as brief as they'd been, proved to be as ineffective as the first dozen or so times he'd tried it. Somehow, he'd thought if he could just put enough pressure on the silk, it would tear and he could win his freedom. Or he could break the timber the bed was constructed of—but it was made from good, strong lumber. As far as he could tell, he'd been on the ship, confined in this room, for over a week. Not only had he failed to have any detrimental effect on that which bound him, he increasingly fell to his captor's efforts to keep him docile.

"It could be worse, warrior," the older Sylannian said.

She was the same one who'd first taken him into custody when he'd been brought aboard. He'd had the vague hope that when she left him alone he'd have much better luck at breaking free. Except, when she left his presence, it was only to be replaced by another of them. However, only she ever spoke to him in his own language, and his grasp of theirs was rudimentary.

As he'd expected, he found her sitting in a comfortable lounging chair in the corner of the cabin. Tarkhan sighed at the evidence that he'd obviously fallen asleep again. It had been another of his captors sitting there previously.

"How?"

"I could shackle you down in the hull where we normally transport the collared."

"Why am I so lucky?"

"Should you prove suitable, you'll have a much different life than most other collared. A situation for which you can thank your Sylannian blood."

"I keep telling you I'm not Sylannian," Tarkhan said.

He wasn't even angry at her insistence that one of his ancestors had passed down Sylannian heritage to him. They'd had this conversation many times, but he still felt compelled to protest. She didn't even bother to respond to his denial, just that hint of a smile and a knowing look in her eyes that he found infuriating. He was about to snarl at her when calls from those on the deck of the boat diverted his attention. In the brief opportunities they'd allowed him to stand, the windows of the cabin revealed they'd been sailing through the heart of what he'd been told was the Sylannian homeland. Each time he caught a glimpse of their surroundings, the islands were getting more numerous and closer together. The double cabin doors were pushed wide open without ceremony and they brought in a covered litter. He watched them settle it on the floor. The cabin barely had room for the thing. His breath came short and sharp.

"Are we here now?" Tarkhan asked.

"Yes. We are at our destination."

"What will happen to me?"

"I will have you transported to rooms that have been prepared for you. Don't look so surprised, we sent word ahead. Once inside, you will find a new life." Her fingers brushed his temples. "Hush now, do not fear. Your keeper will ensure you are well cared for."

Despite her attempt to soothe his sudden fear, Tarkhan struggled and cried out as the Sylannians surrounded him and bundled him into the covered litter. The firm hands of the older Sylannian clamped onto his temples, forcing his head to turn so he was gazing into her eyes.

"You'll only hurt yourself if you continue to carry on. No one must know of your arrival. Sleep."

Tarkhan gasped, feeling darkness smother his mind in its folds.

SIXTY-ONE

Steven's step faltered as he breezed into the room where the Kastlers held their war meetings. The Kastlers held them every day and even though they had long since become tedious, his mother insisted he keep attending. He was no expert on such matters, but while they called them war meetings, there was very little war or defence tactics discussed, but there was a great deal of talk about money and trade. If he'd been them, he would have put far more consideration into how they were going to defend themselves when his brother finally showed up. Not that he felt obliged to point that out to them.

His face froze as he took in the scene of one of the Kastlers' sons, Leo, pawing at one of the young serving girls. The serving girl pressed back, her face to one side as she struggled ineffectually to escape the hands that pawed at her. Fear and hopelessness emanated from her in waves. Steven was thrown back to the moment in the dining room when he'd groped his brother's healer, Kesha, at the table. Kesha's face had frozen, and she'd pulled back from him as far as she could without fleeing the table. Kesha's spurt of momentary fear before Michael had intervened on her behalf was similar to what he was sensing from the serving girl. It was like a mirror was being held up and he was looking at himself. It reflected a self that he was beginning to realise he didn't like.

There were other people in this room. Constance and Peter sat as they normally did at the table and seemed to proceed with their conversation, not paying the slightest attention to the behaviour of their son. There were guards on the door, and other servants all pretending not to notice. Unlike Kesha no one cared enough or had a high enough rank to intervene on behalf of the serving girl. Smoothing his face, Steven strode over to the table, barely looking over at the poor serving girl as he spoke.

"You! My rooms are a mess. Stop fooling around and go do your job and clean them up."

Leo glared at him, not relinquishing his grasp on the girl. Steven tried not to show how angry he was to see the redness on the girl's cheek and the tears streaming down her face.

"Can't you find another servant to clean your room?"

"Oh, you're not finished with her?" Steven said in what he hoped was a vacuous manner, then he frowned at the servant. "Well, did you hear me? What are you doing still lazing about on the table? Go on then. Go to my rooms."

Leo glared at him as the servant used his distraction to edge away. Steven didn't miss that she had to pull her skirts down, or the sleeve of her blouse back over her shoulder, as she scurried across the room, almost at a bolt for the door. She muttered something like 'thank you, m'lord' as she left the room almost at a run.

"Nice of you to join us, Warlord." Peter finally paid attention to him. "I trust you slept well."

Steven pretended he didn't hear the insult in the tone. As a part of his decision to keep playing his part, he was always artfully late for these meetings. Although he never missed much.

While the servants weren't always in the room, they did cover the beginnings of these meetings serving refreshments so could overhear the bits he missed, and also reported directly to his mother.

"Very well, thank you. Although the noise at the changeover of the guards woke me up." Steven yawned and thanked the servant, who handed him a kaf. "Dawn is a disgusting time to wake."

A small burst of power from the servant before they left the room caused steam to curl up from the mug. It was those little, subtle touches that showed him the servants hadn't abandoned him. They understood that this time his arrogance was an act. He sighed, sniffing the smooth, nutty aroma as he took a grateful sip.

"Get a couple more of the guards from Vallantia and get them on duty here," Peter said.

Steven was confused before he realised Peter was glaring at the unfortunate guard standing in front of him and gone back to his previous conversation.

"I'll see to it straight away," the guard said.

"At the rate the guards keep having unfortunate accidents, we're going to run out of people," Constance said, watching as the guard beat a hasty retreat out of the room.

"Um, dare I ask what's happening to the guards?" Steven asked.

"One of them stumbled off the top of the wall this morning." Peter grimaced. "It's probably the commotion that woke you up."

"That couldn't have been healthy," Steven said.

"Made quite a mess on the cobblestones in the courtyard. He was the fifth guard to die. We've lost more men than when we took this place. The drunken fools can't hold their liquor. I've had to issue orders banning them from your father's wine cellar," Peter said, scowling as his attention was diverted to the map on the table. "As if we didn't have more things to worry about than the guards."

"We've received word your brother has run off up to the Heights. Any idea what he's doing up there?" Constance asked.

Steven flicked his eyes up at her over the steaming mug. "How would I know what he's up to?"

"I don't like it when he disappears to places where I don't have people to monitor him," Peter grumbled.

Steven filed that comment away. He gathered the Kastlers were using their network of traders to keep track of Michael and his warband. Not that it would be a hard task, he guessed. Word travelled fast when the Unwanted rode into a town.

"I guess it would be a little unsettling." Steven shrugged.

"You seem pretty pleased about it," Leo grumbled.

Steven blinked, mind racing. "Isn't it what we wanted? Michael, as far away from here for as long as possible?"

"Except we think they are up here somewhere." Peter shoved one of his fat fingers at the map.

Steven leant forward and studied it, noting that Peter's fingers were indeed pointing to the mountain range which was the extent of the Warlord's domain in that direction.

"Doesn't seem to be much up there," Steven said brightly, inwardly smug as he noted the Kastlers' irritation with him.

"The problem is I can't work out any reason for him to be up there, and he can cut around this way." The fat finger traced a path skirting around and ending up on top of Vallantia.

"Meaning he wouldn't get tied up in Callenhain the way we need him to." Constance's tone sounded like she was explaining these details to a simpleton.

"My brother has an uncanny way of finding things out, so I'm certain someone will think to tell him if the Sylannians do attack in Callenhain the way you expect. When is that meant to happen, by the way?"

Peter stared at him, eyes narrowing. Steven smiled vacuously, as if he didn't have any understanding at all about these matters.

"We don't know precisely. Any day now, we expect," Peter said.

"Then I guess it's good that something has drawn them up to the Heights. It's better than him being on his way here, right? Otherwise, he might get here before the attack on Callenhain." Steven eased back into his chair as if he'd solved all their issues for them, blatantly ignoring their point, as if he didn't understand it, that Michael might very well be heading here already via a shortcut through the Heights.

He blithely ignored the look of consternation on the Kastlers' faces as they stared at him. Even Leo looked at him as if he was an idiot. That was a circumstance he was more than willing to allow to continue. The stupider they thought he was, the more they'd discount anything he did.

SIXTY-TWO

Khaliun peered over her shoulder once more as the sounds of battle seemed to draw ever closer. It was an illusion. Those fighting were still well down the path, with the Sylannians unable to break through their line. The Unwanted had been engaging with the enemy down on the trail for what seemed like a lifetime. She could feel and hear the surges of power they increasingly used as they fought. Yet as had proven true with their own experience with fighting Sylanna, the enemy didn't give up. As their fellows dropped, others stepped over the still-warm bodies to keep fighting. In this game, the Sylannians had the numbers.

"Damn it, hurry up!" Orghana snapped to their crews working on the rockfalls

They'd worked in groups building up the rock piles placed at strategic points along the trail. The contraptions their crafters had made to contain the rocks until they were ready had proven simple and were constructed quickly but collecting the boulders of all sizes and stacking them behind the barriers that held them in place had proven to be backbreaking work and nowhere near as quick.

"They can't keep this up much longer," Khaliun said, not bothering to hide her concern. The Unwanted had been battling all day without a break and dusk was fast approaching. "Ulagan, keep things going. We need to get into place to help pull them out of there when they falter."

"We're nearly there. I'll call out when everything is ready," Ulagan said.

Khaliun gestured for Orghana to join her and members of both their tribes made their way down the trail at a trot. A thrumming urgency was pulsing through her. She shook her head, trying to keep it clear. Khaliun was aware, not only from sharing minds with Michael but from her own experience with utilising the veil, it wouldn't be much longer before the Unwanted would collapse.

KHALIUN ALMOST FELT the blows delivered to those of the Unwanted who were in the front. As she watched, she saw the Unwanted's ranks reshuffle, with Michael, Olivia, Nathanial and Damien taking the front positions before their individual rotations were due. She glanced back over her shoulder, almost willing her people to finish their work so those battling the enemy could withdraw. Khaliun's stomach sank as she saw members of the Unwanted collapse, caught by their own and passed to the back of their ranks.

Move! Pull them back to the top. Olivia's command rang in their minds.

It was the first indication she'd had that the leadership of the Unwanted, as busy as they were, had noted their arrival. The first of Khaliun's teams leapt forward to lift the exhausted fighters who'd collapsed between them and carried them up the trail towards safety.

How much longer until you're ready? Michael asked.

Khaliun almost froze as Michael's voice rolled in her head, heavy with fatigue but also combined with determination to stand and keep fighting.

Not much longer, we're nearly done, Khaliun replied before yelling at those toiling above. *Ulagan, get it done, now!*

Khaliun blocked everything else out and dealt with her own job. As more members of Michael's troops collapsed with exhaustion, Khaliun and Orghana sent teams forward to collect the fallen and clear them from the battle. Now, step by step, the Unwanted gave ground. She could feel the triumph coming from their adversaries, which resulted in their attacks intensifying.

We're done, get clear! Ulagan's mindvoice was the equivalent of a mental bellow.

Michael, retreat! Khaliun called out as she dashed forward.

As power seemed to rumble from the sky, Khaliun swore and switched to her othersight and saw multiple bolts of energy crack into the remaining four members. The power seemed to rush into Damien before it leapt between them all. She swore again and pushed the last remaining members of the Unwanted up towards the others behind her to make sure they were assisted to the top. Michael, Olivia, Nathanial, and Damien still stood their ground, pushing back and fighting the Sylannians, giving the rest of their exhausted fighters time to retreat before they did so themselves. She withdrew her own blade and sprung forward into the fray herself, desperately deflecting the stabbing blades of the enemy.

We've got your people. We need to withdraw, Khaliun said as she drew alongside Michael.

Michael spared a glance at her and Khaliun's breath caught as fire seemed to dance in the man's eyes, lick down his arms and shine from his armour and blade. She swallowed as she finally noticed they were all consumed and bathed in the power they drew. There seemed to be little recognition in them, as if they were lost within the energy that encompassed them. Khaliun almost ducked on instinct alone at the sudden influx of power as the four of them drew in yet more of the veil. The hammering blow they flung at their enemy not only caused her to stagger but Orghana and the small team of the clansmen that remained as well.

Waves of peripheral power rolled over her, causing her to go down to one knee. Shaking herself, she saw the four defenders had flung the attackers back down the trail. Forcing herself to her feet, she reached out, grabbing hold of Michael, who was closest to her, and hauling him back up the trail. Trusting her people to do the same for the others.

As they ran past the first of the planned rockfalls, Khaliun had a moment to wonder if enough sanity remained in them to take out the struts holding the rocks at bay. She'd barely had time to finish the thought before Michael, Olivia, Nathanial, and Damien let loose with blasts of power to either side of the ravine as they ran up. It wasn't just the platforms holding the rocks back that shattered. A deafening explosion cracked over the mountains as fragments of the towering rock walls sheered from the cliffs as well. She hit the ground again, dragging Michael with her, trying to cover his body with her own as the fragments from the blast rained around them. Instead of the impact of sharp rocks, she shivered as she was bathed in cold and was astonished to discover a shimmering protective shield above them. It held back the debris and the very air was hazy, as if they were in the middle of a dust storm in the desert. She swallowed again and took some consolation that Orghana, who was on the ground nearby covering Olivia, was just as pale as she imagined she was.

SIXTY-THREE

Kara's eyes darted around her surroundings as she finished saddling her horse. Something had changed in the city, but she couldn't work out what. As interesting as it had been to visit Callenhain these past few weeks, she was glad to be seeing the back of the place. She was grateful that she'd made the time to practice her mind shield the way the Warleader had shown her back when he'd saved Bergan from the Sylannians. Otherwise, she was sure the press of all these minds would have driven her mad long before now.

"What's wrong, Kara?"

Kara realised her fellow villagers were studying her as they worked. Either they'd noticed she was distracted or she'd been projecting her unease on all of them.

"I don't know, something. I think we should hurry and get out of here," Kara said.

The head of her village delegation frowned but at his urging their party doubled their efforts to get packed. Kara dropped her mental shields, just a little. The almost constant background whispering filled her head, and she swallowed. She didn't know how the Warleader and his people stood it. They were all much more sensitive than she was. She hated to think how hard it must be for them to push aside the constant random chatter from strangers. None of it made any sense at all. It was simply random words, the occasional shriek, powerful emotions and mutterings. She was about to pull her mental shields around her again when she stiffened. There, filtering through all the other random thoughts, were those in a language she didn't speak but that she'd heard before. Sylannian. She didn't know where, but they were close. Here. In Callenhain.

"We need to leave. Now," she yelled, springing up into the saddle of her horse.

Her horse danced as her agitation transferred between her and the beast.

"Why the sudden panic, Kara, what's wrong?"

"Sylannians. They're here in Callenhain. I can hear them," Kara said.

The colour drained out of their faces. None of them questioned her knowledge. They were all aware she had a strong mind-speaking gift. Instead, they hastened their efforts to finish preparation to leave. It took longer than she cared for before everyone was ready and they pulled out of the yard. One thing they could be grateful for was their position at the outer edges of the city. As they headed for the gates, the cart rumbling along at a faster pace than normal, she stiffened in her saddle as the screaming started both in her head and in the distance. She saw smoke towards where the river and the docks were located. None of the other villagers had her mind-speaking abilities, but there was nothing wrong with their sight and hearing. All of them picked up their pace, intent on fleeing the city.

As a body slammed into the ground in front of her, Kara scanned the top of the city wall to see the familiar figures of

Sylannians fighting with the guards along its length. She spurred her horse on as the cart made its way through the gate.

"Keep going!" Kara yelled.

Her skin crawled as they rode away from Callenhain and she could only hope the Sylannians were too busy fighting for control of the city to be bothered with those of them who were fleeing.

As the road curved around and they passed the tree line, they finally slowed down. Kara reined in her horse and looked back. The gate they'd fled through was closed and the signs of fighting continued.

"Kara?"

"Head back to Bergan," she instructed him. "Alert every village along the way that Sylanna is invading."

"Where are you going?"

"To the Heights, to find the Warleader."

"Can't you just, well, reach him with your mindspeech?"

"I'm strong, but not that strong. He's too far away and I don't know the people to relay the message. Not out that way. It's why I've been volunteering for guard duty. So I can meet the stronger mindspeakers in surrounding villages. I can't explain it, but it's easier for me to communicate with those I know."

"Take someone with you."

"No, you and the village might need every able body."

"Stay safe, Kara."

She could see he didn't like the idea, but he accepted it. Just like he had when she'd finally confessed that she'd agreed to be the Warleader's eyes and ears in Bergan. While she understood in many villages such knowledge wouldn't go down well, in Bergan's case the Warleader had saved them.

SIXTY-FOUR

The Warlord listened to the clan leaders babble, almost incoherent in their panic. They assured him it wasn't they who had caused the collapse of his Warleader and his entire warband. The Warlord bit back his impatience as they rushed on to tell him all about the fight against the Sylannians up the mountain trail. How it had been blocked and the subsequent collapse of Michael and every member of the Unwanted. That they'd been unable to rouse any of them even though the incident had happened days ago. The Warlord had to remind himself he'd been relieved to be drawn away from the preparations for war when he'd received word of the invasion. He'd been arranging for the elderly and children to retreat from the riverside villages and to settle within the safety of Yalleska's walls. Along with sending weapons and stores to the town guard units of the larger village centres across his domain. He had a pretty good idea what he was about to see. Having heard enough, he held up his hand and got instant silence from all of them.

"Take me to them," the Warlord said.

They stared at him for a moment, then jumped up to comply.

"Of course, Warlord. This way."

He followed the various leaders as they filed out of the hut. If it hadn't been for the fact that Michael wasn't anywhere in the main camp of the clans, he would have ignored them all and gone straight to him. Although given what he'd been told, he suspected they were all up the top of the mountain in the outpost they had informed him they'd built.

"We'll have to ride."

The Warlord nodded. He'd already guessed that much. He wished he remembered the names of the various clan leaders; it might have made things easier. Although he tended to forget nonessential details and all the names of this gaggle of clan leaders definitely fit in that category. The Warlord mounted his horse and, with his warbands following suit, followed two of the clan leaders who'd obviously decided to guide him. As the mountain loomed above, he bit back his irritation. It would take the rest of the afternoon to make their way up the switchback trail that snaked its way to the top, and the outpost he gathered was their destination.

THE WARLORD TOOK in the low stone buildings and the smoke coming from the chimneys in the roof, somewhat relieved. At least there was more protection from the elements than a tent would have provided. Now that he was up here, he could sense that Michael and Olivia were close by and at least alive. While he didn't need anyone to guide him anymore, he allowed the slightly panicked members of the clans to show him the way. He strode into the stone hut as they opened the door for him. The heat that rolled over him was in stark contrast to the icy wind that seemed a constant up here in the mountains. He barely had time to brace as Kesha was suddenly in his arms, her distress washing over him.

"Warlord, I'm sorry, I can't wake them," Kesha said, a catch in her voice.

"It's all right, healer, they'll wake on their own soon enough." He soothed her without thinking about it.

He looked over her head, noting Michael, Olivia, Nathanial and Damien were all in cots in this hut. He could sense the others of the Unwanted close by and guessed they were scattered among the low stone buildings the clans had constructed.

"They've collapsed like this before?" Kesha pushed back enough to look up at him, her eyes seeking reassurance.

"Not often, but yes. I take it they spent a great deal of energy?" The last he said over her head to Khaliun, who sat in a nearby chair.

"I've never seen anything like it," Khaliun said. "They said they'd be exhausted and sleep for a bit, but it's been three days."

Kesha pushed back, wiping tears from her eyes. She'd come a long way from the woman who'd thought she'd been tricked and trapped and hadn't wanted to be with the Unwanted at all. He noted the shimmering protective bubble of the veil that seemed to encompass Michael, Olivia, Nathanial and Damien, and even though he'd expected to see it, he sighed. Nothing could be done until it dropped. It always fascinated him when it manifested. Even though they slept like the dead, the veil still spun from them. As if a part of their unconscious minds still functioned. No one would be able to physically touch them while their protective barrier remained in place.

"They can use great power, more than anyone else I've encountered, but when they push themselves too much, they slip into unconsciousness." The Warlord sent a shaft of reassurance at her. "They will recover."

"How long will they be like this?" Kesha regarded her patients.

"Sometimes it's hours, sometimes days. I can never tell. You won't be able to wake them," the Warlord said.

"I feared the worst. The power they used would have burnt out the minds of normal people." Kesha observed the sleeping trio, fascinated.

"Most certainly; the veil doesn't affect them the way it does regular people." The Warlord didn't mention the Unwanted, unlike regular people, also had self-healing abilities. It was another of the secrets they kept and yet another of the differences that made them remarkably hard to kill.

"This barrier around them didn't materialise until we got them here. Now we can't even touch them," Khaliun said.

The Warlord smiled at her, trying to convey reassurance to all those here in the room. He could only imagine how this had appeared for all of them.

"It happens. They wield the veil in a way that no one else does." He shrugged, not able to explain the phenomenon. "Now, show me this rockfall you created to block the trail."

THE WARLORD THOUGHT he'd long ceased to be amazed at what Michael and his Unwanted could do when they put their minds to it. It seemed he was wrong. He surveyed what remained of what they'd informed him had been a trail to see nothing but rubble. It almost appeared like some of the mountain itself had collapsed and slid down the side.

"They did this?" He regarded Khaliun, his eyebrows rising.

"It was just meant to be the boulders we'd collected to block the path," Khaliun said—her voice held a hint of awe. "We were going to add more after the initial blockage had been made."

"I don't think you'll need to do that." The Warlord's tone was extremely dry. "No wonder they're unconscious. Did they lose themselves?"

"Warlord?" Khaliun said, confusion written all over her face.

"Were they fully in control at the end, or did they seem to operate without conscious control?"

"Ah, it was like they weren't present in their own heads." Khaliun's eyes widened as she remembered the moment. "Power danced over them all, through them. It was like they were on fire."

The Warlord turned to one of his guards who'd accompanied him. The man seemed suitably impressed by the destruction the Unwanted had made.

"Let's get back. We'll have to carry them down the side of the mountain, although I expect some of them should wake sooner rather than later," the Warlord said.

"They'll be groggy and exhausted, regardless. I'll see to it, Warlord, and detail our own to look after them as they wake," the guard said, before issuing instructions to some of the guard unit.

"How will we get the Unwanted down? We can't touch any of them."

"We may not be able to touch them, but I'll lay odds we can pick up the sleeping cots they are lying on," the Warlord said.

He didn't bother to hide his amusement as Khaliun went red. It was clear the woman hadn't even thought about trying to pick up the sleeping cots.

"Did they collapse like this? I mean, after you fought us?" Khaliun asked, her tone curious. "I mean, I know Michael obviously did, but no one mentioned to me that his entire warband collapsed after the battle."

The Warlord considered denying it, but under the circumstances there didn't seem to be any point.

"They all slept for a good deal of time. We had them in the centre of the other warbands not only to protect them but so none of the clan would notice," he said.

Given what the clan had witnessed, he doubted it would make a difference in their relationship. He'd have been terrified if he'd seen the mountainside fall the way it obviously had. The fact that Michael and his people would collapse after they'd pulled a mountain down hardly seemed relevant.

Michael was instantly awake in a way that let him know he must have been unconscious from overuse of the veil. If his stomach's protesting was anything to go by, he must have been out for a few days.

"How long have I been out, Father?" Michael asked.

He didn't have to look to know the Warlord was present and sitting close to where he lay.

"Long enough. What happened? From what Khaliun described, you all flipped out. You haven't done that for a long time."

"Damien happened. He had one of his transition attacks. Mid-battle as we were, we weren't expecting it. His uncontrolled power ran through us as well, and I take it we all went out of our minds there for a bit," Michael said.

"Are you sure you don't want me to take him back to Yalleska until he's settled?" The Warlord frowned.

"Certain," Michael said.

"You four took down the side of the mountain," the Warlord said.

"Ah, we stopped the Sylannians then." Michael regarded the Warlord. "Can you imagine the damage if something like that happened in Yalleska?"

"You scared your poor healer," the Warlord said.

Michael rolled over onto his side and stared at the Warlord, who smiled at him despite his words.

"I should have prepared her better. I didn't expect this to happen. I'll apologise when I see her."

"She's already chastised Nathanial. It was quite amusing to watch. I've never seen him quite that flustered." The Warlord's eyes shone in amusement.

Michael chuckled. His eyes tracked to the door as it opened and he saw Kesha come in with a tray of food, enough that she couldn't possibly eat it all herself. Particularly since she seemed to have an entire pot with her. She stopped abruptly when she saw him awake and, sliding the tray she carried onto the table, she half ran across the room and flung herself on him, hugging him to her.

"Easy, Kesha, I'm fine."

"I thought you were all going to die." Kesha sat back and glared at him.

"I'm sorry. I should have warned you we can slip into unconsciousness after using our powers that way."

"Nathanial said it was Damien who triggered you all," Kesha said.

"It was. How is he?"

"Damien woke up before the rest of you, but he is exhausted and still doesn't have his appetite back."

"It's how it seems to work with all of them. Don't ask me why," the Warlord said.

"Strangely enough, once Damien goes through full transition and out the other side, he'll sleep longer after something like that, but when he wakes, he'll be fine if a little ravenous." Michael shrugged, eyes sliding past her to the pot of food on the table.

"That's what Nathanial said, and Olivia. They both woke this morning. " Kesha's eyes still held concern. "You're the last to wake up."

Michael reached up and pulled her head down, placing a light kiss on her forehead. He was learning that healers, particularly strong healers, were sensitive to the emotions of others. The entire Kallith Clan had been in turmoil. It was no wonder the circumstances overwhelmed her. They'd been trying to teach her to protect her own mind, but it was slow going and, with none of them being conscious to help her, she'd been struggling. She was fine when she was healing, totally focused on what she was doing. It was only in all the other moments her shields got spotty and sometimes seemed to be non-existent.

"Honestly, I'm fine. It's normal for me to sleep longer as well. I was the focus for the four of us." Michael sat up and then stood up, dragging the blanket with him as he sniffed appreciatively at the smell of food.

"They were both starving as well and said you would be awake soon, so I brought enough for all of us." Kesha looked at him earnestly.

The Warlord shook his head, clearly amused, and without comment pulled out a chair for him.

CHAPTER

SIXTY-FIVE

Allani stood on some wooden crates that had been used to form a platform facing the clustered firstwives. She could feel their disdain. So far, the plan was working. She'd managed to keep her own house mostly intact while there were significantly fewer of them after taking Callenhain. Now it was time to ensure even more of them died. They would all rather have been with Jaclyn, taking part in her assault on the home of the barbarian Warleader, but the truth was that they would have died sooner, and by the hands of the daggerwives of Jaclyn's house, if they had been there. In Callenhain, she was relying on the fierce reputation of the Warlord and Warleader. That the Warlord's forces would descend on this city to defend it and not so coincidentally do Jaclyn's dirty work for her and kill off some of the king's strongest supporters. Even so at least here they had a chance of survival if they took to their heels and ran, rather than allowing greed for the riches and accolades that they thought the king would shower on them to cloud their judgement. She couldn't believe they didn't see Jaclyn's play for what it was.

"After we've secured this place, you'll head out and take the villages that surround Callenhain for yourselves," she said, keeping her tone smooth and reasonable. "This land is rich and will bring your houses much wealth and prestige."

"What about the estate house?"

Allani stared at the other firstwife coolly. "Personally, I'd leave them be. They'll starve and have to open their gates eventually. As cowardly as they are by all reports, their walls are filled with guards."

"All the more reason to take it."

"All the more reason to take the surrounding countryside. Of course, if you don't care to carve out your own holdings and territories..."

"What do you mean?" The other woman's eyes narrowed.

"You can't possibly believe the commander, let alone the Monarch House, would allow any of us to hold such a strategic place for ourselves, even if we did succeed?" Her eyebrow rose as she regarded them steadily.

A silence settled on the women who regarded her. She could almost hear the cogs in their minds turning as they considered her words.

"So, the commander has said we'll get to keep the villages we conquer and all the resources they produce for our own houses?"

"How do you think she succeeded in the lands of the traders? She offered some incentive to the houses that fought for her." Allani smirked hoping she conveyed the right mix of confidence and greed. Jaclyn hadn't promised anything of the sort, at least not to these houses. The role assigned to these houses by the Sylannian commander was to be a distraction for the Warlord, and not so coincidentally die, but it wouldn't be helpful for them to work that out.

"Won't the estate and the people in it be a threat to us?" A small firstwife off to one side frowned.

Allani was reminded these women were the heads of houses that rubbed shoulders with some of the most important and high caste houses in Sylanna. They might not have worked out Jaclyn's reason for assigning them to this battle but it didn't mean they couldn't analyse the situation if given the time to do so. Allani opened her senses just enough to see the woman with her othersight. The play of power around her was interesting. She wasn't as powerful as Jaclyn and the inner core of her family, but she was indeed stronger than many. This woman would need to be sent out into the countryside. She was too much of a risk to leave here.

ALLANI SANK INTO A PADDED CHAIR, adjusting the cushion behind her with a sigh. She watched as her fellow wives came into the room and shut the door behind them. While she longed for the luxury of their island home, this place was at least comfortable. Allani waited for the inevitable questions. She was sure it wouldn't take them too long after the meeting they'd just had with the other houses.

"Is it wise sending off the sister houses into the countryside?" one of the other wives asked as they shut the door. "We don't even have this place secured yet. So many have fallen already."

"It isn't our job to take this city," Allani said, watching as her fellow wives stilled at her words.

"Then what are we doing?" one wife asked.

"Distraction. Our goal was to attract the attention of the Warlord and keep him occupied for as long as possible."

"But we're dying out there and their fighting forces aren't even here yet."

"No, the sister houses our commander wants dead are dying." She saw understanding dawning on the faces of the wives around her. "With the other houses spread out all over the countryside, it will take more time for the warlord to round them all up."

"The commander wants those houses dead? But they're some of the king's strongest supporters." The other wife paled. "She's going to claim the throne?"

"It doesn't pay to get in between claimants when the daggers dance for the throne. As strange as it seems, we will be much safer here among the barbarians than we would be back home. Particularly if we ensure the other houses sent with us die, so Commander Jaclyn has no cause to turn her eyes in our direction."

SIXTY-SIX

Steven squeezed his eyes shut as he pressed himself back against the wall, hoping those patrolling the courtyard wouldn't look in this direction.

"What am I doing?"

He took a breath and pushed off from the wall, stuffing his hands in his pockets as he strolled across the walkway around the back of the castle. It had seemed like a perfect plan when he'd come up with it sitting in his rooms looking out of the windows over the grounds. At the direction of his mother, he'd been going for walks, wandering around the grounds and the castle itself seemingly at random at different times of the day, as if he needed the exercise after being cooped up in his rooms. His mother, in particular, wanted to see how far he could push things. How much they would dismiss his activities. One thing he'd noticed, there were fewer of the Kastlers' thugs on the gates and on the grounds in the late afternoon and into the evening. From what he could see, they paid very little attention to him at all. When they glanced in his direction, it was with the distinct whiff of boredom and disinterest. His mother had assessed it was probably because of his known association with the Kastlers. As much as that now pained him to remember, right now it was proving useful.

As he went around the next corner, he caught sight of the small side gate. It was open, as always. Steven took another breath as he wandered across and plunged into the centre of some servants heading towards the gates. As he got towards the middle of the small group, he had to resist the urge to pull his hood up. It would stand out if he pulled it up, since none of the servants had theirs up. As he passed through the gate, his nerves spiked and he held his breath as he passed by the guard, who seemed to be busy cleaning his nails with the tip of his dagger. Steven exhaled slowly.

A small cart carrying supplies made its way through the gates and ran over the guard's foot. The guard dropped his knife and swore as the cart driver stopped, and the guard slapped his hand on the side of the cart, yelling at the driver to keep going. As the driver obligingly moved the cart forward again, the guard bent over, grabbing his foot and swearing profusely.

Steven used the opportunity to edge his way past on the other side of the cart and down the road. He resisted the urge to turn around and tried to ignore the feeling that he had eyes boring into the back of his head. Any moment now, he expected a voice to yell out for him to stop. Each step brought him closer to the bend in the road and the screening trees and it took everything he had not to panic and break out into a run. An unusual urge for him. He never ran anywhere.

Other than a few stray looks, the servants mostly ignored his presence, although he had no doubt they'd noticed him. He was arrogant and had missed a great deal over the years. The only thing that gave him solace now was that it appeared the Kastlers were even more incompetent than he was. Other than when he'd been drunk, or in his own short-lived daydreams, winning a war against his brother was not something he'd ever believed he could do. How the Kastlers thought they could do so when the Unwanted showed up, when even he could slip out of the estate unhindered and unnoticed, he didn't know.

As he saw the city gates in the distance, his heart sank just a little. Normally, he rode between the castle and the town. Steven knew it was too far to walk because he'd stumbled the distance between the two now and then. It definitely wasn't a favourite pastime. Although on previous occasions he hadn't done so on purpose, it was because he'd forgotten where he'd left his horse. Thankfully, probably because of the respect others had for his father and the Rathadon crest on the saddle, someone would bring it back the next morning. That or the ungrateful wretch of a horse had somehow gotten free and made its own way back to its stable. Which is why on those occasions, he couldn't find it in the first place. Steven sighed. Unfortunately, either scenario seemed credible.

STEVEN WAS STARTLED to see the looming city gates. There was something to be said for being lost in his own thoughts. Somehow, it hadn't taken as long to get to the city as he'd thought it would. As he entered the gates with the rest of the crowd, he pulled up his hood. With a quick glance around, he noted the guards loitering around the gates and up on the walls. Although the guards had obviously long since gotten bored with their assigned duties and weren't paying any attention at all. Or at least, he fervently hoped that was the case. If they'd never really cared, it made the fact that the city had fallen to them even worse.

Steven's cheeks grew warm. They'd gotten lazy in the peace that followed when the Warlord had conquered not only their lands, but their neighbours, uniting them all. Maintaining the domestic security of Vallantia, in between the visits from the Warlord's warbands, was their job. The truth he didn't want to recognise intruded again. They'd become weak before the Warlord had come and claimed their lands. Even his father had admitted it. Now it was apparent they were even weaker. His ancestors would roll in their tombs below the Rathadon estate if they realised the depths to which they'd fallen. Or rather, the ones to which he'd fallen. He suspected they'd be rather proud of Michael.

He brought his attention back to the present and strode down the street in the fading light. While his mother had prompted his walks and requested he test how far he could push the boundaries they lived under, he didn't think she really meant him to escape the confines of the estate. He wasn't even sure why he'd decided to push the limits even further and come into town, other than he wanted to see the situation for himself. Steven frowned and stopped near a corner. There were far fewer people out on the streets than he'd normally expect at this hour. A hunched-over figure crossed from one street to the next in short, clipped steps to disappear out of sight. The few people he could see out and about seemed intent to be elsewhere, and given there were very few of them, he figured that elsewhere was indoors.

He started as a wailing scream rang out. At the thud of booted feet on the cobblestones, he spun around to see the only other person in this stretch of street running down the road. The wailing continued, begging someone to stop. Closing his eyes, he swallowed, then continued, hugging the wall as he headed towards the commotion. He was uncomfortably aware of the overloud sound of his own boots on the cobbled road, but he kept his pace steady—running would stand out even more. He hoped he appeared as if he belonged out on the street.

The screaming wasn't far away; he almost wished he was still delusional enough to believe he was a match for his little brother. With one hand on the rough stone wall, he eased his head out far enough to see around the corner and his breath caught in his throat. A man had his arm wrapped around a younger man's waist, trying to haul him away from an older woman who was desperately trying to pull him back. The wailing was coming from her. Blood flowed from the side of her head as another man, swearing profusely, tried to haul her off.

"You two, unhand my property now!"

Before he knew what he was doing, he was halfway across the deserted road, pulling his gloves off, one finger at a time. He had a moment to feel appalled at himself as the fight in front of him froze and the combatants stared at him in varying degrees of shock. The woman gathered the lad into her arms and rocked back and forth, sobbing. The young man regarded him, wide-eyed, while clinging to his mother.

"Who the Powers are you?" one of the men snarled.

Steven frowned and inspected them up and down, and sniffed in disdain as if they were something he'd get his servants to scrape off the bottom of his shoe.

"Peter and Constance must have been desperate by the time they hired you." Steven gestured at the woman and lad. "Come on, both of you. That will teach you to skip out without my express permission."

"You aren't going anywhere!" the man said as he lunged to grab the boy's arm again. "I don't know any Peter or Constance, but I work for the Kastlers. This here now belongs to them."

The man shook the boy for emphasis as he sneered.

"Really, you should pay more attention. Peter and Constance *are* the Kastlers. Your employers, it seems"—Steven looked disdainfully at the two men—"and my very good friends. Now, be good little thugs and release my property."

His eyes narrowed as he closed the distance between them,

slowly drawing his sword, trying to channel the essence of the threat that seemed to come from his brother in bucket loads whenever he did it.

"You... you know the Kastlers?" the other man asked, taking an uncertain step back.

"Are you particularly hard of hearing?"

"Come on, leave that one. We'll find another. We don't need trouble with the Kastlers."

"If you leave now, I might even forget to mention this tedious encounter with them when we meet for a drink after supper."

"But they're at the Rathadon estate." The man paused, frowning at him.

"Thank you, but I am already very much aware of that detail. Now, unhand my property and get out of my sight," Steven snapped.

He looked down at the woman and snapped his fingers at her as he spun on his heels. Steven left the whole scene behind him and walked down the street as if he hadn't a care in the world. There was a burst of incredulity from behind him, then the scurrying of feet as the woman and the boy followed along behind him. Or at least he hoped it was them. He didn't want to ruin his exit to check. Steven tried to keep his haughty demeanour in place as he strutted down the road, just in case the thugs decided to follow. He could hear the woman and lad behind him and feel their apprehension. As they arrived at a cross street, he paused as he tried to think where he could take them, then as an idea occurred to him, he continued around the corner, and down the street. The Arms wasn't too far away from here, and if his memory served him correctly, the publican was yet another childhood friend of his brother's. Or at least, that was what Evan had told him. The information had rather stunned him at the time.

Evan had wondered how Steven could have forgotten those

little details, but it was quite simple, really. He'd been an obnoxious child, full of himself and his own importance. Why would he pay any mind to what his annoying little brother was up to? Newfound honesty surfaced again and forced him to acknowledge that he'd been an obnoxious adult as well. It also occurred to him if he hadn't been wallowing in imagined slights and his own self-importance, Vallantia and its people might not be in this situation right now.

Relief flooded him as they rounded the final corner and he saw light shining from the windows of the Arms, just down the street. Only as he approached the doors did he pause and wonder who would be inside. Evan had already told him that most of the wealthy stayed behind locked doors at night. They would be the usual clientele of the Arms. He backed up a step and peered through the window to one side of the door. He bit his lip as he realised the men inside were not the type he normally associated with this bar. Steven cursed himself under his breath for being a fool. With everything he already knew about what was happening in town and the locals heading indoors before dark, the only ones left to frequent the bar would be the Kastlers' guards. Steven peered through the window, frozen in indecision. He turned his head and saw the woman and lad huddled near the wall. Steven shook himself and returned his attention back to the view of the bar through the window. Relief flooded him as he finally spotted the familiar figure of Ben, the barkeep. Ben glanced across the room, a harried expression on his face, then his eyes widened almost imperceptibly as their eyes met through the window.

Fool, you can't come in the front. Go around the side, Ben said.

Steven swallowed and backed up a step before motioning to the woman to follow him and heading down the narrow alley at the side of the venue. At some point, full dark had settled on the city—something he hadn't been aware of until he'd faced away from the lights shining out of the windows. As he reached a door, he hesitated and looked back towards the main road. The door wrenched open with a hand clamping over his mouth, muffling the shriek he uttered in response, and he was hauled into the doorway. It was a relief when he realised it was Ben.

"Get the woman and boy," Steven said, as soon as the hand left his mouth.

The barkeep glared at him a moment before he ducked out the door.

"You two, it's too dangerous out right now. Get in here," Ben whispered hoarsely.

Steven pressed back against the wall, closing his eyes, trying to push down his own fear. Now that he'd stopped, his brain was shrieking at him over what he'd been doing. The barkeep ushered the woman and boy inside, sitting them on some stools he pulled from under the kitchen bench.

"I... I came into town to see what was happening. A couple of men were trying to take the boy," Steven said.

The barkeep poured some water from a pitcher into a bowl and, picking up a cloth, dipped it in the water. He gently dabbed it on the side of the woman's face, cleaning the blood from her wound.

"It was foolish of you to come here. How did you stop them?" Ben asked.

"I behaved like one of the arrogant rich." Steven chuckled softly. "Well, like myself. I found out the Kastlers are in the flesh trade, so I said they belonged to me."

The barkeep was plainly incredulous. Steven smiled weakly. He couldn't really blame the man, given his past behaviour. The barkeep scrutinised the woman who'd been watching them both.

"They would have taken m'boy if the sir hadn't come," she whispered.

They all froze as the doors to the kitchen opened. A woman came in and as the barkeep instantly relaxed, Steven gathered that he knew her. The woman's sharp eyes took in those of them gathered here, pausing as she noticed him. He saw recognition in her eyes, but while her lips thinned, she didn't say anything. She simply moved around the kitchen and, in short order, pushed a platter of food towards the woman and her son. Then she moved the barkeep out of the way and took over the job of cleaning up the woman's injuries. At a look that passed between the two, Steven finally worked out this calm, competent woman was the barkeep's partner. Ben left her to look after the woman and boy, then grabbed Steven's arm and pulled him over to the other side of the kitchen.

"What are you thinking, coming into town this way?" Ben hissed.

"Evan told me things are bad here, townsfolk going missing. I thought I should check. My father needs to know, although the Kastlers have taken over the estate. It's about time I cared for someone besides myself," Steven said.

The barkeep watched him for such a long time Steven wilted a little inside. Ben had been a long-term friend of his brother and had undoubtedly taken risks and done much that Steven hadn't even been aware of. He transferred his weight from one foot to the other under the man's regard.

"You've chosen a dangerous time to grow up, Steven."

"For the first time in my life, I'm hoping my little brother gets himself back here and saves us all."

The barkeep snorted in amusement before his expression became grave once more.

"Unfortunately, he's tied up right now, so we're on our own until he is in a position to head this way."

"The Sylannians have attacked then?"

"What? I don't know. He was called up to the Heights," Ben

said.

"Oh. That's not anywhere near the river access. Right?" Steven asked.

"No, it's a ride through rough, overgrown terrain between the nearest river access and the Heights. Why?"

"The Kastlers have been killing off the sentries at the other end of the river near Callenhain. They believe Michael and his Warlord will be tied up fighting a war with Sylanna. It's why they've made a move here."

Ben swore, rubbing his face with one hand. Steven stood quietly so as not to disturb him as he thought things through.

"That explains the breakdown in the communication network. I'll see what I can do to send word, but Michael is unlikely to receive any message we send until he comes down from the Heights," Ben said. "Replacing the members of the relay won't be easy."

"Word might already be heading that way. Evan was going to speak to the twins to see if they would go."

"When was this?"

"A few days ago; I don't know if he's spoken to them yet."

"The twins aren't available at the moment, but don't worry about it. I've already taken steps in that direction. It's how I know Michael has headed up to the Heights."

"Ah, I thought I was being helpful," Steven said.

He ducked his head. He wasn't sure why he was so disappointed or why the opinion of this man, a common barkeep, was important to him, but for some reason it was. Of course, some of that was probably because it was becoming increasingly apparent that this man was far more important in his brother's network than he'd ever known. Admittedly, it hadn't been that long ago that he hadn't been aware his brother had a network.

"It was a good thought. How did Evan get into the estate?"

"The same way I got out. Through the servants' gate at the

back. They don't pay much attention and I think the servants helped," Steven said.

"That's how you were planning on getting back in?"

"I hadn't actually thought about how I'd get back in, but I guess so."

"Never mind. That gate will be closed now that it's full dark. You'll sleep here tonight. I'll have people get you back into the estate and your rooms before daybreak," Ben said.

"I'm sorry."

"For what?" Ben's eyebrows rose.

"For being a self-centred fool. For bringing this down on us all," Steven said.

"Past is past and you aren't responsible for the Kastlers, you just allowed yourself to be their pawn. Right now, we just have to survive," Ben said.

Steven swallowed his pride.

"What can I do?"

"Do the Kastlers still trust you?" Ben frowned, staring at him.

"As far as they ever trusted me. I've been trying to keep up the pretence under my mother's orders."

"Good, keep it up. Feed everything to your parents. Word will get to me," Ben said.

Steven thought through the implications of what the barkeep had said.

"The servants."

"It's good you finally care about what is happening outside your walls, but unless I send word otherwise, please, stay put. Now come, I'll show you to a bed. I need to make arrangements for the morning, then get back into the taproom."

Steven followed Ben as he led him through the kitchen to a small door towards the rear. Steven stared at Ben's back. His brother, it seemed, had always been good at picking people, even as a child.

SIXTY-SEVEN

Isabella stared at the axe in her hands, then up at the taskmaster, then back at the axe again. The taskmaster shuffled off and issued instructions to some of the other children. All of them had their tasks they had to complete for the village. Those tasks tended to rotate. She remembered when Owen said he'd speak with the taskmaster, but she hadn't expected the chores she'd been getting. Last week she'd been hauling water from the river and now she was detailed to chop wood.

"Is there a problem, Isabella?" the taskmaster asked.

Isabella saw the taskmaster had walked over and was now standing in front of her. His eyes crinkled as he patiently waited for her answer.

"No, of course not, Taskmaster. I just, well, I've never chopped wood before." Isabella had the sinking feeling she wasn't going to get out of this so easily.

"I believe Owen indicated he'd show you the basic technique, Isabella. You'll pick it up in no time. Off you go." The taskmaster walked away from her, making it clear the conversation was over.

Isabella watched his retreating back for a moment before she headed out of the training rooms. She almost wished she was back in the classes for the littlest kids, listening to stories and learning how to count and read. With a sigh, she pushed the thought aside. All of the changes to her daily regimen were due to her own request. She couldn't really blame Owen for taking her seriously. The tasks she was being asked to do were things she remembered Damien had done before he left the village and became a member of the Unwanted. Before now, she'd never given it much thought. She wandered across the village to where her brother had chopped wood almost daily. There was no doubt in her mind that a pile of logs awaited her attention. She saw Owen leaning on a tree, waiting for her, and he grinned as she drew closer.

"Don't look so apprehensive. This is good exercise." Owen pushed off the tree and sat down on one of the logs, gesturing for her to do the same.

"If you say so, Owen," Isabella grumbled.

"I do. It will help with your overall balance, physical fitness, and upper body strength. All of which are required for fighting." Owen held his hand out for the axe she carried, and Isabella handed it over.

Owen pulled out a small can and dribbled some of the contents on the axe before taking a stone he carried and running it in smooth strokes along the blade of the axe.

"Maintenance of any blade you intend to use is important. Regardless of whether it is a sword or this axe." Owen paused and she realised he was waiting for her response so she nodded her understanding. "You should start with a sharp axe. You use a little oil and then the stone like so. Here, now you try."

Isabella took the axe back from Owen, then the stone, and

replicated the smooth strokes that she'd seen him perform. At least with this activity, she could see how it might correlate to a sword. Although she suspected it would be better practice maintaining an actual sword rather than an axe. Finally, Owen stood, holding out his hand for the axe once more. She complied and held it out to him, then stood back a couple of paces when he took a log from the pile and placed it on the larger one he'd been using as a seat.

"Keep your feet shoulder-width apart, make sure your balance is even, strong stomach and back. Grip the handle like this." He adjusted his position so she could see his grip.

"All right."

He went back to the log, raised the axe above his head, and swung down. The timber cracked, splinters flying as the smaller log split in two. Owen cleared the pieces of the log he'd split, placing them neatly in a pile to one side before grabbing another log. He placed it just as carefully as the first and repeated the whole process.

"Keep your strokes as accurate as you can. Just like the moves we've trained in with your sword practice."

Isabella stifled a sigh and pulled on her gloves, then took the axe from Owen. She positioned herself, taking care with her stance, balance, and grip as Owen had shown her. Owen came up to her side and adjusted her grip, then guided her arms up to the position he wanted them to be, then slowly down again, with the tip of the axe resting on the centre of the log. She waited until he stepped back. She raised the axe, then completed the downward movement until it rested on the top of the log, trying to mimic the action she'd performed with Owen's guidance.

Isabella took a deep, settling breath, then in a smooth motion she raised the axe, following through with the downward motion. She braced as the axe hit the log, the impact of the strike transmitting up her arms. The log sat there with her axe blade lodged in it. It hadn't split as Owen's had in his demonstration. It disappointed Isabella but she saw Owen approved of her efforts.

"Good effort. Now, pull the axe from the log and make sure it's settled and try again. Aim for the split you've already created," Owen instructed.

Positioning herself with care she repeated the action. The resounding crack sounded as the axe struck the log. This time the halves fell to either side of the block. Isabella jumped up and down on the spot, laughing in delight.

"I did it!"

"You did, well done. Now stack the pieces on the pile and grab another log. I want to see you perform that several more times before I leave you," Owen said, but she could hear the undertone of amusement in his voice.

Isabella hummed to herself as she placed the pieces of the log she'd split carefully on the pile to one side under the small awning for the villagers. The pile was there for anyone in the community who might need it and it was a chore that Damien had mostly performed each night, keeping the communal pile stocked. Since he'd gone, some of the adults had taken turns at the task after they'd finished their own business for the day. She grabbed another log and performed the action again, paying attention to her position and form. Owen had been trying to drum into her the importance of performing her tasks accurately. At some point, she noticed Owen had gone about his own business. Isabella continued with her task, humming absently to herself. She was determined, no matter how long it took, that she'd split a log in one stroke. Just as Owen had. Of course, that might mean she'd have to come back and try again tomorrow and the day after. But she was determined that eventually she would achieve her goal.

SIXTY-EIGHT

S teven was awake. Barely. He tried to throttle down his annoyance about the fact that dawn wasn't anywhere nearby, telling himself that he'd been up at this hour occasionally. Usually because he hadn't been to bed yet, but he tried to push that unhelpful thought aside. It was also a little hard to show his annoyance when, to his shock, Ben was a member of the party getting him back to the estate. He'd been certain that the man would hand him off to others to get back to safety and dismiss him rather promptly. Particularly given how much trouble he'd caused over the years, and the man would have worked half the night in the taproom.

Despite all that knowledge, old habits were hard to overcome and he glared at Ben's back as they crept through the streets. It didn't help that all he sensed from the man was amusement. They had pushed him out of bed and ushered him out of the inn with only a single cup of steaming kaf, and now they were moving through the deserted streets of Vallantia like ghosts. To be honest, when he thought past his irritation, he was impressed. It wasn't that they didn't encounter any of the

Kastlers' guards out patrolling, but when they did, those guards simply ended up dead and disposed of in short order. He'd never realised how convenient the river was to dispose of bodies before.

It isn't. Bodies float unless you weigh them down, but there are so many dead bodies disposed of this way right now a few more won't make any difference.

Steven jumped as Ben spoke to him. *Oh, I didn't know they floated, either. Sorry, I didn't mean to broadcast what I was thinking.*

You have one of the weakest mind shields I've encountered. You might want to consider practicing, Ben commented.

I didn't realise.

Only other mindspeakers would notice. Ben gazed at him, a small frown on his forehead. *It's important for you to learn not only because of who your family is but for yourself. As you are it leaves you victim to the influence of others if they have ill intent.*

I guess there would be a few of those, given who my brother is. Steven ducked his head, swallowing. It was yet another area where he came up lacking.

This weakness does not excuse your failings but goes a long way towards explaining some things. People use you to get to the Warleader. Michael does his best to shield his friends from such attempts, but everyone knows who his family is. Knows you are Michael's brother. Other than promoting fear of what Michael will do to them if he finds out they are messing with his family, there isn't much he can do.

Steven swallowed as Ben's words sunk in. *Is that why he does it?*

Does what? Ben frowned at him.

When I've been involved in... Steven paused, wrestling with himself and the sinking feeling a great many people had died because of him. *Plots against the Warlord. Michael hasn't just killed the ringleader. He's killed them all. Did they all die because of me?*

In part, but their deaths are on their own heads not yours. The Warleader wouldn't tolerate insurrection against the Warlord, regardless of who was involved.

But?

The brutality surrounding the deaths of the rebels was an object lesson of what he would do to any others who might try such things, when he catches up to them.

Once they'd cleared the city, there had at least been horses. The problem he was having was that Ben had ordered them to dismount. He wasn't the most experienced person, but there was still a fair distance between his estate and where they were currently standing. He was certain they could have just ridden the horses around the back of the estate. Then waited for dawn and he could have snuck in through the rear gate with the servants. Except, he guessed, every time one of them did that, it increased the risk to the servants. He stared down at his feet and took a deep breath, pushing down his arrogance. It was just his old self trying to reassert itself while he was tired and grumpy.

At a few hand gestures from Ben, the people around him melted into the trees. He followed along behind Ben as they stole through the forest, trying to stick close to the man's back. If anyone attacked, they'd encounter Ben first, which would likely prove problematic to whoever attacked. As much as it made him ashamed, it wouldn't likely be the case if he were in the lead. Playing the arrogant lordling only worked in some circumstances and in the middle of the forest wasn't one of them.

He thumped into something that felt like a solid wall and stumbled back, hitting the ground with an indignant squeak. He was shocked to see that Ben had stopped and that "solid wall" was his back. Ben spared him a withering look before reaching out a hand and assisting him to his feet. Steven's face heated in embarrassment and he was grateful that the low light before dawn hid the evidence. Finally, he peered around Ben to see the reason they'd stopped was a small clearing. His guide led the way forward and Steven followed at a double step as he realised he'd been caught staring around the clearing while his guide had headed on. A rocky outcrop towered over to one side of the clearing, which surprised him. He'd had no idea this existed, yet they couldn't be that far from his family estate.

Ben led him along the base and around a corner. This time, he froze in astonishment. There was a cave entrance where a cloaked person stood. Steven swallowed and groped for his sword before he realised none of the others in his party were alarmed in the slightest. Steven's eyes widened, his mouth dropping open as the person threw his hood back and Ben embraced the older man.

"Smith, sorry for calling you out at this hour, but with the twins elsewhere, you were the easiest way for us to get Steven back where he belongs," Ben said.

"You have but to ask, you know that," the Smith said.

Steven had to resist the urge to squirm under the older man's regard. There was always something about the Smith that made him nervous.

Ben looked at him. "Come on, we don't have much time."

"Then why are we going into a cave?" Steven asked.

"Because it is the mouth of an underground tunnel system, part of which comes out in the Rathadon estate," Ben said.

"Where?" Steven stared incredulously at Ben.

"A place you've likely never been, down in the cells," Ben said.

"Why would my ancestors leave a tunnel open down there?" Steven asked.

"It's not exactly open. There's a fortified metal door, and I believe it was an escape route from the estate, as well as an easy way to get dead bodies from the cells and dump them without dragging them through the castle," Ben said.

"How are we going to get in?"

"A long-dead Smith Lord fashioned the door," Ben said.

"One of my ancestors." The Smith shrugged. "It will open for me."

Steven opened his mouth, then swallowed.

"None of us bite, Steven. What is it?"

"How was it an escape route? If no one but a Smith Lord could get through it?" Steven frowned.

As Ben's smile broadened, Steven couldn't help but think he'd made a mistake. Again.

"You realise we have common ancestors?" the Smith asked.

"Michael can trigger the door. We used to play down here as children," Ben said.

"I... I didn't realise this place existed." Steven frowned. "Michael is a Smith Lord?"

"No, but he does have an affinity for metal. It's strong enough I could key the door to him."

"So anyone with an affinity for metal can traipse in and out of the Rathadon estate?" Steven was horrified at the thought even though he reasoned if he hadn't known about the tunnels it was unlikely too many others did. Then again as recent history had shown not knowing about the secret tunnel and entrance wasn't a hindrance to someone waltzing in and taking over anyhow.

"No, it's locked down to me, the twins and Michael," the Smith said. "If you'd shown any affinity for metal I would have keyed the door to you as well."

Ben watched him with his eyebrows raised, obviously waiting to see if he had any more questions. Steven shook his head. Of course his brother had used the secret access to and from the estate as a child. He'd only become aware they even had cells under the castle when the Kastlers attacked. It was yet another thing no one had seen fit to tell him about. Then again, he probably wouldn't have cared all that much, even if someone had bothered to tell him. Until recently, he would have laughed if someone had told him he'd be sneaking past guards, saving commoners, and traipsing through the forest to go through a cave to get back into his home.

As they descended into the gloomy cave, Steven saw some of Ben's people pull out torches. He opened his mouth then closed it and drew on the veil, the one thing he had an aptitude for. A light popped into existence, floating just ahead of them in the cave. Ben stared at him, his astonishment written all over his face.

"The talent mostly skipped me, but I can make light."

Ben clapped him on the shoulder in a friendly fashion and motioned for him to follow. As they plodded on, Steven had to concentrate on keeping their light source glowing. If he allowed himself to get distracted, it might fade and die and it was much less of a drain to keep going than to shape one into being in the first place.

He blinked as a hand squeezed his shoulder and shook his head. He'd been concentrating on it so hard he'd lost track of his surroundings. Fatigue made itself known, and he gritted his teeth. He would not fail, right here towards the end. He looked past Ben to see the promised metal door. Ben held his finger up to his lips and Steven saw several of the people with them clutching blades in their hands. Everyone tensed and Steven realised belatedly that he should have his own weapon out, as they prepared to fight depending on what they found on the other side of the door.

The Smith approached the smooth metal door and laid his hand on it. It seemed to glow faintly under his touch. Then, with a soft metallic clunk, the door opened and the tension drained in the group as they saw no one in the tunnel beyond.

"My ancestors of old helped build the Rathadon estate," the Smith said. "It still sings to me of how it was fashioned."

"So, the rumour about you being a Smith Lord is true," Steven said, a hint of awe in his voice.

"That kind of talk will get me killed." The Smith's tone was dry. "Let's just say I have a very strong affinity for metal, somewhat like the Smith Lords of old."

Some of the others edged past and into the corridor, taking the lead, placing one foot after the other with care as they made their way to the other end of the corridor. Steven followed along behind, wondering how far they had to go. His fatigue was increasing with the intense cold of the veil, that seeped into his bones. He gritted his teeth and concentrated on keeping the light shining, pressing back the darkness ahead of their small group.

A hand restrained him from walking blindly around a corner and one of Ben's people ducked their head back around the corner and motioned them to follow.

Steven's eyes went wide. The length of the opening was filled with windowless cells carved out of the bedrock. Metal bars lined the length of the space on either side. It appeared to be a natural cavern that had been fashioned into prison cells.

Steven stared down as a crunching sound came from his boots, grinding something into the rock floors.

"These cells are as old as the Rathadon estate itself," Ben whispered.

"I didn't even know we still had cells until recently," Steven admitted.

"Your brother, the twins, Lukas, and I used to explore down here when we were younger. There are remains from those who died here scattered throughout the tunnels. Your ancestors were a brutal lot," Ben said.

Steven froze, his booted foot hovering above the ground mid

step as he realised the crunching when he walked was probably old bones. Glancing around, his dread grew. There wasn't anyone in the cells. He'd thought since this mess had begun that their guards were being held down here in the cells. But not a single soul was imprisoned down here. That meant they were dead or, best-case scenario, they had run off. Despite everything he hoped they had escaped to save their own lives. If they'd swapped allegiance, after what he'd seen in town, if they'd fallen in and helped the Kastlers, they'd earned a death sentence if they showed up again.

"I thought they locked some of the house guards up down here," Steven said, then, noticing the rest of the party was a little ahead of him, closed the distance between them.

"Relax, I've done a few runs through and extracted the house guards that survived," Ben said, then gestured to the crew around them. "Some of these men were your estate guards."

"You weren't worried the Kastlers' guards would notice?"

Ben snorted in amusement. "No, they're a lazy lot. The servants came down to deliver food, the Kastlers' guards didn't."

They came to the other side of the cells. Two of the former estate guards took the stairs a couple at a time to the door at the top and eased it open. Steven saw them relax a little and look back down at them, nodding.

"They'll get you back to your rooms from here. Don't leave the estate again. I'll send word to you if I need anything else. Pass this on to your father." Ben held out a sealed parchment.

Once again, there was that thread of command he heard in Ben's tone. Rather than take it as an insult, as he would have in the not-so-distant past, Steven took the letter.

"Thank you."

"You might want to consider cutting down on the drinking. You're a much better person when you're not drunk," Ben said.

"That has occurred to me as well." Steven smiled tightly.

"Things might have been different now if I hadn't been such a fool."

"Try to practice your mind shield. It may be beyond you, but you are vulnerable."

Ben slapped him on the shoulder and nodded at his people. Even though he was dying of curiosity, Steven thought better of asking what the letter contained. He simply walked up the stairs to join those who would take him the rest of the way.

SIXTY-NINE

The chatter in the tent halted and everyone froze to focus on him as Michael held his hand up. Not that silence was strictly necessary. The thing that had tugged on the edge of his awareness wasn't something he could hear with his ears. He tilted his head to one side and stood smoothly from the cross-legged position he'd been sitting in, the pillows he'd been resting on scattering as he did so.

Warleader!

The voice that called was faint, coloured with a tinge of desperation and equal parts frustration mixed with fatigue.

Warleader, please answer, we need you!

Michael unerringly faced the direction the voice was coming from. Away from these lands held by the Kallith, towards his own people. Olivia and Nathanial came to their feet next to him. He opened himself to the veil and allowed it to fill him, flinging his consciousness out.

Michael, please hear me.

The voice was softer that last time, almost plaintive. Olivia and Nathanial stiffened next to him as he relayed what he was hearing to them. At least the girl had sense and skill enough to direct her mind call directly to him.

I'm here. What's wrong? Kara? It had taken him a moment to register exactly who had been calling for him.

It was never good news when one of his lookouts was this desperate to reach him. This was the second time Kara had had to send word to him, and since the first time the warning had been of a very real threat, he was already tense.

It's that woman you recruited for Bergan again. She sounds desperate, Olivia said,

I wonder what's gone wrong this time, Nathanial said.

Warleader, it's the Sylannians. They've taken Callenhain. Despite her words, the relief that he'd finally heard her was evident in Kara's mindvoice.

Michael stiffened and left Olivia and Nathanial to relay the conversation on to the Warlord and the others in the tent with them. He was peripherally aware of the uneasy stirring of the clan leaders as they heard the report, but shut their reactions out of his mind for now.

What happened? Michael asked.

I don't know how they got into Callenhain undetected in such numbers, but I heard their mindvoices just before they attacked. They launched their attack from inside the city walls. There were so many of them pouring over the city. They took the walls as our group fled. I sent the rest of my party back to Bergan with instructions to warn the other villages on the way and came here seeking you. I kept trying to call out to you but couldn't reach you.

Along with Kara's words, he caught the whispering voices she'd heard, saw fleeting images as she remembered rushing along the roads towards the gates. Saw the Sylannians fighting on the walls of Callenhain. Guards, totally unprepared for the assault from within their own walls, falling to their deaths.

How long ago was this? Michael asked.

A few weeks ago? she answered, fatigue and uncertainty colouring her reply.

"How the Powers did they get into Callenhain undetected?" Olivia asked.

Michael shook his head; he was at a loss to explain it himself but kept the bulk of his attention on Kara.

Do you know where you are now? Michael asked.

No. I was told there is a village at the end of this road, and you would be beyond it up in the Heights, Kara said. *I'm sorry, I didn't have time to make a connection to stronger mindspeakers in this direction.*

Never mind, it's not your fault. Show me what you are seeing, Michael said.

Confusion flashed in her mind, then he caught an image as she scanned her current surroundings. It wasn't much, but it was enough to give him a fair idea of her location.

You're not far from the village. Slow down and rest when you get there. We'll come to you and take it from there, and I'll introduce you to a couple of the stronger mindspeakers in the village, Michael instructed.

He paused long enough to feel her assent and assure himself she'd taken no harm except for pushing herself to exhaustion in her desperation to reach him. As he pulled his awareness back to focus on his surroundings, he heard Nathanial yelling at their people to pack and get ready to ride. Olivia still stood at his side, covering him while his attention had been elsewhere, although the Warlord had already left the tent to make his own preparations to leave.

"I'm sorry for the hasty departure, but it seems we have troubles of our own to sort out now," Michael said.

"So Nathanial told us. Please, go. Help your own people. I doubt the Sylannians are any threat to us here after what you have done for us," Khaliun said gravely.

Without needing to say more, he went through the door that Olivia was holding for him. He didn't run, but his sense of urgency was conveyed to all around him. No one wasted any time in getting ready to ride out.

∽

As they rode into the village, Michael called a halt to the warbands, both his own and the couple that had accompanied the Warlord. While it hadn't taken them all that long to pack and get on the road, Kara should have made it here first.

As he reached the centre of the village, he dismounted, leaving the others to sort themselves out. It didn't take long for the village elder to appear.

"Warleader, a woman has come here seeking you," the village speaker said.

"I'm aware. Where is she?" Michael asked.

"She's in the far visitor's hut. I'm afraid the poor thing was near collapse when she rode in."

"We'll see what we can do for her," Michael said, noting that Kesha had dismounted without prompting and was making her way across the camp, Nathanial in step beside her.

"One of the lads is dealing with her horse," the speaker said.

"Thank you. It would be poor payment for her to lose the animal," Michael said. "Now, if you'll excuse me, Speaker, I'll go and check on her myself."

The speaker acknowledged the Warlord then went back to whatever it was she'd been interrupted from. Michael turned to the Warlord who nodded, but stayed mounted.

"Go, check on the girl. The rest of you stretch, get a drink if you will but we won't be staying long. Make sure you are ready to ride when the order is given," the Warlord ordered.

Michael paused just in the entrance of the small hut, moving one step aside to allow room for Olivia. Nathanial's eyes were grave as they entered, but he didn't comment.

Kesha had a cloth, which she dipped in a small basin of water and used to clean off the dirt and blood from an old half-healed cut on Kara's forehead. Michael winced as he saw the angry redness and seeping of the wound that indicated infection had set in. Once she'd cleaned the area, Kesha placed her fingertips lightly on Kara's temples, careful to avoid the actual injury.

Fluid expelled from the wound, and even he could see it wasn't clean. It was like Kesha was driving out the toxins that had seeped into Kara's flesh from the injury. Nathanial picked up the cloth and dabbed at the excess. Kara flinched, eyes widening.

"It's all right, Kara, she's our healer," Nathanial explained.

"I... sorry, I've never been treated by a real healer before. It feels strange," Kara said.

Michael guessed that now she'd stopped moving, Kara was going into shock. The Warlord appeared at the entrance of the hut, and Michael shook his head at the unasked question. It was doubtful she could tell them anything else more useful than she already had. He stepped back out of the hut, allowing Kesha to finish her work, and faced the small group of the Unwanted who'd congregated nearby. Each of them were good mind-speakers with the ability to feed energy to their horses, and they were all exceptional riders. He took a position next to the Warlord, who raised his voice so it carried to the back ranks of their people as he filled them in on the report they'd received, keeping it brief by necessity. Until they got to Callenhain it was unlikely they'd know more.

"Call in the warbands, you'll be acting in your position of Warleader," the Warlord said to Michael.

Michael accepted the order then focused on the outriders.

"In the Warlord's name, issue orders to the other warband leaders to converge on Callenhain. Only go as far as necessary to mindspeak the other warbands. I don't care if your contact is left insensible with a splitting headache. They can tie them to their horse if they have to. Go," Michael ordered. One and all, the outriders urged their horses into a canter down the dusty road out of the village.

The sound of incoming riders made Michael clench his jaw as he wondered what else was about to go wrong. A moment later he relaxed as he realised it was Khaliun signalling the warbands to stand down. He didn't have long to wait before Khaliun rode into the village with her clan following along behind. Each of them bearing the wolf's eyes tattoo, the symbol of the warriors of Kallith. All of them bristling with weapons, including a great many of their horse archers. While their horse archers were much better with those bows than others, all the Kallith warriors could shoot them. He traded glances with the Warlord, who gave the signal to the warbands to wait.

"With your permission, we will honour our blood oath and come with you," Khaliun said, gesturing to the clans people arrayed behind her. "I've brought those of my tribe that number among the warriors of Kallith; our non-combatants will be cared for by those who remain."

Michael's eyes narrowed as he caught an undertone of anger and determination, not only from Khaliun but from those who rode with her.

"I gather the other leaders were not in favour of you joining us?" Michael asked.

"There was some hesitation among some of the other leaders. I, with the backing of the warriors of my tribe, ignored them. After the assistance you gave us, not only to settle here, but when the Sylannians tried to come at us again over the mountain pass, well, we owe you this much and more," Khaliun said.

"Will the rest of the tribes be safe without your warriors?" Olivia asked.

"They will be fine. There are no others that we are aware of to threaten them. Orghana promises she will ensure those who remain behind will maintain a passage of retreat, just in case," Khaliun said, a tight smile spreading on her lips. "Our path finders will range out to seek other paths to other places over the Heights, in case it becomes necessary."

Michael stared at Khaliun and the silence stretched between them. He knew enough about the ways of the People to know that Khaliun had breached their customs by coming without the consensus of the other leaders. There was clearly much she was not telling him about the events that had unfolded after their hasty departure. Michael indicated his acceptance of the offer to the Warlord.

"Your presence on the battlefield will be most welcome," the Warlord rumbled.

"Not to mention useful, particularly with those bows you wield so well," Olivia said.

"We'll be leaving this place shortly and riding hard, but I'm sure that is something you will all cope with. Keep just behind my own team. At least until you are familiar with how we operate on the road," Michael instructed.

The others made room for the riders of the clans to form up in their midst, with no additional orders being given. While a part of him wished he could speed their way to Callenhain, it was impossible. If it was a full attack, as it seemed to be from what Kara had told them, they would need the other warbands. It would take time, even as fast as they could ride when needed, for the other warbands to gather. That would at least give them time to assess the situation and plan their attack.

SEVENTY

Michael examined the outer walls of Callenhain from the safety of the trees. As Kara had reported, Sylanna had taken the city. And yet there was no sign at all of any fighting, let alone the destruction that generally went with such actions.

"I wonder who smuggled the Sylannians in?" Olivia said.

Michael's emotions ramped up a notch in reaction to Olivia's. They'd been through too much for him not to be aware of what she was thinking. This was the second time Callenhain had fallen to an enemy. It was the second time it had happened without any apparent damage or fighting. The first time her own family had thrown her out of the gates to broker a deal with the Warlord. Like her he couldn't help but wonder who'd become a traitor to their own and allowed the Sylannians into the city to take it with relative ease.

"Just because we can't see damage from the outside, it doesn't mean there isn't some within the city walls," Michael said.

"I'm tipping there is a tie in with the Kastler faction," Nathanial said.

"You think there was another scion of the house still here?" Michael frowned.

"Not necessarily. One could have come and picked up the reins after we left," Nathanial replied, his eyes not shifting from the city. "Or everything was in place before we intervened."

"We really are going to have to deal with that whole family." Olivia's lips pressed into a thin line, eyes narrowing.

"Unfortunately, as always, we seem to have more pressing concerns," Nathanial said.

"Do me a favour." Michael glanced over at Damien.

"Warleader?" Damien responded promptly.

"Don't lose control this time," Michael said.

"I didn't mean to last time," Damien muttered.

"I really detest my family but..." A hint of humour threaded through Olivia's words.

"Blowing up Callenhain is probably overkill," Nathanial finished where she left off.

Damien flushed red at the thought, causing Michael to chuckle and clap him on the shoulder. Passing reassurance onto him as he did so. The lad still didn't quite know how to take their banter.

"You'll be fine. Just concentrate on your job," Michael said.

"I can do it. It's one of the first skills I learnt, even before I was aware of what I was doing."

He didn't ask if Damien really could pull it off, although apparently he guessed what Michael was thinking anyway. Michael sighed. Placing doubt in Damien's head at this point wasn't a good idea. Instead, he faced Khaliun, who stood nearby with their riders arrayed behind her.

"Are you sure you want to do this? We'll try to maintain a shield over you, but..."

"Use of the veil cancels use of the veil, I know," Khaliun said, her expression grim. "If you and yours hadn't risked your lives to help us, I think the Sylannians would have swept over us. The People would no longer exist."

"Just shoot those arrows as accurately as you can. I'll get them to their targets," Damien said.

Michael ducked his head to hide his expression. Allowing his recruit to go off without one of their own to protect him was a situation he wished he wasn't in.

We'll protect him as if he is one of our own, Khaliun promised.

Michael pushed his concern aside, knowing Khaliun was sincere in her pledge.

AT THIS MOMENT, just before the battle, the tension was like a tangible thing. Michael ignored it and reached out with his mind, briefly touching the minds of the other leaders, assuring himself everyone was in place. He'd hated the idea of splitting their forces up this way when the idea had been floated. He still hated it, but the Warlord had overruled him. It made sense to cover the main gates on either side of the city.

Relax, son. We've been doing this a long time. This isn't even the first time we've taken this city, you and I. Besides, I don't quite need a minder yet.

Michael grinned despite himself. The Warlord, his father, was correct. Some of his tension was derived from the fact that the Warlord was on the other side of Callenhain at the other gate. His nerves always heightened when the Warlord was present on the field of battle. Particularly if Michael wasn't close enough to keep an eye on him.

Just keep yourself in one piece, Michael said.

I'd much rather one of us was with him, Olivia said.

He has half the warbands with him, including Aiden. Even he could hear the uncertainty in his own tone, a worry that echoed Olivia's own.

Olivia's eyes slid over to his own and he barely stopped the grimace from crossing his face. Aiden was hardly the most reliable warrior, but his warband was just as good as most of the others and Derick, the man who really led in all but name, was competent. The Warlord had seen to that, at least.

We've been over this. The bulk of the enemy should head in your direction. The Warlord's tone was calm and reasonable.

I know, I just wish you'd at least let me send Nathanial and a couple more of my people to you. Michael was aware he was fussing.

We already have a couple of your people with us. You will need the Unwanted more than us. Again, the Warlord was perfectly reasonable.

But...

We will manage, between Aiden and myself, with the couple of yours to bring down the farmers' gate.

The Warlord was talking sense, but that didn't help. *You know they will fall after taking the gate down?*

They will be safely behind our lines after they take the gate. We'll gain entrance to Callenhain without the loss of life on our side that the brute force method would take without the assistance of the Unwanted. The rest will be normal fighting, the Warlord said.

This time Michael was certain he heard amusement in the Warlord's tone and knew he was deliberately misinterpreting his concern. The farmers' gate was nowhere near as strong as the main gate. In fact, if he was honest, it wasn't a defensive gate at all. It was a small, oversized archway, barely big enough to allow a horse and cart through. The only reason the Warlord needed any of the Unwanted in his team to bring it down was because it was generally barred overnight. Those few members of the

Unwanted would be sufficient to take it down, even if they would be next to useless after doing so. Since he, along with the bulk of their forces, would launch the attack on the main reinforced gate first, the bulk of the defenders within should face off against them. The Warlord's teams, along with Aiden's, should be adequate for what they would face. But it still left Michael uneasy.

Shaking himself, he drew his attention back to the collective warbands on his side of the city. There was no need for him to announce the attack to those with the Warlord. Even on the other side of Callenhain, the start of the fight would be obvious and cue the launch of the Warlord's own attack shortly after.

Everyone ready?

Michael waited as he received the affirmative responses from the various leaders. As the first tinge of dawn hit the sky and the change of duty on the gates caused distraction in their enemy, he called the attack.

Go!

The clans, with Damien in their midst, spurred their horses forward at a gallop, Michael and the rest of the Unwanted streaming in to form the rank behind them. He drew his power and flung a shield in front of the riders. As he did so the warriors of Kallith drew their wicked horse bows and launched the first flight of deadly arrows towards those on the gates. Michael's attention sharpened as those on the gates realised something was happening outside the gates. Power with Damien's signature surged, hundreds of tendrils launching outwards from Damien to wrap themselves around the flight of arrows, speeding them unerringly towards their targets with deadly accuracy. Michael breathed a sigh of relief as the power use was carefully controlled and as the cry went up beyond, he saw many of the lookouts on the walls topple back as the arrows slammed into them. Without pause, the Kallith launched a second flight of arrows at those who foolishly stood up to see what was going on.

Satisfied, Michael drew his attention to the first of his own tasks and sucked in the veil from all around him. The Unwanted, using that as their cue, drew in their own power and, on his silent signal, launched their combined strength. It rushed out from them, Michael adding his own affinity for metal to the mix before their power slammed into the closed gates. The gate screamed in the early dawn as the metal glowed for a moment before buckling. The percussive explosion as the timber of the gates shattered was deafening and glowing lumps of what had been solid metal sprayed those behind the gates.

The clans launched one last volley of arrows through the portal where the gate had stood and over the walls, with Damien doing his bit to assist them on their way. Then they peeled off to the side. The Unwanted spread out and allowed the ranked fighters of the other warbands to come forward between their lines. It was a delicate balance they maintained with their powers. If they overused them during battle and slipped into veil-induced slumber, one of the other bands would have to help get them back to safety, taking them out of their fighting forces as well.

The veil sparkled in his mind's eye as shields sprang up above and in front of the fighters in the lead. Being in the back gave the Unwanted breathing space to recover from their first efforts, although thankfully it had all gone to plan so far. Michael slowed them all down to a trot as they passed through the ruined gates into the town proper. The clatter of the shod hooves of the horses resounded on the cobblestones. As shocking as their entrance had been, the inhabitants had had the sense to stay away. Michael saw teams on foot going house to house, looking for the enemy. The screams and clash of metal on metal gave away when they found their quarry. Michael saw some of the

Sylannian invaders, their strange silken garments puddled around them where they lay motionless on the ground. Some with arrows protruding from their heads and chests. The force of the explosion had clearly thrown others from the top of the wall to meet their death on the unforgiving cobbled streets below.

Hearing a yell from a side street, Michael refocused his attention on the incoming horde of Sylannians running down the street towards them. Michael wrapped his power around himself like a shimmering cloak, then drew his sword and joined the fight.

AIDEN'S EYES widened as he thrust his sword up to deflect the dual blades of the attacker. He flinched as another Sylannian appeared to lunge for him before Derick was there, his horse trampling the enemy in front of him while his sword took out another. Aiden bit back a curse as yet another ululating cry heralded yet another attack group of Sylannians joining the ones that were already surrounding his unit. A glint of metal gave away too late a sword plunging, not towards him but his horse. As his horse reared, then toppled to the ground, Aiden flung himself from the saddle, hitting the cobblestones with an explosion of air from his lungs. Scrambling to his feet, Aiden drew in the veil and desperately flung out his shield, pushing the attackers back as he regained possession of his sword. He spun around and almost wilted with relief as Derick dismounted and, fending off attackers, came to his side.

"Hold on, the Warlord is almost through on the other side," Derick shouted above the mayhem.

Aiden craned his head, seeking his father's forces, but saw nothing but fighting bodies around him. Seeing enemy blades flashing towards him, Aiden gasped, his sword flailing uselessly as he was jerked backwards, sprawling on the ground with a tall, imposing body between him and his attackers. Derick stumbled into the Warlord, who'd come to his rescue, and in a moment that seemed to happen in slow motion, the enemy's blade slipped through his father's guard as he was pushed off balance. The blade drove home into his chest with the weight of the Sylannian behind it. The Warlord stood for a moment, in a pool of calm with the madness of battle swirling around him, and Aiden grinned fiercely as he saw the Warlord topple to the ground, dagger still fixed in his chest. His knuckles whitened on the hilt of his sword, and he took a step forward, eyes glittering. As time resumed its normal pace and the mayhem heaved around him, Derick was suddenly in position, defending the Warlord.

"Protect the Warlord!" Derick bellowed.

Aiden swore as the Warlord's forces surged forward and he lost his opportunity as the battle pushed him further back from where his father lay prone on the ground, surrounded by their own ranks.

Now that the battle was well and truly underway, Michael kept his focus on the task right in front of him. With the skirmishes going from street to street, the Unwanted had split into smaller groups, supporting a squad of fighters drawn from the other warbands. At a flash of blades from a side street, Michael gathered in his power. Before he could lash out to push the attacker aside, a long-handled cast-iron pan caved in the side of the attacker's head. Michael stopped momentarily to stare. The woman with the pan, a local, grinned at him in satisfaction. He nodded in appreciation at her before she ducked back into her house, closing the door behind her. Michael shook his head as the curtain flipped aside and a young girl, probably the woman's daughter, peered out at the carnage unfolding on the street. She was clearly keeping watch for her mother, which explained the exceptional timing.

The squad member next to him, who would have been the one to go down under the assault, nodded her thanks to the girl in the window.

We'll take the side street to the right. Where there was one, there are bound to be more, Michael said to those around him.

Warleader, the Warlord is down!

Michael froze as an image flashed in his head of warband members defending the Warlord against a group of attackers. Relief flooded Michael when he realised that while the Warlord was obviously injured and down, he was still alive.

Where are you? Michael bit out.

The squad paused, understanding something was happening, their posture changing to a defensive formation around him.

Between the docks and trader row.

Michael took stock of where he was before replying. *Hold on, keep him safe. I'm not far off.*

The band member with the Warlord's group acknowledged the order, before their attention shifted elsewhere with a thrust of power as the connection between them cut.

Olivia, how far is your group from the dock side of trader row? Michael asked.

He signalled to the squad around him and moved off at a trot towards the docks. As attackers rose, he ruthlessly drew in power and slammed them back out of his way. He was no longer bothering to conserve his energy levels, lashing out with his sword as he passed and, on occasion, trampling over enemies as they rode.

Not far, why, what's happened? Olivia's tone sharpened as she picked up his urgency.

Father has been injured, Michael said. *From the images of the battle surrounding him, I might need some backup.*

On my way.

Her focus shifted with the draw and thrust of the veil that was distinctly her. Michael cursed as he realised how close they'd been to finishing the bulk of the fighting to clear this section of the city. Although he was under no illusions: it would take days, if not weeks, to hunt out all those who'd gone to ground. As it was, the populace of Callenhain had proven they were quite willing to assist where they could. Particularly as soon as they saw his forces, and they'd dispatched their fair share of the intruders along the way as well.

"The Warlord is down; we're heading towards the docks," he yelled at the leader of the squad that surrounded him.

The woman paled and acknowledged the information with a hand signal, her focus changing as she issued orders to her squad. Michael's horse reared and lashed out as a Sylannian who'd been lying on the ground suddenly leapt up with her blades. The shod hooves of his horse connected with the Sylannian's head and he had time to see it had split open as she fell back and the squad leader struck with her blade, lopping off what remained of the bloody ruin as they rode past.

SEVENTY-ONE

Steven stopped in his tracks, staring at his mother as she stood at the window, gazing up at the wall. He took a cautious step forward to see what had captured her attention. A guard on a balcony on the upper floor stumbled, raising a bottle to his mouth to chug the contents while he steadied himself with the other hand. As Steven watched, the guard lurched up on a chair, threw his arms wide and started singing a bawdy ballad.

Finish the bottle, show them all you can drink them under the table, his mother whispered.

Steven froze as his mother's compulsion rolled out, unable to take his eyes off the guard, who obligingly finished off the bottle and flung it off the balcony.

Dance as you sing, you like to dance, his mother said.

The guard on the balcony doubled his efforts, singing—if it could be called that—at the top of his lungs while lurching from side to side.

"Cut out the racket and come down here!" A guard stood in the courtyard below, staring up at the drunk guard.

Go on, go down to him. Such a short step, his mother said.

The guard on a balcony swayed to a stop, blinking at the guard in the courtyard below him. His mind crushed under Lady Rathadon's will.

"No need to yell, I'm coming," he said.

With a sloppy smile on his face, he clambered up and stepped off the balcony ledge. He didn't even scream as his body slammed into the courtyard.

Steven gasped. "Mother, what are you doing?"

His mother's eyes glittered. "I don't give up what's mine without a fight, Steven."

"You're behind the death of the Kastlers' guards?" Steven swallowed. "What if the Kastlers work out what you're doing?"

His mother eased back into her seat, relaxed as if she'd done nothing more than have some afternoon tea.

"Doubtful; they don't have strong mindpowers." His mother sniffed disdainfully. "Now, what brings you here?"

Steven transferred his regard to his father, who simply sat there, face smooth as he stared at his mother before they turned their attention back to him, quietly waiting. Steven tried his best to ignore the commotion outside and, taking a breath, focused his attention back to why he'd come here.

"I've been a fool."

"Good and bad, life happens. We can only do our best to navigate our way through it." His mother's voice held a hint of sadness.

"None of this was about me. I wasn't the one who was hard done by all these years."

"You were, but perhaps not as much as you imagined," his mother said.

"I thought anything would be better than the Warlord. How could I have known it would be worse?"

Steven swallowed. He still heard the woman's desperate

screams as the thugs who'd taken over the streets of Vallantia tried to drag her son away. He was still horrified by the knowledge that the Kastlers were committing such acts, taking people off the streets and shoving them on boats to be traded to their enemy. All for the fortunes of one of the great trading houses. The evidence that even his mother had been doing more than he had against the Kastlers caused a lump to rise in his throat.

"All of this is bad timing. We are trying to get word to your brother, but it's taking time to track him down," his mother said.

"I believe it's already in hand; he was in the Heights but if the attack the Kastlers expect occurs, he'll probably head to Callenhain next. So, I guess we're on our own for now," Steven said, and passed over the envelope from Ben that he'd almost forgotten he'd come to deliver. "This probably explains it, and more."

Steven ducked his head and drew in a shaky breath. If a storyteller had told a tale about someone messing up as badly as he had, it would have been unbelievable. Steven knelt with his head bowed. He raised his hands placing them from his heart to forehead. A supplicant.

"This is too little, too late, but what can I do? What do you need of me, Warlord?"

SEVENTY-TWO

Michael shoved his concern for the Warlord aside as his unit rounded the corner towards the area known as trader row to see the beleaguered group battling the biggest mass of Sylannians he'd seen since they'd breached the gates.

Olivia, Nathanial? Are you far off?

Just entered from the street to your right, Nathanial said.

One block to go and my team will be with you both, Olivia said.

Cut through the enemy, do not spare yourselves. Michael spurred his own horse forward, aware Nathanial's group was doing likewise, lashing out with a hammering blow at the enemies closest to his own group. *Protect the Warlord, I'll be at your side shortly.*

Yes, Warleader, Derick said.

Bodies toppled, parts of what had once been attached to a living person moments before were severed, and blood washed the cobblestones as Michael, with his unit, carved brutally through the enemy ranks.

"Joining your line," Nathanial yelled above the mayhem, echoing the warning with mindspeech.

Their two fighting units snapped together seamlessly, Michael's powers meshing with Nathanial's as they battled on without pause. A wash of power rolled over him and bodies toppled to one side of them as Olivia's unit merged with them. Michael signalled his horse, who trampled the bodies on the ground as Michael slashed at those still standing.

We'll hold our ground and the Kallith will take out as many as they can while their arrows last, Damien said.

Before Michael could respond, a Sylannian screamed and lunged towards him. Michael manoeuvred to strike at the threat, only for her to topple back with an arrow protruding from her head. Michael lost track of time as unit after unit merged with their growing battle group. He stopped himself from striking off the head of the last person he opposed as he recognised the black and brown fighting leathers of another of the Warlord's warbands. His horse danced sideways as he reined him in. As others kept fighting around him, Michael's eyes tracked to the man lying motionless on the ground. Leaving the mopping up to the others, Michael leapt from his horse, closing the distance to where the Warlord lay. Michael dropped to one knee at his father's side, sparing a glance for Aiden. For once, Aiden's less than immaculate appearance showed he'd at least engaged in the battle.

"He... he went down coming to defend me," Aiden said.

"Explanations can wait until later," Michael said.

Michael stared down at the Warlord with his othersight, his breath catching as the muddy, fading glow of the veil contained within his body sprang into sight. It leaked from the Warlord, dissipating and merging with the swirling veil around them as he grew weaker by the moment. Michael pulled in more of the veil and shared his strength with the Warlord. Metal groaned and Michael spun, his shield expanding to cover the Warlord and those closest to him. Off to one side, double gates of black bars protested as they were pushed open. Michael's eyes widened and he swore as fighters in plain garments, common among caravan guards, spilled out of the compound. The caravan guards yelled their own battle cry as they joined his own forces in fighting the Sylannians.

"Form up around the Warlord; we need to get him to the safety of the compound," Michael ordered.

Michael made room at the Warlord's side as several of the fighters surrounded the Warlord and lifted his unconscious form between them. Their group moved as a unit, step by step, as they made ground towards the compound. As they drew up to the line being maintained by some of the local fighters, it parted, allowing them to fall in behind their own line into a pool of calm.

"Help them fight back the Sylannians and secure the compound," Michael said to the band leader closest to him, who sprang into action without requiring further orders.

"I've alerted the team we left with Kesha," Nathanial said as Michael's second-in-command joined him. "I'll take my team out to escort her here as soon as it's safe to do so."

"Michael!"

Michael swung around again, shocked to see Jenna in the plain brown fighting leathers emblazoned with the Smith's anvil and hammer as she emerged from the guards around her. He braced as she flew to him, embracing him fiercely, and he wrapped his spare arm around her. At a voice bellowing for the gates to be secured, Michael looked up to see Jenna's husband, Theo, directing the caravan guards.

"This compound belongs to your husband's family?" Michael felt relief wash over him.

"It does. We've secured it as best we can. Come, bring the Warlord to the warehouse. We have a couple of healers here who can help," Jenna said, then lead the way.

Olivia yelled orders to their own ranks, who dispersed

around the compound to take over the vantage points. For the first time, Michael noted there were groups of locals everywhere in the compound. Far more than Jenna and her family could account for with their trading enterprises here in Callenhain.

"Survivors?" Michael asked.

"We've taken in the locals that have come our way, both here and at our manor house, and had teams out in the city to rescue as many people as we could," Jenna said.

"I'm afraid I'm going to have to commandeer this whole compound," Michael said.

"It's yours," Jenna said.

Jenna led them into one of the large warehouses, gesturing for those carrying the Warlord to take their burden inside. Michael issued orders to a couple of his people, who promptly took up guard posts at the doors, then he followed along in the party's wake. They ignored those already in the warehouse as they swept across to a door over the far side. Jenna flung it open, revealing a large room. It had a desk pushed unceremoniously against the wall with the chair perched on top. A mattress and blankets on a makeshift base that had a previous life as packing crates took up the space in front of the desk. Those carrying the Warlord lowered their burden onto the bed.

Olivia slipped into the room. "Gavrel, you and the rest of the team find a corner of the warehouse and get some sleep."

"Olivia, I can—"

"Get some sleep." Olivia snapped, then rubbed her face with one hand, the blood and grim from battle smearing up her cheek. "We've all expended a great deal of energy today and we can't afford for any of us to collapse. The teams will be rotating through sleep shifts. The same for the command team. So I'll be getting some sleep myself as soon as this is sorted."

Gavrel held up his hands and with one last look at the uncon-scious form of the Warlord gathered members of his team and left the room. Theo plastered himself against the wall as the team of Unwanted went past and then stood hovering in the doorway.

"I'll get the healers," Jenna said.

"It's all right, I'll send for them," Theo said before turning to bellow orders to someone.

"I take it I've just kicked you out of your temporary accommodation?" Michael said.

"It's fine. We set it up as a convenience when this mess started, we only use it while we're here. We'll take the tunnels back to the estate house, unless you want to move the Warlord there?" Jenna said. "It's secure and he'll be more comfortable."

As Nathanial joined them in the room, Michael shook his head.

"I don't want to move him further until Kesha has seen him. No offence to your healers, Jenna, but we have to get Kesha here," Michael said.

"It's not safe. We don't have control of the city yet," Nathanial said as he channelled a steady stream of his own energy into the Warlord.

"If you'll tell me where your healer is, I can help," Theo said, as he ushered a man with grey-flecked black hair and a younger woman into the room. The couple went straight to the Warlord's side. "There are smugglers' tunnels back to our estate house and to lands out of the city, it's how we've been moving around."

"Nathanial, if you'll consult with Theo? I don't care how you do it, but get Kesha here. Father won't last the night without her aid."

SEVENTY-THREE

Michael looked at Olivia, who rolled her eyes as they heard the Warlord grumble about Kesha's restrictions through the closed door. He wanted to get out of bed, and she was refusing to allow it. To the Warlord's consternation it was her orders his guards listened to, not his. The fighting around Callenhain continued in pockets throughout the city, as Michael had thought it would, but this place was secure. It helped that this was a well set up traders' compound, complete with warehouses, shopfront, and a small pier with access to the major river.

"I'm concerned by how few of them we've flushed out so far."

"We know they've spread out to take surrounding villages. It was a foolish thing for them to do before fully securing Callenhain," Nathanial said.

"I'm not complaining about their lack of sound tactics, but I agree it was a stupid thing for them to do. For them to keep what they've taken, I would have expected far more of them than we've encountered so far." Michael should have been happy with how well everything was going, but somehow it seemed far too easy. This attack didn't gel with some of the recent attacks they'd seen out of Sylanna.

"My rough estimation is there were more of them trying to come at us from the Heights than we've found here." Olivia frowned.

"They may have expected that their people coming through that way would join them?" Nathanial didn't seem convinced.

"Perhaps; something just seems off," Michael said.

Michael broke off from his discussion as Kesha came out of her patient's bedroom. She was remarkably calm, given the argument she'd just had with her patient. Or rather, he guessed the Warlord had been arguing. She'd just said no, and he suspected she used her healing powers to sink the Warlord into sleep to end his protestations.

"How is he?"

"He doesn't take to healing as well as all of you, but he is recovering, although he'll need rest. It would be better if that rest wasn't in a war zone where he'll be tempted to go out and help you fight."

"Can he ride?"

Kesha frowned, then shook her head. "Not right now. If I hadn't been nearby, he'd be dead. He can travel in a few more days, slowly, in a carriage."

"As soon as you give permission, I'll send him back to Yalleska in a carriage."

"He can't go by himself," Kesha said.

"No, he'll go under substantial guard," Michael agreed. "His two warbands and one other."

"He's not going to agree." Kesha sounded genuinely worried.

"I won't be giving him a choice or asking for his permission. I'm the Warleader and he is injured. By his own rules until this mess is sorted or he fully recovers, whichever occurs first, authority for the whole domain defaults to me."

Kesha's eyes widened, then she looked at Nathanial, who shrugged. Olivia chuckled at the other woman's obvious disbelief.

"The Warlord's personal warbands have been following Michael's orders almost as long as they've been obeying the Warlord. The Warlord has reinforced with them what is to occur in emergencies," Nathanial said.

"So, who gets the pleasure of being the third guard detail we send with him?" Olivia asked.

"I haven't decided on the third warband yet. Thoughts?"

"They'll need to be strong enough to withstand the Warlord's demand to head back here," Nathanial said.

"I've already spoken with both the leaders of his own units. They will do as I direct them. They've had a scare." Michael dismissed the concern. He was certain all of them knew what he'd do to them if they failed.

"Send me," Aiden said.

Michael swung around to stare at Aiden, astonished. Aiden had been sitting quietly in the corner while his father was being healed. Michael had to admit the reports he'd received told him Aiden's people had done a good job so far during the fighting in the streets of Callenhain. He may not have been the bravest of men, but his warband was good at what they did.

"Are you sure you can say no to him?" Michael asked.

Aiden's eyes opened wide, his open hands raised as if fending off an attacker. "As Father ordered me, I'm to follow your orders. If those orders are that he is to go back to Yalleska, well, who am I to disregard them?"

Michael couldn't help the snort of laughter. "I'll make sure he knows they are my orders."

"No matter what you think of me, I care for my father." Aiden stared away towards the Warlord's door. "It's my fault he went down. He was protecting me."

"It wasn't your fault. From what Derick told me, you were all overwhelmed." Michael hesitated, then shook his head. "If the fighting gets there, it needs to be someone who can command."

"It's Yalleska. The place is a fortress. I'd pull the villagers into the inner walls and close the gates. I have the experience of my own band leader and my father's that I can draw on for the actual fighting. It isn't always necessary to be in the thick of battle to command, and if that happens, my father will be there as well."

"If that happens, you may have to lock him in his room," Nathanial muttered.

Michael chuckled, although he couldn't disagree with Nathanial's assessment. Olivia simply nodded at him. He wished there was another option, but Aiden was correct. They just had to withdraw into the walls and the leaders of the other warbands, including the band leader currently in command of Yalleska in the Warlord's absence, would do their jobs.

"Go consult with the other two band leaders and get your planning done. I want you ready to ride out as soon as Kesha gives the all-clear. If you and your band leader think you need anything else to ensure the Warlord's safety, even more fighters, let me know." Michael watched as Aiden gestured to Derick, who stood and started to issue orders.

"I'll ask, but with three warbands plus those who remain in Yalleska, we should be fine. Besides, you have your work cut out for you here. You'll need the other bands to clean this mess up," Aiden said.

"Aiden, keep him safe, despite himself."

"Yes, Warleader. We'll do our best," Aiden said, and with an air of amusement added, "Please let me be there when you tell him he has to ride in a carriage."

Michael burst into startled laughter and waved Aiden off.

"You know, if Aiden keeps showing these little bursts of being decent, I might get over my dislike of him," Olivia said.

Michael shook his head. Neither of them liked Aiden, a feeling that had been mutual from the day they met. Fortunately for them all, Aiden seemed to have started growing up. Right now, the last thing they needed was to be bickering amongst themselves.

Aiden sat in silence next to Olivia and Nathanial, as the voices carried across the warehouse despite the closed door.

"You will go back to Yalleska as I order you to do, Father." Michael's voice held a hint of anger.

Not that Aiden could blame him. The argument between the pair had been going on far longer than any of them had thought it would.

"I'm the Warlord and I say I'm not going." The Warlord sounded peevish.

"You are injured, and by your orders command has passed to me. You're going."

"I didn't mean those orders to apply to me."

A silence followed the Warlords obstinate statement. Aiden could imagine Michael was grinding his teeth in frustration and for once it wasn't directed at him.

"They do, and you know it. You didn't put these procedures in place just so the others would follow my orders when you aren't around." Exasperation replaced the anger in Michael's tone. "To throw your own words back at you, you need to lead by example. Would you have our people thinking they can choose only to obey the orders that suit them?"

"I'm conscious now. I'll be out of bed in no time."

"Our healer reports you need rest. You'll follow my orders.

Either you allow us to assist you out to the carriage we've commandeered, or I'll push you into unconsciousness and you'll be carried out. The choice is yours," Michael said bluntly.

Silence stretched between the arguing pair, although Aiden could feel his father's anger at being given such an ultimatum. From Michael, he felt nothing. That wasn't something that surprised him at all.

"I didn't mean you could order me around," the Warlord said.

"That's not how the transfer of command works. You'll get it back when you are fully healed. Not before." Michael's tone was implacable.

Aiden heard his father sigh as his irritation and peevishness spluttered out. He'd come up against that wall that was Michael. It wasn't the first time Michael had defied their father, but it was certainly a rare occurrence. And Michael had won then, too. Aiden wished it was a skill he possessed. It was a feat he'd never managed himself.

"Well, that went better than I thought it would," Nathanial said.

"I thought he'd hold out for at least another hour or two," Aiden agreed.

"He's exhausted just from arguing. He knows he's not well enough to stay, but he had to at least put up some kind of fight," Olivia said.

"I'm surprised you didn't go in to back Michael up," Aiden said.

"Michael had no need for me to back him up on this one. He is right and Father knows it. That doesn't mean he has to like it." Olivia shrugged.

Aiden's attention was drawn as the door to the inner room where his father was staying opened and his father stepped out of the room for the first time in over a week. Michael followed a step behind. Aiden's eyes narrowed as he regarded his father. He'd lost weight. More than he'd thought possible in a week.

"It's a side effect of the healing. I accelerated his body's natural ability to heal. It takes much of his energy," Kesha said from where she stood next to Nathanial.

"You've reversed that speed-healing effect?" Olivia asked, holding the other woman's gaze.

"This morning. He will heal at a normal rate now. He just needs peace to recover." Kesha's eyes were shadowed. "I wasn't kidding when I said he'd nearly gone beyond my ability to heal."

"You and your team are ready?" Olivia asked, her gaze taking in Aiden and the other two leaders who stood waiting nearby.

"We are. We were just waiting for Father to agree and appear," Aiden said, careful to keep his expression solemn.

He nodded at Derick. It was all that was needed. The man went outside and yelled at those going with them to form up. As his father stumbled on his way across the room, Aiden took an inadvertent step forward. The Warlord's plunge to the floor was halted as Michael grabbed hold of him, supporting most of his weight.

"All right, you're right," the Warlord grumbled, glaring at Michael. "I need more rest. Happy now?"

"I'll be happy when you are fully healed and I can transfer command of your domain back to you," Michael said, his eyes shadowed and expression controlled. "In the meantime, let me do the job you trained me for."

Aiden found it amazing that their father admitted he was wrong. Olivia moved forward to their father's other side and helped him as he walked. It was a sign of how bad he felt that he allowed the support. As they passed his position, Aiden fell into step and followed them all out of the doors. It took a little bit more effort to get his father into the carriage. Not because he complained about it again, but simply because the short walk between the bed and outside had tired him out.

"He'll get stronger every day. It's just this is the first time he's been up and out of bed," Kesha said. "He can go for a short walk of similar distance every day, but no more."

Aiden nodded. "I will defer to your judgement."

Finally, when everything was ready, he signalled Derick, who brought forward his own mount, handing him the reins. Michael finished issuing instructions to the other two leaders regarding what he needed of them once they reached Yalleska, then turned to him.

"As soon as he's rested, he'll probably get argumentative. Use the fact that you are following my orders." The command in Michael's tone was clear.

As was the fact that his gaze went from him to Derick and back again. He bit back his own irritation that Derick immediately indicated compliance with the order. It galled him that Michael had the right to directly command all his father's warriors, not just the members of the Unwanted.

"Of course, Warleader." Aiden curbed his irritation; it wouldn't do him any good.

Instead, he nodded to them, then urged his horse forward, keeping to a walk as his command flowed around him and his father's carriage. Michael had ordered extra people to escort them out of the city limits, and then the duty of protecting his father and delivering him safely to Yalleska was up to him. As they went around the corner and headed out of Michael's sight he relaxed back into his saddle and smirked.

SEVENTY-FOUR

Jaclyn lay low in the barge, as did the rest of her family. She had a certain amount of confidence after watching barge after barge of her family being transported into the city without harm. Not that she trusted these smugglers. Those in charge of the barges were watched by a handpicked crew of daggerwives. There was a strong mind speaker with each group who reported when they'd infiltrated this barbarian city safely. It had been a long couple of weeks as her people filtered in unde-tected. With each passing day, she feared their warleader would finish with the distraction she'd set for him and march on Vallan-tia. Before that happened, she intended to be well and truly in control.

Ricardo started as he sensed someone nearby. She reached out and lay a hand on his shoulder.

Calm, my love. They have no awareness that we are here.

Most of these people were blind. Their senses limited to a very few skills. It made her wonder how they'd survived. Then again, it might explain that insanely powerful company under the leadership of one warleader. It was as if their warlord had swept up anyone of any perceptible talent with the veil and put them all in one unit. It had great merit, yet also a very fatal flaw.

A figure on a stone bridge appeared to pause and stare in their direction, drawing her attention. Everyone stilled in response.

Be gone, she whispered, pushing at the mind of the other, trying to convince him he didn't see what he did. Jaclyn breathed a sigh of relief when the figure pushed himself off the rail of the bridge and staggered on his way. She was grateful that she was aided by his intoxication. If he had been sober, she wasn't sure her compulsion would have worked. She peered up at the buildings looming on either side of them as they passed beyond the bridge. Somehow, she hadn't quite conceived of the teeming life within Vallantia. For the first time, she worried that she wouldn't have enough people to enact her plan.

This place is bigger than I expected, Ricardo whispered, echoing her thoughts.

It's a sprawling place. It slumbers, unaware how vulnerable it is in this moment, Jaclyn replied, trying to convey confidence that she didn't feel.

She'd known right from the outset that to keep attacking the barbarians was counterproductive. The newly conquered lands of the traders would suit their people for generations to come. Yet here they were, about to attempt what her own instinct was telling her was foolishness. Every report she'd read on this barbarian warlord and his warleader screamed caution at her. Yet to do elsewise meant death to her and her entire house for defying her king, or she had to rise against her brother and seize the throne with everything that implied. A lump rose in her throat at the mere thought, but no matter how much she pushed back and delayed the dance of daggers for the throne, it was inevitable. Even if this admittedly foolish action succeeded, there was only one final destination. Even if the paths to get there were different. If against all odds she conquered this land for her people, there were no more moves for her to play. She'd have to take the throne or die to blades wielded by her brother's wives.

She studied the habitations on the bank as they floated by. Row upon row of wooden huts on multiple levels, with the upper stories having balconies overlooking the river. Some had external wooden steps leading to the upper floors. It made her wonder how many people resided in these places. They reminded her of the lower levels of her own island court where the low-caste workers lived almost on top of each other. The higher the residence, the more space and status people had. She saw a pier, with boats and barges secured in place next to large, utilitarian buildings. She'd expected they would pull in here, but as they glided past without halting, she traded looks with Myra, who shrugged. Further down the river, she could see the residences were bigger and made mostly from stone. Some even stood alone on their own patch of land.

Before they reached those houses, the barge entered a tunnel, plunging them into darkness as the ambient light from the city was blocked out. When they emerged on the other side, light returned. Jaclyn stared at the lamps that were fixed on poles evenly spaced along the road. She was reminded these people didn't have the spiders, which threw off light as well as producing the silk her people used. Jaclyn hadn't quite realised how useful the creatures were until she'd left the land of her birth and fought in other countries.

She caught a glimpse of tall stone buildings with shuttered windows before they were plunged into darkness again. As they came out from the darkness one more time, she craned her head to check their surroundings and realised they were floating down a narrow channel. What she'd thought of as tunnels were a series of bridges connecting the two banks. As they went around another corner, Jaclyn had the distinct feeling they were going in circles, but she could see they were deeper into the city. Lights glowed to one side, and the barge turned again, floating into a private enclosed dock, the doors groaning as they were closed behind them. The smugglers leapt onto the stone pier and tied the barge to stone pillars built there for that purpose. There was a brief flurry of activity as planks were stretched between the pier and the barge. Her family rose around her, and they flowed off the boat without hesitation.

Daggerwives who'd arrived earlier lined the walls and stood guard on the one waterway entrance at this level.

It's ingenious really, Myra said.

Particularly for smugglers, Jaclyn said.

She gestured to the daggerwives who bundled up the smugglers who'd piloted the barge and took them away to a secure location.

Other daggerwives flowed around them, leading the way up the stone stairs at the end of the dock. The door opened and she was led out to a large open indoor area, which her people had conveniently made into their sleeping area. The windows remained shuttered, blocking prying eyes from peering into this place.

"The smugglers work for a trading family. This is one of the warehouses they used for the storage of goods," Arianne said.

Jaclyn assumed that before she and her sister houses had disrupted the enterprise, this was also where the smugglers had kept the men they were trading. Looking at the size of the place, her eyes narrowed.

If we survive this and get home, remind me to check which other houses may have been trading with these people, Jaclyn said.

You think more of the lesser houses are consorting with the barbarians? Myra sounded disgusted.

This looks too big and well set up to be trading just a handful of men to one traitor house.

Unless it was a new enterprise that they were hoping to expand in the future, Ricardo said.

Jaclyn considered what Ricardo had said and decided he might have a point. That made her curious to meet these traders. She paused, estimating the numbers here in the warehouse, and looked at Arianne.

"Where are the rest of our people?" Jaclyn asked.

"We've taken several of the nearby buildings, First. We've distributed our forces among them," Arianne said.

"Our presence hasn't been given away?" Myra asked.

"No, Primewife. There has been disruption here. The smugglers tell us the trading family has attempted to wrest control of this city from its ruling family. So, the locals attribute attacks and deaths to the traders and their mercenaries," Arianne said.

That certainly made things easier for their own attack. It was unlikely the traders had a firm grip on this place. Jaclyn followed her escort as they climbed a staircase that led to the upper floors. They entered a room filled with chairs, with a hallway and doors down the other end.

"We've set aside the most suitable of the rooms up here for your use, First," Arianne said.

It was basic, things always were when they launched an attack. Then again, it was better than their first accommodation in the land of the traders. Having seen the size of this place as they came in, she had no doubt that they would find and take more suitable accommodation sooner rather than later.

SEVENTY-FIVE

It had been a long week. Damien stared up at the roof of the warehouse they were bunked in and frowned. At least he thought it had been a week, but given how the days were blurring and merging in his mind, it could have been longer for all he knew right now. As the fight had broken into smaller skirmishes going from street to street, the Unwanted had split into smaller groups, assigned to battle teams filled from the other warbands. Their role had been mostly to provide the veil-fuelled muscle. They shielded not only themselves but their assigned team with their powers. As a result, the Unwanted had been on a rotation with down days. Right now, he was on one of those days, but since they were on a war footing, they were restricted to their makeshift barracks.

At least it wasn't just him confined to quarters. Although after they'd all collapsed during the battle in the Heights, he'd had firsthand experience of why they rotated out to rest. None of them, for all the power they possessed, would do any good locked in veil-enforced slumber while their bodies repaired themselves. This battle for Callenhain, mopping up the clusters of the Sylannians, had always been going to take longer than the initial assault. However, he was still at a loose end.

He'd rather be out with the patrols and busy than sitting around. Being restricted to camp wouldn't be so bad if he was good at anything other than killing. Everyone preferred he didn't touch the food or even attempt to help those assigned to meal duty. He would be good as a perimeter guard or hunter if they hadn't been in the middle of Callenhain and if they'd had enough people to spare. As it was, there was plenty of tiscan available here and Michael didn't trust that he'd resist temptation if there wasn't someone else to watch him, so he couldn't go out alone.

He rolled out of his sleeping cot, half growling under his breath, aware that Michael was resting. The leadership group had been up late talking battle plans with the other band leaders. With the retreat of the Warlord, Michael was pulling double duty. Nathanial had gone out with a patrol that had located a larger group of Sylannians to flush out. Olivia was out doing the rounds in the enclave they'd taken over, making sure guards stood duty where they were meant to and everything was still secure. Although Damien was more than happy to be up and awake, ready to defend his teammates if required, in this place, right now, there was nothing for him to be guarding anyone against.

"Damien, could you help me with this, please?"

Damien saw one of the healers grappling with several bags. Some of the other skirmishing parties had instructions to look for healing supplies while they'd been out. Kesha had even provided a list of things she needed. He hadn't paid much attention to the tarp-covered pile in the corner until now, so he hadn't realised how much they'd managed to scrounge up.

"Of course." He relieved the man of most of the bags he was trying to carry.

"Thank you, sorry for being a bother," the older man said.

"No problems," Damien said.

Packhorse may not have been on his to-do list for the day but at least it gave him something constructive to do. He entered the converted warehouse and dumped the bags he was carrying to one side.

"We could use an extra hand if you could you help for a bit? I'd rather not wake Kesha unless I need to."

"Of course, I'm not doing much else right now," Damien said.

He glanced around the room and moved over to one side, watching as another healer rewrapped a dressing on the arm of one of their patients.

"Do you think you could finish this for me?" the older healer asked.

Damien simply grabbed the bandage from him and continued to bind the unconscious patient's arm. He lost himself in monotony, moving around, assisting with changing bandages. Grateful for a task that at least kept him occupied. He didn't think anything of it when they handed him a tray with small vials on it. He followed the healer as they approached the first of the more seriously injured patients. Then the healer pulled the stopper off the bottle and Damien froze. Tiscan. The bottle contained distilled tiscan.

"Damien, what's wrong with you? Come along..."

He heard the words but couldn't respond, his gaze fixed on the innocuous vials. His brain screamed at him that it was pure, distilled tiscan. The world around him seemed frozen and he could hear his own harsh indrawn breath, overloud. Tremors shook his body as he knelt and carefully placed the tray on the ground and backed up. When his back hit the wall, he slid down it until he hit the floor. Eyes still fixed on the vials. Yearning hammered into him.

He pressed shaking hands to his eyes trying to block out the sight. Damien slowly rose to his feet, trying hard to keep his breath short so as not to breathe in or smell the tiscan.

"I'm sorry, healer, I can't. The tiscan. I'm an addict." Damien heard the waver in his own voice, but didn't have the energy to feel embarrassed. *Olivia?*

He forced himself to turn and stumbled out of the warehouse, only to run into Olivia. She grabbed him, staring into his eyes. It took her barely a moment to register the cause of his current state.

"Breathe, Damien, you're all right. I'm here," Olivia said.

He sank into the soothing emanations she channelled into him and allowed her to guide him back into the building they were using as their own quarters.

"Did he use again?"

As he was pressed down into his sleeping cot Damien registered the grim voice was Michael's.

"No, he resisted. A tray of pure distilled tiscan. He gave it back to the healer, called for me and removed himself from the healing hall before I got there," Olivia said.

Damien knew he must be wrong, but somehow, he sensed respect in Olivia's tone and a wash of approval from Michael. He didn't resist as they pushed him down to sleep.

SEVENTY-SIX

Isabella stood looking around uncertainly. She'd finished training and this was her afternoon off from chores, although she'd still chopped some wood for her family and a little for the community pile. While she didn't remember being idle in the past, even on her days off from chores, for some reason, she didn't know what to do with herself. The squealing and splashing from the river gave away that some of the younger children were playing. She could see others industriously building a cubby in the trees near to the edge of the commons. Another group sat with their heads together, gossiping with each other.

She reached up and rubbed her shoulders absently as her gaze caught on the bathhouse. While her family hut had its own small wash basin, most of the huts did, the bathhouse had tubs big enough to soak in, if you were of a mind to do so. She decided she was. It seemed she'd collected an assortment of aches in muscles that she hadn't known existed before.

Isabella went to the low stone building on the edge of the commons. It had large tanks on the roof, with a winding staircase leading to the top. The tanks filled with rainwater but otherwise were kept topped up by those on water duty. She flipped over the sign near the door to signal the bathing room had an occupant before she entered, then used a quick burst of power to open the tap over the far bath, allowing the water to flow into the tub. She unbuttoned her vest, hanging it on a wooden peg on the wall before pulling her tunic over her head and placing it on the next peg. She sat on the wooden bench to remove her boots, careful to keep an eye on the water level. As she stood, she used another small pulse of the veil to shut off the water, then took off her trousers and concentrated on the water, pulling more power to heat it. As steam rose from the water, she sighed in satisfaction. She placed her trousers on the bench, near her weapons belt, then trod up the wooden stairs and stepped into the steaming bath, sinking into the depths. As she settled against the wall of the tub with a sigh, her unbound hair spread across the water's surface. Isabella closed her eyes and allowed the water to soothe her aches.

She didn't bother to open her eyes when she heard the door open; she knew it was Sonja. She'd only seen her friend in passing these last few months as she was constantly finding herself at different tasks. Without much thought, she flipped the faucet for the second tub, allowing the water from the tanks above to fill it.

"You're getting strong, like your brother," Sonja said.

"So it seems; although he's much stronger than me." Isabella sighed.

"He should be. He's older," Sonja said as she disrobed. "Aren't you afraid?"

Isabella laughed. "Of many things, but afraid of what, in particular?"

"The veil children like you—they say they usually die. That your powers will grow until they burn out your mind," Sonja said quietly. As the faucet shut off and then steam rose from her bath, Sonja wasted no time climbing into the tub.

That was one thing Isabella liked about Sonja. Other than being one of the few in the village of a similar age, she was blunt. She didn't dance around a subject trying to be delicate.

"Well, my brother's mind hasn't burnt out yet, so I'm hopeful mine won't. Not much I can do about it, though."

"Not that I don't appreciate you heating the water for me. I'd have a cracking headache if I tried it and you don't even look fatigued, but they say you should minimise your use," Sonja said, water lapping over the edge of the tub as she shifted position so they were facing each other. It certainly made conversation a little easier.

"I spoke with Damien's Warleader before they left. He said to use my abilities, just like exercising a muscle, it makes things easier." Isabella rolled her head to one side to look at her friend. "I think Michael knows more about the subject than anyone here."

At the thought of Michael, she couldn't help the smile. While she didn't really see what Sonja saw in Damien, she appreciated her brother's Warleader. In a way, it reassured her that her previous apathy on the subject was due to there being very slim prospects in her home village. Not because there was anything wrong with her. Sonja sat up and stared at her, water sloshing over the rim of the bath at the sudden movement.

"Damien let his Warleader near you?" Sonja said, staring at her.

"Well to be fair, if Damien had tried to tell me what to do after everything returned to normal, I would have probably done the opposite." Isabella's cheeks flamed, and she hoped the steam from the bath hid it from her friend.

"Isabella! You're smitten with your brother's Warleader?"

Sonja's eyes widened. "I never thought I'd see the day you acknowledged boys weren't all horrible!"

Isabella giggled and splashed Sonja with some water from her own tub, grinning as Sonja spluttered from the dousing.

"Did you get a good look at him?"

"Mmmm... he's certainly fine to look at." Sonja sobered. "Isabella, did you miss the part where the man is a monster? All those stories we've heard about the fearsome Warleader who does the Warlord's dirty work? That's him."

"In case you missed it, Damien is one of them now," Isabella pointed out.

"Well, but Damien didn't have a choice. He was forced to join their ranks. So he killed the baker, he betrayed you. He was a horrible man, and I can't say I'm sad he's gone." Sonja shuddered.

"Aren't we a fine pair? You are pining over my brother, and I am fantasising about Michael, the second most feared man in our realm. Both the type of men our parents would warn us to stay away from and neither of whom are here."

Sonja giggled, and the mood lightened again.

"Is that why you're fooling around with swords? Trying to make yourself into the kind of person who this Michael would like?"

"No. Well, not entirely." Isabella closed her eyes and tried to relax. "I'm not worried that the veil will channel through me at such levels it will burn out my mind, but I am worried the Warlord will go back on his promise to Damien."

Silence filled the bathhouse, the steam lazily filling the cabin. She heard the water lap as Sonja moved.

"You hope that if he takes you that you'll be skilled enough to be one of his fighters?" Sonja said softly.

"Of the fates that await me if he comes back here, that seems the most palatable, but I'm thinking it is an unrealistic hope."

"What do you mean?"

"Not that long ago you made a comment about my looks. What other possible use would the Warlord have for someone like me? What threat could his Warlord have made that would cause Damien to kill the baker the way he did? It wasn't just because the man was a lech, otherwise the baker would have been dead long ago."

Isabella swallowed. Somehow, now she'd verbalised her worry, it made it more real in her head.

"I know you, Isa, you couldn't be like the Warlord and his people. I'm sure Damien knows what he's doing. He won't let anything bad happen to you."

"Damien isn't who you think he is any more, Sonja." She held up her hand to stop Sonja's immediate protest. "He's my brother. I love him, but he's one of them now. He's just as much of a killer as his warleader and his Warlord. If they can turn Damien into that after such a short period of time, they can do the same to me as well."

"Isa, no, everything will be fine."

"Don't you understand? I'd rather become the type of person others fear than become the Warlord's plaything."

"Damien would never allow it," Sonja said, absolute conviction in her voice.

"My brother wouldn't have much say. Neither, I fear, would Michael."

"You honestly think the Warleader would care?"

Isabella smiled softly, thinking back to that last night before her brother had ridden out with his squad mates.

"If I became one of his people, I think he would. I just have to get much better at fighting before they ride back through here." She pulled a face at Sonja, her mood lightening again. "Besides, I've decided."

Sonja's eyes widened. "Decided what?"

"I'll be of age next year."

"I'm aware of that, Isa." Sonja's voice was hesitant. "Why do I think I will not like whatever it is you've decided?"

"Michael is going to be my first." Her eyes slid across to her friend and she laughed at the shocked expression on her face.

"I know he's attractive, but you really want to sleep with him?" Sonja asked.

"Who else am I going to sleep with, a visiting trader?"

Sonja's face clouded. "Is this another of your schemes to avoid the Warlord?"

"He's the first man I've been attracted to. I was beginning to think there was something wrong with me." Isabella rolled her eyes.

"Does he know you've decided he's going to be your first?"

"I'd say so. Apparently, my shielding is shocking."

"You? But you're already the strongest here," Sonja spluttered.

"Compared to the rest of the village, yes, but apparently not with them."

Sonja's eyes widened, then she burst out into startled laughter. "Oh my, so there you were, having lustful thoughts and he could sense it?"

Isabella nodded, covering her eyes with her hands and sinking under the water.

SEVENTY-SEVEN

Something was up. Damien could tell because Michael, Olivia, and Nathanial were having a hushed discussion over to one side. That might not be unusual in the current times, but they kept glancing in his direction as they did so.

"Callan, if we could have a moment of your time?" Michael asked.

Damien traded glances with Callan, who shrugged and rolled out of his cot. Damien watched as his teammate crossed the warehouse and, at a gesture from their leadership group, took a seat with them. He couldn't help but notice when Callan looked in his direction before once again giving his full attention to Michael.

Damien swallowed. Even that, given his not-so-distant past, wasn't necessarily strange. Michael had briefed those detailed to keep an eye on him when neither he, Olivia or Nathanial could be around to watch him. Although he hadn't done anything wrong that he could think of since those awful events in Callenhain. That thought caused him to pause and he swallowed, poking at his memory to see if he could detect any inconsistencies. But he seemed to remember the last week almost perfectly. Even if some of it was a blur, his squad mates assured him that was normal when they operated at this tempo. He shuddered at the memory of his encounter with the tiscan vials the other day, although he thought it was a positive sign he'd been strong enough to resist. His leaders had been doing their best to keep him occupied and away from temptation since, which he appreciated.

"Damien," Nathanial called and gestured to him.

He swallowed and racked his brain again, trying to work out what he'd done wrong. They all appeared so serious as they stared at him. Shaking his head at his squad mates who made fun of him, he jogged across the warehouse to his leaders, hoping he hadn't done something stupid that he didn't remember.

"Relax, sit down. You aren't in trouble," Olivia said.

"I can confirm you didn't go on a bender last night that you don't remember," Nathanial said, correctly guessing where his anxiety was coming from.

"Just as you remember, you came in. Ate a little food, then crashed into your sleeping cot, along with the rest of the squad you were out with," Michael added.

Damien ducked his head and sat, not even trying to hide his relief.

"I want you to take a double squad out on patrol and check the surrounding villages." Michael paused to look at him, smiling at what Damien assumed was his dumbfounded expression. "We know from the warning we received that some of the Sylannians have attacked some of the smaller villages out of Callenhain."

"If you find a village is clear of any incursions, mark it off and report back to us."

"Make sure you deploy scouts and don't stumble into a village. If you find Sylannians, keep watch and send someone back to alert us."

"Don't risk yourself. We'll send more teams to assist in taking them out."

Damien swallowed, his eyes flicking from one to the other trying to assess if they were serious.

"You want me to lead a squad?" Damien asked.

"You'll do fine. Besides, we will send experienced people with you," Michael assured him.

"Listen to the advice of your team, as any good leader does, but you are the leader, so the decision and responsibility will ultimately end up with you," Nathanial advised.

"Everyone has a first time; no better time than the present to see what you are capable of," Olivia said.

"I'll do my best."

"That's all I need. If a leadership role isn't something that ends up suiting you, well, it's good to establish that as well," Michael said.

"There is also no shame attached if you do this and decided you'd much rather be someone's second in future conflicts," Olivia said.

"I believe you will do well, or I wouldn't be asking this of you. I'll be assigning Callan as your second, but we'll take some time to consider the rest of your team and get back to you," Michael said.

Damien took a breath to settle his nerves. "I have one suggested change to the orders."

Michael regarded him steadily. "Go on."

Olivia nodded at him.

"There's no point in me leading a hand-picked team if we're just going to come running back here to report." Damien swallowed and plunged on. "That's what scouts are for. If you trust me to do this, then let me do it. I won't be foolish with the lives of those you place under my command, but let me make the call.

If it is a situation I think we can handle, we'll do it. Otherwise, we'll hunker down and call for backup."

There was silence as Michael stared at him for such a long time that Damien was about to mutter an apology before he stopped as a grin appeared on all three of his leaders' faces.

"Well done. You passed the first test. Speaking up if something isn't quite right or you think it can be done better is an essential requirement." Michael leaned back, satisfaction radiating from him. "Very well. You have discretion. Attack if you think you can deal with the situation."

Damien took a breath as his nerves doubled, even if he'd just brought it on himself. His original assignment would have been much easier than the one he'd just given himself. He darted a look at Callan to see how he was taking the news and was surprised he couldn't detect even a hint of jealousy. Callan thumped him on the shoulder as they both went back to their sleeping area.

SEVENTY-EIGHT

Damien rode along easily, or at least he hoped he appeared calm and at ease. In reality he was far more nervous than he should be for simply riding out of Callenhain on patrol. A voice whispering in his head that this was the first time he'd done so as the leader of a patrol didn't help. Neither did the fact that this was also a mixed patrol comprising not only a unit of his fellow Unwanted, but the bulk of the warriors were from one of the other warbands. A team of the Kallith had even been placed under his command as well.

Relax, you'll do fine.

You don't mind? Damien asked.

He didn't feel the need to qualify what he was asking.

Callan chuckled, which caused Damien to look over to see him shaking his head.

Not at all.

You've been in the Unwanted much longer than I have.

I'm much happier being second rather than in a leadership role. If anyone minds, it's probably Nathanial.

Damien looked at Callan to see if he was kidding and saw a grin on the man's face.

He suggested you, I think. Why wouldn't he be happy? Damien asked.

Damien found his mind instantly worrying at the problem, if indeed it was a problem. Nathanial had proven to be not only a leader but a friend during his time riding with the Unwanted. The person who'd helped him through some dark times and that he could go to for anything. No matter how bad they were.

I tend to act as Nathanial's second. If this goes as well as I suspect it will, Michael has already indicated I'll be reassigned, which means Nathanial is going to have to train up a new second.

Damien ducked his head and hoped his cheeks weren't as red as he suspected them to be.

Thank you for your trust. Particularly since you are the ones who'll pay the price if I stuff this up.

You've got good instincts, Damien. If you didn't want to be tested for a leadership role, you shouldn't have kept drawing attention to yourself and doing well.

Damien went to protest that he done no such thing when Callan threw images at him: When he'd spoken up and suggested the Unwanted raise fog to obscure their approach before battle. The fight with the Kallith when he'd called warning of the flight of deadly arrows heading for them and set them on fire. His recent role in the action that got them into the gates of Callenhain. Damien shook himself and noted his surroundings.

"Let's pick up the pace. We've got a bit of distance to cover today," he ordered. "Once we pass the outer limit markers, send out the advance team."

Callan passed back the order, and they all spurred their horses up to a ground-devouring trot. Damien decided if Callan didn't have an issue, then he doubted any of the others did either. Michael had said they were going to pick his team carefully, so he was unlikely to have been given anyone who would cause him undue trouble.

As he saw Shallan, his senior scout, waiting just off the path, Damien signalled his squad to stop.

"Sylannians?" Damien asked.

"Yeah, their behaviour is odd. They look like they are settling in to stay," Shallan said.

Damien went to dismount before Callan shook his head.

You're our band leader, not the scout. Trust your people.

Right, old habits.

Damien thought through his options. It would be much easier if he could see the village in question.

"How many of them did you count?"

"About a dozen. Doesn't look like the villagers put up much of a fight."

"How far are we away from this village?"

"Not far. You'll be able to see it from the trees just over the hill."

"I need to see this. Callan, get the squad off the road and out of sight. Then you are with me," Damien said.

He dismounted and passed the reins of his horse to Callan who took them and rode the short distance back to the squad, issuing instructions. It didn't take long before the squad faded back into the trees that lined the road. Callan jogged forward to join Damien. Without another word, Shallan led them up the hill, leaving the road and walking through the trees.

It didn't take long before he was standing looking down on the village in the gully by the river below. It was a small village, even smaller than his own home village. Still, until they'd been hit by the Sylannians, it seemed like they'd been doing well enough for themselves. Their huts lined the river and were well-maintained. They had some small crops, mostly little gardens behind each of the huts.

"It's a fishing village. Between their catch and the herbs and roots they bring in from the forest, they do quite well for themselves, selling the excess to Callenhain. Or they did," Callan said.

"How the Powers do you remember that about such a small place?" Damien didn't bother to try and hide his astonishment.

"I checked the map and studied the villages on our path last night," Callan said.

"Nice work," Damien said.

"It's a part of my job as a second to take the pressure off. I did the same for Nathanial." Callan shrugged, dismissing the praise.

Damien squatted down and continued to watch the activity in the village below. Sure enough, barely a dozen Sylannians were in the village keeping order. It made him wonder where the rest of them were.

"There's a string of these villages in a row, right?" Damien asked.

"There are, they are fairly close together," Shallan said, pointing along the ridge line they were standing on. "If we head over to that outcrop we'll probably be able to see the next one."

Damien restrained himself and allowed Shallan to lead the way. It didn't take them long before they were at the vantage point. Shallan needlessly pointed towards the other village. It was substantially larger than the first one, with far more Sylannians in it.

"Can some of your team get closer to get a more accurate count of numbers in that second village?"

"Of course."

"Let them know; we'll move forward to the smaller village and deal with the group of Sylannians there."

Shallan and a couple of her companions melted into the trees, disappearing from sight. Damien made his way back towards where they'd left the horses, thinking through the attack that was to follow. He couldn't afford to mess this up. Particularly since he'd been the one to insist that it was pointless to keep running back to Michael for help all the time.

"We're going to attack right away?" Callan asked.

"No. We'll wait a couple of hours. If the villagers are still fishing, I'll bet some Sylannians go on each fishing boat. That will reduce numbers in the village even more."

"Wouldn't they go fishing any time?"

"City boy." Damien chuckled. "Best time for fishing is in the early morning hours around dawn and a couple of hours before dusk."

"So that should give us a rough time to expect the ones who go with the boats to be back?"

Damien's nerves settled. It helped a great deal that he had been able to come up with some sort of plan that sounded reasonable.

THE FISHING BOATS had left some time ago and, just as he'd predicted, a couple of the Sylannians went on each of the fishing boats, halving their numbers. It also had the bonus of pinpointing which of the buildings the Sylannians had taken over for themselves. Protecting the remaining villagers would also be a little easier since Shallan confirmed the Sylannians herded them into the communal hall.

All right, everyone, you have your orders. Let's do this, Damien ordered.

He barely waited for the acknowledgement he received from his people before he wrapped the veil around himself and ran. He cleared the trees, trying to cover as much distance as he could before the Sylannians noticed they were under attack. By the time the guards noticed, he was close enough to spot the precise moment they realised those descending on them were not their own. He saw the flash of panic on the sentry's face, before her blades flashed up and deflected his own. The Sylannian lunged, trying to plunge one of her blades into his stomach. He stepped forward, which twisted his torso sideways just as her blade skimmed past. Without hesitation, he brought his other hand up, his hunting dagger slashing across her throat. He spun, seeking another target, only to find there was none. They'd vastly outnumbered the Sylannians to the point the fight had seemed anticlimactic.

"Damien."

He turned at the warning and saw a horde of weeping locals, adult and children alike heading in his direction. Damien barely had time to get his weapons out of the way before he was surrounded. He found his arms full of wailing people and he looked over, faintly alarmed, catching Callan's eye. Not that he was any help, any more than the rest of his people. They all just stood there, grinning at his predicament. Or at least they did until they found themselves under a similar assault.

"Please, everyone. You're safe now. I need you all to calm down."

Damien did his best to send out calm from himself in waves. He checked the progress of the setting sun, knowing the fishing boats would be heading back soon.

"The boats. They have more of their people on the boats." One of the older men tugged at his arm, pointing towards the river.

"We know. Can you help get everyone back in the building? We need to clean up before those boats come in. Don't worry, you'll have several of my people with you to keep you all safe." Damien sent waves of reassurance over them all as he spoke.

The older man straightened his shoulders and bellowed at his fellow villagers. They began, with only a little reluctance, to stream back to the community hall.

"You three, go with them," Callan said, pointing to several squad members.

"Let's get this cleaned up, then get out of sight of the jetty until the boats come in," Damien ordered.

He went to grab the enemy he'd killed, only to have two of his people grab the body and haul it over beyond the tree line. They'd have to help the villagers dispose of the bodies properly. For now, out of sight would do. They were all scrambling to take cover, although this time close to the jetty where the fishing boats would dock. Shallan was halfway back across the square when she skidded to a stop and doubled back. He was about to call out to her when he noticed Shallan stoop and pick up the broken remains of a bucket, throwing them behind the nearest hut. Sometimes it was the smallest detail out of place that could trigger a warning that something wasn't quite right.

He paused, watching them all seeming to disappear into the shadows. They were pulling the veil to them, making themselves harder to perceive. Damien gave one final glance around the now-quiet village and nodded to Callan and the two team members with him, Shallan and Gavrel, clearly acting as his protective detail, just as he would have done for Michael, Olivia or Nathanial. There was no need for him to check that his guard were also the three strongest in the veil after himself. Damien half jogged over to the small shed at the edge of the wooden jetty. Without having to look, he knew it would contain a collection of nets, hooks, and fishing pots. Calmness settled on him as the veil pooled around him and the coolness washed over his skin. Of late, it was soothing with the power threading over and through him. He wasn't sure when it had changed from pain to comfort.

They didn't have long to wait before the fishing boats appeared and pulled up to the jetty. He saw a couple of the villagers jump off first and tie up their boats. As the Sylannians stepped off onto the jetty, he saw one of them pause and glance around with a frown.

Now!

Damien launched himself at the Sylannians closest to him, ignoring the arrows that sang nearby, the splash of water giving away the deadly accuracy of the Kallith arrows that slammed into those who'd remained on the boat. He registered a couple of his people going into the water after them to make sure they were dead. They would leave none alive to warn the Sylannians in the next village.

Damien checked the bodies with his othersight, seeing without a doubt that the Sylannians were dead. Those of his people who had dived into the river appeared a short time later, their teammates assisting them back onto the jetty. Then the wailing started again as the villagers they'd rescued earlier ran to embrace their fellows. For the second time that day, Damien found himself with his arms full, comforting people around him. It was an odd experience, particularly as one of the Unwanted.

SEVENTY-NINE

Kesha felt a tug at her consciousness and she fought with herself for a moment before she finally sighed. It was the member of the Unwanted who watched over her and he would pull her out of her healing trance himself unless she came back herself. They'd received several strong lectures from Nathanial on the subject. It made sense for her to save her strength in case of an emergency. She finished what she was doing, putting a few pain blocks in place, then withdrew from her patient's mind and body. She stood, using the moment to stretch her aching back. That was the thing about healing talent. There were times she got lost in her healer's trance, spending far longer healing another than she should.

Kesha inspected her makeshift healer's hall. While the sight of so many injured people saddened her, at least these people would live. There were many who'd lost their lives since the war began. It was heartbreaking. She turned to Lem, who'd shown up to help not long after they'd set up the healing hall. After a brief reunion she'd put him straight to work. While Lem had little of the healing talent he was brilliant with tonics, knives, needles and thread. He'd quietly taken over the day to day running of the healing hall and carefully rostering their limited number of healers so someone was always on duty.

"Send for me if I'm needed." Kesha kept her voice low.

"Go rest, Healer Kesha, you've done the heavy lifting. We can manage for a few hours," Lem said.

Kesha left the healer's hall, aware her guardian followed her. Her sleeping cot was in the warehouse across the alley and she blinked at the sudden bright sunlight. It had been night-time when she'd begun her work. As she crossed the laneway, she glanced automatically towards the far end, checking that the guards stood at the entrance. She saw a slight movement, which she was sure the guard did on purpose, and sighed with relief. All was well, and they were still secure in this pocket of safety in Callenhain.

As she reached the sleeping quarters, one of the guards opened the door for her and tension drained from her when she stepped into the room and sensed that charge around her. With the Unwanted congregated in one area, it was like there was a background hum of energy. She'd grown used to it and fancied it somehow helped her recharge better, but it was one reason other people felt uneasy in their presence.

"I swear, the Sylannians are getting stupid. I can't work out why they are going out in small groups the way they are to take smaller villages," Michael said.

"Do we really care? It makes them easier to pick off," Nathanial said.

At hearing the hushed conversation, Kesha changed her path and joined Michael and Nathanial in the corner. She glanced over to those who were sleeping and saw Damien and Callan were among their number and gathered Olivia must have been checking on those maintaining the outer perimeter guard positions. Both men greeted her as she approached them and Nathanial waved her to sit with them. Kesha was about to do so when she saw blood covering his neck, hand, and some on the ground near him.

"Nathanial, you're hurt. Why didn't you send for me?"

"I'm fine, Kesha. I'll heal." Nathanial fended off her attempts to take off his leathers to check his injury.

"Nonsense." Kesha grabbed his vest, unbuckling it while he protested.

Kesha glared at him, and he subsided with a weak grin.

"Honestly, Kesha, you'll see. I'm fine. It's just a little injury I got helping clear the last village. We thought we were done so relaxed and a couple of Sylannians jumped at me from the underbrush," Nathanial said, although he allowed her to push back his linen undershirt from his shoulder.

"Not with that amount of blood you won't be. Seriously, Nathanial, what were you thinking—" Kesha stopped, staring at his neck.

There was a scar, one that appeared as if it was freshly healed, with only what appeared to be a small tear in his skin. She pulled a cloth from her belt, grateful she always had several on her when she'd been working in the healing hall, and dipped the corner in a nearby pot of water and carefully cleaned around the wound. She could see the veil swirling around him, through him, and could almost swear she could see Nathanial's skin knitting, healing itself in front of her eyes. Which was impossible.

"I would have insisted Nathanial go to you for treatment if it was necessary. A simple cut like that." Michael shrugged. "We heal."

"I'll go sleep in the next shift, I promise." Nathanial's eyes danced in amusement.

Kesha blinked as she became aware she was staring. She'd always known they were different but to heal this way? Then she found herself washing the trail of blood that trailed down his neck. As she cleansed the blood on his upper chest she paused, plucking at his shirt.

"Are you sure you don't have any other injuries?" Kesha asked as she stared at his blood soaked linen shirt and not so coincidentally his chest.

"I'm certain, I still had my armour on, I'd just loosened the neck guard. Stupid mistake, I should have known better."

Aware of a moment of silence and the fact she'd stopped tending Nathanial and was just staring at the evidence of a well-muscled chest and upper arm, Kesha felt her face heat. She tried to focus on the cloth as she rinsed it but was unable to help herself and her eyes slid back to Nathanial's self-healing neck.

"How are you doing this?" Kesha's hand reached out, her fingers brushing the freshly healed skin. Her senses tingled at the play of energy within him.

"We're different." Nathanial shrugged.

"People can't do this. I can't even heal myself this way."

"True. Regular people can't, but even you've mentioned that it seems like some people's own bodies help with the healing."

"Not like this. I can't see how you're doing it."

"If it makes you feel better, I can't work out how you do what you do either, yet I can see you are doing the healing," Nathanial said.

"We don't spread it around but not all of our reputation is because we are all brilliant with the sword," Michael said.

"This healing ability makes us all a little harder to kill," Nathanial said.

"The Warlord doesn't heal like you." Kesha's eyes caught Michael's.

A pained look passed over his face. Kesha realised he had two sets of parents, neither of which healed the way he seemed to. It was a fact he could hardly have escaped noticing.

"No, he doesn't. Which is why I've sent him back to Yalleska." Michael's lips compressed at the last.

"I still can't quite believe he agreed to go."

"He didn't have to agree. With him being injured, by his own orders I am in command," Michael said.

Kesha stared at Nathanial, and he shook his head at her. In this she trusted his judgement. Kesha watched as both Michael's and Nathanial's attention transferred to the man who approached them. Unlike the Unwanted, the rest of the Warlord's forces wore brown fighting leathers with the Warlord's crest: a taloned hawk with two crossed swords. On the shoulder of the uniform of the man who approached, there were three triangle shapes, which Nathanial had explained represented Yalleska Peak and meant the wearer of the uniform was a band leader.

"Sorry for the intrusion." The band leader paused until Michael waved off the apology. "Jenna sends word that they have a patient at the manor house who needs your attention, Healer Kesha."

"Of course," Kesha said.

Nathanial sighed as he stood. "Give me a moment, I'll get my team together."

"No, Nathanial, you need to rest. I'm sure one of the other teams can act as escort to Jenna's place." Kesha rested her hand on his chest. "I've been there and back several times now without issue."

"I've only just commenced my shift. My team can act as Kesha's escort," the band leader offered.

Kesha held her breath as Nathanial stared at the other man before finally nodding and launching into a string of instructions. She bit her lip as most of the orders had to do with keeping her safe. Michael just watched the display, amusement dancing in his eyes. The other band leader, for his part, took the barrage of orders with good grace and, while she didn't know the man, she could swear he was amused as well. When Nathanial was done with the band leader, he stood, gesturing for Kesha to do likewise and methodically adjusted the fit of her leathers. Kesha waited patiently as Nathanial did up the flap that closed around her neck.

"Listen to your protection detail and don't overextend yourself," Nathanial said, kissing her gently on the forehead before pinning the band leader with his gaze once more. "Call me if you need assistance."

"Or rather, call me," Michael said to the band leader, waiting long enough for the man to nod before shaking his head at Nathanial. "She'll be fine. You need to go and rest. Now, before you fall over."

Kesha covered her mouth with one hand as Nathanial looked like he wanted to argue, then finally raised his hands, conceding the point. With one final glance in her direction, he sighed and walked over to his sleeping cot. His groan as he sank into it, forearm resting over his eyes, told her he really did need the rest. Kesha blushed as she found the band leader waiting patiently for her. After Michael dismissed him, the band leader gestured for her to precede him out of the warehouse.

EIGHTY

As they galloped into the village, those of the clans who rode with him let loose their arrows in a deadly rain that felled Sylannians in the village. As the first bodies fell, the call went up and the enemy swarmed out of the buildings like angry bees whose hive had been disturbed. Then Damien was in the midst of the mad battle. Time seemed to both speed up and slow down as he charged towards the centre of the village. As a Sylannian loomed before him he had a moment's notice before his horse reared, lashing at the attacker's head. The crack of her head splitting open was almost lost in the screams and clash of blades.

As he and those around him came in line with the water well, they vaulted from their horses. Damien lunged, his sword catching the Sylannian who was trying to kill a horse with the rider still astride.

A cry rang out that made Damien spin and he saw a young boy holding a large kitchen knife in the air as he charged at the attackers. The scream had come from the lad's horrified mother. Damien cursed and lashed out with both the veil and his weapons, shunting a group of attackers to one side as he struck at the one closest to him.

He spun again, grabbing the boy and, channelling more strength down his arms, threw him back, just as the sword from one of the Sylannians was about to take his head. Feeling hands grab him, he drew his attention back to his own fight and flinched back as a dagger plunged straight at him. As he turned his head, something grazed his cheek. He staggered as his attacker released him, falling back with arrows protruding from her. Damien spared a moment to thank the powers that someone had been looking out for him, then took a breath and fought on, trying to keep his attention on his own part in this fight. He could wish the locals had stayed where they were being detained and left the fighting part to them, but unfortunately, they'd decided to get involved. Although seeing some of them lashing out with the vicious hooks attached to poles they used for fishing, he had to admit, some of them were better at fighting than others. But unlike the previous village, where everyone except the Sylannians had come out unscathed, not all the villagers were going to survive.

Steady. There are always losses in battles like this, Callan said.

I know. It doesn't mean I have to like it, Damien said.

At some point, Callan had fought his way back to Damien's side, though Damien didn't know when he'd gotten separated from everyone.

It was when you went after the kid. Very heroic. There was a bite to Callan's tone. *Don't do that again.*

I couldn't just let the boy die. His mother's wailing got to me, Damien said.

You won't do anyone any good if you die doing something foolish.

I didn't, though. Breathe, Callan, I'm fine, Damien said.

Talk stopped as they fended off a flurry of attacks from multiple enemies. The Sylannians were trying to surround them.

A quick scan confirmed that while Callan had reached his side, none of the others had. Damien strengthened his shield, using it to buffet some of those he was facing while striking at another. He and Callan fought together, battling those that confronted them. Another flight of arrows cleared a couple of the Sylannians around them, but their blades were soon replaced by others. There was a desperation in their fighting as if they were panicked or trapped. Hearing a yell from one side, he saw the locals with the vicious fishhooks and blades running forward to stab and slash at their attackers. Damien spared a glance to see the long poles they were mounted on kept most from getting too close to the locals wielding them. He blocked the thrusting blade of one of the Sylannians, then saw a hook lash around his enemy's neck and pull back. As the blood splattered, he moved onto the next attacker. More of his people were fighting to get to his side, but he couldn't spare the concentration to see how far away they were.

On blocking a blade, he finally registered the person in front of him wasn't a woman but a man. He flinched, thinking he'd mistakenly attacked a local, then registered the dark eyes, hair, and the silks the man wore. Suddenly the reason for the Sylannians desperation was clear. They'd fight to the death to protect one of the Sylannian men. Damien sucked in more power and reached out with the veil, grabbing hold of the man and pulling him forward. He ignored the desperate Sylannians who battered at him with their powers and swung his sword, channelling even more of the veil until it shone. The etching on the blade flared with the sword and flame closer to the hilt, licking and dancing like a real flame. Damien cut the man in two.

Damien knew he'd pay a price for drawing that much power at once, but was grateful it hadn't sent him spiralling into debilitating pain or bring on a veil attack. He released the dead male and launched himself at the remaining Sylannians. As the rest of his people finally joined ranks with him, the tide of battle turned. Not that the enemy surrendered. As always, they fought to the death.

With a final volley of arrows from the clans, the last attackers slumped to the ground.

That was a good decision to leave the clans people behind our lines, Callan observed as one of those closest to him toppled back.

Their skills with the bow far outweigh their ability with the sword, Damien said.

He reached out with his mind, scanning the village for any sign of Sylannians but found none. Weariness hammered into him, yet he had more work to do before he could rest.

He jumped as the locals cheered, looking at them in astonishment. With the number of them who had fallen in this fight, he'd half expected recrimination and blame. While there was sadness and loss, the feeling of overwhelming despair had lifted from the village. What he sensed from them was gratitude that the Unwanted had come to fight for them. Even though they were just an insignificant fishing village.

EIGHTY-ONE

Isabella found herself lying flat, staring at the wooden floor beside her bed before she registered the screaming. She hadn't even been aware that she'd moved. Light flared and she flinched, glancing up at the window. Her breath sounded harsh and unreasonably loud, causing her to swallow. She rolled her eyes at her own stupidity. With all the screaming and yelling going on outside, it was unlikely anyone would hear her breathing, no matter how loud she thought she sounded. Easing herself up, she crawled across the floor, avoiding the windows, cursing herself for not closing the shutters the night before. The evening breeze had been pleasant when she'd gone to sleep, but now she wished she'd thought of security. Isabella reached out with the thinnest of threads of the veil. She grabbed the edge of the shutters and eased them closed, careful not to make a sound. She breathed a sigh of relief and stood, pulled on her training clothes and grabbed her sword and knife. It was almost habit now, after all this time training under Owen, although she was under no illusions as to her ability. She'd been taught enough to be aware of how much she had to learn.

Noise from the other bedroom told Isabella that her parents were up and moving as well. It wasn't like they could have missed the commotion outside caused by the unmistakable sounds of fighting. It wasn't the Warlord, since he'd already claimed their village. She didn't think bandits would be stupid enough to attack a place claimed by the Warlord, either. Rumour suggested some tried their hands at such things on occasion. Might even get away with it for a time, but eventually they were tracked down, rounded up and dealt with severely. Usually, the punishment meted out by the Warlord's warbands was their lives. As much as she feared the man, everyone else did too. So that left one likely group.

Sylanna.

She slipped out of her bedroom and saw her parents coming out of their own room as well. They motioned to her and led the way towards the back door. This might have been the first time Sylanna had attacked them but it was something they'd planned for. The front door opened towards the river. The back door led to the forest. The slamming of the front door made her jump, and she spun. They'd run out of time. Sylannians poured in through the door and she caught a flash of bright colour from their clothing and the glint of the blades they held in the low light.

"Go, Isa!"

Isabella's father grabbed her and pushed her towards the back door as he yelled and charged at the women, brandishing his own weapon. Isabella tried to protest only for her mother to grab her arm and, after yanking the door open, shove her outside.

"Run, Isabella."

Isabella opened her mouth to protest, but her mother slammed the door, blocking her line of sight into the house. Isabella backed up, one careful step after the other, scanning the village. She pressed one hand against her mouth as she realised it was like some of the battles from her brother's nightmares. Some buildings on fire, bodies lying unmoving on the ground. She jumped as someone grabbed her from behind, her scream stifled by the hand that clamped across her lips.

"Hush, Isa, it's me. We don't have time for tears and panic, come!" Owen said.

Isabella saw the grim expression on his face, bathed in the red light cast by the flames of a nearby building. She broke into a run as Owen half dragged her into the surrounding forest. While she could still hear the one-sided fight that continued behind her, they'd be screened from view. The noise in the village would almost certainly cover their retreat. Long after this night was a distant memory, that first scream that had woken her from her sleep would haunt her nightmares.

ISABELLA STOOD behind a tree with the veil wrapped around her, watching as the Sylannian woman came further into the trees.

Just a few more steps, she whispered to herself.

As the woman stopped and scanned the bush around her, Isabella froze, wondering if the woman had heard her thoughts. While she'd thought she'd get better at keeping her emotions to herself as her powers grew, in practice she found she leaked more and seemed to have far less control. It reminded her of Damien's deteriorating state before the Warlord and his warleader came to Ranlith. Her anxiety rose as she thought of going through veil sickness as Damien had.

As a voice called out from the edge of the village square, the woman answered while scanning the forest once more before frowning and walking back to her companion and the town. Isabella swore softly to herself and dropped the cloaking of veil she'd had around her. She spun and almost ran straight into

Owen, who gave her a look before he sheathed his blade and, with a hand on her back, directed her back to their small camp.

Isabella sat down on a rock and watched as he busied himself around their camp and handed her a plate of food. She took it and ate a few mouthfuls, glancing up at him now and then as they ate.

"What?" Isabella asked.

"If you'd managed to kill that woman, they'd notice she was missing and find out we are here," Owen said.

Isabella ducked her head and applied herself to her food, hating the fact that he was right.

"We have to help them." Isabella pleaded, her gaze flicking from her plate to Owen.

She'd kept going back to stare at the village. So many of the huts had been destroyed and bodies had been piled up to one side and burnt. Some seemed to be alive, but no matter how many times she'd gone back, she'd never set eyes on either her parents or Sonja.

"I'm sorry, Isabella, I'm only one person. If an opportunity to break some of the others free presents itself, I will do my best, but I cannot guarantee anything."

"They're dead, aren't they?"

He regarded her sombrely, not rushing to deny it. Isabella's lip tremble and tears traced their way down her cheek.

"I haven't seen your parents, either. I'm sorry, Isabella, there was nothing you could have done for them."

Owen rose and crossed the distance between them. Without saying a word, Isabella buried her head in his shoulder and cried. He just held her, rocking her back and forth while she mourned her family. Isabella felt as if she was caught in a storm, with the veil swirling around her, and she whimpered as the whispered voices of others sounded in her head.

Isabella, please try to regain control. The Sylannians will sense you.

Owen expanded his own mental barriers, but he couldn't do much to shield her. She was already much stronger in the veil than he was. She only hoped it was enough to prevent the Sylannians from sensing her. Isabella bit back a cry of pain as her bones ached with cold as the veil flooded into her. Then it was like every part of her was blistering. Fire raced through her, followed closely by pain. As if her whole body was being ripped apart and reforged into something else entirely. She was sure if she opened her eyes she'd see her skin and muscles peeling back to expose the bones beneath the flesh. Only the feel of Owen's arms around her as he held her and tried to shield her told her that wasn't the case. No matter how it felt.

As the flood of the veil that had poured into her stopped as suddenly as it had begun, she collapsed, exhausted. Isabella didn't stir, even though she was aware when Owen picked her up and carried her to her bed. With the veil's departure, every bit of her ached. She could feel every hair in her head, burning and throbbing after the assault on her body, right down to her fingertips. Pain seemed to be pulsing in time to her heartbeat. Isabella fled gratefully into sleep to escape the agony.

EIGHTY-TWO

Kesha unconsciously breathed a sigh of relief as the gates closed behind the last of her escort as they rode into Jenna's estate. She'd done this trip between their own place near the docks and the estate house several times now, but the journey still made her nervous, even with the knowledge that this area of the city was well and truly back under Michael's control. The grounds were filled with the makeshift camps of locals who'd been able to make it here for sanctuary—Jenna and her husband hadn't refused sanctuary to anyone, even though they'd been bursting at the seams. As with the other times she'd been here, there were guards maintaining careful watch. Jenna and her husband had drawn together a force consisting of those who normally rode as guards for their trade barges and caravans, as well as those from other trading houses and some of the surviving town guard. Kesha dismounted, waiting patiently until two of Michael's people who'd ridden with this unit came forward along with the band leader and they all ascended the stairs of the manor house.

Jenna appeared at the doors, and embraced her in genuine welcome despite her obvious fatigue.

"Thank you for coming, Kesha, I know you must be stretched with all the draws on your talent these days, but the man our patrols brought in is beyond our own healers," Jenna said.

"Of course I came and don't fear. Nathanial and the Unwanted make sure I don't burn myself out," Kesha said, following the other woman into the house with her temporary guards following along in her wake.

Jenna led her into what, in normal times, had been the dining room. They had cleared out the grand table and chairs that had once taken pride of place in this room in order to make room for a healing hall. As Jenna gestured to an unconscious man on a low cot with a healer sitting beside him, Kesha checked with her othersight and saw the thin stream of healing talent passing from the other healer to her patient.

"I'm sorry to call on you, Healer Kesha. I stabilised him and forced him to sleep so his body could heal on its own," the healer explained, standing to make room for Kesha. "But I fear his condition is beyond my ability to heal."

"Never fear sending for me. You've done well," Kesha said as the other woman blushed and moved to one side.

Kesha took the low stool and one of the Unwanted came to her side and rested her hand lightly on her shoulder, pulsing the veil into her. Kesha sighed as the veil flooded in, fatigue being banished in its wake until she buzzed with energy.

She laid her hand on her patient's temple, drawing on her healing gift as it was fuelled by her Unwanted supporter and assessing his injuries. She could see the signs of the other healer's work and added her own power to aid his healing. Kesha's attention was drawn to the angry redness in his head and she left the remaining injuries to repair under the influence of the healing she'd already triggered in his body. As she guided a healing pulse of power through her patient, it washed over his brain and wrapped around him like a blanket shielding his head as she worked.

Kesha relaxed, relieved as she saw the redness diminish. Only the fatigue that weighed heavily on her gave an indication she'd been working on the man for some time. There was now low-level activity in her patient, normal for most people during a sleep pattern. As close as she could work out, it meant he was dreaming, a very good sign.

She moved on, checking down his body one more time, noting that the signs of internal inflammation had died down. Satisfied, she gently removed the sleeping compulsion the other healer had put in his mind. She wanted him to wake up naturally rather than abruptly. Having done her work, she stood and stretched before easing back on to a small wooden stool. As she'd suspected, she didn't have long to wait until he stirred but despite his easy awakening, the man surged upright in his cot, eyes wide. Those who stood guard over her stepped forward, although they hung back when she raised her hand. Patients reacting violently upon waking was one of the reasons Nathanial insisted she have guards with her while she healed.

"Easy, I'm a healer. You're safe now," Kesha said, using her powers to soothe the man and his fears.

As she caught images from his mind, she swallowed. Sylannians. She wasn't surprised this man had been hurt by Sylannians, but he'd been in a boat, near buildings that were like none she'd seen. She caught another image of people, both adults and children, being dumped overboard into the water. Of dark eyes that stared into his own, accompanied by a strong spurt of fear. As the man slumped back onto his cot, she looked at the member of the Unwanted who stood next to her.

"Can you get Michael for me?" Kesha regarded her patient a

moment longer before adding, "Or Olivia, whichever of them is awake and on duty. Don't disturb their sleep."

The guard nodded at her and while she didn't move so much as a muscle, and Kesha didn't hear anything, she had no doubt her request was passed on. Kesha considered what she'd learnt from her patient, who lay regarding her. She could also feel the wariness he showed towards her guards, who'd moved in closer. Kesha saw the flash of recognition as the uniform of the Unwanted came into his field of vision. Although there was a deep sense of relief in him that he wasn't in the hands of the Sylannians.

"How did I get here?" the patient asked.

Kesha waited as one of her assistants offered the man a drink, cautioning him to sip the liquid. If he consumed too much too soon, he'd make himself sick.

Jenna stepped forward, drawing the man's attention to her. "You were unconscious in an alley and one of our patrols brought you in. However, I can't tell you how you came to be in that alleyway in the state they found you."

Kesha sensed his confusion. He had no idea how he'd ended up in the alleyway either. Although it wasn't uncommon for those who'd suffered head injuries to forget things. Including how they'd been injured.

Kesha glanced up expectantly as Michael and Olivia were shown into the dining room by Jenna's husband. The guards who'd been standing on her shoulder keeping an eye on her patient stepped back at a gesture from Michael. She could sense the spurt of fear from her patient, his eyes wide as he stared at Michael. He definitely recognised Michael.

"You asked for us, Kesha?" Michael said.

Michael sounded so pleasant and calm, yet he must know the man on the bed was terrified about what was going to happen to him.

"I believe this man knows how the Sylannians ended up here in Callenhain," Kesha said.

Michael transferred his gaze to her patient. She shivered as Michael's power flowed around her to her patient and he assessed the man. If anything, her patient was even more petrified than he was before.

"I won't promise I won't hurt you. I can't do that since I don't know what you have to say, but our healer will be most displeased with me if I undo all her hard work," Michael said.

Michael stepped closer and sat down on a stool that materialised due to some hasty shuffling by her assistants. Her patient's eyes nearly rolled in his head as he tracked Olivia's movement as she took a stool on his other side. Kesha considered withdrawing, but decided if Michael had wanted her to leave, he would have told her to do so.

"I suggest you tell us your story. All of it. Without trying to absolve any of your own actions," Olivia said.

"It's unfortunate for you, but we're going to know if you are lying to us. So, tell me events as they are. I can accept people make mistakes," Michael said.

Kesha found herself fascinated despite herself. The pair were firm but doing their best to project calmness and sitting the way they had somehow made them less intimidating. Michael wasn't quite telling the truth. He could force his way into the other man's head and extract what he wanted. The fact that it would probably destroy the other's mind and it was a practice he found personally abhorrent was what held him back. But her patient didn't need to know that, and anyway, he was leaking. If she had caught those images and feelings that flared in his mind, then Michael and Olivia certainly would.

"I'm a... I was a smuggler," her patient said.

"Who did you work for?" Michael asked.

"A trading house, owned by the Kastlers," he whispered. He continued, words tumbling out of his mouth as if he didn't want to think about them, "We were trading with the Sylannians with the only thing they wanted."

"What was that thing?" Olivia asked.

He paused, looking over at Kesha, his lips quivering. He was close to breaking, but Michael had allowed her to sit here out of respect, not so she could interfere. Besides, as much as she'd rather not be here witnessing this interrogation, her presence might be the only thing that saved the man's life.

"People, mostly men, taken from the streets. In return, they gave us silk. The house believed the silk was like nothing else that could be sourced anywhere. That it was invaluable."

"You'd done this run more than once, I take it?" Michael asked.

"Yes. Many times. It takes time to round up... men, from the street."

"What happened this time?" Olivia asked.

"We tied up to the pier to prepare for the Sylannians to unload the cargo. We'd barely tied off when the Sylannians leapt onboard. I... there was so much blood and then, then she told the barge master we were to bring them here. The barge master told her if we did what she wanted, you'd kill us all. The Sylannian didn't accept it. She said if we didn't bring them here, you wouldn't have the chance to kill us because she would."

Kesha saw Michael and Olivia exchange glances and inserted a question of her own.

"What happened to the captives?"

Her patient stared at her with an air of desperation. He almost seemed to latch onto her presence. As if it was easier for him to concentrate on her than either Michael or Olivia.

"They killed them, all of them, and threw the bodies into the water. It's why the barge master believed their threats."

Michael closed his eyes and Kesha could sense he was battling his own instinct to kill this man for what he'd already admitted and been responsible for. When Michael opened his eyes again, Kesha was surprised to see he seemed remarkably calm.

"What did you do?" Michael asked.

"I did what I was told to do. I helped smuggle the Sylannians here, and they launched their attack."

"Can you take us to where this Sylannian in charge is?"

"No, I don't know exactly where she is, only the ones I brought here."

Michael and Olivia both stiffened and Kesha was glad she wasn't the one under their intense regard.

"The Sylannian in charge, the one who said she'd kill you. Did she stay in Sylanna?" Olivia asked.

Kesha could hear that Olivia suspected the answer was no.

"I don't know. We had two barges. My barge left first, and I brought the Sylannians on board here. It took several runs. We smuggled them into the city in batches. I can show you the warehouse where the one who led the attack here was based. I don't know if the leader of this group is still there."

Michael looked at Theo. "Do you know the location of the warehouses used by the Kastlers here in Callenhain?"

Theo nodded and stepped forward. "The one on the docks or the one near the markets?"

The smuggler swallowed. "The ones near the stock markets."

"I know the ones he means," Theo said.

Michael thanked him, then turned his attention back to the smuggler, staring at him long enough that the man trembled.

"Where did the other barge go?" Michael asked.

Her patient flinched at Michael's sharp tone but answered.

"I don't know. That one stayed behind with the barge master. As far as I know, they are still on the island we traded with. That's all I know."

Kesha flinched at the cold anger that flared from Michael before his mind shuttered again. Kesha took a small step back as Michael stood, staring down at her patient, who froze on his cot, holding his breath as Michael glared down at him. He motioned to his people.

"You'll stand guard over this one. Nothing is to happen to him; he will not be allowed to escape," Michael ordered.

"Yes, Warleader," the guard said, then took a position to the side of the sleeping cot.

"Can you assist us in locating the warehouse where the leader of the Sylannians here is hiding?"

"We'll assemble a team to guide you," Jenna said.

"After all of this is done, if I allow you to live, you will have to work off your debt to the people of the Warlord's domain for the harm you have caused," Michael said.

Michael spun and strode from the room. Kesha had been around the Unwanted enough to know the rumbling outside in an otherwise blue sky reflected the depth of his anger.

EIGHTY-THREE

Michael didn't know what he'd expected, but this wasn't it.

Um, just checking. Am I unconscious and dreaming right now? Michael asked.

Not unless we all are, Nathanial said.

Olivia simply shook her head. She seemed as dumbfounded and confused as he was. They'd all been ready to fight when they'd burst in on this place where the Sylannians heading this invasion were hiding out. Instead of a fight, what they encountered was a bunch of Sylannians kneeling in the centre of the room, heads bowed. Their empty hands were on display, palms up. All it took was a quick scan of the room to spot the pile of weapons off to one side.

"Secure the weapons," Olivia ordered.

Michael heard the reports of his people as they cleared room after room in the building without a single drop of blood being spilled. Except for those guarding the various entrances to this rabbit warren, his people filtered back into the main room. They formed in a circle around these Sylannians who hadn't uttered a word let alone lifted a blade.

Suddenly wary, Michael sent his abilities out, seeking anything that screamed to his senses as being out of the ordinary. Yet in this exhausted, mostly sleeping city, uneasy as it still was, there wasn't anything that seemed out of place. As he stepped forward, the tension rose in his people, energy jumping from one to the other to the point the veil itself cracked and rumbled. All of them were far more nervous right now than if they'd stormed in and engaged in the fight they'd been expecting.

"What do you want?" Michael asked.

It was a small relief that the smuggler had advised him that these women were fluent in his language, which was much better than the smattering of Sylannian he could speak. Michael had no doubt these women wanted something, or else they'd be fighting to the death right at this moment instead of kneeling in the centre of the room.

"It's the Commander of Sylanna you want."

"Why is that?" Michael's eyes narrowed as the Sylannian avoided his question.

"She is the sister of our king and the biggest threat to his reign. Why do you think she sent us here?" the woman said.

"I don't know. To try to conquer our lands?"

Apparently amused, the woman chuckled and gazed up at him under her eyelashes, appraising him. Michael fought the urge to move and place himself behind Olivia as he caught what she was thinking about him, as he was certain their captive intended. Most Sylannians were too accomplished at mind games for it to have been a mistake.

"My apologies, Warleader—I'm told that is your rank?"

"It is."

"You have quite a reputation. Our king wants her to die. She is just doing the best she can to ensure the survival of herself and her house."

"I repeat. What do you want?"

"You can't have failed to notice we didn't fight as well as we could have. I had to make this attack look good, but I'm sure you've managed to round up and dispatch the other houses that came with me," the woman said.

Michael watched as the woman at the centre finally stared straight at him while the women around her continued to look passively at the floor.

"It wasn't that hard," Michael admitted.

"Jaclyn didn't care if they survived. I can help you, Warleader, I just ask you to grant me and mine our lives and refuge in your land."

"How else can you help me besides the fact you've apparently just betrayed your own king?"

"I merely follow the orders of Jaclyn. She has the authority in the king's name. So, in fact, I have not betrayed my people at all."

"Who is Jaclyn?"

"Jaclyn is the most feared commander in our history. None have survived like she has. You will not beat her easily. She doesn't fight for herself or her brother. She fights, as she always has, for the survival of her house, for her children. Jaclyn will destroy anyone she believes is a risk to them."

"Where is this fearsome commander of yours?"

"I don't know. She didn't divulge her plans to one such as me. My house had exactly two options. Die under the blades of Jaclyn's daggerwives on our home island or come here to fight you," the Sylannian said.

Michael frowned at the woman in front of him, trying to process all the tiny bits of information she'd inexplicably shared with him.

What does this woman want? Michael asked.

Survival. It seems she's suggesting that is all this commander she is speaking of wants as well, Nathanial said.

Michael didn't question Nathanial's certainty on this one. Of all of them, he seemed to understand the motivations among the desperate.

"So you expect me to let you live?"

"I expect to die, even though I still cling to the hope you will spare my life."

I don't recall a single Sylannian who was willing to divulge information about their people before. They might prove useful, Olivia said.

He weighed her observation against the healthy dose of scepticism he detected in her comment.

"Bind them," Michael ordered.

His people leapt into action, restraining the unresisting enemy. Once they were done, he left without a backward glance. The Unwanted followed with their prisoners. None of them were about to trust these women, no matter what they said or how they behaved. At least not until they had proven themselves. Michael was waiting for their real motivation to become apparent.

EIGHTY-FOUR

Jaclyn regarded the smuggler as he knelt before her. She had to admit he'd at least proved useful so far. As far as bases went, this wasn't such a bad one to start from.

"Tell me about the Warleader's family."

"Well, everyone knows about them," he said.

"In case it has escaped your notice, I'm not from around here."

"Their family, the Rathadons, were the warlords of old here in Vallantia and surrounds. There were many warlords in those days. Then the warlord of Yalleska went on the war path, and defeated everyone in his way including the Rathadons. The Yalleska warlord left the former Rathadon warlord crippled and took his son. He was only a young boy back then."

Jaclyn considered the man, thinking back on the reports she'd studied about these people.

"The Yalleska warlord is the one you simply refer to now as the Warlord?"

"Yes. No one else is allowed to use the title."

"The boy, a son of the warlords of old, grew up to be the Warleader?"

"Yes, First. Everyone says he's the most trusted of the Warlord's people."

"Does he hate his family?"

"It's whispered in the streets that he doesn't get on with his brother. Steven is said to get involved with conspiracies. He's even mixed up with the Kastlers," he said.

"Who or what are the Kastlers?" Jaclyn frowned.

"The trading family I work for. The ones who've been organising the deaths of the Warlord's sentries."

"Ah, your employer," Jaclyn said. It was starting to sound like a game of intrigue at the court with everyone betraying everyone else the second their backs were turned.

"Yes."

"Where do I find these ancient rulers?"

"What?" He stared at her, obviously confused.

"The Rathadons. Where do I find them?"

"I expect at the Rathadon estate. Speaker Rathadon, the old warlord, he and his wife don't get out much. Steven lives there as well."

Jaclyn took a deep breath and pushed down her irritation by reminding herself how useful this man had proven to be so far. He grovelled, probably to whoever had power over him and right now that was her.

"Where is the Rathadon estate?"

"Oh, it's a short ride out of town. It's a huge place with walls and gates and everything. You can see it rising above the tree line from the other side of the city. I'm told it's like its own little world in there. It's why the Kastlers took the place. He said if he controlled the Rathadons he controlled Vallantia. There used to be a map around here somewhere. I could show you where it's located," he said.

"Wait, so your employer is responsible for this recent disruption? He launched an attack on the Rathadon estate?"

"Yes, he paid for a lot of mercenary types, or that's what he calls them. I think it was foolish. The Warleader will find out and I don't think the Kastlers' paid mercenaries will stand against the Warleader."

"Why is that?"

"Well, they mostly aren't real mercenaries; they are little better than thugs—bullies who'd stand on street corners in the dark and beat up the unsuspecting." He shrugged. "I'm not sure I've ever met actual mercenaries here. I mean, they used to exist, but these days they either all ride for the Warlord or they are dead."

"So you think the Warleader will easily beat these thugs your employer has hired?"

Laughter burst from the smuggler's lips. "I doubt he'd break a sweat doing so. Sane people go to a great deal of effort to avoid the Unwanted."

"The Unwanted?"

"That's what the Warleader's personal warband is called, the Unwanted. I don't know why, except I guess no one wants to be around when they show up." The smuggler stared at her and swallowed. "To be honest, I'd rather not be around when the Warleader gets here—and he will."

"Don't worry, you belong to me now and we are much better at waging a war than the Kastlers' thugs."

"It won't make any difference," the smuggler whispered.

Jaclyn stared at the man for a time. He was pale, and she could feel the spurt of fear that came from him at the thought of the Warleader showing up. He feared facing the Warleader more than he did displeasing her. Finally, she motioned for the daggerwives to take the man away. Jacklyn issued orders for the map of the city the man spoke about to be dug out from wher-ever they'd stashed it while cleaning out this place.

Jaclyn stood with Ricardo and Myra on either side of her, with the representatives from the sister houses and their head dagger-wives arrayed in front of them. These were the most trusted houses that had fought by her side while her house had been in the former homeland of the traders.

"The attack on the barbarian habitation of Callenhain is well and truly on its way and we're told the one they call the Warleader has engaged our fighting units there," Jaclyn said.

"So the mind speaker relay is up and operational?" one of the other firstwives asked.

"It has been from almost the start, for barbarians it was a remarkably good idea. We didn't ferry anyone in here until we were certain the bulk of their fighting force was otherwise engaged," Myra replied.

"The fighting forces there have spread out to the smaller villages and towns..."

"Why would they do that?"

"Surely it makes them more vulnerable?"

"Because it will take far more time for the barbarians to track them all down than if they were all in one place," Myra said.

"They buy us time for our own attack and to settle in before the barbarian warleader and his forces head this way," Ricardo said.

"Which I have no doubt he will," Jaclyn said.

She was perfectly calm despite the unrest of the others. The questions were to be expected and unlike the houses who'd gone to participate in the other battlefront, these would see the impli-cations quickly. She could feel the knowledge of the inevitable death of the sister houses, isolated and alone in a barbarian land, settle on them. Also, the relief they and their houses were here and not there being sacrificed for Sylanna.

"We expect the first stage of our campaign here to go smoothly," Myra said, continuing the briefing.

"The Kastler trading family have done half our work for us—this place is in disarray." Jaclyn allowed her confidence to show.

Myra waited as Jaclyn's influence spread and the others calmed. "We have two targets to take, one marginally harder than the other simply because our forces are already here inside the defences of their walls. The second attack party will have to breach their walls first."

"So we'll be separated?" One of the other daggerwives frowned.

"We will, but we do not expect that circumstance to last longer than a day," Jaclyn said.

"We assess we will easily secure both the city and the estate of the former rulers of this place," Myra said.

"I and my house will go after the estate house, which is a short distance from the city itself," Jaclyn explained as one of the daggerwives behind her pointed to the large map the trader had found for them. "The rest of you will take the city from the mercenaries that currently control it."

"From what we've observed, they aren't very good mercenaries." One of the first wives snorted in amusement.

"Are you sure you won't need more of us to assist you with the estate house, First?" another asked.

"As you've noted, these so-called mercenaries aren't very good at their jobs. We're reliably informed the bulk of the people who fill the estate are the serving class. Once we've secured the walls and taken the remaining Rathadons, we shouldn't have any problems."

"We are told the elderly Rathadons are beyond their fighting days, disfigured and crippled. Their son, brother to the Warleader, is totally incompetent to the point he makes the mercenaries look good," Ricardo said, scanning the others in the room. "Yet the old, crippled leader is well respected by his people here. Once we hold his life in our hands, we believe we will have no issues from the bulk of the population."

"We're simply trusting the smugglers in all of this?" a first-wife asked, frowning.

"We've taken the minds of several barbarians. It not only allowed us to learn their language, but also to corroborate at least some of what the smugglers have been telling us," Myra said. "Some of our daggerwives have also been out in the city to secure information as best they can without giving away our presence."

"These people also aren't very adept at shielding their minds. They believe what they are telling us," Jaclyn said, glancing around to see if there were any more questions. When there were none, she continued. "This is how I want you to secure this city."

She received instant attention from all in the room as, with the help of Myra and Ricardo, she detailed what she required from the sister houses. There was enough leeway in the plan they outlined for independent action to deal with the unexpected. These houses would enact the plan they were given and take this habitation. Once they'd done so, that confidence they'd all displayed in the battles for the former homeland of the clans would return.

EIGHTY-FIVE

Olivia stood up, massaging the muscles in her shoulder. She was aware that both Michael and Nathanial noticed her sudden mood change. Now that they had the city and surrounds under control again, it was time to confront that one issue. She had to admit if even only to herself, she'd been putting it off.

"It's time I went to visit my dear family and ask them what the Powers they think they are doing," Olivia announced.

"I admit the reports we've received from the scouts are damning, but let's try to stay calm," Michael temporised.

Olivia rolled her eyes at him. She could tell he didn't believe a single word he'd just uttered.

"I'm going with 'they panicked when the attack happened and slammed their gates shut, leaving the city and everyone in it who looks to them for protection to fend for themselves'," Olivia said dryly.

Nathanial stood, his mouth opening, then closing as he ducked his head before sighing. "I'd like to say you are going to be surprised and they have an exceptionally good reason for being a no-show in this fight, but unfortunately, I think that is exactly what they did."

Olivia appreciated the honesty. With Michael and Nathanial falling in either side of her, she headed out. Damien and his team scrambled to get ready and left with her. They wound their way through the devastated streets, the scars of the battles that had been fought along their length apparent from the rooftops and in the residences. It would take time for those signs to fade, but overwhelmingly, those who'd survived were grateful they'd come to help them. People stilled and watched as they rode past, not a single hostile thought in their direction. Everyone guessed exactly where they were going. There was a deep undercurrent of hostility and anger, but it was directed at her family.

"Go get 'em, m'lady!"

"Those cowards with all their guards could have tried to help!"

"Teach 'em a lesson."

She did her best to ignore those who cried out for blood as they rode, although she couldn't blame them for the sentiment. The support of the Unwanted solidified around her like a comforting blanket as they closed ranks around her. They were just as aware as she was that the people were no threat to them right now, but none of them would take any risks, particularly given recent events. Just because they'd mostly cleaned up this part of the city of invaders, it didn't mean they hadn't missed pockets of them. Although at this point the residents of Callenhain were actively engaged in the clean-up efforts and informed their fighting units where the Sylannians were holed up.

Finally, she pulled up, staring at the closed gates of her family estate. The gates and walls were free of any signs of fighting. It appeared their prisoners had told them the truth. The Strafford estate had remained untouched.

"I'm not an expert at this kind of thing, but those walls look surprisingly intact," Damien said, half under his breath.

She couldn't disagree with his observation or the feeling of disgust coming from him. A low-burning anger lit up in her.

"So, it's true. They've done it again," Olivia said.

"I'm sorry," Michael said.

"You didn't do this. You don't have to be sorry for it."

"I'm not sorry for the act; you are correct, I didn't do this. I'm sorry this has reopened old wounds," Michael said.

"They haven't changed in all these years," Olivia said.

"Did you really expect them to?" Nathanial asked, his voice quiet.

It wasn't really a question, but Olivia shook her head anyway.

"Whatever happens, they can no longer remain in power in Callenhain. They are too great a risk," Olivia said.

"If you choose to appoint someone else to oversee Callenhain in your absence, I will, of course, support you," Michael said. "But it would be better if it waited until after we have settled this little war we are fighting."

She closed her eyes as she struggled with the emotions that ran though her, and took a deep breath, falling back into her role as the second-in-command of the Unwanted. In a way, she could accept what her family had done. It was what they were. What they had always been. She wondered what it was that made them different. She did not display any of the spineless incompetence of the rest of her family. Michael and Nathanial had pointed that out to her on many occasions and besides that, the Warlord didn't tolerate such people in his fighting ranks.

I'm glad you are finally learning that you are not your family, Nathanial said.

Nathanial was looking at her, his eyebrows rising. Her past wasn't pretty, but most of them had similar stories. History was not such a nice place, no matter how many tried to daydream and convince themselves it was.

Olivia spurred her horse into a gallop towards the main gates of her family's estate. Michael and Nathanial rode to either side of her, with the rest of the squad forming up behind her. As they bore down on the gates, Olivia's temper rose another notch. Gritting her teeth, she drew sharply from the veil.

Olivia... Michael trailed off.

She threw her power forward into the gate, the metal bands glowed then the whole thing exploded.

Never mind, Michael said.

They will not get the added pleasure of making us wait outside the gates while they decide if they are going to open them, Olivia snapped.

Blasting the gates to splinters had done nothing to dampen her anger. It still simmered, with the veil rumbling like an approaching storm in response.

"How come when I lose it I'm unconscious and when Olivia does it she just gets more scary?" Damien whispered.

"When you do it, you're out of control. Which is a different type of dangerous," Nathanial said.

"Olivia didn't accidentally blow up the gate. She intended to. She was furious," Michael added. "She'll sleep like the dead later."

"Right now, it's her fury driving her forward," Nathanial said. "It's something to keep in mind when your powers settle down."

Olivia threw an irritated look at them. Michael and Nathanial just stared back at her innocently.

"Does she know her eyes are glowing?" Damien whispered.

"Probably. She's seen Michael get mad before and, if I'm being candid, me as well. It's not a new phenomenon," Nathanial said, then added brightly. "Yours do it too, in case you didn't realise."

"Actually, I think Olivia is demonstrably better at the angry thing than either of us. I don't think even her family will miss the point," Michael said.

"I don't know, they can be pretty dense," Nathanial disagreed.

Olivia felt the thread of amusement in their tone and sighed. While she judged Damien was genuinely curious, Michael and Nathanial were deliberately trying to get her to calm down, chipping away at her anger in a way that only they could. She almost rolled her eyes as there was silence behind her, waiting for it. She could almost hear Damien thinking things through.

"So what you're saying is once I've gone through transition, anything up to and including blowing up a gate is all good. As long as I'm really angry?" Damien asked.

"Gates are fine. Just try not to blow up entire castles," Michael said. "Castles are harder to replace."

"You'll have to control your power use carefully. If you collapse into a veil-induced slumber after blowing something up it will kind of take away the impact," Nathanial advised.

"I'll try to keep that in mind," Damien said.

"I'd suggest picking your target so you can make a good impression with both the destruction and your entrance," Michael added.

"All right, that is enough out of the three of you." Olivia dismounted in the outer courtyard then spun, planting her hands on her hips, and glared at them.

Damien's eyes widened and he managed to look just as innocent as the other two did.

"Of course, Olivia, we don't want you to blow up the estate either. Damien here might think it's competition," Nathanial said.

"After all, he already took down the side of a mountain," Michael said.

"Hey, that wasn't just me! That was all of us."

"Of course, Damien, you're just the one who lost it and tripped the rest of us." Michael chuckled under his breath.

"As if it's not enough that I had to put up with the two of you. Now there's three of you," Olivia growled under her breath.

Michael smiled softly at her and closed the distance between them, and pulled her into his arms.

We would suffer the burning of the veil for an eternity for you. We hate to see you hurting. If you want your family estate brought down, we'll do it. Right down to the very last stone.

Olivia took a moment, soaking in that acceptance for what she was, flaws and all. Somehow, coming home always brought out the worst in her.

If you want your family to die, fine. They die. We won't judge, but don't make the decision with your judgement clouded by anger. You will second guess yourself after, my friend, Nathanial said.

As Nathanial joined her, she leant her head to one side, resting it on his shoulder.

What have I done in this life to deserve the pair of you to back me up? Olivia let out a breath, her anger dispelling with it.

You've been there to talk us down off the cliff. You've always had my back, Michael said.

You're the family I never had, Nathanial whispered.

Olivia sniffed as her anger cooled, under the unconditional acceptance and trust of not only the two people closest to her in this life but from all the Unwanted.

Olivia stared back at the pale faces of her family, who sat in a ring of chairs in a private sitting room. Her parents didn't dare to look anywhere else but right back at her. It seemed after her previous visit and the way she had dealt with the Kastlers'

nephew, they might finally be learning. Normally they'd be looking to Michael with everything she said, as if crosschecking that he approved of her actions and requests. Baren, however, stared at her, defiance in his eyes and posture.

Your parents are terrified, Nathanial said.

Watch your brother. He's working himself up for something, Michael said.

"You will not fail the people of Callenhain so completely again," Olivia said.

"Olivia, you could hardly expect we could fight the Sylannians," her father said.

"We woke up, and they were everywhere," her mother said.

"No, we don't owe her any explanation," Baren said to their parents, then surged to his feet, hands clenched.

"Baren, don't..." her mother said.

Baren thumped his chest with his hand, staring at Olivia defiantly, ignoring their mother's warning. "I ordered the gates sealed. I did what I had to in order to protect what we have."

"A part of your job description is to protect the people from invasions like this. At the very least, you could have taken as many of the people into your walls as you could," Olivia said. She dismissed her parents and concentrated on Baren, eyes narrowing as she watched his hand drop to his waist.

"It's not our job to protect anyone but ourselves," Baren said.

"How did you come to that rather startling conclusion?" Olivia asked, the cold of the veil in her tone.

"You're the Lady Strafford, remember? At least when you can be bothered to grace us with your presence. It's your job to fight the invaders, not ours." Baren took a step towards her. His spine stiffened as he puffed his chest out, and one hand went to the hilt of his sword. "The commoners aren't worth—"

Baren's words cut off. The sword he'd tried to draw fell back into its sheath as Olivia's dagger plunged into his chest. Her mother screamed and her father stood, taking a step towards Baren as he collapsed, hands pressed against his wound.

"Leave him," Olivia snapped, staring coldly at her parents.

Her father sank back into his chair, hands raised. "I'm sure he wouldn't have fought you, Olivia."

"Then he shouldn't have drawn a weapon," Olivia said flatly. "I will be appointing a steward to oversee everything you do and report directly to me. If you fail again, I'll pick another to act as Speaker of Callenhain. I would, of course, give them permission to take over the estate as their residence in my absence."

"But... you wouldn't. Where would we live?" her mother asked, bottom lip trembling.

"That wouldn't be my concern."

With that final threat, Olivia left her family staring, waves of horror following her as she walked out the doors with Michael, Nathanial and Damien but a step behind her.

EIGHTY-SIX

At hearing his name being called in that familiar bellow, Aiden rolled his eyes at Derick.

What's the bet he's finally well enough to realise we aren't on the direct road to Yalleska? Aiden asked.

I won't take that bet. Derick sounded amused rather than worried.

Aiden reined in his horse until he was level with the windows of the carriage to see his father frowning at him.

"Yes, Father?"

"Where are we? This is not the road to Yalleska," his father grumbled.

"We've diverted just a little to check on Ranlith."

"Why? I thought we were going back to Yalleska." His father's eyes narrowed but remarkably, he kept control of his temper.

"It's not far out of our way and you and our Warleader did promise, given Damien's sister is likely to be just as talented as he is, all the warbands would make an effort to go through and check on her welfare."

"I'm not sure either of us meant you to take this upon your-self, Aiden," his father said.

"It will only add a couple of days to our journey and, to be honest, the girl looked like she was close to going through transi-tion. I thought it best to check on her. Besides, I'm sure Damien will feel better that we are doing so and none of us want him to lose control. Again," Aiden said.

His father leaned back, frowning, but didn't offer any more argument. Unfortunately, the healer had been correct, and the enforced rest was helping his father get better every day. Although on the good side, after losing the argument with Michael, his father hadn't offered them any resistance at all. He'd half expected that first morning on the road for his father to wake and demand to be taken back to Callenhain. Instead, he'd been the perfect invalid and done as he was told. Aiden waited another moment in case his father thought of something else to ask, then when nothing was forthcoming, he spurred his horse forward again. He was about to comment to Derick when one of their scouts appeared around a bend in the road, looking concerned. He'd learned that was never a good sign.

"Sir, the village has been taken."

"What?" Aiden said.

"Sylannians appear to have taken Ranlith."

"How did they get all the way out here?" Aiden swore.

"Probably took the river, it's only a day's travel that way," Derick said grimly.

Aiden sat back, trying to look like he knew what he was doing as Derick smoothly took control and started issuing orders. For the first time, he was glad that they had not only his own band but those that normally rode with the Warlord as well. It was unfortunate their scouts hadn't been out too far in front; since they hadn't seen any sight of the Sylannians they'd reasoned that they were in safe territory. It seemed they'd been wrong in that assumption, and now they were far too close to Ranlith for his comfort.

As Derick and his father's band leaders issued orders, the door to his father's carriage flung open. Despite the protestations of the driver, his father stepped carefully from the carriage.

"What is it?" the Warlord demanded as he slowly made his way over to them.

"There are Sylannian invaders in Ranlith, Warlord," Derick said.

His father's expression was unreadable as he focused on Derick and the two other band leaders.

"We're planning on rescuing the villagers, of course?" It wasn't really a question since there was the thread of an order in his father's tone.

"Of course, Warlord. We are just making plans now," the Warlord's band leader said.

"The scout reported there don't seem to be many of the Sylannians here," Derick said.

Both men moved aside and made room for the Warlord as he finally crossed the distance between them. He studied the rough map they'd sketched in the dirt and pointed.

"The meeting house is on the other side. It's the only other stone building other than the bathhouse, which is there." He pointed closer to the line they'd drawn. "Near the river."

"I remember," Derick said.

"The Sylannians would have taken over the meeting house for themselves," the Warlord said.

"The locals have been corralled into one of the animal pens over here." The scout squatted down and drew a square over to one side of the impromptu map.

It never ceased to amaze Aiden how some of the members

could be so confident in front of his father. Then again, he guessed the scouts, out of all their members, were used to having to report what they'd found to whoever was in command.

"They're under guard?" his father asked.

"Yes, Warlord. A team of six of the Sylannians watches over them. They're tied up," the scout answered.

"But they are all together?"

"Yes, Warlord."

"Can you take a small group of our fighters and lead them over to the side closest to the villagers and set them free?" the Warlord asked.

The scout ducked his head, considering the request. The silence stretched. Aiden was about to reprimand the man before he finally answered the Warlord.

"Yes, Warlord, I can do that."

"Some of those with skills at hunting would be best, you think?"

"It would be easier, yes, Warlord. They already know how to move in the forest."

"Good, go pick your people. I assume you have some in mind?"

"Yes, Warlord."

"You'll lead your team to the other side. Wait until you hear us attack, and using the distraction it provides, get the villagers free to safety," the Warlord ordered.

"Yes, Warlord," the scout said, and at a gesture from Derick went off to gather a small team.

Aiden stayed quiet as his father took control of the attack planning, grateful that he was here and had done so. Even if Michael would not approve—and that was putting it lightly. When he'd decided to come this way, he hadn't expected to actually find Sylannians or to have to fight. Now he was regretting his impulse to swing by and try his luck with Isabella without her interfering brother around.

As his father spun and strode back to the carriage, Aiden shared a look with Derick. It seemed he was equally relieved that the Warlord had taken over, then Derick groaned and pointed his chin in the direction his father had gone. Aiden spun and saw his father strapping on his weapons. He nearly groaned out loud himself and wondered who he'd bullied for them to materialise. With both Derick and the other band leader looking at him pointedly, Aiden growled in pure frustration.

"The old man would pick now to be difficult," he muttered.

Straightening his back, he marched over to where his father stood, arming himself with his weapons belt.

"I'm going."

"Of course you are, Father. I'm certainly not going to leave you unguarded out here. As you've pointed out to me before, Michael would kill me if I was that stupid." Aiden kept his expression bland, having no issues at all in throwing Michael's name into this whole argument.

His father stopped, clearly not expecting the response he'd received.

"You're not going to try and stop me?"

"Not at all, Father. I'm afraid you'll still have to ride in the carriage, though."

"Get me a horse," his father demanded.

"Unfortunately, Michael foresaw you might get difficult on this precise issue and there isn't a horse for you," he said blandly at his father and held his hand up as the old man went to protest. "If you'll get back in the carriage, we'll make sure you arrive in the village safely."

With that, Aiden ignored the fact his father's face had gone red and switched his attention back to the leaders of their respective warbands.

"You know what you are doing. Let's go liberate this village."

He rolled his eyes. "I'll stay with the Warlord and follow along behind with him in case he gets any other ideas about engaging in this fight."

EIGHTY-SEVEN

Nathanial traded glances with Olivia as Michael ran his fingers through his hair and got up to pace like a caged animal. He could feel Michael trying to curb his frustration with their current situation. There were too many places they needed to be all at once.

"It would have been easier if those Sylannians had fought us when we entered their hideout," Olivia said.

"I can't kill them in cold blood when they handed themselves over like that, but that just makes them one more problem."

"As if we didn't have enough of those. For what it's worth, I agree, although you already know we both do."

"We can't leave them in custody here," Olivia said.

Nathanial found he couldn't disagree with her assessment. If they left the Sylannian prisoners in her family's custody, by the time they got back the whole of Callenhain would probably belong to Sylanna.

"I don't see any other choice but to divert to Yalleska and leave them there," Michael growled.

Which would mean it would take even longer for them to get

to Vallantia. If the smuggler and their prisoners could be believed, the Sylannian commander and her house were either here in the Warlord's domain already, or would be soon. Given there wasn't even a hint of where the other Sylannian force was, he'd tip the only logical target was Vallantia. This incursion had been a distraction. Even if it had been a substantial one.

"I know you want to get moving to Vallantia, but I think we need to take more time to finish off here," Olivia said.

"If we run off with the job half finished, we'll only have to come back and have an even worse mess to clean up," Nathanial said.

"I know. We have to take the time to do this properly. I just hate not knowing what's going on," Michael said, growling in frustration. "Of all the things the Sylannians had to show competence in, they had to take out the communications network before they attacked. If they hadn't, it would be a simple enough to receive word about Vallantia or wherever the Sylannian force lands."

"Still no word from Ben or the twins?" Olivia asked.

"No. I don't know if I should be concerned by that or not."

"You could always force contact with Ben?" Olivia said. "Under the circumstances, he'd forgive the blinding headache, in a week or so after he recovers."

Michael paused from his pacing, then shook his head. "No. I suspect he's already deployed the twins as a temporary relay."

"If they've encountered some of the splinter groups and other smaller raids along the way, it could explain the delay," Nathanial said.

"If that's the case, I'll receive word soon enough." Michael sighed and slumped in the chair he'd deserted a moment before. "I was impressed that Damien gathered his team and came with us the other day. He even thought to deploy his unit to perform security for us while we dealt with Speaker Strafford, without being told to. It was a small thing but a big step. Your thoughts on how he's going?"

"Callan tells me he's settling in really well leading his combined battle group. They've cleaned out two different incursions of Sylannians in small surrounding villages so far," Nathanial said, relieved at the change of topic.

"I think he's shown he can follow orders and make good decisions, with good results, without having to ask us first," Olivia said.

"I had my doubts, but it was a good call," Michael said.

"I thought it was time. He lost a lot of confidence with his relapse," Nathanial said.

"He knows I trust him, other than with tiscan?" Michael asked.

Nathanial nodded. They'd been walking a dangerous line with their latest recruit. Then again, they did with so many of their people, all with different issues as they settled in. Damien had too much potential to allow him to languish in the back ranks of the Unwanted.

"I think he does now," Olivia said.

"He was afraid you would never trust him again," Nathanial added. "Another reason I pushed for us to give him a trial at leading."

"I've been impressed with how he's taken responsibility. There are many who never do." Michael shrugged.

"I have one thought about how to save time on one of our tasks," Olivia said.

Nathanial stared at her, not missing the slightly tentative tone in her voice. Michael's eyebrows rose as he too stared at her. Nathanial found his curiosity was piqued.

"Well don't keep us waiting," Nathanial said.

"We all agree Damien has done well with the leadership duties we've given him with his patrol?" Olivia asked.

"He has; going forward, I was thinking of assigning him permanently in that role for those occasions where we must work independently. Sorry, Nathanial, you're going to have to train up a new second."

"I figured as much," Nathanial said.

"Give Damien and his squad the duty of escorting the prisoners to Yalleska. Then, once we are certain we are done here, we can head to Vallantia," Olivia said.

Michael frowned. It was clear from Michael's hesitation that he wanted to test Damien and see his capabilities, but he didn't want to risk giving Damien too much too soon. Still, Nathanial thought the idea had merit and shouldn't prove too difficult.

"Having that little distance from us will help him settle into his role and assist the team to really become his team," Nathanial said.

"You don't think it's too soon?" Michael asked, looking at them both.

"Perhaps, but we're probably always going to think it is too soon. I'd rather we give the trust and see how he performs now than in the middle of battle. Which is what I fear Vallantia will be," Olivia said.

"So he can deliver the prisoners and report to the Warlord, then cut over the top close to the mountains and come to join us in Vallantia from there," Nathanial said.

"He'll be, at the most, a couple of weeks behind us," Olivia said.

"Which will give us time to assess the situation and draw up our own attack plans," Michael said.

They broke off as the doors opened and Damien came through the doors with Callan and their squad.

"Rest up. We'll probably be out again in the morning," Damien said.

Seeing all of the leaders over in the corner, he had a quiet conversation with Callan, who laughed and slapped him on the shoulder before heading off to his own sleeping cot. Damien sighed and joined them.

"Your report on today's activities?" Michael asked.

Damien stepped forward to the nearby table with the map of the region on it. Nathanial joined both Michael and Olivia at the table as Damien pointed out a couple of villages.

"We cleaned out this one first. The two squads worked well together today. The Sylannians here weren't that organised. They didn't even have sentries out. It was over in a few hours."

"Casualties?"

"On our side? A couple of minor injuries to three of the regulars who ride with us. I sent them straight to the healers as soon as we got back here."

"I'd be wondering what you'd been getting up to if there was none on the other side," Nathanial said.

Damien chuckled, shaking his head as he continued to study the map. He then pointed to another small village near their assigned patrol for the day.

"Given we finished up early with our assigned target, I changed our route back and we went past this one as well. There weren't any Sylannians in that one, so it can be crossed off the list. It's why we're back a little later than normal, but I judged it worthwhile."

"Good work. I'll have a change of assignment for your squad. The leader of the other squad will be informed he's permanently assigned to you until further notice, but the Kallith unit will be reassigned elsewhere. I'll brief you tomorrow and you'll probably ride out the day after," Michael said.

Damien was curious, but Nathanial saw that he pushed down his immediate instinct to ask what he was going to be doing next and excused himself when it was clear that the debrief for today was over. Nathanial watched as Damien went back to his squad, filling them in that tomorrow would be a day off but to expect other duties the day after. Then, taking his own advice, he crashed in his own cot to get some rest. Since all of them had been up and on the road well before dawn and it was now verging on evening, the rest was certainly well deserved.

"You want me to take the prisoners back to Yalleska? Then cut across and join you all in Vallantia?" Damien repeated.

He looked from face to face just to make sure he'd heard them correctly and his mind wasn't playing tricks on him.

"We're doing some final sweeps, but I think we are finally done here," Olivia said.

"Given the information we've received about the possibility of another attack force, we'll head to Vallantia. We want to get there as soon as we can," Michael said.

"I can escort the prisoners, but I think you should take the other squad with you," Damien said.

"There are quite a lot of prisoners, Damien, are you sure you won't need the extra assistance?" Michael asked.

"We should be fine. They haven't been any trouble at all from what I've heard, even trying to help with camp duties where they can," Damien said.

"They are certainly the most unusual Sylannians I've encountered." Olivia raised her eyebrows. "Nathanial, you're blushing."

"I swear one of them was trying to flirt with me the other day. I can handle them screaming and trying to plunge a dagger into me but the flirting thing is unsettling," Nathanial grumbled.

Damien stared at Nathanial, who finally noticed the silence of those around him and shrugged.

"That wasn't a complication I was thinking of, but I'll keep it in mind." Damien chuckled under his breath. "I'm sure Callan and the others all know the way to Yalleska, but I'll check."

"They do. They've all been there quite frequently," Michael assured him.

"Are you sure you trust me to do this?" Damien asked.

He couldn't help but ask. Setting out on patrols which lasted, at the most, a handful of days had been one thing. He'd been here under their eye almost every evening since his targets had been those within an easy day's ride of Callenhain. This would mean he wouldn't re-join them for weeks.

"If I didn't think you were capable, I wouldn't be assigning you the task," Michael said.

Damien ducked his head, feeling his face flush.

"Thank you, Warleader. I'll do my best. Now, unless there is more, if you will excuse me, I'll go let the squad know and we can get ready for our departure tomorrow morning."

Damien waited until Michael agreed and waved him off. He returned to where his squad was bunked. He almost stopped at that thought. *His squad.* It wasn't something he'd expected with the Unwanted, at least not this soon. Particularly with the problems he'd had. Granted, Michael had assigned him some of their more seasoned members and Callan as his second, but he was still aware of the weight of responsibility that settled on him. He didn't want to let down either Michael or the Unwanted.

EIGHTY-EIGHT

Aiden stood in the newly liberated village, both relieved and irritated. While he'd been successful at keeping his father out of the battle, he hadn't had much luck getting him to stay put once they did get here after Derick had advised him the battle was over. The Warlord had been out of the carriage and running around everywhere since they'd gotten here. Insisting on personally checking in with each of the rescued villagers and issuing orders to the members of the bands as to the care they were to receive. One thing was clear, Damien's sister was nowhere to be found in the small group of villagers who'd survived. He sighed. That was such a shame; he'd been trying to come up with a reason to order the girl brought with them back to Yalleska. Not that he'd admitted as much to his father, but Derick had guessed his motivation, probably even before he'd known why he'd decided to come this way. As an alert was called out, Aiden was a little embarrassed to see his father had his sword drawn before he'd managed to draw his own. Aiden belatedly drew his own weapon, hoping no one had noticed his lapse.

Their people were tense as a man cautiously made his way from the tree line into the village towards them. His hands were up, palms out, showing they were empty. Not that it mattered that much, since he was clearly armed. Those responsible for the Warlord's security drew closer to him. They were alert, but not concerned.

"Stop right there. Who are you and what do you want?" Aiden called out.

The man stopped and drew his attention from the Warlord to look at him.

"My name is Owen. I live here in Ranlith."

"Why weren't you with the others?" Derick asked.

"I live on the outskirts of the village. They completely missed me. I tried to keep an eye on everyone but I'm just one person. There wasn't anything I could do," Owen said.

Aiden turned to his father, who gestured the villager was to be brought to him.

"Were there any other survivors?" the Warlord asked.

Owen hesitated and shook his head. "No."

He's lying. Derick's eyes flicked over to him.

I did pick that up. I wonder why? Aiden said, his interest sparked as he moved to his father's side.

"I'll save you some embarrassment, Owen. You aren't very good at shielding. I know you just lied," Aiden said pleasantly. "So perhaps you'd like to try that again, only this time with the truth, and I hope you have a very good reason for lying to the Warlord."

Owen looked at him, his eyes widening as he saw the blade Aiden still carried in his hand. If he was honest with himself, he'd almost forgotten he had drawn the thing but they might get some answers this way.

EIGHTY-NINE

Isabella woke slowly, feeling sluggish. She reached out delicately with her mind, relieved that at least her head wasn't pounding this morning. It confirmed what she already knew: that Owen wasn't in their camp. Unable to sense him nearby, she withdrew her consciousness. The last thing she wanted was the Sylannians to sense that they were here. Not that it overly concerned her. Owen often got up early and went hunting while she slept.

Finally prodding herself into movement, she performed a few duties around their camp before she sat on a fallen log and sipped a mug of kaf. She wondered how long ago Owen had set up this little hideout and why he'd done so. It was obvious it had been here some time and it was well stocked. She went to take a sip of her drink and realised she'd already finished it while she'd sat there thinking. Placing the mug aside, she stood and checked the position of the sun. The morning was mostly over. She bit her lip. Owen had been most insistent that she should stay in their camp. Lips firming, she shook herself and picked up her weapons, leaving their makeshift camp as she strapped on her belt. It would upset her, but she couldn't help but go to check on those who were left.

It didn't take her long to make her way back through the forest towards the village. They weren't that far away, and even though there was no path she trod it by heart now. Their secret hiding hole was just far enough that those in the village wouldn't notice the sound, sight and smell from their camp.

Isabella paused, hidden by the shadows thrown by the underbrush, watching the village, her eyes wide as she tried to understand what she was seeing. While she'd been sleeping, the control of the village had changed again. There were more people than she'd seen in a long time, and the Sylannians were nowhere in sight. The village's survivors were clustered off in a corner, being cared for by some of the outsiders. The uniform the outsiders were wearing was familiar—the Warlord's people. Isabella found herself running towards the village, then came to a sudden halt as she breached the tree line and raised her hands to show they were empty as she found swords pointed in her direction.

"Isabella, you should have stayed in the camp."

She saw Owen standing off to one side talking to the giant of a man that was the Warlord and another of the Warlord's people.

"You were gone when I woke. I just came to check."

"Let the girl through. Unless I am very much mistaken, that is Damien's little sister," the Warlord's voice rumbled.

"It is; put up your blades. Damien wouldn't be very happy if you hurt her," said the man standing near the Warlord and Owen.

He's Aiden, the Warlord's son, Owen told her.

At a gesture from the guards that surrounded her, she walked towards the three men. Her breath shook, and she was aware of the sudden press of minds around her. She closed her eyes briefly and tried to push the random thoughts of others out of her head.

They'd been alone, just the two of them, with the minds of those in the village far enough away that she'd almost forgotten what the constant mental chatter of others was like. She hadn't even noticed how much it had been affecting her until she'd left the village proper.

As she reached the spot where the Warlord stood, relief flooded Isabella as silence wrapped around her mind. She reached out with one hand, steadying herself against a tree.

"What are you doing? Leave her be," Owen said.

"Just helping her," the Warlord said mildly.

"She doesn't need your kind of help any more than Damien did. Isabella was doing just fine."

"She isn't. Her shielding is next to non-existent and Damien probably would have been dead by now if he'd stayed here. There is more than one reason he rides with my Warleader," the Warlord said.

"We were teaching him, he was fine—"

"You mean you drugged him insensible most of the time?" Aiden said blandly. "As a consequence, he's a tiscan addict. A circumstance that nearly cost him his life and freedom."

"Didn't it ever occur to you to wonder why he didn't cope with anything that meant he had to stay around others too long?" the Warlord asked.

"He just wasn't good at baking or..."

"Granted, he is a very good fighter, even better now he's had more extensive training. It was the drugs addling his mind and the press of the thoughts from others driving him off to pursuits like hunting to get away."

"We've seen it before with strong mind speakers. They go mad unless they get help learning control." Aiden transferred his gaze to her.

"Thank you," Isabella said to the Warlord.

The men stopped and stared at her. Isabella concentrated on

the Warlord, who was the one shielding her mind. She peeked up at this monster that she had feared since before her brother had been taken. While she still feared this man and she wished the Warleader was here instead, she was still grateful for his help.

"You're welcome. I think you'll have to ride with me, no matter what the other survivors here decide to do," the Warlord said.

"Why?" Owen bristled with suspicion, hand moving towards his sword.

Isabella placed one hand against Owen's chest in warning. She'd lost too many people she cared about already without losing him as well.

"Because she needs at least some training in her use of the veil or it will consume her. I doubt any here have the capability of training her."

"Why would you care?" Isabella asked, trying to merge this man who seemed to have some concern for her welfare with the mental picture she had of him.

"Your brother cares for you." The Warlord shrugged.

"You threatened me to get him to do what you wanted." She heard the note of accusation in her tone.

"I need your brother functional and able to concentrate on this war without being concerned about you. We all do."

"Why? You have your Warleader, and his entire warband. Why do you need Damien as well?"

"Let me tell you a secret, Isabella. I don't have anywhere near as many people with the abilities of Michael and his Unwanted as everyone thinks—and the Sylannians outnumber us."

"You don't?"

Isabella inspected the men and women camped around her, all of them bristling with weapons. Opening up her senses, she tested those around her and drew in her breath sharply as she realised that, against all odds, she was more powerful than any of those she sensed with the Warlord. Although she guessed they would all know how to use the veil to their advantage better than she did. She glanced back at the Warlord as she felt his gaze on her. Heat rose in her cheeks as she realised he had been waiting for her to come to her own conclusion.

"We don't. As it turns out, your brother is one of the stronger members—or will be when his abilities finally settle. He's comparable to Michael, Olivia, and Nathanial, as I judge you will be. If you survive. Which will be far more likely if you come with me."

Owen shook his head. Isabella stared over at her fellow villagers being cared for by the Warlord's people. Yes, they'd run, saving their lives, but there was little for them here now. Certainly not any safety. She swallowed, remembering Damien's bargain with the Warlord to save her.

"Will you ensure they'll be all right if I agree to go with you?"

Isabella tried to keep her regard of the Warlord steady. She wanted to appear calm and confident, even if inside, she was trembling. Although something in the way he looked at her suggested he knew how scared she was.

"I would have done what I could have for them anyway, but of course," he agreed with a nod.

"Father, you need to go and rest. If you take harm, Michael will kill me," Aiden said.

Isabella stared at Aiden for a moment then back at the Warlord, noticing that he appeared a little pale. Her eyes widened a little and she almost flinched expecting him to yell but all he did was sigh and reach out to place a hand on her shoulder.

"Come, it will be easier for me to maintain a shield on your mind if you are camped closer to me. I fear my son is correct. Michael will take it poorly if anything goes wrong, and someone will be bound to tell him if it does," the Warlord said.

"Thank you," Isabella said.

"You too, Owen. I know you won't trust Isabella is safe unless you are close by," he added.

Isabella twisted her head to look up at the Warlord. She was sure that instead of anger it was amusement she sensed coming from this man. It didn't fit with his fearsome reputation at all. Everyone said he set fire to villages, killed and took whoever he wanted. Yet this wasn't the man she was seeing. She straightened her shoulders. It wouldn't do for her to be careless and let her guard down. The Warlord could just be trying to lull her into a false sense of security to get whatever it was he wanted from her. A chuckle escaped her lips unbidden as she realised he didn't really need her cooperation or consent. He could have just dragged her off, but despite what "everyone" said about him, the Warlord hadn't done that at all. In a small corner of her mind, she wondered if perhaps "everyone" had been wrong.

NINETY

Aiden sat in what passed for a tavern in the town they'd stopped in. He'd commandeered it when they'd arrived. With his father injured, he didn't even have to come up with any excuses as to why he wasn't going to camp rough. While it might have made perfect sense to Michael and Olivia, helping to make their movements unpredictable, he preferred comfort. At least with his father safely installed in one of the rooms above, they could all relax a little.

"If it wasn't for that interfering healer, the old man would be dead already," Aiden grumbled.

"Cheer up, he still might die." Derick shrugged and took a swig of his ale.

Aiden stared at his captain. As much as he wished Derick hadn't intervened and stopped him from finishing the job on the battlefield, he'd realised almost straight away it would have been a mistake. Those closest to the Warlord were loyal and even with the madness of the battlefield they hardly would have failed to notice if he'd plunged his own blade into his father. Derick might have been put in place by his father and had proven to be extremely competent, but Aiden had no doubt of his loyalty.

"Unfortunately, if that was likely Michael's pet healer wouldn't have agreed to allow this," Aiden said.

"It's a pity. If the Warleader hadn't insisted on him going back to Yalleska to recuperate, he might have been prodded into going back out to fight," Derick suggested.

"That's another one who just won't die."

"Perhaps with luck that goal might still be achieved and the Warleader will die in the conflict," Derick said.

"I doubt it. He's too good at what he does." As much as it pained him to admit it, there was more than luck at play when Michael entered the battlefield.

"All of your plans will amount to nothing if he doesn't," Derick said.

"As soon as my father dies, I'll be the warlord. Michael will do as he is told or die along with everyone else," Aiden said.

"The bulk of the Warlord's fighting forces follow him," Derick pointed out.

"I know," Aiden said shortly, his eyes narrowing. "But if Father will just die, I'll be installed in the stronghold while my dear brother and sister are fighting the Sylannians. By the time they realise it will be too late."

He'd been doing his level best to improve how people perceived him. As far as he could tell, everyone except his own people still preferred Michael. He got the distinct impression they'd even choose Olivia or Nathanial to lead them rather than him. Catching movement on the stairs, Aiden saw Isabella being shepherded into the common room by her ever-present, self-appointed guardian. Owen glanced at Aiden as he guided his charge over to the far corner of the bar. The man clearly held a healthy distrust of him. Aiden turned his attention back to his band leader.

"What?"

"It will be difficult to get that one into your bed. What with Owen acting as her chaperone, and your father's interest," Derick said shrewdly.

"That obvious?" Aiden asked, although he made a mental note to hide his interest a little better.

"You and half the men in this taproom." Derick rolled his eyes and poured more ale into both of their mugs.

"I think I have an advantage over the others in this taproom. Yet another thing to add to my to-do list."

"How did the Warlord take your excuse for why we diverted to go through Ranlith in the first place?"

"Given the results and securing Isabella, he didn't really care why we went that way." Aiden shrugged.

"She'll be like her brother," Derick said.

"Most likely, but regardless, that girl will warm my bed as soon as my father dies."

"Then we're going to have to separate her from her guardian," Derick said.

Aiden observed the pair, who didn't notice his interest since they seemed to be engaged in an earnest discussion.

"What do you suggest?"

"Assign him to one of the warbands as soon as we get to Yalleska," Derick said, certainty in his voice.

"You think he'll agree?" Aiden tore his gaze away from the girl to look at Derick.

"Don't give him a choice," Derick said, his tone blunt. "We can spin the Warleader's orders to suggest he appointed you to be in charge of defences while the Warlord is recovering. We're at war, after all, and he is a fighter. Assign him to a warband and make him bunk with them in the barracks."

"She will obviously be in the keep," Aiden said.

"The way the Warlord is behaving, he will want her close by," Derick said.

"How fortunate; that would put her within my reach as well." Aiden smirked and took a long swallow from his own mug.

Derick nodded, then signalled the barkeep, who took down a flask and poured the dark liquid it contained into two small glasses before passing them to his boy, who promptly brought them to the table.

"What's this?" Aiden asked.

"It is a local brew—strong smell and taste. I arranged a test on a local addict and it masked the smell and taste of"—Derick's eyes flicked around the tap room before he leaned forward, picked up the small glass and whispered—"the tonic we'll need to control your tool. If we can contrive a circumstance to get our hands on him, I've ordered a barrel of the stuff to take with us when we leave tomorrow."

Aiden rose his glass in salute and threw back the dark liquid that sent an explosion of berries and spice into his mouth and a fire down his throat. His eyes raised to Derick in appreciation. It was one of the reasons he really liked the man. He was extremely competent and searched for ways to solve problems rather than just say they couldn't be done.

CHAPTER

NINETY-ONE

The Warlord twisted to watch as Isabella came into his rooms, wincing as the movement caused his injuries to protest. As Michael's healer had indicated, all his activity, particularly in Ranlith where, he could admit now, he had pushed himself to show there was nothing wrong, had strained his healing injuries. Kesha had informed him there was only so much she could do and even with her healing powers, he still needed rest. He hadn't really believed her until his own body had proven her point.

He waved Isabella over to the sitting area by the windows. It was his favourite place, looking out over Yalleska town down in the valley and his territory beyond. He waited as she crossed the room and tentatively sat on the edge of a large leather chair that made her look like the child she still was.

"I was born down in that village," the Warlord said.

Isabella stared at him, then out the window at the sprawling village.

"You weren't the son of the Warlord?" Isabella asked.

551

"I was, but he didn't know it. He owned my mother; she was his bed slave."

Isabella paled, her eyes going wide. He could feel her warring with herself. Her emotions going from sympathy to disbelief back to sympathy again.

"You, but how..." She stumbled to a halt and her hands rose up as she took in her surroundings.

"He was a brute of a man, as you'd expect in those days. When my mother became pregnant with me, she bribed the leader of the warlord's private security detail and he helped smuggle her out of the stronghold. He continued to look after her and me. The village, what there was of it, was one hovel stacked against another. People living in squalor. The children used to go through the garbage thrown out by the warlord looking for scraps." The Warlord paused, looking over her, to see her hand was pressed against her mouth.

"I'm sorry."

"One day, an altercation broke out between a couple of men over my mother and her top was ripped, exposing her slave collar. Someone reported her to the warlord. He took her back and killed her in a public execution as an example to the other slaves."

"I don't know what to say."

"The man who'd become my father brought me to the stronghold, passing me off as his own son. I ran around under the warlord's nose, was fed and trained to fight. Much later, when I was bigger and stronger, I killed him. My stepfather and his warband followed me while others feared me after that. I became the Warlord by being meaner, more brutal than any around me. That man taught me well."

"I... I didn't know." She ducked her head. "I know you don't allow people to be owned. Everyone knows, but I didn't know why."

"I didn't expect you did. I didn't tell you my past to make you feel sorry for me."

The Warlord watched as Isabella stilled at that. He could hear her thinking through what he'd just said.

"Why did you?"

"The rumours of my exploits these days grow in the telling. A great many are perpetuated by me and not completely accurate. They are a show of strength. If people fear me, they will be less likely to cause trouble. You are not my prisoner, Isabella. I brought you here for your protection and to help you understand your abilities. If you choose to ride with your brother and the Unwanted, well, you may do so."

"I'm not sure I can fight and kill," Isabella said.

"You need someone to teach you how to use your emerging abilities. Too many like you die. I can help you for now, but you may need to ride with Michael, eventually. That doesn't mean you have to become a warrior. He already has a non-combatant: the healer riding with him." The Warlord added the last as an afterthought.

While he'd seen she'd been wearing a sword when she came into the village, he judged it wasn't something she was comfortable with or had much practice with. At least prior to her brother being taken.

"Couldn't I just go back to my village?" She looked up at him, eyes almost pleading with him.

"You could, except I doubt your village will exist for much longer if indeed it does now. You also need to face the very real possibility you would pose a risk to them all," he explained carefully, willing the girl to understand.

"I... I could never harm them," Isabella said.

"You wouldn't mean to, but you are not like others. You are already struggling with the press of minds around you. I've seen this before. Your full powers are only just starting to emerge. If

I'm any judge before too long it will drive you to distance yourself from people, or even to madness. At best, without help, you'll live the life of a hermit in the forest. When your abilities surge you don't have control, it will lead you to kill someone regardless of your intent. You are a threat to everyone around you." He held up his hand as she went to protest. "No one here is strong enough to shield others from your more dangerous abilities, let alone train you. I judge you are the same as your brother. The same as Michael, Olivia, Nathanial, and the rest of the Unwanted."

She sat in silence for a time staring at him, the horror of what he'd said evident. He could also see the hesitation in her. She didn't actually disbelieve anything he'd said. Even though she desperately wanted to.

"What am I?" Isabella whispered.

"What you are is not your fault. Just what you are born to be. There are very few in this world who can help you grow and understand who you are. For now, at the stage you are at, I can help. I'm stronger than most but not like the Unwanted. There will come a time when I think you will need the learning Michael can give you. I need you to understand that. Until then, you are my guest and under my protection."

"Even against your own son?" Isabella blurted.

The Warlord frowned in irritation. "Is that boy bothering you?"

"Not precisely, it's just..."

"Just what? You can tell me. I'm aware Aiden is not an admirable man."

"I... I could sense it, with the baker, what he wanted long before Damien killed him," Isabella said.

"You sense the same thoughts when my son looks at you?"

"Not exactly the same but, sometimes it feels like my skin is crawling. When I look around, I see him watching me. I think he's better at hiding his thoughts than the baker was. If Damien were here, he'd kill Aiden as well," Isabella said, her eyes darting up to catch the Warlord's before she lowered her gaze to inspect her fingernails.

"I'll speak to him and yes, you are under my protection, even from my own son, which I will make sure to impress on him," the Warlord said.

"Thank you," Isabella said.

He could tell by her hesitant tone and pinched expression he'd given her much to think about. He relaxed back into his chair, happy for her to think things through for herself.

NINETY-TWO

Aiden rolled off the woman, breathing heavily, a fine sweat covering his body. It was one of the luxuries he'd missed being away from Yalleska as long as he had. The woman was one of his father's captives who was grateful to be dragged up to his bed and spend time in relative comfort while he had sex with her. He opened his eyes to stare into the dark pools of the Sylannian woman's eyes, then gasped as her hand grabbed him and she expertly proved she could make him rise again so soon after they'd just finished. Sylannian women, so he'd found out, were extremely well trained in satisfying their men.

"Again, master?" A playful expression on her face.

"Ah, my pet, I've missed having you brought to my bed. Unfortunately, I do have some chores I need to get done today," Aiden said with a hint of regret as he gazed at her.

She pouted at him, but her hand stopped its efforts and rose to rest on his chest instead.

"Who was the girl you were thinking of while you were bedding me?" she asked.

Aiden chuckled. Trust her to know he'd been seeing a pair of blue eyes staring into his own instead of her brown ones.

"A future acquisition, my pet, so you'll have some company soon enough. Don't worry, I won't push you aside."

So as not to get distracted, he rolled out of bed and grabbed a robe for himself and another for her. He held his hand out to her. She sighed but came to him and he slipped the robe over her shoulders, kissing her gently on the back of the neck.

"When I'm warlord, your accommodation will be a lot more pleasant."

Not letting go of her hand, he led her to the door and pulled it open to see the guards waiting in the corridor.

"See her back to the cells." As an afterthought, Aiden added. "Make sure she has something nice for dinner and a drink. Not the normal slop they get down there.

"Of course, Aiden." The guard gestured for the Sylannian to walk in front of him.

He didn't have to do more than that. She'd travelled the hallways between his rooms to the cells many times. Even though he'd been away for some time, halting their bed sport, he was sure she wouldn't get confused.

Aiden stared up the stone staircase that led up to his father's rooms. The girl was with the old man. Aiden frowned. He didn't know if his own powers had improved or if practice and riding with Michael all that time had honed them. Even though he hated to admit it, perhaps there had been advantages to riding with the Warleader and his Unwanted.

Aiden returned to his room and relaxed back onto the bed.

"Now, my unwitting slave, what can I torment you with today?" Aiden said, closing his eyes and concentrating on the link between him and Damien. He noted with satisfaction Damien was much closer and should arrive in Yalleska in the next day or so. More than enough time for him to drive Damien to the edge of reason.

NINETY-THREE

Damien observed as everyone set up camp with an efficiency born of a lifetime on the road. It amazed him there wasn't as much push-back as he'd expected. Even though the prisoners hadn't given them any trouble at all on the journey so far, he'd rather they weren't in a village with them. Of course, his nervousness might just be because he was more worried about how the unsuspecting villagers in the village they descended on would react.

Damien was almost at a loss since the team insisted on setting up his sleep space along with their own. He'd learnt early on they'd glare at him if he tried to do it himself. Instead, he went to one side of their makeshift camp and tried to calm himself. His nerves were counterproductive right now, but the thought of messing up was killing him. As he often did, he found his mind turning to Isabella.

She will die...

It will be all my fault.

Damien shuddered and closed his eyes as he pressed the heel of his palm to the bridge of his nose. His own mind repeated the phrase and obligingly threw up an image of his sister, dead on the ground. He tried to push aside the panic this evoked. Damien didn't even know why he continued to torture himself this way. Isabella was safe at home with their parents. Yet no matter how many times he told himself his sister was safe, ever since leaving Callenhain, his own mind had continued to torment him to the point he wasn't getting much sleep. Damien half turned to confess his current problems to Callan, then shook his head. There wasn't much Callan or his team could do about him thinking such things. He'd survive it. He took a deep breath and faced the camp again to see the prisoners huddled together, a couple of his squad keeping watch over them.

"Drag out the spare sleeping pallets for our prisoners, their behaviour on this trip deserves recognition," Damien ordered.

Damien saw the women's eyes flick to him, one and all, obviously startled by the order.

"Of course Damien, we'll see to it," Shallan said.

Shallan and a couple of her team mates moved into action, looking through what they had with them and pulled out the spare supplies they'd packed to fashion sleeping pallets for their prisoners. It was one of the things he'd asked them to pack as a reward and motivation to entice good behaviour from his prisoners.

"Please, we can help. Perhaps cook the meal so you can all rest a little?" Allani's eyes darted around as the squad stilled. "We won't try anything. I know you are perfectly capable of telling if we try to poison your food."

Damien kept his face blank, even though he had no idea how to check his own food for poison. From the way the rest were reacting, he wasn't the only one who didn't know how to do that particular test. Either way, it was best his prisoners didn't realise that.

"Thank you for the thought; we will prepare our own food,

but we'll give you supplies so you can make your own if you will," Damien answered, then looked over to Callan. "If we can loosen their bindings just a little to allow them some movement? Within reason."

He waited long enough to see Callan nod and issue orders to a couple of others who'd already set up their own sleeping spots for the night. Satisfied, Damien walked over to a nearby tree, ignoring the eyes of his prisoners that were still on him. He could feel their astonishment, but a certain amount of consideration, even to an enemy, was something he could afford to show. Damien slid down to the ground, resting his head on the trunk, and closed his eyes. If nothing else, the warmth of the last light of the day on his face, along with the faint breeze was restful. More so than his sleep had been of late.

NINETY-FOUR

Ben slid the bar across the front doors, locking it in place. He commenced his rounds and closed the shutters on the windows, one by one. Not for the first time, he regretted the fact the bar had so many windows. Particularly on these early mornings when his customers had stayed until nearly dawn. He reached up to pull the wooden shutters closed when his hand froze. The sky was starting to push aside the darkness of the night and he placed his palm against the window and stared out at the city wall. It was several blocks from the Arms, but his place was on a hill and from this window a section of the city wall was visible. Ben's breath caught as he caught sight of what could only be a body that plunged from the top of the wall to the ground. He dropped his mind barrier to be flooded by shrieks of pain along with images of blades, silk and fighting carried to him through the veil.

He unconsciously faced in the direction of the Rathadon estate and concentrated.

Speaker Rathadon! Ben waited a moment, then swore before he called again only to receive no answer.

Lady Rathadon!

He wasn't hopeful that she would reply, either. Both the Speaker and lady were advancing in years and at this hour, it seemed, deep asleep. He thought about calling Steven, but he feared he didn't have a strong enough connection to the man to make the conversation private. As difficult as things were right now, it wasn't like the man had been even remotely trustworthy before recent events.

He checked out the window and saw a flurry of activity and more bodies plunge from the wall to the cobblestones below. His lips thinned. It was too late for him to be able to get out of the city to the Rathadon estate. It had been too late before he'd happened to see the first body toppling from the top of the wall and heard the whispered death cries of the victims.

Evan! Ben was about to yell again, then stopped mid-holler.

Ben? Evan's confused reply sounded in his head.

His eyes narrowed as he realised that Evan's mind voice was stronger than he'd expected it would be. The man might not know it but either the stress of the invasion or perhaps actually using his mindspeech more had obviously triggered his abilities in a good way.

Evan, pay attention. I wouldn't ask, but you're closer to the Rathadon estate than me...

Of course I am. I stayed the night...

You what? Ben frowned, confused for a moment, then relieved as the words sank in.

Steven and I got drinking. Well, it isn't like there's much else for us all to do being locked up this way, so I stayed the night. Or rather I'm about to... I haven't been to sleep yet...

You're drunk. Ben was torn between being relieved that Evan was already at the estate and exasperated that he was drunk.

You know, I think you might be correct!

Ben almost groaned at the cheery tone; he could almost see the sloppy smile on Evan's face.

Listen closely, Evan, get Speaker and Lady Rathadon, as well as Steven, and get them out of the estate via the tunnels. He explained, trying to keep his instructions simple.

What? Why? I was about to go to sleep, Evan grumbled.

Ben throttled down his temper. At least Evan sounded a little more alert, showing he perhaps wasn't quite as drunk as he'd first thought.

We're under attack by the Sylannians. They are already inside the city. Vallantia will change hands again before full daylight.

But...

Go, he ordered. *Now! Get out via the tunnels if you can.*

Ben almost sighed with relief as he saw the flashing image of a door being flung open and Evan running down the hallway. Having done what he could, he turned his attention to his next task. Drawing on the veil, he closed his eyes and concentrated, narrowing his mind-call to one person he was well acquainted with, but who was on the edge of his abilities to contact.

Adam! He paused for a heartbeat before swearing softly. *Adam, Powers, wake up!*

He drew in even more power to support his call and holler to the other man at the top of his mental voice again when he stopped.

Ben? Sorry, it's early. What's wrong? Adam asked.

Get word to your brother to pass on to Michael. Vallantia is under attack by Sylanna. I wager the city will fall again before full daylight.

I'll try, but I don't think Colin is in position to reach Michael yet.

Wait, so he doesn't even know Vallantia fell to the Kastlers?

No. Colin had a few issues along the way—those damn unpredictable attacks slowed his party down. Are you safe?

Ben swore, barely reining in his temper. *I'm fine, for now. The attack has only just started. But keep in mind, I'll be going to ground.*

Stay safe, Ben.

Adam's attention faded as he focused on his brother and Ben withdrew from the connection. He'd done what he could for now to send out word. His gaze was drawn to the wall and he saw another body fall from the top. Ben shook himself into action and reached out, snapping the shutters closed, and moved around the room at a half run closing the rest. The screaming and the sounds of battle weren't necessary for him to know the attack had started. He could sense it in the change in the whispering in the veil, the half groans and cut-off gasps of those being killed. There were always some of those sounds in a city this size, it usually formed a background noise that he tended to block out. Now there was more of it. A lot more than a handful of people dying in unfortunate circumstances.

He ignored the whispering, crying voices, even while leaving himself open to them so he'd have some sense of how the battle was progressing as he spun and ran for the stairs. He wouldn't do Speaker and Lady Rathadon, Michael, or anyone any good in the coming battle if he was taken out at this early stage.

It was past time he gathered his family and went to ground.

NINETY-FIVE

The bond that connected Samuel to his wives was agitated, more than it usually was although the problem didn't appear to be him. So he guessed he should be grateful for small mercies. Samuel picked up a cheek of yellow drop fruit and bit into the soft squares his wife had thoughtfully cut it into. It was the explosion of sweet and tart together that he loved. Samuel caught a dribble of juice as it ran down his chin then sighed as the agitation increased to an irritating buzzing in the back of his head. It was like a trapped insect desperately trying to get out. Now that he was aware of it, it was hard to ignore.

"What is it, Chelsie?" Samuel asked.

Chelsie sat lounging back on one of the low chairs. Her mood went from being deeply satisfied to scowling at a report she'd been handed.

"Your sister reports she's taken out the traitor house and is launching her attack on the barbarian lands. How did she know?" Chelsie asked.

"How did she know what?" Samuel said, pushing himself

away from the table and his fruit somewhat regretfully. If he didn't sort out Chelsie's mood, he'd never get any peace.

"How did she work out which island was the traitor island?"

Samuel frowned trying to remember exactly what his sister's instructions had been. "Well, we... um... we told her... Didn't we?"

"We didn't know who the traitors were, let alone where they were. Only that they were rumoured to be a lower-caste house."

"She must have received her own intelligence," Samuel said, waving his hand dismissively. "You know how she is."

"There wouldn't have been time. You gave her the orders and she went straight there, to a low-caste family on the edge of our territorial lands." Chelsie scowled. "It might be nothing, but I think we should send out some of our own to have a discreet check out that way."

"Why? We know the traitors are gone."

"We know she must have hidden her children somewhere; we just don't know where. One explanation for her knowledge of the location of the traitor house would be if she already knew about it."

The frown on Samuel's forehead cleared. He gazed up at Chelsie, whose eyes glittered with malice.

"She finally made a mistake. Do it," Samuel said.

NINETY-SIX

Surrounded by her daggerwives, Jaclyn ran along the trail through the forest. Her scouts advised her that once they broke through the trees they'd see the burning lights that would act like a beacon to their destination. The smugglers had proven quite useful once again in ferrying the bulk of her forces out of the city itself to a place upriver. While she'd left some of her people in the city to keep hold of the smugglers and ensure they couldn't run off giving warning of the attack, the bulk of her forces were with her. She wanted no mistakes in ensuring the Rathadon estate and its residents were in her custody. The city itself after that should be easy since her own people would only have to replace the Kastlers' guards. They'd spent days watching their patrols and she'd concluded they shouldn't be a problem for her own daggerwives or the sister houses she'd brought with her. She wanted the gates and walls intact, giving her a defensible base of operations to bring in more of the sister houses securely and expand her hold on this land.

She broke through the tree line and slowed to a stop, breathing lightly, like the others of her inner circle. All of them were able to supplement their strength with the veil. It was why they were chosen. She didn't allow herself to think about how small that inner circle really was—for this task, it was enough. She pushed aside the little inner doubt that her brother's wives were correct that the Warleader of this land would be more than a match for her. If there was the one thing she'd learnt from her campaign in the land of the traders, it was to break the impossibly big task into smaller tasks.

She stared at the looming estate. It was big enough that it was like a separate world. The estate house was a multi-storey affair, all in stone, that looked like it sank into the bedrock beneath. Walls made of rock ringed the estate; the gates were reinforced with metal. There were obvious guard posts around the walls, although she didn't detect anyone in them. The Kastlers and their people were lazy.

Taking this place was one of her smaller tasks.

JACLYN REACHED UP, her fingers catching in the irregular small holes in the rock, then pushed with her leg, allowing her other arm to reach up to the next handhold. It was the great thing about these old rock walls. Along with the holes that seemed to be drilled into them, they possessed uneven edges to catch with her hands, small little outcrops just enough to wedge her feet onto. If anyone had been left watching from the tree line, they probably would have perceived the wall as a seething mass as her family scaled it without the need of ropes or hooks. No self-respecting Sylannian, having been born in the multileveled island tree homes, needed such assistance to climb.

On reaching the top, she took a moment to scan her surroundings, aware of the few brief fights that took place in the lookouts. Jaclyn frowned, seeing small holes, similar to those on the wall she'd just climbed, wondering what they were for, then dismissed them. These people would know the why of building in stone better than she did. She watched as the dawn lightened the sky and spread across the treetops. Those in the estate would soon be waking. They had only a few moments left to maximise the advantage they'd gained. Her daggerwives ran around the walls, descending to the courtyard below. Blades flashed, taking out guards asleep at their posts, making their job just that little bit easier.

As the sun tipped over the walls and spilled into the courtyard, the doors to a low building off the main estate opened and guards stumbled out. They joked and pushed at each other before those in front froze as they registered what was in front of them. It was in that moment the first rank of her daggerwives launched themselves at them. With the sounds of battle ringing off the walls, those inside would wake and understand, too late, that they were under attack.

Jaclyn drew her blades and glanced around the mayhem that seethed on all sides of her, although she had little concern about the outcome. Dismissing the battle in the courtyard as easily won, she sprinted towards the large double doors of the estate. She guessed there would be a bar on the other side of them, and if they left their run too late, it would be dropped, making her job harder. As she ran up the stairs, she pulled in the veil, and shoved her hands forward, pushing that power into the doors. They slammed back, which caused a couple of people on the other side to be flung against the wall and slump unconscious.

With her family around her, she sprinted into the estate. Teams peeled off at every door and hallway to clear the path and disarm all within. Their pet smuggler had told her the elder Rathadon lived on the lower floor due to his injuries, but so far her people who'd been peeling off and taking every room they encountered reported nothing other than the lower class, the servants, who she was told served the ruling family.

She was about to mount the broad staircase leading to an upper floor when she caught sight of guards drawing their blades further down the hallway in front of her. Trusting instinct once more, she abandoned the stairs and ran towards the guards. As the one to her left raised his sword for an overhead blow, she raised one of her own blades to block while lunging with the other to stab the guard in the neck. The man on her right fell almost in tandem with his fellow guard as Myra plunged her knife up and into his heart.

The daggerwives flung open the door and burst into what seemed to be a large sitting room with windows that had a view over a garden. On a quick scan of the room, she saw the door off to one side. Her family poured into the room, checking every possible hiding space as they swept it. Her head daggerwife, with her squad close behind, smashed into the door, the others following them into the room beyond. Finally, Jaclyn entered to see her daggerwives with their blades held at the throats of two elderly people. Then her eyes fell on the still figures of several of her own daggerwives bleeding out on the floor. She raised her eyes to the daggerwives who now restrained the old couple.

"How did our own get so sloppy that an old, crippled couple managed to take them down?" Jaclyn demanded.

"We disregarded the male, First."

"He isn't as incapable as our informants led us to believe." The daggerwife refused to meet her gaze. "Neither is the old woman; we didn't expect them to fight."

"While we were battling with the old woman and trying to disarm her, she took down two of our own. The old man stabbed the third in the neck while we were occupied with his wife," said one of the daggerwives restraining the old woman.

"You said you wanted them alive, First." The daggerwife swallowed.

Jaclyn's eyes narrowed as she finally dismissed her daggerwives. Any of them who got killed by an old man and woman deserved their death. She took in the scar running down the side of the old woman's face and the old man's clawed hand. Although he was not whole, he could clearly grasp a dagger.

"Speaker Rathadon, I have heard a great deal about you. Apparently not all of it accurate. We have much to discuss, primarily about your son," Jaclyn said.

She'd give the old man his due. Despite not having full use of his limbs, he still had fight in him. She could see it reflected in his eyes. Although, interestingly, she couldn't hear anything from his mind. From him or his wife. That was extremely unusual, and gave her pause. Most people in a panic tended to broadcast their feelings whether they willed it or not. Most old cripples would have been distressed about the events that had just occurred. Yet it seemed there was more to the old former Warlord of Vallantia than many gave credence to.

"There's more, Firstwife," the daggerwife said, walking forward to hand over twin blades. "The woman fought with these."

Jaclyn frowned at the daggerwife's pale complexion and scrutinised the blades, taking in the etching. Jaclyn's eyes rose to meet the challenging gaze of the old woman.

"Who are you?" Jaclyn demanded.

NINETY-SEVEN

Steven swore to himself and pulled his pillow over his head as the screaming started. It didn't prove any more effective at cutting out the sound of battle than the last time he'd heard such sounds in the courtyard. He wondered why it was that everyone always decided to attack at obscene times of the morning. Although he guessed he really should be grateful to Michael for coming to save his hide. The pillow was wrenched off his head and he saw Evan's pale face above his own.

"Get up, you fool, we have to hide."

"Why would we need to hide from Michael? Granted, he probably won't be happy with me, but he never is," Steven grumbled.

"It isn't Michael," Evan bit out.

"What, but... who is it this time?" He winced hearing the almost childish wailing tone in his voice.

"Sylanna, by the looks of them. Lots and lots of them." Evan glanced over his shoulder, almost as if he expected invaders to come bursting through the doors.

"But I thought they were allies to the Kastlers?"

"If so, I don't think anyone's bothered to inform them of that little detail."

Steven allowed his friend to pull him from his bed, bewildered at the events. He pulled away from Evan, who was trying to guide him to the door, and stumbled over to the heavy drapes. He pulled back the thick curtains and stared down into the courtyard. Any faint hope he had that his friend was wrong was dashed as he saw the writhing mess of fighting below. Although it appeared to be extremely one-sided with the dead mostly being the Kastlers' people. Despite the circumstances, it wasn't a state of affairs he could dredge up even a hint of sympathy for. Those below had signed their own death warrants when they'd dared to take the Rathadon estate. He allowed Evan to pull him away from the window and they ran across the room.

"Hold on." Steven stopped abruptly and grabbed his boots, sitting down on a chair to haul them on.

Evan groaned and grabbed his weapons belt off the weapons rack and assisted him as he strapped it on before they both bolted to the doors.

"We need to get to the basement; there's a tunnel where they take the dead out of the cells."

"No."

"Come on, Steven, we don't have much time."

"We need to collect my parents first. I'll not leave them here."

With that he spun and ran to the end of the hallway, taking the small winding staircase the servants used to move to and from the lower floors. It amazed him how much he'd learnt since the Kastlers had taken over his home. He hadn't even known the back staircase existed before recent events. Only the sound of his friend's boots on the stairs behind him let him know Evan was following him.

As the sound of doors splintering and screaming grew louder, he hit the lower floor and sprinted towards his parents' room.

Without ceremony he ran inside, only registering that the doors had been open when he was halfway across the sitting room. As hands grabbed him and he found himself slammed into the floor, he realised the room seemed to be filled with women. He struggled ineffectually as his hands were bound. His captors flipped him over and he found himself staring into a pair of dark brown eyes.

"So, you would be the ineffective big brother to the one they call the Warleader." The woman's voice almost purred.

He had a moment to wonder how this woman spoke their language, then, looking at the predatory glint in her eyes, decided he didn't really need to know. He tried to twist around and almost wilted with relief as he caught sight of his parents, bound and sitting on the lounge. His mother had blood running from a cut to her head but otherwise appeared unharmed.

"I know you probably think this was a good idea but by the time my little brother comes after you, and he will, you will regret this day," Steven said, tearing his eyes away from his mother to look back up at the woman.

"Why is that? It seems the Kastlers thought it was a good idea," she said.

"The Kastlers had an over-inflated sense of their own competence," Steven said, wondering where his sudden certainty and boldness had come from.

"I'm much better at fighting than the Kastlers. Don't you want to see your brother die?"

Steven couldn't help the chuckle that escaped from his lips. It seemed these people had gathered a great deal of information about them if they were aware of that little detail. Then again, it wasn't something he'd ever tried to hide and his position on that particular topic had only changed recently. Funny the impact mercenaries and thugs invading his city and his home had.

"Many people have wanted the Warleader to meet an unfortunate fate. None to date have ever succeeded."

"Well, I happen to know your brother is a little busy on the other side of your lands right now."

Steven blinked, hope surging before it was dashed. She obviously meant Michael was occupied on the other side of the Warlord's domain. Which meant he was over towards Callenhain, not that he was just outside of Vallantia. That was so much wishful thinking.

"Regardless of where he is, he'll come, then you'd best hope his temper doesn't get the better of him."

NINETY-EIGHT

Tarkhan paced around the sitting room as his mind idled to the familiar pulses urging him to calmness. There were many women who tended to him in this place, but he didn't know their names. The main one who primarily had his care he simply called Keeper. She'd told him that was her title and job. His keeper had gradually given him more comfort and a certain level of freedom as he stopped trying to fight her control. Shame flooded him. He didn't know how long it had taken her to tame him, but it hadn't seemed to take long. At first, he'd etched a mark into the wall near his bed every time he woke, but he'd eventually lost hope and given up. There was no way for him to really tell the passing of the days and nights. While he resided in several rooms, and he even had access to an exercise room down the hall, none of them had a window. He was buried deep within this place they'd brought him to. The keeper didn't try to break into his mind like the Sylannians had the first time he'd been captured, but day after day her will washed over his mind, urging him to calmness, to acceptance.

He'd even stopped mentally prodding at the silken collar that wrapped around his neck. Every time he'd tried to free himself using variations of the technique he'd learned the first time he'd been captured, it failed. Just as his keeper had explained it would. So, he gave up. That step had prompted her to unbind the silken bonds that fastened him to his bed and the beams of his bedroom. She had given him permission to move about these two rooms that were his. They even took him down a long hallway, when he asked, to a large open exercise room with padded mats on the floor and allowed him some physical activity. Three rooms and a hallway were all he'd seen since he'd been here. The keeper warned him if he tried to leave these rooms his more restrictive bonds would be put back in place. After being kept in confinement for so long, he valued even the small freedom of moving about his rooms as much as he wanted to, so he hadn't even tried to open the outer door that led to the hallway. There'd be no point anyway. The door was locked from the other side. His keeper wasn't that trusting. Tarkhan smiled cynically. Even if the door hadn't been locked, he wouldn't have tried to go outside. Not anymore. The whispering in his head urging his submission to her will was all pervasive.

"Come and take a seat, Tarkhan," the keeper said.

"Yes, Keeper."

Tarkhan sank meekly onto a low lounging chair against the wall and closed his eyes, shuddering as she rewarded his obedience with a small burst of delight. He'd lost touch of who he'd been. If he'd been told before his capture that humans were just as susceptible to obedience training as animals, he would have laughed at them. Yet that was exactly how she was training him. Just because he knew what she was doing, however, didn't mean he could stop it from being effective. He much preferred his keeper being pleased with him than unhappy with him.

"You are doing much better, Tarkhan, now that you have come to terms that your life has changed."

"Have you been breaking in people like me for long?" Tarkhan asked, watching her carefully.

His keeper walked over to him, one of her hands tilting his head up while her fingertips on the other brushed his temples. He shuddered as the contact between them intensified her will as it rolled over him, crushing and washing away even any hint of defiance. Tarkhan realised if the Sylannians could use these mind gifts on others while they were fighting, his people would have fallen to them years ago.

"Most of my adult life. As you have discovered, it is a skill I am very good at. So do not fret, there is no shame in your submission."

"Yes, Keeper." Tarkhan's voice was the merest whisper.

Grief for what he'd lost welled up in him as he realised the keeper was correct. He'd finally submitted, lost all will to fight back. Fighting and defiance hurt. He was sick of pain and had no desire to court any more of it. The keeper pulled him into her arms, rocking him gently. Her fingers stroked his temple, words whispering in his head, calming him, pushing aside his loss and fear. The outer door opened, and the keeper stood.

"Leave us," the woman said.

"Yes, Firstwife," the keeper said.

The other woman, who was distinct with broad swaths of maroon and cream in her robes, waited as the door closed behind the retreating form of the keeper. The silence stretched between them as her gaze racked him from head to toe. Finally, she strolled over to him, her steps so smooth and graceful she almost seemed to glide. As she sat next to him her hand rose and he didn't even flinch as she stroked his temple. Tarkhan gasped as strong emotions washed over him. Caught up in their wake, he could do nothing but stare back into the eyes of this woman.

"You only have one purpose in life now. You may even find it pleasurable. Should our breeding be successful, I will reward you greatly."

"You, want me to... breed... with you?"

Tarkhan was stunned. She grabbed his hand and pulled him, unresisting, to his feet.

"Come, my warrior, should our liaison produce a child and it grow up strong and healthy, it might even rise up one day to rule an empire."

"What do I call you?" Tarkhan swallowed, wondering what had possessed him to ask such a thing.

The woman laughed, causing relief to wash over him as she led him towards his bed. She wrapped her arms around him, pulling his head down so she could whisper into his ear, all the while stroking his temple and urging his submission to her will and needs.

"Should you have need to scream a name while we breed, you may call me Chelsie."

NINETY-NINE

Damien stared up at the fortress where it loomed on the mountaintop with a single winding road snaking up to it from Yalleska village. It stood multiple stories in height, with towers on each corner and levels constructed in the caves beneath, or so he'd been told. A wall ran around the castle with imposing gates. He could see the traces of the veil. Layer after layer seeped into the ancient stone. A dull thread of power had been laced into the stonework by those with an affinity for stone. This had once been an ancient keep of the Smith Lords of old or so legend had it. Damien might not have an affinity for stone or metal himself, but that didn't stop him from being able to see the work of a master or, more likely, given the size of the fortress, many of them. After all, warlords, not just the current one, had a tendency to take whatever and whomever they wanted.

With a glance back at his prisoners, he spurred his horse on, determined to be within the walls before nightfall. The sooner he dropped his charges off, the sooner they could all re-join the Unwanted.

"We're going to have to spend the night," Callan said.

Damien wished he could refute Callan's assessment. The idea of spending more time than he had to in the Warlord's company didn't appeal to him. From the wave carrying a collective mental groan, he gathered none of the squad was looking forward to an overnight stay at the stronghold. Although he was bone-weary and wondered if having a proper sleep in a cot in the barracks might help.

"Once we get rid of this lot, is there somewhere in the village the rest can stay?"

"Of course, Yalleska town isn't that small. It's used to having to put up the caravans from the villages that arrive to drop off the tithe."

"Then let's get this done with. Keep a low profile, then you can take the squad to stay in the village. I might have to suffer for the night but it doesn't mean the rest of you do."

"Thank you but I'm meant to stay with you. Michael would kill me."

"I promise I won't go near tiscan. I've learnt my lesson on that one. Besides, I have a funny feeling the Warlord will tie me up half the night with questions after I pass on Michael's briefing."

"I don't—"

"Wouldn't there be more risk of me encountering the stuff in town rather than at the stronghold?"

"Well, yes, but..."

"Good, it's settled then. You and the rest of the squad can have the evening off in town while the Warlord becomes my minder for the night. He knows about my little problem, and I doubt he's going to let me use any more than Michael or the rest of you would."

Damien relaxed in his saddle when Callan subsided, although he could tell the man was still uneasy but also did not want Damien to think he wasn't trusted. The predominant thought from the rest of the squad was relief that they wouldn't have to stay at the stronghold, even if there was a little guilt that Damien would have to.

∾

Damien watched as the doors to the cells were locked then turned, relieved that at least one burden had been lifted from him. The prisoners were now the Warlord's problem.

"We usually separate the men from the women," the guard said.

"I'll explain it to the Warlord. Trust me, the Sylannian women are far easier to manage if you keep the male with them." Damien said then waved his hand at Callan. "Go, before anyone can think to say otherwise."

"Are you sure?" Callan asked.

"For the final time, yes. I'll be fine. Get out of here. I have my keeper." He pointed to the waiting guard. "I'm absolutely certain they will pass me from guard to guard until I'm shoved in front of the Warlord. I'll go and report, keep the Warlord company while he bombards me with questions. Sleep in a spare bed in the barracks and catch up with you all in the morning."

Callan looked at him, a frown creasing his forehead.

"If it helps move this dispute on, that's exactly what is going to happen. We have orders. There is someone waiting to escort him." The guard shrugged, looking entirely bored with their circular conversation that had been going since they'd descended into the cells. "He's to be taken directly to the Warlord."

Callan finally nodded, although clearly not particularly happy. Damien waved to them, then followed the guard who led him up a dank stone hallway.

"This your first time here?" the guard asked.

"Yes. It's bigger than I imagined," Damien said.

"This is part of the original cave system. The cells and passageways were fashioned from them," the guard explained. "A legacy from the Smith Lords."

Damien gathered the guards who worked down here didn't get too many visitors. At least not visitors who were free to walk out again.

"Isn't it a risk? Cave systems like these can have multiple openings," Damien asked, looking up at the smooth rock walls as they passed. He imagined it had taken some time for the rock workers to create this place.

"They've long been tracked down and sealed. The warlords who've held Yalleska over the years have been here almost as long as the Rathadons and Straffords." The guard gestured towards a path that led up to the left. "Also, like the Rathadon and Strafford castles, the stronghold was originally built by the Smith Lords. If anyone can track down exits and close them, it's a Smith Lord."

Old light stones, made by a stonemason with an affinity for bedrock, were spaced down the long hallway. Although they threw their light, pushing back the darkness, it was still dim. Damien drew the veil to him. Biting his lip in concentration, he willed light to appear as he remembered Michael had done on more than one occasion. He grinned in delight as a small glowing globe popped into existence in front of their party. The man in front of him swore and looked at him, his eyes wide.

"Sorry," Damien muttered.

The man continued to stare at him for a moment longer before he continued up the hallway.

"No problems. You lot as ride with the Warleader are an uncanny lot," the guard said.

The cheery globe of light bobbed along in front of them,

unconcerned by the guard's shocked reaction. It was obvious Damien had been in company with the Unwanted far too long. He'd forgotten how normal people reacted to such displays. It was also plain the poor guard probably wasn't one that rode out with the warbands, so he probably hadn't encountered the Unwanted and the almost-casual displays of power that others couldn't even dream of possessing.

Damien repressed a sigh of relief as the guard who'd been leading him opened a locked and barred door to let him out of the corridor into the stronghold proper. The air was fresher than that below. Yet another guard who was vaguely familiar waited for him and waved his fellow guardsman off. The first guard grunted and left without a word. The sound of the bolt sliding back into place and the rattle of the key in the locks heralded the fact his former guide had locked the door again.

"Wouldn't that make it terribly hard for the rest of you to get down to the cells?" Damien asked.

"That door is always kept barred from the inside, but it isn't the only entry into the cells below."

"Ah, so that door isn't used much?" Damien frowned, trying to understand.

"It isn't. This section of the stronghold is closer to the tower where the Warlord resides, which is where I need to take you," the guard said.

"I guess that makes sense, to keep it locked. If I hadn't seen how secure the cells were I'd think it was a security risk," Damien said. At mention of the Warlord he realised this man was one who generally rode with the Warlord whenever he'd shown up.

The guard shrugged, his mouth closing on what he was about to say as he stared to a spot just above his head.

"I know it's dusk, but I don't think we need extra light quite yet." The older guard's eyebrows rose as he stared at him.

Damien sent a pulse of power to extinguish the faithful little globe of light that he'd forgotten about. It hiccupped, as if it sensed he didn't really want it to go away then exploded with flecks of light bursting in all directions before fading.

The guard flinched, then threw a glance at him that was clearly unimpressed. Or at least, he was pretending to be unimpressed. Unfortunately for him, Damien could sense he was more amused than angry. Damien would give this guard one thing: he was calm, unlike the guard who'd guided him up from the cells. He guessed this guard, had encountered the Unwanted more than often enough to be more comfortable.

"Come, the Warlord wants to speak to you. I take it this is your first time here?" the guard asked.

"Was it my total ignorance that gave it away?"

"Unless I miss my mark, you're the Warleader's new one?" the guard asked.

"I guess. I doubt the Warlord takes in many new recruits." Damien shrugged.

"The Warlord takes in plenty of new recruits. The Warleader does not," the guard said with an amused glint in his eyes.

Damien mulled over that last bit of information. He checked the other man out and saw the veil swirling around him. He had more power than most; all of the warriors attached to the Warlord's warbands did, yet nowhere near the levels of those in his own warband. All of them, regardless of their natural abilities with the veil, were certainly more trained in its uses. At least when it came to fighting, they were. They'd refined fighting technique with use of the veil to a fine art over the years.

"You don't mind? Not riding with the Warleader?" Damien found he was genuinely curious. Generally being under close quarters, he'd not mixed much with the others outside of the ranks of the Unwanted.

"Not in the slightest. Besides someone has to be there to mop up while all of you fade to the back and quietly collapse,"

"I didn't realise that was widely known."

"It isn't, but for those of us who have trained to back up the Unwanted in battle, we need to know." The guard shrugged in an easygoing manner. "I'm the band leader of one of the bands directly attached to the Warlord. So, yes, I know." He shrugged.

Damien assessed this confident, affable man that strode with him, leading him through the maze of passages. They paused as a door opened and Aiden stepped out.

"Ah, Damien, my father is waiting to speak with you," Aiden said.

"I was just guiding him there now," his guide said.

"I'm sure you have better things to do..." Aiden said.

"It's all right, the Warlord asked..."

"I'll show him the rest of the way. I'm heading there myself, anyhow." There was a clear note of dismissal in Aiden's tone.

Damien saw the other man frown, his eyes narrowing, although finally he gave way to Aiden.

"As you wish." The guard turned to look at him. "Anyone will be able to give you directions back to the barracks when the Warlord is done with you. You can bunk in with my unit for the night."

Damien thanked the guard before continuing to walk with Aiden. He frowned at the older man. Aiden threw a glance over his shoulder at the retreating back of the guard. When he finally spoke, his voice was hushed to the point Damien had to stop himself from leaning forward to hear.

"I had to warn you, I'm so sorry, Damien," Aiden said.

"Warn me about what?" Damien frowned.

Damien unaccountably found dread starting to settle on him and tried to shake it off. He took a breath, trying to settle the knot in his stomach, but it seemed to catch in his throat. Closing his eyes briefly, he forced himself to breathe. Aiden's agitation was clearly contagious.

"My father rode through Ranlith on his way back here." Aiden kept his voice low.

"And?"

As the silence seemed to stretch between them, Damien felt like ice had drenched over him, fear and anger clamouring in his mind.

"Your sister, she's with him now..."

Damien flinched as an image of the Warlord with his arm around Isabella flashed in his head and, reached out with his mind to search for the Warlord. Seething anger flooded his mind. He jerked back to his present as Aiden pushed him into a small corridor.

"Let go of me," Damien grated.

"Calm down, here, drink. You won't help Isabella like this," Aiden said.

As flask was pressed into his hand, Damien drank from it almost absently to appease Aiden, while he continued to search for the Warlord. It did nothing to ease the anger that bubbled away in his mind. He grimaced at the sickly-sweet taste, but feeling the burn of the spirit, he took another swig of the flask anyway. A hint of a bitter undertone to the drink tasted familiar and he realised he'd almost drained the thing. As his mind found the Warlord's presence, he pushed his nagging concern aside and shook his head, trying to push back the anger that kept rising in him. It wouldn't help his sister one little bit but every time he tried to calm down, the anger rose again. He held the flask out to Aiden.

"Sorry, I nearly sculled that whole flask."

"Oh, under the circumstance, please, finish it. I came prepared. I have another." Aiden pressed it back to him.

Damien tossed back the rest of the contents in a couple of mouthfuls. He felt a little guilty since the flask had been full when it had been handed to him, but as Aiden had indicated, he had another.

His focus changed as he strode to the stairs, taking them two at a time, aware that Aiden was at his side. The top of the stairs opened into a large, open chamber, and other than the leather chairs near the window on the far side, the room was surprisingly empty. His gaze narrowed on the double doors on the far side and he didn't even miss a step as he strode towards them. His jaw clenched as he saw the guards stationed at the doors and forced what he hoped was a pleasant expression on his face.

"Father is waiting for us both," Aiden said.

Damien swallowed, glad that Aiden spoke since he wasn't sure he wouldn't snarl at the guards to get out of his way. He saw his hand shaking and tried once more to force himself calm. He almost doubled over in pain as something like a physical blow hit him, fear flooding his mind, a whispering voice bringing up all the nasty things the Warlord could be inflicting on his sister.

The guards, clearly having been expecting them, opened the doors. Damien strode between them, reaching out with ethereal fingers to slam the doors behind him so hard even the shutters on the windows shuddered in response. A gasp drew his attention. Isabella stood, looking pale, a hand pressing to her lips.

"Damien, no. It's not how it looks..."

Fire was racing through his entire body as he went to draw his weapon, then he froze as Isabella's words reached him. As fear and anger rose in his mind again, Damien's hand clenched around the pommel of his sword. He heard his ragged breathing as he realised the voice in his head was urging him to protect Isabella, to kill the Warlord. The Warlord held up one hand as his other grasped for a sword he wasn't wearing.

"Damien, I didn't—"

Damien shook his head and raised a shaking hand to his head

as the voice became louder and more insistent, almost shrieking at him. He stopped, eyes widening as he realised the voice in his head urging him on wasn't his own. Pain lanced through him and he staggered. He wondered if his face was a pale as it felt when a part of his brain recognised he'd been drugged.

"Tiscan, why would he give me tiscan?" Damien whispered to the Warlord as he saw the man's eyes widen.

The Warlord staggered and looked up confused, a half-uttered scream on his lips as he hit the ground.

"Damien, what have you done?" Aiden screamed.

The words seemed hollow, echoing at him from a distance, and he swayed, the words making no sense to him at all. Then Aiden was grappling with him, a blade being pressed into his hands. With a crack, splinters rained around the room as the guards came crashing in. Damien found himself tackled to the ground, the dagger Aiden had pushed into his hands moments before being ripped away. His mind scrambled, trying to grasp the power that had been there moments before and failed. He stared up as Aiden's face loomed over him and as darkness closed over him, it occurred to him.

Aiden had just set him up to take the blame for the death of the Warlord.

THE EMERGENCE SERIES CONTINUES...

Defiance (Emergence, Book Three)

Find out more by visiting https://www.catherinemwalker.com

About the Author

Catherine M. Walker was born in a small country town in Western Australia but now resides in Perth, Western Australia.

Sacrifice is the second book in Catherine's second epic fantasy series Emergence.

If you'd like to know more about Catherine's work, including following the progress of her new series visit:

https://www.catherinemwalker.com

www.ingramcontent.com/pod-product-compliance
Lightning Source LLC
Chambersburg PA
CBHW060721190726
48285CB00001B/16